The unVeiling

A NOVEL

5/23/03

To Will Ramsey +
Millennium III Publishers.
God bless you in your
journey.

Dr. Jay Z

REV. 1:3

The unVeiling

A NOVEL

Some wondered if
it would happen in their lifetime...

Others didn't believe
it could happen at all...

...UNTIL NOW!

JAY ZINN

WinePress Publishing
MUKILTEO, WA 98275

The Unveiling
Copyright © 1997 by Jay Zinn

Published by WinePress Publishing
PO Box 1406
Mukilteo, WA 98275

Cover by Jay Zinn

Printed in the United States of America.

Library of Congress Catalog Card Number: 97-60469
ISBN 1-57921-015-5

ACKNOWLEDGEMENTS

My beautiful wife, **Roseann**, who lovingly supported and encouraged me, and allowed me the countless hours to work on this book.

Mom and **Dad**, who made me a reader, gave me a wonderful upbringing, and listened to my childhood stories I used to pound out on the old Royal manual typewriter.

Tom Taylor, the man who led me to Christ, January 9, 1972, when I was in the Air Force. I hope this book finds you, Tom.

Richard C. Benjamin, spiritual father and apostolic mentor who believed in my calling to preach and teach God's Word. He assisted and advised me in countless ways over the years to achieve that call.

Kevin J. Conner, spiritual father and mentor in teaching, who inspired me and taught me in the biblical keys and tools for unlocking significant truths of Scripture.

Cecil Murphey, author, friend and mentor who took me beyond the elementary skills of writing into becoming my own editor. His input has been invaluable for my future in writing.

Mark Geier, the first man to challenge and urge me to put my end-time studies into a book so that others might benefit by them.

Nina Young, who helped me to get started through her encouragement and the books she lent me on novel writing.

Randy Colver and **Peter Stevens**, two friends who spent hours on the technical and grammatical editing of the first draft of this book, and offered me their invaluable insight.

Tim and **Corina Barbee**, the first to read the entire first draft, offering the critiques, editing and encouragement that helped me believe I could actually see this thing through to publication.

Sandra Marker and **Pam Sevenbergen**, partners in writing from our editing group who continue to assist me in my journey of learning and practicing the skills of writing.

Ed Turner, an ex-police officer who assisted me through numerous phone calls on the details of weaponry.

Ernie Martin, of Persuasion Marketing Group, who assisted me in creating the book cover for my novel with his technical expertise in computer graphics.

REVIEWS

"*A story so compelling, you won't want to put it down. If you like Frank Peretti, you'll love Jay Zinn.*"

Corina Barbee, Fairburn, GA

"*COMPELLING!...CONVINCING!...CONVICTING! I compare Jay Zinn's writing to that of Tom Clancy, along with the uncanny ability to stir up and provoke faith in the reader. The Unveiling is one book you'll recommend as you anticipate the next!*"

Mary Henderson, Pastor's wife, Colorado Springs, CO

"*After leading to Christ, Jay Zinn took me under his wing and impacted my life through his anointed preaching and teaching. I'm confident you will experience the same after you encounter his writing. Be prepared for the power of Jay's pen— the hovering hope of the Holy Spirit permeates his novel, The Unveiling.*"

Evangelist Rick Stanley, Elvis Presley's step-brother and the co-author of the books: *A Touch of Two Kings* and *Caught in a Trap*.

"*Memorize the name of Jay Zinn. You'll be seeing that name a lot from now on. This is his first novel, but he's definitely heading toward the top.*"

Cecil Murphy, author of 65 books including *Invading the Privacy of God*, and was the ghostwriter for such bestsellers as *Gifted Hands* and *Rebel With a Cause*. Atlanta, GA

"Dr. Zinn was able to zoom me into the present and future times with familiar surroundings in his novel. The characters are you and me, family and friends—neighbors, believers and non-believers. He creatively walks us through the stages when the revelation of God actually unfolds before your eyes. This is a book you'll want to buy ten copies of, because once you've read it, it will put you on a mission—you'll want everyone you love and care about, even people you meet, to know about this truth in the way it is presented."

Collette Robinson, Singer, Atlanta, GA

"Jay Zinn is a born story-teller. He took the book of Revelation and put it into a story I could relate to. After I read his novel, I was able to tell others about the events in Revelation—something I could never do before."

Adjua Adams, Atlanta, GA

"I think **The Unveiling** is a good book because it has just the right effects and graphics. It was the best book I ever read. It is one of those books that you can get into and not be able to put down. The book had a little bit of everything for everyone."

Shannon Gonzales, age 9, Bonita Springs, FL

"Believable characters that you can identify with; and exciting plot that makes it hard to put this book down; accurate biblical facts concerning end time events, all of it comes to life. Dr. Zinn has brought all these aspects to us in his work, **The Unveiling**. Thank you, Jay, for an inspiring, hopeful, account of things to come."

Cricket Huffman, Fayetteville, GA

"Wow! This novel inspired me to reread Revelation. Jay Zinn has painted a colorful, vivid portrait of our tumultuous final days on earth. **The Unveiling** is riveting reading for anyone who wants to be prepared for the 'end times.'"

Mary Jergenson, Spring Valley Deputy Clerk. MN

"A fantastic novel, by an extraordinary author, with an unusual depth of insight into God's final chapter."

Julie Hilts, Co-founder of Children's Hope International, Eagan, MN

"In *The Unveiling*, Jay Zinn captures the action and suspense that any John Grishom book has to offer—but through a Christian perspective."

Brittany Stanley, age 14, Fayetteville, GA

"Over the years I've avoided fictitious accounts of end time events to not confuse biblical with sensational. Because I know Jay, his commitment to scriptural integrity, and to careful, accurate interpretation, I was anxious to read *The Unveiling*. Eye-opening and intriguing, this creative work paints the picture in luminous clarity."

Tom Huffman, Fayetteville, GA

"*The Unveiling* was a wonderful book. I read it to my children and it gave me an opportunity to get out the Bible and read them the passages from Revelation. It was very action-packed and even though I have read and studied the book of Revelation for many years, having it told in story form and in a way that you can relate to the characters, makes it very interesting. It made my children hungry for the Word, and has challenged us all to check our hearts to see where we stand with the Lord."

Carla Gonzalez, Pastor's wife, Bonita Springs, FL

"An enthralling book! Kept me on the edge of my seat for literally hours. This is the only way I could read a book on end times."

Joanna Winter, 16, Fairburn, GA

PROLOGUE

The station guard waved his gun in Bob's face.

"Move it, Jansen!" he said, as he shoved him through the wood-carved doors into the cold, night air.

Outside, a blanket of smog slapped him with the nauseating stench of a road kill. He gagged at the sight and smell of the cadaverous flesh of martyrs stacked eight-feet-high to the left of the church. When he realized their heads were all missing, a chill ran up his spine.

"Quit dragging your feet!" the guard said with his gun in Bob's back. He pushed him ahead toward the noisy crowd seated in the stands of a small arena. As Bob walked into the spotlight he felt the crowd staring at him like starve-crazed beasts. He surveyed their faces and followed their eyes to the raised wooden platform, fifteen-feet high. It was lit up by a light from the steeple tower of the old church.

At the top of the platform, a blood-stained block lay below the mechanical arm of a twenty-first century guillotine. A laser gun protruded from the arm, designed to move laterally across the neck of its victims and then retract to its former position. Bob had heard about this machine from the stories Martha and Cap' used to bring back from their food hunts. A queasiness stirred in his stomach. He began to sweat.

"Death to the rebel!" someone shouted from the stands. "Kill the dog!" another yelled.

The crowd began to scream profanities to the rhythm of their stomping feet, and rattled the stands beneath them.

With a sharp poke of his gun the guard shouted at Bob above the clatter, "Climb, Christian!"

CHAPTER 1

The world changed and so had attitudes.

Governments had grown hostile toward Christians, the world's economy was collapsing, famine raped a quarter of the world's population, and a pandemic of natural disasters plagued the world. For Jack Mitchell, all these elements created a different approach to pastoring a church.

Jack missed the good old days of conferences. The subject matter usually dealt with counseling techniques, enhancing Sunday School programs, church growth principles; the normal stuff a pastor should know. He only wished it could have stayed as simple as that. Now they had to brace themselves for a bedlam of judgments.

It hadn't been announced yet, but the conference notes were pretty clear. He used to look forward to this day leading up to the return of Christ.

Now he wasn't so sure.

Jack scanned the somber audience of pastors in the Rai Conference Center. Nearly ten thousand men and women had converged on the city of Amsterdam in Holland. Normally, a pastor's conference would have been buzzing with excitement, especially one this size. All seemed to suspect, however, that an unpleasant announcement was coming. It created a cloud of nervous anticipation over the assembly. No one talked. Everyone either sat deep in thought or engaged in prayer in the last few minutes before the opening of the conference.

Jack studied the twelve men seated on the platform. They were apostolic leaders from of a variety of denominations—similar in clout to the influence the disciples of Christ might have had on the church of the first century. Over the last ten years they had guided the church through a number of obstacles created by the world's changing climate. Their insight into the times had provided invaluable wisdom for pastors.

Jack glanced at the podium at Nathan Kelly, one of the apostles, who welcomed the pastors and introduced the eleven other speakers on stage before he launched a short speech to set the tone.

"Pastors," Kelly said, "the prophetic train is in motion and gathering momentum. Two years ago, God visited me in a dream. In that dream, he showed me three visions which were confirmed by several of my colleagues who received the same dream. At our last conference, we shared those visions with you, and everyone who embraced the warnings were prepared when they happened."

Jack nodded. It had helped his church avoid a number of problems.

"In the first vision," Kelly continued, "we saw the opening of the fifth seal in Revelation, chapter 6. It began with an all-out assault on Christians in China and the persecution spread throughout Asia to the Middle East."

Jack sadly recalled the slaughter of the two missionary families his church had sent to China. Within a week, after the last conference, word had come back that those families were arrested and executed.

"Next, the Lord showed us the rise of a global super-church that would rise to unite major world religions through a common cause for a New World Order. That movement appeared three years ago in Central America and has spread rapidly through other continents. Today, this superchurch is called the *World Church*. In my opinion, she's the Harlot of Revelation 17. So beware, her organization is dangerous and growing fast."

Jack knew how dangerous this World Church was. He had a run in with her members in his college town. They had infiltrated his church through the students and lost eight families to them.

"Third, we saw two years of drought and floods coming to the United States which came to pass this year. America is still recovering from the damage and the economic chaos it created."

Kelly took a sip of water and wrapped his fingers tightly around the corners of the podium. "Ladies and gentlemen," he said, "I'm afraid there's more coming and, like the irresistible fist of God, there's no stopping it."

By now, Jack knew where Nathan Kelly was going with this. The book of the Revelation had laid it out pretty clear. He surveyed the saddened faces to his left and then to his right. Some heads were bowed, others watched the speaker. *What will become of them, Lord? Will they hold up under the pressure? What will happen to their congregations? What will happen to mine?* Kelly's voice cracked and pulled Jack's wandering mind back to the message. "The reason we invited you to Amsterdam is to share another warning from God we received two months ago. In a vision, we saw an earthquake coming that will ripple across the surface of the entire planet. We believe this is the quake that will mark the opening of the sixth seal in Revelation 6. It's scheduled to happen this year. When? We don't know, but it is imminent."

Shaken by the grim reality of more judgments, Jack shifted in his seat and stared at the floor. *Dear God, I knew it would come, but not in my lifetime.*

Kelly continued. "Sadly, dear friends, it won't end with the quake. Another divine judgment will come followed by another and then another, and so on. Each judgment that comes will be more severe than its predecessor. They'll come like a row of falling dominoes, and will escalate in strength, until the last one falls on the day when Christ returns."

Jack stared blankly at his conference notes. *Dear God, help us.* He glanced back at Kelly who was wiping his brow with a handkerchief.

"At our last world conference," Kelly said, "we placed our emphasis on world evangelism. Though we urge you to continue your efforts in this, our emphasis through this conference will be on *preparation*. We want to prepare you to sustain optimism through these arduous times, to keep faith in the sovereignty of God, to know that when the skies turn gray, the Lord is still in control and will offer us a way to escape."

Nathan Kelly closed his opening speech like a father encouraging a frightened son or daughter who wakes up from a nightmare. "...we must rise to the occasion, beloved, and cling to God with all our hearts. We are on the threshold of the final days of our Christian pilgrimage. Our journey through the end of time has begun."

Kelly closed with prayer and dismissed the pastors for their first morning workshop. Jack slowly rose from his seat. The last phrase of the message flashed in his head like a neon sign. *Our journey through the end of time has begun...*

CHAPTER 2

Jack Mitchell sat in the hotel suite of Nathan Kelly. Nathan was his pastor before Jack answered his own call to the ministry. They had been close friends for twenty-eight years, and to this day, he still regarded him as his spiritual mentor and advisor.

"I'm glad you could come," Nathan said as he handed Jack a glass of Coke. "Is Rhonda with you?"

"No sir, afraid not."

Nathan sat down on the couch. "Finances?" he asked.

"Yeah, money's been tight these days. She had to take her old job back at the hospital, so she couldn't make it."

"I'm sorry. Tell her I missed seeing her."

"I'll do that."

Jack stared at his glass and watched the fizz sprinkle about the ice cubes. A cloud of concern hung in the air from the content of the conference that day. He didn't know where to begin with the zillion questions bouncing around in his head. But his questions could wait. Nathan was troubled about something. "You appeared burdened today," Jack said.

"About the judgments?" Nathan replied. "It's hard not to."

"No, I mean *beyond* the judgments. I'm a pastor, I know

how it works; faking optimism around the people while something's going down behind the scenes."

"Is it that obvious?"

"To those who know you."

Nathan tapped his fingers on the arm rest. "You're right. There is something else."

"Can you tell me?"

Nathan sighed and nodded. "God visited me last night with another vision. I couldn't share it with the pastors today. It's got me concerned."

Jack leaned forward with his hands clasped in his lap. "What did you see?"

"The World Church is positioning a leader to head their organization. I'm afraid it's the beast under the Harlot of Revelation 17."

"The Antichrist?"

"That's right."

"Did you see who he was?"

"Yes and no."

Jack stared at the Bible laying next to him on the coffee table. He recalled the studies they had in the past on this subject. "You taught me once that the Antichrist might be a fallen apostle. Is that what the Lord showed you?"

"That's what he showed me, but there's an unsettling component about it."

"What's that?"

"He'll come out of the twelve men seated on the platform this morning."

"What?"

Nathan frowned. "That makes me a candidate, doesn't it?"

"No way!" Jack said. "Not the twelve. I can't imagine any of you leaving the faith."

Nathan placed his hand on Jack's shoulder, "If Judas Iscariot could walk with Christ for three years and betray him, are these men and myself any less vulnerable?"

Jack furrowed his brow and stared at his mentor. "Maybe it's another apostle, outside the twelve."

"No, I'm afraid not. The Lord said he'd be coming from our group."

Jack shook his head. "Man, this is hard."

"Yeah, I know. I could use someone to help me carry this burden. It's been weighing on me heavily. Would you partner with me in this with prayer?"

"You're not going to tell the others?"

"How can I? We're all candidates."

"But why me?"

"Who else can I trust, now, but you? You've been like a son to me. Our travels, our studies together over the years...you're as close to me as any one."

Jack sat quietly for a moment, groping for words to comfort his friend. He knew there was no way that Nathan Kelly would leave the faith. But he also knew the man's humility. A man who never took his walk with God for granted. A man who knew the power of deception and that no one, not even an apostle, was immune to the temptation of sin. Because of this he could appreciate Nathan's concern.

Jack grabbed his friend's hands and looked deep into his eyes. "I'll pray every day, my brother...that God will keep you from falling. But I know...I just know it won't be you."

Nathan half-smiled with his eyes full of tears. "I appreciate your confidence in me, Jack, but I must confess I've been asking myself the question all day...Lord, is it me?"

CHAPTER 3

Bob Jansen stared at his open book.

He didn't see the words, but just kept thinking about the days when life was less complicated.

With a sigh, he pushed his economics text aside and got up from his desk. He went to the window and stared into the early winter darkness. It had snowed off and on all afternoon. He reflected on the winters he had enjoyed as a boy. Sledding down old man Harris' backyard. The snow forts and snowball fights. The empty fields that beckoned for snow angels or patterns he'd make by dragging his feet. He remembered it all. A time that seemed so long ago.

Now everything had changed.

The world offered little hope for the future. The economy had crumbled. His once prosperous dad now barely paid the bills for his college education. He wondered if he would finish his last semester, and wasn't the only one who was concerned. The student body at Canterton University had dwindled to less than half of the six thousand students of his sophomore days. No one could afford it. Scholarships and grants were extinct. Finances, for most, had dried up.

Now, at twenty-one and in his senior year, a big, sad world

out there stared back at him. The clock had turned back to the days of the Depression—soup lines, suicides on Wall Street, crop failures from floods and droughts. America's dance with the deficit was over. The country was bankrupt. The economy of four European countries had collapsed within the past month.

Why now? Why did the world have to go nuts now? Nothing but gloom and doom awaited him. Yeah, doom and gloom. That's the term he heard a student use the other day. It sure fit the way things were.

"Something bothering you?" Shayne Taylor asked as he looked up from his textbook.

"Yeah, my brain is fried…"

"For the whole last hour, I'd say. I couldn't help but notice all the huffing and sighing going on over there. You didn't even turn one page."

"Well, why should we bother anyway? What good will a degree do us if there aren't any jobs? What if everything vaporizes by the time we're ready to graduate?"

"You know, you're right. Why should we study for a future we can't be certain of?"

"A future that'll never exist."

"Yeah. So what do you want to do then?"

Bob threw one of his books against the wall. "I don't know, but I sure don't want to sit around here."

"And I won't get any studying done with you moaning and moping around." Shayne slammed his book shut.

"Then let's go out. Do something…"

"On Wednesday night at 6:15? Canterton's a ghost town, remember? No money, no students. No students, no bars. No bars, no girls."

"See what I mean," Bob said, "no future." He turned to the window again and stared at the snow flakes shimmering like ghosts under the street light. "Think you'll make it back for our last semester?"

"I don't know. My funds are getting low. Scary isn't it?"

"Yeah, it is." Bob watched the snow flakes feather their

way to the ground. "Why don't we go out anyway and just cruise a while? Maybe some girls will be out tonight."

Shayne stood and closed the other books on his desk. "Well, it's a long shot, but okay. Anything's better than worrying about what will or won't happen tomorrow."

"Yeah," Bob said as he reached for his parka. "Anything's got to be better than this."

CHAPTER 4

The cloud disappeared when they saw the girls.

The two brunettes had just walked out of an apartment on campus, when Shayne and Bob cruised by. Shayne turned his red Mustang around to go back for another look.

The timing of their return synchronized perfectly with the girls getting into their car. They glanced at Shayne and smiled.

Bob tapped Shayne on the arm. "Hey, did you see that? Let's follow them."

"Yeah, it might brighten things up a bit." Shayne watched in his rearview mirror to be sure he drove slow enough for the girls to catch up. When they did, Shayne drove parallel with the girls' car in the two lane right-of-way. They exchanged glances and smiles all the way to the next light. When they came to a stop, Bob rolled down his window and motioned to the driver to roll down hers. She did.

"Hi," Bob said as he leaned his arms out the window. His breath steamed in the cold, winter air. "Where are you girls going?"

"No place you'd care to be," the driver replied.

"Hey, try us. You never know."

Shayne peered around Bob and watched the driver as she conversed with her friend and then turned back to Bob. "You can join us if you like, but I doubt if you'll stay," she said.

Shayne leaned toward Bob's window and yelled, "Wherever you stay, we'll stay!"

"All right," she replied and smiled, "follow me."

—◁▥◁▥◁—

"What rotten luck," Bob said, as the girls pulled into the parking lot of Canterton Community Church. "They're religious UFOs—Unidentified Female Objects."

Shayne shrugged his shoulders. "Maybe they're stopping to talk to us," he said and pulled up beside the other car parked under a light pole.

Bob stared at the girls as they got out. A gentle breeze blew back their flowing, brown hair from beneath their wool caps. "Oh," he groaned, "I think I'm in love."

"Come on, lover boy. Let's go."

Bob and Shayne got out and exchanged names with the girls. The driver's name was Laura Greene, and her friend was Whitney Conner. Bob unconsciously raked his eyes over Whitney's attractive features. "So what're you boys doing tonight?" she asked.

Bob looked at Shayne and then at the church. "Uh...you two planning on going in there?"

"We are," Whitney replied. "Would you like to join us?"

"Yeah, how about it, Shayne?" Laura asked.

"Well, I don't know," Bob said.

Shayne frowned at his friend and looked at the girls. "Would you excuse us, please?" he said, and pulled Bob back to the car. "Are you crazy?" he whispered. "We find some real babes and you want to dump them because of a church? How do you know they're religious? Maybe they're just going to a wedding or picking up their kid sister."

"Listen, pal, I'm not going into that church. I know we we

24

need something to brighten our miserable college lives, but church is not what I had in mind.

"Ah, come on, what can it hurt? Let's go in with them. If it gets weird, we'll leave."

"How?"

"We'll sit in the back row."

Bob looked over his friend's shoulder at Whitney. "Okay, I'll do it."

Shayne grinned and gripped Bob's shoulders. "All right," he said, and strolled back to the girls. "Hey, we decided to join you."

"Great!" Laura said. "We'll get our things."

Bob moaned when he saw them reach in the car for their Bibles. *Strike one! We know this ain't no wedding.*

When they entered the foyer of the church, they found themselves immersed in a sea of friendly faces. The exuberant mood of the people surprised Bob. Didn't they know the world was messed up; that the future was bleak? Most of the people he knew sure did and tried to escape the reality of it through drugs and alcohol. Apparently, not these people.

At 7:30, the sound of upbeat music burst through the doors of the sanctuary. The girls each grabbed Shayne and Bob's hand. They led them into the auditorium down a crowded aisle, and into the front row.

Bob sharply poked Shayne, "What happened to sitting in the back?" he whispered.

"I know, I know. Just cool it, will you? It's not going to kill us."

"Wanna bet?"

When the music ended, a man with gray-streaked hair walked onto the platform. With a smile, he adjusted his wire-rimmed glasses and asked them to find their seats.

Shayne leaned over to Laura, "Who's that?"

"Jack Mitchell, our pastor. He just got back from Amsterdam. Everybody's anxious to hear what he learned from the apostles."

"Apostles?" Shayne said.

"Messengers sent by God," Bob replied.

Shayne frowned at him. "Since when did you become an expert in church matters?"

"I grew up in a church," he whispered, "and if these people believe apostles still exist, we'd better get out while we can."

Whitney overheard his comment. "Stick around," she said. "You might find this interesting."

Shayne refused to leave, so Bob resigned to ride out the service. As the pastor spoke, Bob studied the people around him, still puzzled by the absence of gloom in their lives. *How can they be so cheerful?*

Bob decided to listen to the pastor and soon found himself pulled into the message, unaware that the next hour would start him on a journey that would change his life.

CHAPTER 5

"I can't spare you the bad news," Pastor Mitchell said.

The pastor's message quickly eclipsed Shayne's initial purpose for going into the church. As he listened to the predictions of coming judgments, a hunger for more understanding burned in his heart. When he left the dorm earlier that night, the world's current condition made no sense. Now he learned from Pastor Mitchell that the Bible had predicted these things.

"So, the first five seals of Revelation 6 are the prophecies fulfilled to date," the pastor continued. "Sadly, however, it's only the beginning..."

"I heard about this once," Bob whispered to Shayne.

Shayne ignored his comment, completely focused on the message.

"The next divine judgment in Revelation is the earthquake and celestial signs of the sixth seal. The apostles predicted this will happen sometime this year..."

The congregation buzzed with excitement. Shayne looked at Bob. "Did you ever hear that in church?"

Bob shook his head and looked back at the pastor.

"For the unsuspecting soul," Mitchell continued, "a

quake of this magnitude will be a terrifying experience. But for us, if we keep our eyes on God, it's an opportunity to bring many to Christ."

Shayne shifted in his seat. His right foot shook nervously. How would he cope with all this when he could barely handle the things that were happening now?

"In the meantime, we have an immediate problem to deal with for Canterton Community Church. Ten years ago, we saw the need to have small groups of Christians meet in their homes. We incorporated this into our congregation to create closer relationships, and it's been a great success. The time has come, however, for our small groups to serve an additional purpose.

"Since the crash of the economy, we've been unable to meet the payments on our building. The bank has given us the rest of January, and then they'll have to foreclose."

A wave of protests rippled through the audience while Pastor Mitchell raised his hands to calm them.

"Brothers and sisters, this shouldn't surprise us. I've talked with many pastors in Amsterdam who were experiencing the same hardships. It's happening all over the world. But they're still having church, like we can, through small groups. It's the only thing left we can do."

"What do the apostles say about this, pastor?" a member asked from the audience. "The apostles recommended small groups with urgency; not because of financial difficulties, but to prepare for the day when persecution hits the free world. The third world churches have already crossed this threshold, which is why they're forced to meet underground."

"But this is America!" another member shouted.

"America isn't exempt, my friend. You've seen the rise of political opposition. We don't live in a *Christian-friendly* society any more.

"Along with our antagonistic government, the aggressive campaign of the World Church has infiltrated our campuses and churches. Hundreds of students across America have joined her movement. I've warned you about this organization.

Once she rises to full strength, with the government on her bank roll, an all-out assault against God's Church will be imminent."

"Aren't we overreacting a little, pastor?" someone asked.

"No friend, we're not. If you were to talk with a third-world pastor, you'd know. Many pastors at the conference told me they and their people are being hunted like animals for sport. Millions of Christians have been driven from their homes and churches. Thousands are martyred daily."

"Why haven't we heard about this?" another asked.

"Selective journalism and media coverage, perhaps. I don't know for sure. But I know it's happening from the first-hand testimonies of pastors I talked with at the conference."

A wave of whispers swept through the audience.

"I wish I had encouraging news for you, but these are serious times. We can only face it with confidence in the sovereignty of our God. Some of us will survive, while others may go on to be with the Lord. But, no matter what happens, God will give us the grace to go through it. From this day forward, I urge you to be prepared, and keep your eyes on Jesus."

As Pastor Mitchell closed the meeting with an invitation, Shayne's stomach churned. Two opposing voices struggled in his mind; one saying, *Go, Shayne. This is for you.* And the other screaming, *No! Don't do it!*

Laura gently touched his arm. "Would you like to go up, Shayne?"

He turned to gaze into her beautiful brown eyes. They sparkled with pureness. Her prompting was all he needed.

"Yes," he said. "I'm ready."

CHAPTER 6

Bob stared out the window of Shayne's Mustang on the way back to the dorm. He hadn't said a word since they left the church.

"All right," Shayne said, "Why're you so quiet?"

"Why'd you do it?" Bob asked.

"Do what?"

"You know what. You went forward for prayer. It's not like I get enough harassment from those World Church fanatics canvassing our dorms, now *you* had to go and get religious on me."

"But I wanted to. It made sense."

"Yeah, enough to leave me stranded for a whole hour?"

"You were with Whitney, weren't you?"

"Sure, but you know I don't go for those religious prudes." Bob folded his arms and stared out the window at the flurry of snow in the headlights. Had he known the night would turn out this way, he would've stuck with his books at the dorm. Now his roommate was on his way to becoming a Bible thumper like his parents. Fanatics: Jesus this and Jesus that! The University had become a sanctuary for him from their zeal. But tonight's experience had dredged all that anger he had against their hypocrisy and legalism. They were never

30

happy with him. He just couldn't be spiritual enough for their standards. They couldn't get it through their heads that he didn't want to be like them. He didn't like their brand of religion. Masks and shackles was all it was. He hated it. It was junk. Pure junk.

"So," Bob said, "where'd they take you to get brainwashed?"

Shayne grinned and shook his head. "They took me to a room to explain the commitment I was making."

"And?"

"I became a Christian."

"No, I mean, *what* happened to *you* when you did that?"

Shayne glanced at Bob. "You mean when I prayed?"

"Yeah."

"Why?"

"Because I've seen it before. You go down, you get saved, but did something *really* happen to you?"

"Yes, something *did* happen…"

"Like what?

"Like a big weight had been lifted off my shoulders."

"What else?"

"Things seemed to fall in place…like it wasn't just my world anymore. You know, like it was God's world now. He had the controls and the mess out there didn't seem to be as scary. Everything's different. *You* even look different."

"What does that mean?"

"Well…different…like you're a brother…"

"Brother? Hey, leave me out of this. I'm not interested in this *born-again* stuff. I've heard it all my life."

"All right," Shayne replied, "I won't push it on you."

"Good."

Shayne poked Bob's arm, "But you don't stand a chance against Whitney's prayers."

"Oh great. Somebody *else* is praying for me now."

"Yep. Laura told me Whitney hasn't shown that much interest in a guy since she became a Christian a couple of years back."

"Really?" Bob leaned forward and stared at the snow dancing across the windshield. He had to admit, Whitney *was* the most attractive girl he'd ever seen in a church. With her in the picture, maybe he should give this more thought. He didn't have to convert. "Think she'll want to talk to me anymore?"

"Sure. Why don't you come with me to the small group meeting Friday night. She'll be there."

"With Laura, right?"

"Of course!"

Bob smiled, but then he remembered his other plans. "Wait a minute, I had something else going on Friday, like going out to celebrate the end of our midterm exams."

"Okay then, go and celebrate. I'm going to the group."

"Laura's really gotten to you, hasn't she?" Bob teased.

Shayne shrugged. "Whitney will be there, too."

Bob shook his finger at Shayne. "See there, you're already crowding me with this religion."

Shayne laughed. "But isn't it better than what the World Church cult has to offer?"

CHAPTER 7

"I don't trust John Drakon!"

The members of the World Church council stared wearily at their colleague, Hugh Parker.

Garrett Riley, chief officer of intelligence, smiled and shook his head. "We've heard that before, Parker..."

"There've been hints of a conspiracy—"

"But our operatives uncovered nothing."

Margaret Aldredge, the presiding matriarch of the World Church leaned forward, "Gentlemen, please," her hazel eyes focused on Parker. "*What* hints?"

"I've heard things..."

"What? Rumors? Whispers?" she replied. "We need proof."

"I received a phone call from two agents. Said they had something on Drakon, but they disappeared two days later. I tell you Margaret, he's up to something."

Aldredge sighed and leaned back in her chair. "Garrett, has your department checked into this?"

"Yes, but—"

"No excuses," she said pulling off her reading glasses. "Find out what happened to those men. And you, Parker, don't bring this up again until I've seen a file of evidence on my desk."

"But I—"

"Wait." She held up her hand to silence him, "We're talking about Drakon here." She perused the faces of the other members. "In case anyone else on this council endorses Parker's suspicions, may I remind you that Drakon has fifteen years of impeccable service in our organization. His uncanny ability to predict trading in the stock market has given us resources that surpass the world's most prominent financial barons. His genius at political and commercial strategy handed us our power with the World Trade Organization, the World Bank, the United Nations, and the top ten heads of state.

"Because of Drakon, our Church holds the purse strings of the entire world. And with it, *control*. Need I say more?"

No one responded and they all stared at Parker. He leaned back in his chair and folded his arms, defeated again by Drakon's popularity. Unfortunately, Drakon would know what he said. Without proof of Drakon's treachery, Parker could only fear for his life now.

Minutes later, the secretary announced Drakon's arrival. "We'll continue with item three, tomorrow," Margaret Aldredge said. "Send him in."

What John A. Drakon lacked in looks, he made up for in stature. His sleek, silver hair crowned a moderate height of five feet and eleven inches. He wore an immaculately tailored pin-striped suit that enhanced his stately appearance.

As he approached the large oak table, he surveyed the faces of the twelve-member council. He knew so well their thoughts, and their fears. His green, cat-like eyes deeply set under bushy eyebrows intimidated the stoutest of men, especially Hugh Parker.

"Dr. Drakon, what news do you bring from the conference in Amsterdam?" the matriarch asked.

"Our operatives report that the Christians grow weaker by the hour. Due to the economy, many are retreating to underground meetings and are forced to let the banks foreclose on their churches."

"Excellent," Margaret Aldredge replied. "That leaves their buildings for us. What else?"

"The statistics cited at the conference agree with ours. Nearly a third of their members have defected. Hundreds of thousands of Christians are abandoning their faith every day to join our cause for a New World Order."

"And what brought this about?"

"We've been able to persuade the weak and nominal Christians to embrace our teachings."

"And the pastors...?"

"Not a problem. They're as open to our message as the others. If they don't see it our way, we name a price: life or death. Sooner or later, they see the wisdom to comply and merge their congregations with ours."

"How have we dealt with the conservative clergy?" Garrett asked.

"Our *search-and-kill* operation in the third world countries has produced effective results. The assistance of the local police has accelerated our efforts and the puppet-governing officials care so little about the pastors, they let us go about our work without interference."

"But what of the pastors in the free world?" Aldredge asked.

"We're still maintaining our covert position. A good half of them have come around, while the rest are being monitored. We maintain a file in our data banks on every resisting pastor. If they so much as give a hint of protest toward our legislative procedures in their local and state governments, they'll disappear within the week."

The matriarch sat back in her chair and smiled. "Everything is coming together beautifully. A suitable time for our next phase."

The eleven councilmen nodded.

Margaret Aldredge turned to Drakon. "Have you spoken to Reuben Aster about our proposal?"

"I have. He's in Tel Aviv now, ready to meet you."

CHAPTER 8

John A. Drakon knocked on the door of Aster's suite.

A broad shouldered man, six-and-a-half feet tall, greeted him. Drakon had never seen a more stunning individual. His wavy, black hair and deep blue eyes were enhanced by his olive-toned skin. These dominant features served Aster well in dealing with political and state officials whether they were men or women, but especially with the women.

Aster led Drakon through the living room to a veranda separated by a large gold-plated Menorah. He motioned to Drakon to sit down at a table next to the balcony window which overlooked the waterfront of the Mediterranean. A meal had been prepared for them.

Drakon sniffed the savory aroma of food. Little dishes of hummous and baba dip, kibbi, a tubile salad, grape leaves and felafel were laid out as appetizers. For the main course there were plates of grilled chicken, beef, lamb and kafta kabob.

"I've read your report," Aster said in a deep baritone voice. He poured dry red wine into Drakon's glass. "You've done well, John."

"I'm afraid the credit belongs more to you, Reuben. *Your* ideas are what brought us this far."

Drakon had worked with Aster nationally and internationally for the last ten years. When he first met Aster, he knew he had met the one who was destined to rule the world. To Drakon, Aster embodied a genius for world greatness beyond any leader he had read about in history.

"Look at that view," Aster said, pointing to the horizon with his glass. The partially opened window of the balcony elicited a slight winter breeze off the waters. "I love the smell of the salt air, the cry of seagulls, the chirp of the sandpipers." He leaned forward and smiled. "When we get past this stage of our covert operations, we'll make Israel our permanent home."

"It's been long coming," Drakon said as he surveyed the dishes of maza. "Tomorrow will be a milestone to that end."

Aster grew still and stared briefly at the horizon. "It's going to make things easier to tie up the loose ends with this council. Maintaining two simultaneous covers has grown increasingly difficult. Amsterdam was hard for me. Tomorrow we will end our charade with the council. Then, I'll have one act left to play out with these Christians until everything's in place."

Drakon tipped his glass affirmatively and took a drink of his wine to wash down his bread and hummous. "And none too soon. Parker's been picking away at my cover. I had to terminate two of his agents who were snooping around."

"A minor nuisance. We'll be rid of Parker tomorrow."

Drakon chuckled. "How about you? Anyone suspect you yet among the twelve?"

"Nathan Kelly acted strange toward me in Amsterdam."

"Think he knows anything?"

"I'm not sure, but he was cold, not as friendly as I've been used to."

Drakon tapped the table with his fork. "You want him erased?"

"Not yet. Just put a shadow on him. We need to concentrate on the remaining three heads of state. Once we have them committed to the ten-kingdom alliance, I'll leave this little club of apostles, and then we can take care of Kelly."

"We should've taken him out years ago."

Aster poured Drakon more wine. "Relax, John. It served us well as a cover and kept us abreast of their strategy. Once we have the alliance and our World Federation established, the Christians can do little to stop us."

"How's it coming with those three prima donnas in the alliance?" Drakon asked.

"Still politically ambitious, but we'll bring them in line soon. If not, I'll simply replace them."

CHAPTER 9

The hour had come for the council to position Aster.

Having a figurehead to embody the principles of the World Church was long overdue. The organization had grown into the largest affiliation of religious entities in the world and needed a leader to bring personality and charm to the organization, someone to represent their cause to the world.

Until now, they had been in contact with Aster through Drakon under the code name *chameleon*. Today they would meet him face to face and inaugurate him into his destiny.

The members of the World Church council sat quietly around the large oak table as Drakon and Aster entered the room. "Members of the council," Drakon began, "Dr. Reuben Joshua Aster."

The council stood and applauded their special guest. They quickly exchanged greetings and sat down.

"Dr. Aster," Margaret Aldredge began, "I've been an admirer of your talents and genius for ten years now. We've been monitoring your covert operation a long time and have found you to be first among the elite. Your infiltration into the rank of the twelve most powerful leaders among the

Christians is nothing short of a miracle. I can speak for the council, and myself, that we couldn't be more pleased with your credentials."

Aster gazed deeply into the hazel eyes of the matriarch and winked. "Compliment received, Madame."

Hugh Parker, the council's vice chair, jumped in. "Dr. Aster, the world's economic plight has provided us now with the greatest opportunity for solidifying our next phase toward a New World Order. Are you prepared to accept our offer to make you the ambassador of our organization?"

"I am, but I have three concerns before I can begin to function in that position."

"Concerns?" Parker asked, leaning forward in his chair. He cast a suspicious glance at Drakon. "What do you mean?"

"My concerns are about three members of the heads of state in the alliance we're forming. They have political ambitions that could undermine our objectives and must be subdued. Until I am convinced of their commitment to the team, I can't risk exposing my identity to the Christians by taking this role prematurely."

The council whispered among themselves in apparent misgiving. Garrett Riley, the council's intelligence officer, addressed Aster. "We've heard nothing of this from our operatives. Every head of state in the alliance has shown great support for our cause."

"According to Drakon, all but three," Aster replied.

The council stared suspiciously at the two men.

"We've seen no report," Riley said.

Hugh Parker glared at Drakon. "You've given Aster highly sensitive documents..."

"Wait," Margaret Aldredge said, and looked at Drakon. "I'm sure you have a good explanation for ignoring protocol, John. But if this report *is* true, I'd like to hear Dr. Aster's recommendation."

Aster scanned the members of the council. "I believe we should maintain our present course while I continue to move freely among my peers with the Christians. In the meantime, persuade the three heads of state to lay down their personal ambitions and line up. When I'm assured of their loyalty and Drakon confirms it, I can drop my Christian cover and become the voice of the World Church."

"And if they don't line up?" Parker asked.

"We replace them with *cooperative* heads of state."

Parker surveyed the stone-cold faces of his colleagues unaware of the billowing cloud of smoke forming behind him.

The matriarch leaned forward to speak when the cloud moved directly between the council and Aster. She gasped.

"Don't be alarmed," Drakon said. "Just be still."

All the members of the council froze in their chairs, staring at the pulsating cloud as it rumbled. Bursts of light, like static electricity, shot out of the cloud and a nine-foot creature suddenly appeared in the smoke. With a deep-throated voice, the entity said,

> "I am the spirit, Shenzar. Hear me.
> "Aster has been chosen to become a great tree whose branches will cover the earth. Under his branches, the nations of the world will find rest. There is none like him among the gods, for he will save the world and rule it. Listen to him!"

As quickly as the creature appeared, he vanished. Two bolts of lightning shot from the pulsating cloud and encircled Aster and Drakon.

The electrically-charged room blinded the eyes of the council. When their sight returned, the cloud was gone.

They stared at the aura of energy that crackled around Aster and Drakon's charged bodies. Then Aster spoke firmly with authority in his voice. "When the time is right, I will lead this organization under my true identity. In the meantime, I'm placing Drakon in charge of the council."

Parker jumped up and glared at his colleagues. "Didn't I tell you Drakon was up to something?"

He turned to Aster. "Just who do you think you are, you

and these hocus-pocus illusions? I don't know how you did it, but I'll not be conned to believe in it, or the message. This council is the greatest power in history, and *you*, sir, will not waltz in here and take over."

The other members nodded nervously.

"Drakon," Aster replied. "Show them."

"With pleasure." Drakon said. He smiled deviously at Parker and pointed a finger at him and Margaret Aldredge. "You two are dismissed from your posts. Leave the room."

The matriarch jumped up beside Parker. "Outrageous!" she said.

"Then leave the hard way," Drakon replied and looked above them.

Parker followed Drakon's eyes to the ceiling. A fiery pillar had appeared over the heads of the council. "Noooo!" he screamed as a white-hot flame leaped out of the fire and engulfed both him and Margaret Aldredge.

The other members of the council gasped in horror as they watched their colleagues shrivel in the flame like two foam cups. Their smoldering bodies fell back into their chairs and the room became filled with the nauseating odor of burned hair and skin. The destruction was swift. All that remained were their charred bodies and skulls, with a grisly smile from their teeth.

The council members stared at the smoking remains.

Aster leaned his hands on the table and studied the pale faces of the council. "It's fortunate for you that Drakon and I are here to fill these vacant seats."

No one spoke.

"Okay then, it's unanimous," Aster said. "We accept the nomination. I will replace Aldredge as the new chairperson, and Drakon will replace Parker as the vice chair. All in favor say aye."

"Aye," they replied.

"Any objections?"

The council members shook their heads.

"Okay, that settles it." Aster smiled and looked at Drakon.

"John, I want you to set up our World Church headquarters here in Tel Aviv. As for me, I'll concentrate first on the president of the United States, and then I'll go after the other two heads of state later."

He turned to the council. "Drakon will have the honor of announcing my name to the world. I advise you not to upset him.

"And, Mr. Riley? You've been heading up our covert operatives?"

Riley nodded.

"I want you to step up our efforts on the third world front. Every pastor who refuses to join, kill them.

"For now I want the rest of you to cozy up with the loyal heads of state in the UN. Ensure their commitment to our cause and the ten-kingdom alliance. If you detect anything that spells desertion from any of them, I want to know about it."

"Until the timing is right," Aster continued, "I don't exist. If Drakon or I find any of you breathing my name to anyone outside of this council, you'll swiftly join your crispy friends here. Understood?"

They nodded and held their noses to ward off the odor of their dead colleagues.

Aster and Drakon turned to leave the room and stopped at the door. "Oh, one more thing," Aster said. "Parker was right. Drakon *has* been up to something for fifteen years. He's been laying a foundation for the 21st century ruler of the world. Me."

<hr/>

As Aster and Drakon left the room, the eyes of the beaten council stared numbly at the smoldering bodies of Aldredge and Parker. The day they had waited for so long, the day they had expected to appoint their *puppet* ambassador...had become a day they'd regret for eternity.

CHAPTER 10

Friday night had come. The exams were over.

Bob Jansen and Shayne Taylor stood at the door of the fraternity house that was having the small group meeting. Tim Patterson, a first-string linebacker on the football team, greeted them at the door and welcomed them in.

"Hey everybody," Whitney Conner said as she grabbed Bob's hand and pulled him toward the group. "This is Bob, and his friend, Shayne."

Several students greeted them and led them into a room where the chairs were arranged in a circle. Bob noticed a picture of Jesus on the wall, along with the various posters of musical artists and scriptures. It reminded him of his parent's home, filled with religious embellishments they treated like shrines. He should've gone out and celebrated with the guys instead.

"Okay!" Tim Patterson shouted. "Why don't we get started."

Everyone took their seats in the circle of chairs and quieted down.

"Let's begin with someone telling the group about a significant event that happened in your life this week," Tim said.

Whitney raised her hand. "I've got something to share," she said. "First, I survived the week of midterms." The other students nodded and smiled from their similar experience.

"And," Whitney continued, placing her hand on Bob's shoulder, "I met a new friend at church."

Bob felt his face turn red.

"I got to pray with Shayne," Laura said, gazing at him with a smile. "He prayed to receive Christ Wednesday night."

The group reacted warmly and applauded for Shayne.

As Tim Patterson kept the testimonies going around the circle, Bob listened intently to each one's experience that week. Surprisingly, he found himself wanting to be a part, but had nothing to share. He couldn't relate to someone outside of his own common experiences or interests. Yet, he found their stories appealing, which scared him.

When they finished their testimonies, Tim grabbed his Ovation guitar and led the group in singing for the next twenty minutes. He began with joyful, upbeat songs and then went into slower songs of worship.

Bob didn't know any of the songs, but he enjoyed watching the group. He'd never seen such sincerity before. Fanatics, he'd seen, but the spirit of this group was different somehow. He gazed around the room at their happy faces. Their eyes were closed with their hands raised in the air.

Even Shayne, his old marijuana-smoking friend, was caught up in it; raising his hands to Jesus like the rest.

When the music stopped, they all sat quietly with their eyes still closed, like they were waiting for something.

A red haired girl broke the silence. "I believe someone here is down to their last dollar and needs a few bucks to carry them through the weekend."

Bob glanced around the circle. No one looked up. He didn't recall seeing anything like this before. Was it supposed to be some big revelation? That description could fit anybody these days. It certainly fit *his* situation. He smiled and shook his head when no one responded.

Tim Patterson finally spoke up, probably for Bob and

Shayne's sake. "The Bible calls this a *word of knowledge*. It's something that God reveals to meet a need. Who does this relate to?"

Conviction gripped Bob's heart. Maybe no one else had this problem. Maybe it really *was* for him. If so, the girl was right. He waited a little longer. Still no one responded.

"It's me," Bob said, raising his hand reluctantly. "I'm the one who's broke."

The group glanced up from praying and smiled.

"Let's take an offering for him," Laura said. Everyone agreed and a hat was immediately placed in the middle of the group.

Bob watched in disbelief as they took money from their purses or wallets and filled the hat with cash and change. Tim took the hat and counted the money. "Fifty-two dollars, exactly," he said, handing it to Bob. "Will that help you for a while?"

Bob stood with the money in his hands. "Wow! I don't know what to say. Thanks! Thanks a lot!"

The students clapped happily for him.

Tim proceeded with the meeting and other words of knowledge were brought and responded to, followed by a lengthy discussion over Pastor Mitchell's Wednesday night message. The meeting ended after they held hands in a circle and prayed for the school, their church's transition, the country, and unsaved friends.

Everyone left early that night, exhausted from the week of midterm exams.

———

Bob sat deep in thought on the way back to the dorm.

Neither of them spoke.

When Shayne pulled his red Mustang into the dorm's parking lot, it was 9:30. The still, lifeless campus reminded them that most of the students had already left for home during their semester break.

Canterton University, named after the city, was nestled in the rolling hills of Virginia on the banks of the Roanoke River. Its claim to fame came into public view when their alumnus, Samuel Thomas, became the current president of the United States. Most exciting for Shayne and Bob was the president's scheduled address for their graduating class in June.

Next to their dorm was the campus itself. The red brick buildings were mostly veiled with a fingering maze of ivy vines, now powdered with snow. Shayne particularly enjoyed the elms that lined the streets, towering like soldiers with their sabers raised to form an arch.

"Well? Did you like it?" Shayne asked.

Bob pulled out of his thoughts. "I just don't get it," he said.

"What's that?" Shayne asked.

"Why they gave me this money. You know how tight it's been for everybody. Even the rich kids. Yet they put cash in that hat without giving it a second thought. Why?"

"Because they care, maybe...or they're Christians..."

"But I've never seen Christians do anything like this."

"Really?"

"Yeah, really. I've been in church most of my life, but there's something different happening here. These Christians don't fit the images I grew up with. They act normal. They're religious, but they act normal."

Shayne didn't know what to say. He didn't have a religious background, so he couldn't relate to his friend's confusion and decided to leave it alone. He patted Bob on the shoulder and opened his door. "Let's go in, I'm tired."

"Whitney invited me to church Sunday," Bob said as he got out of the car.

Shayne shut the door and leaned on the car roof. "You going to go?" He tried to sound disinterested.

"I might."

Shayne smiled and picked up a handful of wet snow. "You sure it's religion that's got you confused...or Whitney?"

He tossed the snowball at Bob's head and ran for the dorm.

CHAPTER 11

"Mr. President, your 10:30 appointment is here."

Samuel Thomas glanced at his watch. "Send him in, please," he replied. He stepped from behind the desk of the Oval Office to greet his guest being ushered through the door. "Reuben Aster! This *is* a surprise. What brings you to Washington?"

Aster gazed casually around the room. "Two years in office with soaring approval ratings, Sam. Even in *this* economy, America still loves you."

Thomas adjusted his wire-rimmed glasses and smiled. "The polls are showing the best ratings in history."

"Better than JFK?"

"Even better."

"Then I got here just in time to bring you back down to Earth," Aster said, walking toward the couch.

President Thomas stared at him and walked toward his chair in the middle of the room. "How refreshing your candor is in this dreary life of power and prestige. A nice change from my coddling administration."

Aster sat on the couch and admiringly stroked the top and leg of the coffee table. "Nice wood. Cherry?"

"Uh…yes, it is." Thomas sat down in his chair next to the couch. "Tell me, Reuben, do you still abide by that celibacy rule of yours? I've got a great secretary on the other side of that door—"

"Forget it. Not with my schedule. Besides, extracurricular activity with the opposite sex is politically hazardous these days."

"Didn't know you were running for office?"

"I'm not."

Thomas stared curiously at Aster. "So what can I do for you? You come to cash in on the promises I made you during the campaign?"

Aster smiled. "You do get to the point, don't you. A quality I've always admired. Yes, I've come to cash in."

"Thought so. It seemed a little odd that a leader of conservative Christians would risk a personal visit to Washington. Could get messy if a story leaked out that you were hobnobbing with the upper crust of the left wing."

"The least of my worries."

"Then why a personal visit? Why not your usual mode of contact through your operatives?"

"I've heard rumors that require my personal attention."

"Rumors?"

"About you backing out of the program. Important people are wondering how committed you are to the alliance."

"I fully intend to participate with the alliance."

"That's not what I hear."

"Check the records. Look at the bills I've gotten through congress. I've done everything you've asked me to do."

Aster leaned forward. "We're that close," he said, holding up his thumb an inch away from his index finger, "that close to the *pivotal* step for the New World Order. But these American Christians keep holding things up. We've got to tighten the reigns, Sam, shut them down."

Thomas gripped the arms of his chair. "What do you want me to do?"

"You've got seventy percent of the House and Senate in

your pocket, including every seat on the Supreme Court—"

"On *your* bank roll, you mean."

Aster stared quietly for a moment at Thomas. "How hard would it be for you to pass a creative bill that could weaken any public gatherings for Christians? Create something like more stringent building codes or zoning laws if they want to meet. Anything that can distract them, slow them down."

Thomas stood up. "Wait a minute. I've spent my entire political career fighting to get where I am today, and I can't jeopardize those efforts. We started turning up the heat on those fanatics ten years ago. We've taken their tax exemption from them, started a trend of church fires….what more is there to do? They're struggling already. I know they can still gridlock us in the House or Senate, but we'll be rid of them."

"It's going too slow."

"But I need more time. This isn't a third world country, you know. There are Christians in office who still carry enough clout to make trouble. We can't rush into this."

Aster stood up and moved toward Thomas. A crimson streak formed on his right temple. "I want things to move faster, Sam. The alliance is your priority. If we don't shut these meddling Christians down, we can't initiate the constitutional convention quickly enough to establish the World Federation."

Thomas wiped the beads of sweat from his forehead. "The alliance will have to wait until the second term. By then, we'll have every right wing fanatic replaced by our own people and will pass new laws that'll knock the Christians out completely. It'll happen, I promise. But too much too soon, Reuben, could backfire on us."

"Us?" Aster said, glaring at Thomas. "You sure it's not *you* and your political ambitions you're worried about?"

"No, that's not true—"

"It's a hungry world out there, Sam. They don't care about you or your office. They want a future that transcends the has-been clout of America. The ten-kingdom alliance will be the new superpower; not Samuel Thomas, and not America."

51

Thomas dabbed at the beads of sweat, now running profusely down his forehead. "Confound it, man, can't you see I *can't* do anymore. I've done all I can do for now."

Aster frowned and held up his hand. "I can see the rumors are justified. Apparently, you've forgotten the power and money that gave you this presidency. What a shame when the reports get out about the organization that funded your campaign."

"That'd be stupid. It would expose your own people."

"Not our money, Sam...foreign and corporate lobbyists. Such fabrications are no problem to spin no matter how popular you are. Heros' wings are easily clipped in volatile times like these."

"Your plans are premature, Reuben. It won't work."

"Oh, but they will. After we ruin your career, we'll put a bullet through your head."

"You wouldn't dare!"

"Japan and Europe called me this morning to confirm their commitment to the alliance. We need the United States to complete it. Do you really think I wouldn't dare? Do you think I'm going to let a puny career politician like you mess with destiny?"

Thomas jumped up from his chair. "Get out! Get out before I call security!"

Aster chuckled and moved toward the door. "I'm giving you three weeks, Sam. Three weeks to come up with a plan that'll shut down the Christians *and* their politicians sooner than your political agenda. We have a narrow margin of time we're dealing with here. Next time I call, you'd better have something or you're on your own."

Aster opened the door and looked back at the president now standing behind his desk. "Three weeks, Sam," he said. "Goodbye."

CHAPTER 12

He was trapped.

Trapped like a fly in the web of Aster's political influence and power.

President Thomas stared at the door where Aster walked out. Beads of sweat still rolled down his forehead. His body shook uncontrollably. He reached in his drawer for the bottle of Valium and swallowed a couple of pills.

The secretary buzzed his office.

"Mr. President, Malloy is here to see you."

Thomas wiped his brow with his handkerchief. "Send him in, Carla."

Cliff Malloy had been head of the Central Intelligence Agency for twenty years. He'd served under three presidents with an excellent record.

"Mr. President, you okay?" Malloy asked as he entered the room. "You're as white as a sheet."

"I'll be fine, Cliff. Please...sit down."

"Sir...are you sure you're okay? I can get the doc——"

"No. I'll be fine. Just give me a moment to explain." President Thomas strolled to the couch and lowered himself into a reclining position with his feet propped up. Malloy sat in the chair across from him.

"Cliff, you've been a friend of the family for thirty years now. I remember how diligent you were to protect Dad when he held office. Ever since I was a boy, I've dreamed of following in his footsteps, and worked hard to get here. I wanted to make Dad proud."

"I'm sure he'd be proud, sir."

"Before he died, I promised him I would run for president, and do my best to serve America in a way that would honor his name. But when victory seemed to be eluding my campaign during the primaries, I succumbed to temptation and took the plunge."

Malloy cocked his head and frowned. "What's going on, sir?"

President Thomas sighed and stared at Malloy. "Reuben Aster bankrolled my campaign with the funds of the World Church organization."

"What!?"

"I know, Cliff. I know. It was foolish of me. I should've never listened to my campaign advisers."

"So, what's this guy's price for the presidency he bought you?"

"It doesn't matter. I can't agree to his request. I've done too much already. If I give in, he'll have me selling America to a world federation."

"World federation? Are we talking encroachment on U.S. sovereignty?"

President Thomas sat up and looked Cliff in the eyes. "You must kill him. He's a lunatic possessed with controlling the world through this ten-kingdom alliance he's forming. He's already got nine of the strongest countries signed on."

"And he wants the United States to be number ten?"

"Yes. I've been holding him off as long as I could, but my time's run out."

Malloy stood up. "I'll get right on it, sir."

"Be quick about it. I've only got three weeks to comply to his impossible goals. He'll kill me, I assure you."

"I'll keep you posted on our progress."

"Keep your strike force small. No more men than is absolutely necessary. He's capable of having his own operatives within your ranks."

"I'll hand-pick them myself, sir. Why don't you lie back down. Get some rest. I'll take care of this leech."

President Thomas smiled feebly and walked Malloy to the door. "You're a good friend, Cliff. Dad always liked you. He felt safe on your watch."

"Thank you, sir. I'll do the same for you." Malloy patted Thomas' shoulder and left the room.

Emotionally drained from his encounter with Aster, the president returned to the couch and laid down with his right arm over his eyes. His left hand dropped onto the cherry-wood table in front of the couch. Little did he know that a tiny bugging device had been planted under the table earlier by the skillful hands of Reuben Aster.

CHAPTER 13

"...or you're on your own."

Cliff Malloy rewound the taped conversation of Aster with the president. "...I'm giving you three weeks, Sam. Three weeks to come up with a plan..."

Malloy clicked off the tape and turned to agents Hank and Derrick, his closest associates in the CIA. "What have we got?" he asked, pushing back his chair from the desk. He reached behind him for a brown-spotted banana on top of a cluttered stacks of files, and began to peel it.

"It's unbelievable, chief," Hank replied with an opened folder of documents in his hand. "The man's life is a complete blank before he surfaces in his involvement with Christian activists. Like someone erased his records. No parents, no birth certificate...nothing."

"Interesting." Malloy threw the banana peel in his trash can and took a sip of his tepid coffee. "So what's he been up to?"

"It's strange. His life is full of contradictions."

"How's that?"

"He's got his hands in everything. On one side, he's ranked among the twelve most powerful Christian leaders in the world. An apostle they call him. On the other hand, he's been in an intricate partnership with the activities of the World Church, who aren't particularly pen pals with Christians."

"An undercover operative…"

"That's not all, chief," Derrick cut in. "I've been digging up some serious stuff on this World Church. They've got bigger plans than religious domination. Not only do their financial resources surpass every organization and financial giant in the world, we've uncovered a trail of World Church funding into the campaigns of major world leaders over the last ten years."

Malloy ran his fingers through his short, graying hair. "The nine heads of state in this ten-kingdom alliance Aster's been forming?"

"Yes, sir," Derrick replied. "The alliance is no fairy tale. It's a world-class conspiracy with Aster in the middle of it all."

"And he's more than an undercover agent, chief," Hank said. "It appears he's been a catalyst in the inner circle of World Church operations, he and another guy named John Drakon."

"Fascinating," Malloy said.

"Apparently their objective is world domination through this alliance, sir," Derrick said, "and the United States is slated to join them. From there they plan to create a World Federation."

"Which threatens U.S. sovereignty," Malloy said.

"Precisely," Derrick replied, "And guess who the World Church plans to head up this ten-kingdom alliance?"

"Aster," Malloy replied. "Well, gentlemen, looks like we've got ourselves a very big fish to catch. Does the surveillance team have the van ready?"

"Yes, and we've located the apartment. Our men are bugging the suite as we speak."

"Good. Join me at 1700 hours."

CHAPTER 14

The U-haul truck sat parked in front of Aster's hotel.

Inside, Malloy and his two agents were in full view of Aster's balcony. They sat cozily among instruments, computers and hardware that resembled the walls of a sound studio. With Aster's room bugged, Malloy hoped to get more information on the alliance before he killed him.

Drakon and Aster returned from their evening meal and entered the suite. As Aster switched on the lights, Drakon grabbed his arm and motioned for silence. He scanned the room and felt the residual energy of recent activity. He turned to Aster and pointed to his ears.

Aster caught on.

Drakon walked quickly to the radio and turned up the music. He then motioned for Aster to return to the hallway. Aster went first and then Drakon, shutting the door behind him. "Let's move away from the door," he whispered.

They took a few steps and Drakon whispered to Aster,

"We obviously have company. I suggest we go out on the balcony and find our eavesdropping guests. I saw the truck parked out front when we came in."

Aster grinned. "The president's protectors have come. Let's give them a *warm* greeting."

Drakon chuckled. "With pleasure."

They reentered the suite, turned off the music, and went out on the balcony. A flurry of snow obscured their vision until they discovered the truck parked directly below across the street.

"Mr. Malloy," Aster said loudly for the bugging devices. "What a predictable disguise, your U-Haul coffin."

———◦◦◦———

Malloy threw off his head set and jumped up from his chair, "What the—"

Derrick switched their monitors to audio.

"Don't be surprised," Aster sneered over the speakers in the truck. "I've been waiting for you ever since your discussion two days ago with the president. You're not the only one who can bug a room."

Malloy scowled and looked with disbelief at Hank and Derrick.

"Poor Sam," Aster continued. "I feel sorry for him. Pity he had to waste such good agents to save his puny hide."

Malloy caught the threat in Aster's voice and ran to the back of the truck to open the door.

"I'm disappointed in you, Malloy. You've been careless. Your files should have revealed myself as a greater foe than you anticipated. But enough of the chit-chat. I have important matters to attend to. My associate, John Drakon, will tuck you in for the night. Sweet dreams."

Malloy raised the back door in time to peer through the snowfall and locate Aster's balcony. A lone figure, silhouetted against the light inside, stood with his arms raised.

Malloy's eyes widened when a fiery ball of light appeared

between the man's hands. Then a commanding voice shouted through their monitors, "Be gone!"

A bolt of light shot out from the fiery orb and streaked toward the van like a missile.

At that instant, the head lights of an oncoming truck shined in Malloy's face and momentarily blurred his vision. He shielded his eyes from the light and looked up at the balcony. He smelled something burning and saw a blue, reddish streak of light trailing directly to the gas tank alongside the truck's cab. The tank was smoking and glowing red!

"Get out of here!" Malloy shouted to Hank and Derrick as he started to jump out the back.

It was too late.

The force of the explosion ripped through the equipment and blew out the panels, leaving the truck engulfed in flames. Hank and Derrick died instantly.

Malloy, however, was caught by the explosion in midair when he jumped, and was hurled seventy feet into the bed of the truck that had just passed. As he landed, his head struck the corner of a crate which knocked him unconscious.

━━◦Ⅲ∫Ⅲ◦━━

Aster and Drakon watched the event with amusement, convinced that Malloy and his agents were dead.

The distant wail of sirens soon filled the air with the crackle and snap of the blazing flames.

"What a beautiful night in this nation's capital," Aster said coolly.

"A perfect way to end the day," Drakon replied.

"Too bad President Thomas decided to jump ship. He could have had such a wonderful future. Now we've got to replace him."

"Tomorrow?"

"Yes. We'll need to pay our chief of staff a visit."

Drakon grinned. "Becker will have his work cut out for him, molding that sniveling VP into a president."

"Yes, but unlike Thomas, that sniveling VP will gladly avoid the tragedy his predecessor is about to experience."

The two men looked at each other and laughed, oblivious to the unconscious form of Cliff Malloy, lying in the back of a southbound truck that would wind its way into Virginia.

CHAPTER 15

Another night of insomnia.

The third night Pastor Mitchell lay awake, still mulling over the changes his church would be facing. Usually, when his mind was restless, he'd heat up a cup of milk to help him fall asleep.

They were out of milk.

Wide awake, he put on his wool coat and drove to the Qwik Mart three blocks from the house. Just as he parked in front of the store, a truck pulled in beside his car.

"You're out pretty late on the road," Jack said to the driver as they approached the door together.

"Yeah, but at least I'm still alive. Nearly got killed by an exploding truck in Washington."

"Really?"

"It's a fact."

"God must have been watching out for you, friend."

The trucker frowned and lowered his eyes. "Don't believe in God," he muttered and quickly entered the store.

Jack followed him inside, respecting the man's desire to distance himself from any more comments about God. Obviously, an opportunity to witness wasn't the reason for Jack's insomnia.

Jack purchased a quart of milk and returned to his car. As he opened the door, a groaning sound caught his attention. He surveyed the parking lot and saw no one.

"Oooohhhh!"

There it was again. Somewhere in the direction of the truck. Jack glanced back in the store, and saw the driver perusing the sandwich cooler. Jack strolled over to the rear of the man's truck and peered into the back.

"Ugh!" he gasped at the sight and smell.

A bleeding and burned man lay on his stomach beside a wooden crate. His tattered leather coat and under garments revealed severe cuts and gashes on his back and legs.

"Help me...please...somebody," the man said.

Jack looked back at the store and moved toward the door to get help.

"*No one must know*," a voice whispered.

"Huh?" Jack stopped and looked back at the injured man.

"*No one must know*," the voice said again. Jack turned to see who it was. It wasn't the injured man, but he saw no one else. A chill surged through his body. He pulled up his collar. *God must be speaking to me.*

"Oooohhh!" the man groaned again. Jack looked inside the store, but no one was watching. He returned to the rear of the truck. "Can you move, mister?" he asked.

"Don't know," the man replied weakly. "I'll try."

Jack opened the tailgate with his eye on the driver inside. He jumped into the bed of the truck and gently lifted the man's shoulders.

"Ouch!"

"What's wrong?"

"My back's on fire."

Jack looked at the red and white layers of shredded skin mingled with pus and blood. "I'll be more careful, but we've got to move you out of this cold. Try to move with me, slowly."

He gently pulled the man's legs forward until they dangled over the tailgate. He pulled him up carefully and placed one arm around his neck. Then he eased the man's feet to the ground.

"Lean on my back and I'll hold on to your arms over my shoulders. I'll pull you over to the car."

The man groaned and said, "Okay."

Jack glanced again in the store. The trucker now stood at the counter with the clerk, both oblivious to the activity outside.

While he dragged the injured man toward the car, the stranger went limp and passed out. Jack's feet began to slip on the snow and he barely retrieved his balance. He held tight to the dead weight of the man's body and shuffled his way to the car.

As he laid the man in the back seat, the door of the store chimed. The trucker walked out. He went straight to the cab of his truck and never looked back at his cargo. The truck growled into reverse, then into first gear and pushed through the snow-covered lot into the cold wintry night.

Jack leaned back against his car and sighed. *That was close!* He looked into the back seat at the unconscious figure and shut the passenger's door.

A light layer of snow blew off the ground as he shut the door, exposing a black leather wallet. Jack spotted it and picked it up. *Must belong to this fellow.*

He placed it in his coat pocket and hopped in the car. He thanked the Lord for helping him and prayed briefly for wisdom. He looked again in the store at the clerk, who stared at him out the window. Jack waved. The clerk waved back and returned to reading his paper.

No one had seen a thing.

It was the way God wanted it.

CHAPTER 16

Rhonda Mitchell, Jack's wife, was a professional nurse.

She put the final wrapping and bandages on their strange guest, and stared at him for a moment as he lay unconscious on his stomach. She figured twenty percent of his body on his arms, hands and back had received second degree burns. He also had multiple bumps and bruises, including a deep gash in his skin above the right temple.

God sure spared your life, mister.

Rhonda said a prayer and turned out the light. She closed the door softly and came downstairs to join her husband.

"Thanks for attending to him, sweetheart," Jack said. "You're a great nurse."

"He's hurt bad, dear. Looks like he's been in a fire or an explosion of some kind."

"Is he going to make it?"

"He'll make it, but if his burns had been any deeper or covered any more of his body, he'd be in critical condition."

"How long do you think it'll take him to recover?"

"If we apply the ointment three times a day and the bandages are changed…maybe three to four weeks. He'll be in a lot of pain. You sure we can't take him to the hospital?"

"I'm afraid not. God spoke to me clearly out in that parking lot that no one must know about this."

"But why?"

Jack picked up the black leather wallet on the lampstand beside him. "Maybe this is our clue," he said holding it up. "I found it on the ground. Must have fallen out of his pocket when I put him in the car."

Rhonda took the wallet and opened it. "Clifford James Malloy, CIA. Jack, this is the CIA director! What's he doing in the back of a truck in Canterton, Virginia?"

"I don't know."

"Do you think God meant, when he spoke to you, that the CIA shouldn't know about this, or that nobody in *Canterton* should know?"

"I'm not sure. Perhaps it would be best to wait until Malloy wakes up and let *him* decide."

Rhonda sat on the couch and stared out the living room bay window. The stately elm trees, lining the street, had been dusted with a fresh layer of snow.

"Why us, Jack?" she asked. "Why did God send you tonight to find this man?"

Jack shrugged his shoulders. "Who knows." He gazed at the ceiling and chuckled.

"What's so funny?" Rhonda asked.

"God's sense of humor. Malloy's an agent who has served under three liberal presidents. What's funny is that we have a liberal intelligence officer being cared for in the home of two, so-called, right wing fanatics."

CHAPTER 17

"No! Not the tanks!" Malloy yelled.

"Hank!—Derrick!—Run!"

Delirious with fever, Malloy struggled to get up while Jack and Rhonda held him down on the bed.

"Conspiracy!" Malloy screamed, straining against the firm grip of Rhonda and Jack on his arms. "I've got to stop him! Stop Aster! He's going to kill the president!" He struggled once more to get up and then collapsed.

"What're we going to do?" Rhonda asked as she relaxed her grip. "He needs better medical attention. If we keep him with us we're going to need a miracle."

"Give me your hand," Jack said. "We'll pray." He knelt beside the bed and laid his hand on Malloy's burning forehead. "Father, in Jesus' name, we ask you to remove this fever."

They continued to pray for about five minutes more and then sat back to watch the patient.

Beads of sweat formed on Malloy's head.

Rhonda placed her hand on his face and smiled. "God is answering our prayer. The fever's starting to break."

Jack raised his hands. "Thank you, Lord!"

"Let's let him rest now, dear," Rhonda said. She took Jack by the hand and walked around the bed. They took one last look at Malloy and shut the door.

Downstairs, Rhonda prepared dinner while Jack reclined in the family room of their hundred-year-old home. He reflected over the last eighteen hours since he found Malloy while he watched his wife in the kitchen. Jack was thankful for his beautiful companion. For twenty-five years she had sailed through a myriad of challenges. Once again, she shone through another unusual circumstance common to the role of a pastor's wife.

Jack's thoughts shifted to an old ache in his heart. How he wished they could have had children. They had prayed so long for God to heal the endometriosis she had.

They were blessed in other ways, however. The kids from the university had become their own children. They were wild and naive; many in desperate need of practical wisdom. Jack and Rhonda had nurtured many students through their four years of school and then sent them out ready to make their mark on the world. Many graduates continued to write. Some even called, which made all the years without children less painful.

"What're you staring at, dear?" Rhonda asked.

"You," he said. "Have I told you lately how beautiful you are?"

She smiled. "Not since the last student we took in."

"What's that supposed to mean?"

"I know your pattern. First, you feel sorry for some puppy-eyed kid who needs a home, then you tell me I'm beautiful and ask me if we can keep them."

"That bad, huh?"

"It's been two months since our last student moved out. You sure this compliment isn't attached somehow to keeping Malloy?"

Jack jumped up and playfully grabbed his wife. "No, it isn't."

"Hmmm," she sighed, snuggling into his arms. "Too bad dinner's on the table. We can't let it get cold."

CHAPTER 18

"Mr. President, relax."

Lamar Becker, the White House chief of staff, brought George Cane his coffee.

The president took a sip and looked nervously at Becker. "It's easy for you to say...you've been in this game a long time. I only became vice president as a favor to Sam. But now, by the fate of an assassin's bullet, I've inherited the role of someone I could never measure up to. You know it, I know it—"

"But the world doesn't know it," Becker said. "That's where I come in...to help you through this. We'll have you being *presidential* before you realize it. It'll grow on you, George. Look how well you handled the swearing in today, and the press conference. You're going to do fine."

Cane set his coffee down and paced the floor. "How can I possibly fill Sam's shoes? It will take a miracle for me to get reelected."

"That's why I invited Dr. Aster here today."

"But are you sure he can help?"

"How do you think Samuel Thomas got elected? It was Aster who paved the way for him. He'll do the same for you."

"Why didn't Sam tell me about him?"

"Like I said, he and Sam had a special relationship. Aster was a key political strategist behind the scenes. Trust me on this. The man has connections...and very deep pockets."

Cane jerked when the phone buzzed in his office. He stared at Becker.

"That's your line, sir. Better get used to answering it."

Cane nodded and picked up the phone. "Yes?"

"Mr. President," the secretary replied, "a Dr. Reuben Aster is here for your 3:30 appointment."

"Uh...thank you, Carla. Send him in."

Lamar Becker opened the door and reached out his fat hands to welcome their guest. "Mr. President, this a personal friend of mine, Dr. Reuben Aster."

Cane strolled out from behind the desk. "Dr. Aster, it's good to meet you. Lamar's told me a lot about you. I understand you can help me establish some clout in this Oval Office. Please," he motioned to a chair, "have a seat and tell me about it."

The three men sat down and Aster began. "Mr. President, I *can* help you, but I'm operating from a delicate position. I can't allow others to know of my involvment with you, except for present company alone. I work covertly to give myself flexibility as well as to safeguard those I help, like yourself. I need assurance of complete anonymity."

Cane glanced at his chief of staff. "Can we do that?"

"We can," Becker replied.

Cane smiled. "Go on please, Dr. Aster."

"The first way I can help," Aster said, "is to give you documented proof that will pin-point the people who plotted the assassination of President Thomas."

George Cane turned toward Becker. "This is getting good, already."

Becker winked at Aster and leaned toward Cane. "Mr. President, if this information will bring these murderers to justice, the people will love you for it."

"Yes," Cane replied. "An excellent way to begin my term in office. Who are these assassins, Dr. Aster?"

"The religious sect of right wing Christian extremists. They've been opposing our efforts toward a New World Order for three decades."

"I thought they were pacifists."

"No longer," Becker replied. "They've grown into a militant nation among nations. They've got to be stopped, sir."

CHAPTER 19

Four weeks had passed since Cliff Malloy's accident.

His burns and wounds were healing well, thanks to Rhonda's skill as a nurse *and* her prayers.

Jack thought they should keep quiet about their faith since Malloy's office and political persuasions were less than friendly toward Christians. They would do this at least until they found out more about this CIA director who had so mysteriously entered their lives. In the meantime, their comfortable bedside manner, day after day, gave them access into part of their patient's personal life.

They found out that Malloy was an only child whose mother had died when he was sixteen. He grew up with a tough father who served under two presidents as the director of the CIA. Malloy was also an ex-marine, a skilled marksman, and had never married. He shared just about everything with them except the details of his job or the events surrounding the accident.

Jack decided it was time to probe a little further. "Cliff...Rhonda and I have a few questions we'd like to ask you about your accident and how you arrived here."

Malloy smiled and sat up. He was lying comfortably on his back now.

"What happened to you?" Jack asked. "How did you get in that truck?"

Malloy's countenance turned into a solemn stare, gazing past the Mitchells out the window.

"You said a lot of things during your fever," Jack continued. "Serious things you might have withheld under normal circumstances. Though I didn't recognize you at first from the burns, I discovered who you were when I found your wallet."

"And what did I say?" Malloy asked calmly.

Jack sat on the side of the bed. "We heard you repeating a word that sounded like *aster*. You kept saying it, over and over. Then you screamed out the names of two men, Hank and Derrick, and talked about a plot to assassinate the president."

Malloy's face turned pale as though his memory had been jogged. "Sam!" He grabbed Jack's shirt and pulled himself up. "The president? How is he?"

Jack glanced sadly at Rhonda, then back at Malloy. "I'm sorry, Cliff. The president is dead. He was assassinated the same day we found you."

"No!" Malloy gasped. He slumped back down into his pillow.

Jack put his hand on Malloy's shoulder. "We didn't want to say anything until you were better. We heard you speak about the plot in your delirium the next day after we found you. But before we could decide what to do with the information, the news came out that night that the president had been shot by terrorists."

Malloy clenched his fists. "No. It can't be."

"The world's still in shock over it. When the vice president was sworn in, he vowed to bring the assassins to justice."

Malloy wiped the wet trail of tears off his cheeks.

"Your name has come up in the news," Rhonda said. "They all think you're dead."

"Have you told anyone about me?" Malloy asked.

"No," Jack replied. "We decided to hold off until we were sure you were well enough to give us direction. I felt strongly that we should keep quiet about this and hide you here."

Malloy covered his face with his hands and said nothing for awhile. Finally he gazed into Jack and Rhonda's eyes. "You were wise to hide me," he said. "I don't know how or why I was so lucky to fall into your hands. Not only have you saved my life and nursed me back to health, but you've kept me safe. I'm indebted to you both for what you've done. I need to be alone right now so I can sort things out. Then I can give you more instruction."

Jack gently touched Malloy's reddened hand of newly formed skin. "No problem," he said. "Get some rest, now, and we'll talk later."

CHAPTER 20

"Bob! Bob Jansen!"

Bob recognized Whitney Conner's voice and stopped. He struggled internally with the option to run or face the woman he had managed to avoid all spring.

Back in January, after the Friday night small group, he never went to the Sunday church service with Shayne Taylor, like they had planned. That was because he suffered from a serious hangover when Shayne tried to wake him. He'd gotten drunk the night before and spent the entire fifty-two dollars the small group had given him. He felt so ashamed and embarrassed he moved into a room by himself and managed to elude Shayne and the girls altogether... until now.

"Hey!" Whitney shouted as she ran up.

Bob kept his back to her and started to walk.

"Bob, stop! Look at me," she said, grabbing his arm.

Her warm, gentle voice melted his heart, and he slowly turned to gaze into those lovely blue eyes he had tried so hard to forget. Embarrassed and ashamed of his cowardice, words escaped him.

"Are you okay?" she asked. "We've been worried about

you—Shayne, Laura, the small group. What happened? Did
we do something to offend you?"

Bob took a deep breath. "I don't know what to say,
Whitney. Please go. You don't want to bother with a guy like
me. I'm a jerk. Why don't you guys forget about me and go
on. I'm not worth the effort."

"You're wrong," Whitney said, still holding on to his arm.
"You *are* worth the effort. What have you done that's so awful
to justify abandoning your friends and the people who tried
to help you?"

Bob wanted to run, but Whitney's hold on his arm and her
concern were irresistible. He gave in and told her about his
drinking binge.

Whitney smiled and laughed.

"What's so funny?" Bob asked.

"Is that what this cat-an'-mouse game has been all about
for the last three months?"

"That's right."

Whitney shook her head. "Okay, it *was* a stupid thing to
do, spending all that money on beer. But it was a mistake for
you to think we'd allow something like that to change our
relationship. We care more about your soul than the money."

The guilt was too much. Bob stepped back from Whitney.
"Look, I don't need your religion. I just want to be left alone."

Whitney stepped up and peered into his eyes. "Why are
you so afraid...?"

"I'm not afraid," he said, stepping back again. "You people are the ones who are scared. Religion's just a crutch for
you guys to lean on in hard times. You watch. It'll change as
soon as the economy turns around. I've seen it all my
life...just a bunch of hypocrisy."

Whitney put her hands in her wind jacket and looked
away for a moment. "I'm sorry you feel that way, Bob, but I'll
still pray—"

"Don't. Don't waste your prayers on me. I've gotten this
far without God..."

"How far, Bob?" Whitney frowned. "How far have you

gotten without God? Do you really know? Are things getting better for you? Look around. Look at the world. If you want to keep living in denial, fine. I'm sorry that I bothered you. Good day."

Bob stared sadly after Whitney as she walked away.

Way to go, jerk! The girl tries to help you and you kick her in the teeth.

For the first time in months, Bob looked seriously at himself. Why *was* he being so stubborn about having God in his life? Would it really be so bad? Why did he fight it so hard? Maybe he blamed his parents for destroying any foundation for him to believe. But deep down, he knew *they* weren't to blame; he couldn't blame God for their marriage falling apart, either.

As he turned and walked in the opposite direction, Whitney's words kept haunting him...*How far have you gotten without God?...Are things getting better for you?...If you want to keep living in denial, fine.*

CHAPTER 21

The three and a half months went slow for Malloy.

But he felt good, fully recovered from the burns and wounds. When he first told Rhonda about the exploding gas tank, she was convinced that an angel had been dispatched to stand between him and the blast. His body should have been covered with full flesh burns from an explosion that close. It was a miracle he came out alive.

Now, on this spring day in May, a suitcase sat at his feet packed with a few of Jack's clothes.

He was ready to go.

Malloy nursed his last cup of coffee thinking about his new friends. Jack and Rhonda had become the dearest people he'd ever known. No one had shown more loyalty to him than these two. Was he ever surprised when they told him they were *Christians*. What an ironic twist of fate to think that he, Cliff Malloy, had taken a liking to Christians *before* he knew what they were.

But these weren't the people he had stereotyped when he fought against their cause. He'd always pictured Christians through the eyes of his father or the politicians he'd protected throughout his career. They were painted as fanatic, right wing extremists who always wanted to legislate morality or impede the progress toward a New World Order. But that's how he *used* to see them.

How wrong he had been.

Jack and Rhonda were the *real* thing. Christians who demonstrated a selfless love he'd never experienced. He was embarrassed by the ignorant disregard and unwarranted prejudice he'd harbored against them.

Since he arrived at the Mitchells' home, Jack and Rhonda managed to get through the calloused wall of his heart; nearly persuading *him* to become a Christian. They never forced it and carefully framed their invitations with the price one had to pay to become a serious follower of Christ. Tempting as it was, however, he fought it; afraid he couldn't do what he had resolved to do if he decided to go with God.

"What a beautiful morning," Rhonda said cheerfully as she entered the kitchen. She eyed the packed suitcase on the floor next to Malloy. "Looks like you've decided to go."

"Yes. I see no more reason to stay and intrude on your generous hospitality, thanks to your fine doctoring."

Rhonda half-smiled. "We knew this day would come. We'll miss you sorely."

"I don't know how to repay you folks, you've been so kind."

"You don't owe us a thing, Cliff. We'd do it again, even if it were someone else."

"But there *is* one thing you could do..." Pastor Mitchell said entering the kitchen.

Malloy grinned. *Here it comes.*

"You could let us know after you're gone when you've decided to give your life to Jesus."

"There you go again, Jack," he replied. "You sure make it hard for a guy to remain a heathen. I promise you one thing, though..."

"What's that?" Jack asked.

"If I ever take the plunge, you two will be the first to know. Fair enough?"

"Fair enough."

"As long as it's soon," Rhonda added.

Malloy glanced at both of them and shook his head until they burst into laughter. He knew he'd never get away from their prayerful commitment to see him get *saved* even after he left. The hook was too deep.

CHAPTER 22

The air smelled rinsed by the spring May shower.

Bob Jansen loved that fresh scent. He took a long, deep sniff from his perch on the campus wall. The bees were out gathering their pollen from the smorgasbord of flowers, while red-breasted robins dotted the green landscape, gorging themselves on the abundance of worms from the moist soil. The warmth of the sun, breaking through the clouds, felt good on his back. But with all this loveliness, Bob couldn't enjoy a beautiful spring day like he used to. His senior year had come to a close and he couldn't even be glad about that.

Finals were around the corner, and then, graduation. Another reason to be happy, but not for Bob. His life was falling apart.

Three months ago, he had moved to another room and then to another dorm to escape the conviction he felt when he saw his old roommate, Shayne Taylor. By doing so, he not only rejected his best friend, but he lost his connection to Whitney.

To add to his misery, the college placement program had failed to locate a job for him. The same thing happened to

most of the students due to the worsening effects of a growing economic crisis.

His future was bleak at best.

To escape the pain, Bob drank heavily. He even began to
dabble in drugs, something he vowed he'd never do. The
mood-altering chemicals affected his incentive and learning
capacity so badly that his grades dropped below average.

Now that his college days were ending, his Dad's support
would stop, leaving him to face the reality of looking for that
elusive job to sustain, not only his domestic needs, but his
addiction to drugs.

He had no where to go, no where turn and he could never
live with one of his parents again.

"Hello, Bob," a sweet familiar voice said behind him.

Whitney!

Bob turned to gaze at the sculpted face of this angel who
kept turning up in his life.

"Hi," he replied shyly and hung his head. "I didn't think
you'd want to talk to me again…after the way I treated you
before."

"That was weeks ago," she said, jumping up next to him
on the wall. "You must have been having a bad day."

Bob chuckled. "I can't remember the last time I had a *good*
day."

"Then maybe I should leave…"

"No," he said, grabbing her arm. "It's okay. I promise I
won't bite this time."

Whitney smiled. "I've been thinking about you lately.
How're you doing?"

Bob lowered his head and stared at the pavement. "Not so
good," he sighed, striking his heel against the wall. "My life's
sort of become a mess."

"Can I help in any way?"

Bob turned to Whitney and frowned. "Why do you care?
I don't understand."

"I don't know," she said, shrugging her shoulders. "I guess
Jesus gave me a burden for you."

"Jesus? I don't know what that means to me. I've heard about him my whole life, but he never showed up when I needed him. Like now."

"Maybe he tried and you wouldn't let him." Whitney placed her hand on Bob's shoulder. "Sometimes he tries to help people through people like me."

Bob sighed, struggling inside with conviction and contradictions. He wanted what Whitney had. It seemed so real in her life. But the images of his parent's legalism, their divorce, and his drug addiction all held him back like iron bars in a prison.

"Jesus can free you from the drugs," Whitney said.

"How'd you know I was using drugs?"

"Word gets around."

Bob turned his head.

"Look at me," Whitney said. She pulled his face to hers. "I have friends that were delivered from serious addictions. You met them in the small group last January. Tim Patterson was one of them. They're all straight now and doing well. Jesus can do the same thing for you."

Whitney was getting through. Hope began to stir in Bob's heart. He wanted to be free of the guilt and pain that had pressed down on him these many years.

"You're right," he said. "I know you're right, but—"

Before he could finish, the ground rumbled beneath them and rocked the block wall they sat on, throwing them both to the ground.

"Earthquake!" Bob yelled, as he held Whitney tight. He glanced up and saw the buildings of the campus sway like buoys on a churning sea. They growled and shuddered in protest to the shaking. Two buildings across the street succumbed to the rolling ground and crumbled in a roar of dust and debris.

Bob and Whitney bounced along the cracking pavement for three minutes until the first shock of the quake subsided. When the subsequent tremors ended, an eerie darkness settled over the campus. The birds no longer chirped.

Like a veil placed over a lamp, the sun became shrouded. Bob gazed curiously above the university's tower clock at the full moon appearing in the darkened sky.

It was turning red. Blood red.

Suddenly a burst of light lit up the night from a blazing shower of meteors.

Screams of terror and crying came from every direction on campus. Under the light of the shower students ran about like frightened animals in a forest fire, stunned and disoriented by the nightmarish event.

The display continued for a full half hour before it stopped, leaving the campus totally immersed in darkness. Candles and flashlights soon dotted the horizon from the buildings or homes that survived the quake.

Was it over?

While Bob sat dazed by the experience—still holding Whitney—he recalled Pastor Mitchell's warning back in January:

> ...the next divine judgment in Revelation is the earthquake and celestial signs of the sixth seal. The apostles predicted this will happen sometime this year...

CHAPTER 23

The tremors stopped after three terrifying minutes.

Lamar Becker lay on the floor staring blindly into the darkness. He didn't move until he was certain the ordeal had passed.

"President Cane!" he called out.

No answer.

Suddenly a flood of light burst through the windows of the Oval Office. Streak-tailed meteors filled the dark sky.

Becker pushed back his disheveled hair and walked to the window, staring at the astonishing display of meteors until the last one faded away.

The phone buzzed next to him, somewhere on the floor.

He dropped to the floor and groped around in the darkness to find it. He didn't go far when he noticed a reddish hue of light on the oval carpet. Goose bumps covered his body when he saw a scarlet-colored moon peeking through the curtains.

The phone continued to buzz and woke President Cane on the floor. He had hit his head and passed out.

Becker grabbed the phone and found the intercom. "President Cane's office, Becker speaking," he said, still staring at the moon.

"This is security. Is the President all right?"

Becker peered through the darkness in the direction he heard the President moan. "President—"

"I'm okay," replied Cane as he picked himself off the floor.

"He's safe," Becker said to security. "What's happening out there?"

"We're not quite sure, sir. The emergency power just kicked in. We're checking out the damage."

⸗⁂⸗

Bob Jansen stared at the blood-red moon beside the tower clock.

This isn't possible. It's only 12:30 in the afternoon.

"Whitney, are you all right?"

"I'm okay," she replied.

"Is this it? The earthquake your pastor said would happen this year?"

"It could be. Probably the opening of the sixth seal…"

"Is it all over then? Is this the end? Does this mean it's too late for me to be saved?"

"No, it's not too late," she said, squeezing his hand.

Bob waited no longer. He knew what he had to do. He'd seen it many times in his church back home when people prayed for God to save them. He fell to his knees and clasped his hands, gazing into the black sky.

"Oh please, God…please forgive me. I've been a fool to run from you. Please save me. I'm sorry I turned my back on you and my friends. I want to change. I need your help. I need to get free of the drugs. I can't do it without you. I can't face the madness in this world by myself. I believe in you Jesus. That you've risen from the dead. I want you to be my Savior. Please Jesus. Please forgive me."

Bob threw himself on the ground and wept, oblivious to his surroundings. The only thing that mattered now, the utmost concern in his life, was his desperate need to be saved.

As Whitney's hand rested on his shoulder, a warm sensation filled his heart and calmed his restless mind. He could feel God's forgiveness sweeping through his heart. He was saved.

With tears running down his cheeks, Bob sat up and peered through the darkness in Whitney's direction.

"Welcome to the family, brother," she said. "I've been waiting a long time for this. How do you feel?"

"Forgiven. Peaceful. Light-headed."

Whitney squeezed his shoulder. "That's the Holy Spirit inside you now. He just moved in."

"It feels good. My mind even feels clearer."

"Anything else?" she asked.

"Well, I'm not depressed anymore and I'm not scared of what's happening right now. Like I feel safe in God's hands."

"Praise God!" Whitney said with a clap of her hands. She gave Bob a hug and then stood as he helped her up. Bob took her carefully by the hand through the darkness across broken sidewalks and debris. Soon a light appeared in a building, then another, and another, until the lights dotted the campus horizon like fireflies. The cries of the people searching for family members and survivors under the rubble caused him to think of his own parents and friends.

"I hope Shayne and the others are okay," he said.

"We should try to find them."

"Yeah, but how?"

"Let's head for Pastor Mitchell's house. Maybe they'll be there."

As they hiked through the maze of rubble and the bizarre darkness, Bob felt confident somehow that they would find their friends alive and safe. He couldn't wait to see their faces when he told them he'd been born again. Though the day had turned into darkness outside, the darkness inside of him had turned to light.

For the first time in a long time, Bob's future looked bright again. He had Jesus now to help him face his tomorrows.

CHAPTER 24

Malloy didn't leave the Mitchells until noon.

They had persuaded him to stay for lunch so he could start his journey on a full stomach. It was Rhonda's apple pie that really detained him.

"We'll miss you, Cliff," Rhonda said, standing on the front porch to see him off. Jack stood at her side.

"Thanks for everything," Malloy said.

Jack gave Cliff a hug and then grabbed his shoulders, "Come back and visit us, friend, when the coast is clear. Maybe by then you'll be free to let us in on the details behind your accident."

"I hope so," Malloy replied and said goodbye as he walked down the steps of the porch.

At the bottom of the stairs, a deep groan rumbled underground. The concrete slab of the sidewalk jerked below him and snapped like a sheet of styrofoam. Malloy frantically grabbed for the railing to break his fall, hoping he was imagining it all until he saw Jack and Rhonda thrown down on the porch above him.

The house creaked and groaned from the shifting ground. The trees and poles swayed violently along the street. The wires snapped in two.

After three horrifying minutes, the quake finally subsided. Then, an eerie stillness blanketed the sky. Not a bird, nor a cricket, could be heard. Only the crackling of electric sparks spewing from the broken wires on the ground and in the trees.

"Jack, look! The sun!" Mary shouted.

Like a veil thrown over a lantern, the sun's rays disappeared. Total darkness covered the neighborhood.

Malloy stared at the blood-colored moon until a splash of meteors exploded in the sky, falling to the earth like ripened fruit that had been violently shaken from a tree.

"It's happening!" Jack yelled. "The sixth seal. Just as the apostles predicted."

None of the three moved for the next thirty minutes while the captivating display of *signs* and *wonders* lit up the blackened sky.

Ending as suddenly as the meteors came, the darkness returned against the red hue of the moon.

Rhonda's heart pounded so hard she thought Jack could hear it. She reached over and groped for his hand. "You okay, dear?" she asked, squeezing him tight.

"Yes, are you?"

"I think so, except that my heart needs to stop racing."

Jack searched in the darkness for their friend. "Cliff! You okay down there?"

"I'll be okay if someone can tell me why it's dark at 12:30 in the afternoon. Am I seeing things or *not* seeing things?"

"No, you've seen something all right," Jack replied. "Follow our voices up the steps. We'll make our way into the house and get some candles and flashlights. I'll try to explain all this to you through God's eyes."

CHAPTER 25

Bob and Whitney found Shayne and Laura hiking through the debris on the campus.

They exchanged stories about each other's experiences while they made their way to the Mitchells' home. Shayne was ecstatic over Bob's conversion. That was the highlight for him.

When they arrived, they found Pastor Mitchell and Rhonda safe with their home still intact. Once everyone had shared their stories, they started in on their questions to Pastor Mitchell.

Before everyone came, Jack Mitchell had been showing passages in the Bible to Malloy about God's judgments in the last days. Now, after he answered everyone's questions, he picked up where he left off with Malloy to read from the notes he had retrieved from his attic study.

"Here it is," he said, shining the flashlight on the page. "There was a similar event in history like the one we experienced today. Listen to this dated May 19, 1780, in *Our First Century* by R.M. Devens:

> 'Almost, if not altogether alone, as the most mysterious and yet unexplained phenomenon of its kind in nature's diversified range of events, during the last century, stands the dark day of May 19th, 1780—a most unaccountable darkening of the whole visible heavens and atmosphere in New England—which brought intense alarm and distress to multitudes of minds, as well as dismay to the brute creation, the fowls fleeing, bewildered to their roosts, and the birds to their nests, and the cattle returning to their stalls. Indeed, thousands of the good people of that day became fully convinced that the end of all things terrestrial had come.'"

Jack scanned the faces of his attentive audience. "Here's another document about the same event," he continued. "It's from *Gage's History of Rowley, Massachusetts*:

> 'The darkness was such as to occasion farmers to leave their work in the field, and retire to their dwellings. Lights became necessary to the transaction of business within doors. The darkness continued through the day.'"

"That's incredible," Bob said. "Boy, am I glad I didn't wait any longer to get saved."

Jack smiled. "So are we, Bob."

"Aren't there events like this somewhere in the Bible?" Whitney asked.

"Yes, there are," Jack replied. "In Exodus, God sent darkness over Egypt for three days. In the gospel of Matthew, when Jesus hung on the cross, darkness covered the land from noon to three in the afternoon, followed by an earthquake when he died. Prophets such as Isaiah, Joel,

Haggai, even Jesus, all predicted that *signs* and *wonders* would appear in the heavens, before Christ returned. The countdown has begun. I believe the sixth seal of the Revelation was opened today."

"Show them your notes about the meteor shower," Rhonda said.

Jack nodded and thumbed through the pages. "This was recorded in *The New York Journal of Commerce*:

> 'The falling stars did not come as if from several trees shaken, but from one. Those which appeared in the east fell toward the east (same with the north, south, west). And they fell not as ripe fruit falls ... but they flew, they were cast...straight off, descending...'

"...and again by R.M. Devens in *Our First Century*:

> 'Extensive and magnificent showers of shooting stars have been known to occur at various places in modern times; but the most universal and wonderful which has ever been recorded was that of the 13th of November, 1833, the whole firmament, over all the United States, being then, for hours, in fiery commotion...During the three hours of its continuance, the day of judgment was believed to be only waiting for sunrise.'"

"That nearly describes what we saw today!" Laura said. "It's really starting to happen isn't it? Jesus is coming back."

Silence blanketed the room.

Jack watched everyone stare soberly at their shadows dancing on the walls from the flickering light of the candles. He could almost read their thoughts, perhaps similar to his own. History indeed had repeated itself. Only this time with no speculation. Today was the beginning of a dire future for Earth's inhabitants.

He looked at his Bible lying on the table where he had read a passage earlier to Malloy from the prophet Joel:

> Before the great and terrible day of the Lord, I will display signs in the heavens. The sun will be darkened and the moon will be turned to blood.

CHAPTER 26

Lamar Becker updated Aster on the damage report.

"After the three days of darkness ended," he said, "the sun revealed a global mess. There's no way to count the myriad of casualties still lying under the rubble. Millions were swallowed up by the earth. Others died of heart failure. Cities, towns, and villages on every coastline have been hit by massive tidal waves. It's chaotic out there. The survivors are pilfering the quake victims while governments are scrambling to restore law and order—"

"Gentleman," Aster said to Becker and Drakon, "don't you see it? This quake is the perfect opportunity for justifying a World Federation. With Japan and Europe coming on board, we have nine kingdoms set to ratify a constitution. The United States is all we need."

Aster turned to Becker. "What's the political temperature on the Hill?"

"Hysteria. Everyone's open for a quick fix. Couldn't be a better environment for initiating a con-con (a constitutional convention to amend or replace the U.S. Constitution)."

Aster grinned. "We only need 34 states to authorize a call for it. Do we have the votes?"

"*Before* the quake we had 32 states," Becker replied. "Under *these* conditions, I'm certain we'll have the votes."

"Then get your networks rolling. Contact the WCPA (World Constitution and Parliament Association). Tell them to call every governor, congressman and senator who supports our cause and inform them that a con-con must be passed if the world is to survive. Instill urgency into them. Delay could propel the world towards anarchy if we don't act quickly."

"And the World Church?" Drakon asked.

"Inform the council to set a date for the United Nations to assemble for an emergency meeting. Then tell our nine heads of state to prepare the necessary documents to ratify a World Constitution. Get them to persuade their neighboring allies to jump on board if they want to escape economic disaster. We need at least twenty-five countries to establish the constitution, then we can set our world government in place."

"What if the Congress balks?" Becker asked.

Aster smiled. "Wouldn't you say the present condition of the U.S. calls for a state of national emergency?"

Becker grinned. "Yes, I would."

"Can you convince President Cane and his administration to do this?"

"Of course."

"And the National Security Council?"

Becker chuckled. "Sir, you're a genius. To declare a state of national emergency would give the administration and the NSC absolute power of emergency management..."

"As well as bypassing Congress and the representative system of government," Aster replied. "If a constitutional convention fails, we can still hand U.S. sovereignty over to a world government through the power of emergency management."

"A great plan!" Becker said.

"What about the Christians?" Drakon asked.

"Once we've established our World Federation and its government structure, we'll induct a global police force and turn them loose on these Christians...*after* we frame them with conspiracy."

"Ah, yes," Becker replied. "Like Nero framed the Christians of his day for burning Rome."

CHAPTER 27

A week had passed since the earthquake.

Malloy welcomed the first rays of the morning sun from the Mitchell's back porch. He was relieved to see it shining again after three whole days of depressing darkness.

It was a mild spring day in May. The birds chirped gleefully, and the smell of fresh brewed coffee gurgled from the pot that sat on the rattan table next to him.

The neighborhood buzzed with activity from chain saws, hammers and bulldozers, digging through the rubble of the quake's aftermath.

Though anxious to get on with his plans, Malloy decided to stay and help the Mitchells pick up the broken glass and debris, and repair the damages to their home. The little harm they suffered surprised him in a quake of that magnitude. It was indeed a miracle.

A need to warn the Mitchells about Aster kept goading him these past few days. He felt they should know about Aster's plan to crush the Christian sect, but would it really matter? Would it help them or endanger their welfare to be privy to this information?"

Malloy turned toward the screeching of the screen door.

"Man, that coffee smells good!" Jack said, walking out on the porch. He came up and poured himself a cup.

"I need to ask you something," Malloy said.

"Okay," Jack replied, and sat on the porch rail.

"Everything you've shared with me—this earthquake, the prophecies—it's got my attention."

"Good."

"You told me the Bible predicts the rise of a one world government led by this Antichrist character. Will this happen after the quake?"

"After an alliance of ten-kingdoms emerges."

Malloy's stomach churned. He realized the startling parallels to the information he had. "Then I think I know who this Antichrist might be."

Jack stood up from the rail. "How?"

"Remember, during the first days of my stay, you heard me repeat a word you thought was some type of code?"

"Yeah, you kept saying *aster*. It's the Greek word for star. I thought it might be a code name for another Star Wars or something."

"What if I told you it was the name of a man?"

"Aster's a man's name?"

"Yep. Reuben Joshua Aster."

Jack's mouth dropped open.

"The guy's big stuff," Malloy said. "Had President Thomas shot because he wouldn't play his game."

"What game?"

"The alliance made up of the ten kingdoms you just mentioned to establish a World Federation. Aster needed the United States to be the tenth kingdom and Thomas stood in his way."

Jack paced the floor and muttered something under his breath.

"What are you thinking?" Malloy asked.

"I know this man."

"You should. He's one of the twelve leading apostles among the Christians."

"How'd you know that?"

"I've read his profile. Seemed odd, but it made sense after I realized it gave him access to the Christian movement and their operations to resist a New World Order."

Jack turned and stared at the leaning trees in his back yard. "Then it's true what God showed Nathan Kelly. One of the twelve would fall and become the Antichrist."

"Nathan Kelly? He's one of the twelve, isn't he?"

"You know about Kelly, too?"

"Jack...I worked for the CIA. We monitored all you Christian activists. You were the enemy; the right wing extremists who opposed the mainstream philosophies of our government. It was my job to know."

"Are we *still* the bad guys?"

Malloy smiled. "Not to me, except for Aster. He's still public enemy number one on *my* list."

"Aster," Jack said, as though the name triggered something in his mind. "Cliff...come with me. I think I might have something that'll interest you."

CHAPTER 28

Malloy followed Jack to his attic study.

The ceiling arched low, leaving enough height for the two of them to stand in the center of the small room. A mahogany desk sat under the window of a dormer where a stream of light came in and illuminated the computer and keyboard.

Malloy curiously surveyed the hundreds of books, notebook binders and papers which filled the shelves along the walls. Many were still on the floor from the quake. "Excuse the mess," Jack said. "I'm still putting stuff back." Jack grabbed a notebook off the floor beside his desk and thumbed through the pages. "Hmm," he said, stopping to read over a page. "It's been there all along…right under our noses."

"What?" Malloy asked peering over his shoulder.

"Reuben Joshua Aster. The man's name amazingly belies his identity."

"I don't get it."

"All right, I'll break it down. We'll take one name at a time, starting with Reuben."

Malloy sat down in Jack's green recliner. "Okay."

"Israel got it's name from a descendant named Jacob. God changed Jacob's name to Israel. He had twelve sons. The first was Reuben. Reuben betrayed his father and lost his right as firstborn to the inheritance. Now pay attention to this pattern: *twelve men...one betrays...falls from position.*"

"Got it."

"This same pattern is repeated in the New Testament: twelve apostles...one betrays Christ, which is Judas...he falls from an apostolic position."

"Still with you."

"Nathan Kelly believed, and has taught for years, that this same pattern might be repeated in the last days before Christ returns. Twelve apostles, one betrays Christ and falls from—"

"Aster...?"

"You got it."

"So because of this pattern," Malloy said, "you think Reuben is an appropriate first name for Aster?"

"It could be."

Malloy smiled. "So what about his middle name, Joshua? How does that fit in?"

"Joshua is another way of saying Jesus. Jesus is the Greek equivalent for Joshua. Since *antichrist* literally means *in the place of Christ*, the middle name of Joshua could signify his intentions to replace Jesus and become a new Messiah; that is, another Christ in the place of the real Christ."

"Fascinating. I like this study. Now what about his last name? You mentioned it's the Greek word for *star.*"

"Right. A star in the Bible is symbolic for *saints* and *spiritual leaders.* Aster's been a spiritual leader in the church for years. You may find this hard to believe, but he actually did a lot of good. Somewhere along the way he became deceived and turned from the faith. The Bible calls it *apostasy.* It means to fall from, abandon or defect from the truth...the same thing Judas did."

"And how does this fit in with a star?"

"Revelation, chapter 9, shows a picture of a star falling from heaven and being given the key to the bottomless pit. Chapter 11 says that the Antichrist comes out of that same bottomless pit."

"So a fallen star...a fallen Aster, who happens to be a leader among the twelve..."

"Do you see the pattern? Twelve...betrayal...falls from position. Reuben Joshua Aster."

"Incredible. This Bible of yours is intriguing. Like, it's alive."

Jack smiled. "It's alive for those who will to listen to it."

Malloy paused to ponder the unusual excitement that stirred in his heart. He couldn't describe the feeling that gripped him like decoding clues on a treasure map.

Suddenly a thought provoked him down another path. Could this process of interpreting apply to Drakon, Aster's partner?

CHAPTER 29

Malloy enjoyed the name hunt.

It surprised him to discover how relevant the Bible was to the world's present conditions, and how accurate. Had he been duped all these years into ignoring the most valuable book in the world? A book that could answer man's questions about purpose, about destiny? He had one more question.

"What can you tell me about John Drakon?"

"Drakon?" Jack replied. "He dropped out of active ministry years ago. Can't remember when. He used to have a powerful gift in prophecy. I'd never seen anyone used greater than John Drakon, especially at conferences—" Jack paused.

"What?" Malloy asked.

"Drakon spoke at a lot of conferences with Aster. Are they connected somehow in this conspiracy?"

"He's Aster's right-hand man. Both of them are key players in the infrastructure of the World Church."

"The World Church?" Jack curled his right index finger over his lip. "Things are starting to add up."

"Do you think his name means something?"

Jack reached for his Bible on the floor and turned to the

thirteenth chapter of Revelation. "There's a false prophet that's predicted to work with the Antichrist. If Aster is the Antichrist, then it's conceivable Drakon is the prophet. Look here…"

Malloy peered over Jack's shoulder at the passage.

"The symbolic implication of verse 11 is that a prophet will rise out of the church. He's like a forerunner of the Antichrist. It says he has two horns like a lamb, but speaks like a dragon."

"Dragon? Kind of sounds like Drakon doesn't it?"

Jack stared at Malloy. "What'd you say?"

"I said, dragon sounds like Drakon."

"Cliff, you're on to something there." Jack dug around through the pile of books that had fallen onto his desk and found his Greek lexicon. He thumbed through the pages. "Dragon…dragon…there it is. The Greek word for dragon is *dra-kon*. Drakon's name means *dragon*.

Cliff smiled. He really liked this. "How about John Arnion? How do those two names fit?"

"Let me think. There are two significant *Johns* in the New Testament: John the Baptist and the disciple, John."

"And…?"

Jack tapped his fingers on the desk. "Forerunner!" he said, snapping his finger.

"Huh?"

"John the Baptist was the forerunner of Christ. He announced the arrival of Jesus, the Messiah, to prepare the people to receive and follow him. Precisely the same purpose the false prophet has to proclaim the Antichrist to the world. That's what Drakon plans to do for Aster. To proclaim him and get the people to follow him."

Malloy rubbed his hands together. This was getting good. "Now what about his middle name, Arnion?"

"That's a tough one. Never heard of a name like that before."

"Maybe it's a Greek word like Drakon and Aster's name."

Jack peered at Malloy, "You're becoming quite the

scholar, Cliff. You'll make a good Christian, yet."

"Please, just the word study, thank you."

"All right." Jack smiled and returned to his Greek lexicon. "Let's see, now...arnion...arnion...ah, here it is. It's the Greek word for *lamb*. That's it," he said, closing the book. "He had two horns like a lamb. So we have *John*, a forerunner; *Arnion*, the two-horned lamb; and *Drakon*. He speaks like a dragon because Satan's referred to as a dragon in scripture. It's Satan who's behind the whole scheme."

"Bravo," Malloy said with a clap. "We've got them pegged now."

Jack glanced at the passage again, and then stared at Malloy. "What did your files reveal about Drakon's activity over the last few years? Didn't you say he was an intricate part of the World Church?"

"That's right."

"Did he do much in the way of commerce?"

"If he was involved with their infrastructure, he had to have his hands into commerce. The World Church has emerged as the largest financial organization in the world. There's nothing equal to the fortunes they've amassed over the last two decades."

"Which ties in with the two horns..."

"How?"

"It's believed by several of my colleagues that the two horns are symbolic of *commerce* and *religion*. Drakon's involved in both." Jack leaned back in his chair and stared at the ceiling. "That's why Revelation 17 and 18 speak symbolically about the one-world church as a harlot who gets rich off the merchants of the world."

Malloy sighed and sat down again in the green rag-torn recliner next to the Jack's desk. The overwhelming truth settled heavily on him. "I think we're in trouble, pastor...big trouble."

Jack gazed soberly at Malloy. "You don't know the half of it, Cliff. There's a lot more going to break loose than this. It's a good time to accept Jesus into your life and make him your Lord."

Malloy rolled his eyes, shook his head and chuckled.
Doesn't this man ever give up?

CHAPTER 30

Malloy ignored Jack's comment about salvation.

He had a job to finish. Becoming a Christian now was the farthest thing from his mind.

"I've got to stop Aster, Jack."

"It can't be done."

"Why not? Why would God give us this information if he didn't want us to do something about it?"

"It's hard to explain. All I can say is that God will allow this to happen, just as The Revelation predicts. There's nothing we can do to stop it."

Malloy rose to his feet. "But, I can't stand idly by and let them get away with it. I've got a score to settle for President Thomas."

"He's dead, Cliff, and you're dead, too, remember? You're not the director of the CIA anymore. Aster's probably replaced you with his own man by now."

"I'll find another way..."

"And get yourself killed this time? Listen to me. These men are not human. They've sold their souls to a creature who's been around since the beginning of time. They're operating under the powers of hell. God plans to let it happen to fulfill his ultimate purpose."

"What purpose? I don't understand."

"The clock is running out for the human race to turn from their sins. Look around you. It's a sick world out there. You should know that better than anyone. God won't ignore the world's sins. He's predetermined a time to bring judgment on the ungodly and end it when Jesus returns. You can't change that, Cliff. Nobody can. You can only change your mind and get on the winning team, God's team."

"Like you're winning now?"

"I know how it looks, but our battle isn't about living. It's about dying to our sinful desires and placing God on the throne of our hearts. The day will come when God's people will rule the earth. But it will only happen God's way; not the way the world is accustomed to ruling."

Malloy sat quietly, battling the contradictions inside. He wanted to yield. He knew Jack was right, but he didn't want to lose the hate and revenge he had stored up against Aster. "I'm sorry, but I can't change. The CIA's in my blood. Don't get me wrong, I've been listening more than you think. Becoming a Christian appeals to me because I like the kind of people you and Rhonda are. But I can't become a Christian until I finish the job the *old* Malloy set out to do."

Jack stood up and placed his hand on Cliff's shoulder. "Are you sure you want to jump back into that whirlwind of peril? Wouldn't it be safer to start a new life here in Canterton? Aster thinks you're dead. You can change your identity. He'd never find you."

"I couldn't live with that, knowing what I know, and what I've got to do."

Jack sighed and patted Malloy's shoulder. "Okay, it's your decision."

Malloy stared for a moment out the dormer window of the attic and said, "I think I'll go for a walk. Thanks for the Bible study."

Jack started to pick up more of his notes off the floor. "No problem. We both learned a lot this morning. Enjoy your walk."

As Malloy started down the stairs, Jack had a parting question to ask. "How did it get this far?"

Malloy stopped and turned. "What?"

"How did Aster manage to get so deep into the heart of our government?"

"Money, I'd say. Times have changed since the economy turned sour. People got greedier, didn't want to adjust their lifestyle. Integrity's gone, too. No one has the guts to stand up for what's right anymore."

"Then who's been protecting America?"

"Nobody cares, Jack. It isn't America's world anymore. Times have changed, and the world's been primed for a New World Order. I know, I've been a part of the movement. There's no patriotism left in any country out there. Only whatever it takes to survive."

Jack and Malloy stared at the floor in silence.

"Ironic isn't it?" Malloy continued. "Government, media, journalists; all painting Christians to be the radical misfits whose mission it is to impede progress. The truth is, following Christ is the only hope this world has left."

Malloy turned and descended the steps with his hands in his pockets. He had a lot of planning to do.

<hr />

Jack and Rhonda never saw Cliff Malloy again. He stayed out long after the Mitchells had retired to bed.

The next morning, Jack came downstairs and found a sealed envelope on the kitchen counter with their names on it.

Five minutes later, Rhonda came down and found Jack wiping his eyes.

"Honey, what's wrong?"

Jack handed her the note. "It was on the counter," he said, as she opened the letter.

Dear Jack and Rhonda,

Words cannot express how grateful I am to you for saving my life and nursing me back to health. But even greater than that, you've opened my eyes to see and know the truth about Christ. Because of your love, sincerity, and a genuine lifestyle of faith, I'm seriously contemplating the possibility of becoming a Christian someday.

For now, however, there's something I must do before I make such a commitment. Hopefully, God will use me to alter the course of events and make this world a safer place to live.

I'm going to finish the job I started. Please pray for me. I'm going to need it, lot's of it.

Sincerely,
Cliff Malloy

Rhonda looked at Jack with a puzzled expression.

"He's going after Aster, honey. He's going after Reuben Aster."

CHAPTER 31

Bob Jansen envied his friend, Shayne Taylor. He wished he had Shayne's faith and courage to get married in a time like this.

The rays of sunlight danced on Laura's lovely wedding gown as they threaded their way through the trees of Canterton's river park. Pastor Mitchell read the pledges Shayne and Laura would repeat as husband and wife.

Bob stood next to Shayne as his best man, tugging at the collar of his tuxedo to let the heat escape. Laura's radiant face beamed with smiles at her bridegroom through the whole ceremony. Bob had never seen two happier people.

Whitney Conner stood next to Laura as the bridesmaid. Bob kept glancing at her, enamored by her deep blue eyes and lovely brown hair. The garland of flowers on her head graced her attractive face like a gold frame. His mind soon wandered from the ceremony as he saw himself and Whitney standing before the pastor instead. He'd be the happiest man alive if...

"The rings please."

Shayne nudged Bob. "Snap out of it, pal. The rings."

Bob blushed as he fumbled in his pocket for the gold rings

and handed them to Pastor Mitchell. He glanced at Whitney.

She smiled at him.

The wedding concluded with the vows and Shayne and Laura kissed each other as husband and wife.

Bob could imagine himself doing the same with Whitney, someday.

———

During the reception, Bob strolled over to the wall of the river park and stared at the muddy waters of the Roanoke River. Sections of the wall still lay in rubble as a grim reminder of the quake.

While the guests buzzed in conversation in the reception line, mixed emotions ran through his mind about the wedding and his own future. How terribly responsible Shayne must be feeling to have a wife now. How would he support her under these conditions? The economic depression had grown worse, the soup lines were longer, and the shelves of the grocery stores were barely stocked. Transportation by train, air, or roadway had been curtailed by the universal damage of the quake. People couldn't travel, and only the rich could afford to.

A lot of the graduate students, like Bob and Shayne, had stayed in Canterton to help rebuild the city. They made a little money working on construction crews, repairing the roads and bridges and clearing away the rubble. It was the only work available.

Shayne had shown Bob the one-room efficiency apartment he and Laura would live in, but it cost twice as much as normal. How was Shayne going to do it? He certainly had more faith than Bob. And what about children? How could they even think of having any kids with the judgments of God looming around the corner? Could marriage or a family really fit into these times? Would it work?

All these thoughts plagued him because of the blossoming desire in his own heart. He loved Whitney. But was it wise to ask her to marry him? Sure he graduated from college, barely, but he had no *real* job to support her. The one he had now was temporary. How impossible everything seemed to him now. He'd never be able to marry.

"Beautiful view isn't it?"

Bob jumped and turned toward the visitor. "Whitney!"

"I'm sorry. I didn't mean to startle you."

"It's okay."

"I saw you standing here alone and thought you might like some company."

"Thanks," he said, trying to cover his excitement.

Whitney leaned against the wall and stared at the shimmering waters below. "Wasn't that a great wedding?"

"Yeah, but I'll miss them."

"They'll be around."

"I know, but it's different when your best friend gets married and you're still single."

Whitney remained silent and continued to watch the river.

"You ever wonder," Bob asked, "how hard it might be to get married, I mean, with all this end-time stuff going on?"

Whitney turned and looked into his eyes. "If you marry the right person, it could work."

"Think so?"

"Sure," she replied, gazing back at the water. "You can't stop living because things get tough. I think it would help to face life's hardships with a man who loved God; someone who could encourage your faith when times got worse."

Bob stared at her. How he'd love to be that man for her. But what did *he* have to offer? She deserved someone better. "Well, whoever that guy is for *you*," he said shyly, "will be a lucky man."

Whitney turned and looked deep into his eyes...

"Hey Bob!" Shayne called from the reception party. "Whitney! You two going to have any cake? Come over here and get it before it's all gone!"

With his right hand on his stomach, Bob courteously

extended his arm to Whitney like he had in the wedding procession. She put her arm through his and they strolled back toward the reception.

How Bob ached to tell her his true feelings, to explore her heart and see how she felt about him. But the images of the quake and the accompanying signs were too fresh in his mind to allow it.

CHAPTER 32

"Jack, it's on!" Rhonda shouted up the stairs.

News had leaked out to the media that a national state of emergency had been declared by the White House to the House and Senate. To avoid national panic, President Cane had scheduled a detailed national report to clear the air.

Jack ran down the stairs from his attic study and glided into his Lay-z-boy recliner.

"Fellow Americans," President Cane began, "several months ago I took office at a heart-wrenching time when our beloved President, Samuel Thomas, was assassinated. To this day we feel the pain of that horrible injustice.

"Adding to our grief, the world has since been rocked by an unprecedented global disaster. The earthquake which touched every inch of this planet, continues to thwart recovery in many countries by successive tremors. Famine has accelerated throughout the world, roadways and airports have been ripped apart, and shipyards are filled with grounded or sunken ships in the aftermath of the quake's tidal waves."

Jack held Rhonda's hand to comfort her. He knew things were bad, but not *this* bad. Most of the news covering the world's plight had been obstructed by the recovery process.

The President continued. "Third world countries have been hit the hardest, and have limited resources and technology to cope with the damages. The entire world is in a state of panic and economic shock.

"For the last three days, our administration has been meeting with members of the House and Senate. We've also met with nine heads of state from the most prominent industrialized countries in the world. Together, we've devised a plan to help each other through this difficult hour. A meeting of the United Nations has been scheduled to convene in two days."

Jack sat forward in his chair. "Here it comes, Rhonda."

"Our department has called on every state in America to implement a constitutional convention."

Jack shook his head in disbelief.

"According to Article V of the U.S. Constitution, only thirty-four states are required to apply, yet an overwhelming forty-five states have responded. Our purpose for this is to unite with the rest of the world toward a New World Order that can overcome our crisis. We have agreed to set aside our national sovereignty in favor of a new constitution for a World Federation.

"Oh my," Rhonda said, squeezing Jack's hands. "Is this real?"

"God help us," Jack replied.

"Ninety percent of the world's governments have prepared to come to the United Nations to discuss and negotiate the details of the document. It won't be a complex or heavily structured system of government. The ruling body will be small enough to make swift, effective decisions.

Jack hung his head and stared at the floor, tightly controlling his anger. He felt helpless. Things were happening too fast. *Give me wisdom, Lord, please.*

"Though this may seem rushed to you," the president continued, "we have no recourse but to act quickly. The longer we delay, the more we jeopardize the balance of economic survival throughout the entire world.

"As of today, America will operate under emergency management. To expedite this, recruiting stations will be set up to increase the numbers in our military. Troops will be dispersed throughout every city in the nation—"

"Martial law," Jack said to Rhonda.

"We'll also be taking a national census, calling on every American citizen to participate so that we can serve you better—"

Or control us better.

Jack grabbed the remote and clicked off the TV. "So it begins," he said soberly. He ran his hand through his gray-streaked hair and glanced at Rhonda. "Honey...I need to meet with the elders."

CHAPTER 33

Nathan Kelly clicked off the TV.

He leaned back in his chair with his thoughts postured toward God.

The President's speech didn't surprise him. He saw it coming. But, as it was for many Christians, reality had a way of stretching one's faith to call upon the grace of God.

A small reading lamp lit up his shoulder with the apartment shrouded in darkness. He liked it that way. Less distracting when he prayed.

After two hours of prayer and meditation, he spoke out loud, oblivious to the stealthful intrusion of two men lurking in the shadows. "So, Aster," Nathan said, reflecting on the message of the president, "the curtain rises on Act I of your plot—"

"It's more than an act, brother Kelly," a voice spoke from behind.

Nathan jumped up and peered into the dark hallway that led to his bedroom. "Who's there?"

Aster and Drakon stepped out of the shadows toward the light.

"You!" Nathan said. "How did you two get in here?"

"By the bedroom window you left open," Aster replied coyly. "You should be more careful with all the looters out and about these days."

"Why're you here, Reuben?"

"We thought we'd stop by for a friendly chat."

"Breaking and entering is hardly grounds for a friendly chat. What is it you want?"

"Want?" Aster smiled at Drakon. "Why your cooperation, of course. How'd you like the president's speech tonight? Wrote it myself. Thrilling news, wouldn't you say?"

"You're wasting time, Reuben. Get to the point."

"Very well," Aster replied. "I've come to ask...no...to *tell* you to stop teaching your ridiculous theory that the Antichrist is a fallen apostle. My Christian friends might get the wrong idea."

"You sure it's a theory?" Nathan asked.

"No. It's a fantasy."

"Are *you* a fantasy, Reuben? I've heard from reliable sources that you've been in bed with the World Church."

Drakon started for Kelly. Aster put his hand up to stop him. "You must understand, Nathan, that John and I have received a new assignment. A calling, you might say, to unite the world in peace and brotherhood. By taking control of the world, we can save it from destroying itself."

Nathan folded his arms. "I pity you. You've betrayed God and murdered his people. The prophecies about you are true."

"I don't believe in those prophecies," Aster sneered. "I tired of them years ago. I'm into something more tangible, with quicker results. Why don't you join us? It's a better cause than Christianity. We've managed to ally every major religion on earth and get them to set aside their differences. With your help and influence, we can persuade the apostles and the Christians to join our global family. Together, we can build a better, safer world and promote the interests of universal humanitarianism."

"Humanitarianism? You hypocrite. It's no secret that your

World Church has terminated every religion in the third world who refused to joined you. Those who did, joined only because they were bullied and subdued into converting."

"Nathan, you're hurting me. It sounds so cold the way you put it."

"And what will you do if I don't join you?"

Aster grinned. "In the interest of survival and a destiny for global peace: a simple matter of termination."

"Like you terminated the president?"

"Something like that."

Nathan frowned. "Why'd you even bother to come here and play this silly game? You know you don't have any intentions of inviting Christians into your movement. You only intend to annihilate them—unless they deny the faith like you two."

Aster clapped. "Brilliant...brilliant. You always were the brightest among the twelve."

Nathan tired of Aster's ego. "This conversation is over. Leave my apartment, now!"

A crimson mark formed on Aster's right temple. He glared at Nathan and stepped back. "Take care of him, John."

"With pleasure," Drakon said. He raised his right hand in the air with a ball of fire forming between his thumb and ring finger.

Nathan stood fearless. He knew from Scripture what the prophet could do. But before Drakon hurled his fiery orb, Nathan shouted, "In the name of Jesus, get out!"

CHAPTER 34

The name of Jesus stirred up a flurry of shadows.

Demons, that had accompanied Aster and Drakon, now scurried about the dark corners of the room scrambling for cover.

Suddenly, a rushing wind from a score of angels swirled above the heads of the men.

Nathan Kelly could see them. Their swords flashed brightly, poised in their hands for battle. Four surrounded him immediately, while another grabbed Drakon's out-stretched arm to restrain his release of the fire.

The celestial warriors chased back the sniveling demons who scampered about the room like a pack of terrorized dogs.

Then Shenzar appeared to enter the fray and assist Drakon in the termination. His strong, ten-foot frame slowly pushed back the angels who had encircled the apostle. With the arrival of their new ally, the emboldened demons pounced on the angelic foes; scratching, kicking, and biting with inter-mittent shrieks.

The angels fought valiantly as steel upon steel rang men-acingly above their heads in self-defense. One of them stood directly in front of Kelly, shielding him with his nine-foot body while he skillfully held Shenzar at bay.

When Nathan saw the demonic, towering giant overpowering his bodyguards, he fell to his knees and prayed below the brush of activity around him.

Soon a fog-like thickness filled the room. Nathan stopped praying and opened his eyes to discover another score of angels had been dispatched by God to assist him.

Instantly, they turned the tide and pushed back the enemy. Shenzar motioned to the demons to retreat and then vanished. Nathan stared curiously at the glowing angels while they surveyed the room. The angel holding Drakon's arm, pushed it back down to his side, until the fireball was gone. The angels turned to Nathan and smiled with an affirmative nod and then disappeared.

Perplexed and released by the divine protectors, Aster and Drakon backed away. They never saw the angels themselves, only Shenzar and the demons.

Drakon glared at Kelly while he rubbed his sore wrist, bruised by the grip of his captor.

"You'll do well," Aster said to stop spreading your lies. There is no Antichrist, and the world will never become the doom or gloom of the future you've painted with your mistreated prophecies."

Nathan turned his back to them and returned to his chair. "Shut the door behind you," he said as he sat down.

"Mark my words, Nathan," Aster sneered, "your every move will be monitored. You're a dead man if you don't heed my warning."

When Aster and Drakon left, Nathan put his head in his hands and prayed, "Thank you, Lord...thank you for delivering me by the hand of your angels."

CHAPTER 35

Pastor Mitchell's elders arrived the next day.

They all sat quietly in prayer, with an occasional glance at their pastor. Jack continued to pray in his recliner until the last elder arrived, seven in all.

"Brothers," he began, "the noose is tightening around our freedom. After listening to the president's speech last night, I was shocked when today's polls revealed an overwhelming support for this new plan. I fear deception has gripped our country, not only among the citizens of America; but every branch of religion, both Christian and cult alike."

The elders nodded soberly.

"Few seem to recognize the peril of this plan, and there isn't a voice strong enough in Washington to challenge it. Our nation is dying, gentlemen. It will ebb into the horizon of global socialism until a one-world government emerges.

"What can we do?" asked one of the elders.

"We must continue to equip the church for the events which lie ahead. Encourage our people to prepare their hearts and get their homes in order. Life under the regime of martial law won't be easy."

"What about the mandatory census?" another asked.

"We must be careful. This census could be a prelude to the *mark of the beast* in Revelation 13. If my assumption is correct, they'll want a statement regarding our religious preferences. Pray for wisdom in this; wisdom to know how to avoid another Holocaust like WWII. Especially pray for the weak, because many will be tempted to deny Jesus in order to save their skins. We must instruct them to endure to the end and never deny their allegiance to Christ. Not even in the face of death."

Jack studied the saddened elders. "I know it's hard to believe, but don't forget, exciting days are ahead for the Church. Any moment now, according to Matthew 25, Jesus could come for his Bride. If our lamps are full and ready to meet him at the midnight hour, we have a chance to escape the ruthless world government under the Antichrist."

"When do you expect this?" another elder asked.

"Soon. When the World Federation is established, the stage will be set for the Antichrist to move closer to world dominance. I believe he's at work now behind this movement. It wasn't the president who gave that speech last night, it had the imprint of the Antichrist all over it. The president is only a tool in his hands. With all of this developing now, the debut of the Bride is imminent."

The elders shuffled nervously in their seats.

"We can't fight what God has ordained," Jack continued. "It won't be long before the Holy Spirit is restrained, then nothing will hold back the fury of darkness unleashed on the earth. We must cling to Jesus and ride out the storm, doing what we can to preach the gospel to those who will hear."

CHAPTER 36

Four angels hovered at four diametrical posts above the earth's atmosphere. The illumined globe hung suspended between them.

In one voice they cried to the winds of the north, south, east and west, "Cease! Be still!"

The ocean bodies of the planet grew calm below. Every tree stopped swaying and the birds found themselves unable to glide on their usual currents of air.

Then a celestial being, one like God's Son, appeared on the eastern horizon. He had the seal of the living God and cried out to the four angels, *"Don't hurt the earth, the sea, or a tree, until the seal is on the foreheads of God's servants."*

Whitney Conner's sleeping figure lay serenely on her bed. The two-leaved windows in her apartment bedroom opened silently of their own accord for the illumined angel. A soft glow filled the room as the creature entered the room and stood beside her bed. He gently touched her forehead.

Startled by the touch, Whitney opened her eyes. "Hello?" she said nervously, and sat up in her bed. "Who's there?"

She was alone.

A slight breeze brushed against her cheek and she glanced at the window. "Now how did that get open?" she asked aloud.

She went to the window and examined the dark street below. She saw nothing until she raised her eyes to the night sky. There on the horizon, a trail of light streaked from her window like pixie dust in a Peter Pan movie. In a few brief seconds, it faded and disappeared.

How odd!

She stared at the stars for awhile and breathed in the brisk night air of the approaching fall. She then closed her window and started back across the room.

In her stride, she caught a faint glow of light to her left from the corner of her eye.

"Who's there!?" she asked, stepping back. Rigid, she peered in the direction of the light. It had vanished. She waited for a reappearance, but nothing happened. Certain it was her imagination, she moved again toward her bed and—

"Oh!" she gasped jumping back.

There it was again! The sudden appearance of a small glimmer of light.

Her heart pounded faster as she waited, too frightened to move. Again, no reappearance. Nothing until she moved forward.

There it was again! Vanishing as before when she jumped back.

By now her eyes had adjusted to the darkness and she saw the outline of her mirrored dresser standing in the corner where she'd seen the light.

Could the dresser have something to do with this encounter? It seemed to connect somehow with seeing the light. She resolved to pursue the mystery, this time more boldly. Moving again she discovered the small faint glow from

Jay Zinn

a reflection in the mirror.
It came from her forehead.

CHAPTER 37

Pastor Mitchell opened the front door for Whitney.

Rhonda stood at his side and welcomed her in.

"Whitney, what's the matter?" Rhonda asked. "You sounded upset on the phone?"

"Forgive me for getting you up this late, but I had to talk to you."

"Have a seat, dear, I'll heat up some coffee."

"That won't be necessary, Mrs. Mitchell. Can we just talk?"

"Sure," Rhonda replied and ushered her into the living room.

As Whitney sat down on the couch she paused to frame her first question. "Pastor, remember when you taught the book of Revelation to the church?"

"Yes, it was a couple of years ago."

"I was a young Christian, then, and didn't retain much; but I did remember something about 144,000 people. Before I came over, I looked it up in the Bible. It appears to me that the sealing of 144,000 will happen soon after the earthquake we just had. Am I right in assuming that?"

"That's what I believe," Jack said.

"Then who are they? I've heard some of my friends say they were 144,000 Jewish evangelists."

Jack smiled at Rhonda and then at Whitney. "Did you get us up at two in the morning for this?"

"Not quite," she replied soberly, "but I experienced something tonight that I can't explain. Something supernatural—"

Rhonda sat forward. "Supernatural?"

"Yeah, and for some reason I believe it has something to do with this 144,000."

"What happened?" Rhonda asked.

Whitney bit down on her lip and stared out the window. "I think an angel visited me tonight."

"An angel?" Jack said.

Whitney nodded, hoping they wouldn't think she was crazy. "Please, tell me about the 144,000, pastor. I've got to know. I believe it's a clue."

"Okay," Jack replied. He reached for his glasses and Bible on the coffee table. "First, I find it difficult to interpret this to be 144,000 Jewish evangelists. The context of this passage in Revelation 7 clearly describes the 144,000 as coming from twelve different tribes of Israel."

Whitney frowned. "I don't understand."

"Jews don't come out of all the twelve tribes. Their roots trace back to the tribe of Judah, with the tribes of Benjamin and Levi in there. So it can't be correctly interpreted as being all *Jewish* evangelists."

"Then who are they?"

"Personally, I think it refers to members of spiritual Israel made up of both Jews and Gentiles in the Church."

"So at least they're all Christians?"

"Yes."

"But why only 144,000?"

"I'm not sure. Obviously, they're sealed for protection. Maybe for a specific purpose, like a divine assignment."

"What assignment?"

"The passage doesn't tell us, but we find another 144,000 described in the fourteenth chapter of Revelation. I believe *that* could be a clue to understanding the purpose for the 144,000 in chapter 7."

"Are they the same people?"

"Some believe they are, but I don't believe that. The fourteenth chapter specifically says they're all virgin men, but they could be different than the 144,000 in chapter 7."

"Okay, well, let's forget their purpose. What about the seal on their forehead, do you think we'll be able to see it?"

Jack laughed. "My these are serious questions you have. Yes, I think God and his angels will see it, but I don't know if we'll be able to."

"Whitney, what does this have to do with the angel?" Rhonda asked.

Whitney shifted in her seat.

"Pastor...Mrs. Mitchell...the angel touched my forehead tonight and woke me up. I saw the window in my bedroom open and got up to close it. When I looked outside, I discovered a fading trail of light that went from my room toward the horizon."

"Are you sure?" Rhonda asked.

"Absolutely. If you'll turn out the lights, I'll show you something."

Jack looked bewildered at Rhonda. He went to the wall switch and turned off the lights.

"Do you see it?" Whitney asked.

As their eyes adjusted to the dark, Jack and Rhonda stared curiously at the faint glow on Whitney's forehead. "Yes," Rhonda whispered in holy awe, "we see it."

Whitney sighed. "Praise God, then I'm *not* going crazy. Do you think it could be the seal of the 144,000?"

"I have no way of knowing," Jack replied.

"Well, if it *is* the seal, why would God pick me? What assignment could he have for me when there are millions of others to choose from?"

"That's a question I'm afraid I can't answer, Whitney," Jack replied. "I just don't know."

CHAPTER 38

The next day, Bob Jansen waited anxiously for Whitney to answer her door. He was holding a bouquet of flowers in his left hand while his right hand fumbled with a black velvet box in his pocket. He decided if Shayne could get married in faith, then he could, too. He'd just work things out along the way. After all, Whitney believed it could work with the *right* person. Finally, she came to the door.

"Bob! It's good to see you!" Whitney glowed with affection. "Please…come in."

Bob had to stare for a moment, taken back by an unusual change in her countenance.

"Anything wrong?" Whitney asked.

"Wow, you look different. Kind of all lit up or something."

"Really?"

"Yeah, I can't describe it." Bob handed her the bouquet.

Whitney blushed. "Oh, Bob, what beautiful flowers."

Bob took her by the hand as he walked in and shut the door behind them. "Whitney," he said, groping for the right words, "it…it's been a month now since Shayne and Laura's wedding. I've been lonely without a roommate and, you know, sort of missing the way things used to be when we did things together."

"Yeah, I know. It's been lonely since Laura moved out, too."

"I've been thinking," Bob continued. "We've known each other for nearly ten months now, and I've grown very fond of you. I...I was wondering if you might share the same feelings about me?"

"What're you getting at, Bob?"

Whitney appeared uncomfortable, which made this harder. Should he go on?

"Well...what I mean is...ever since the wedding, I've realized my feelings for you are stronger than just friends."

He swallowed hard and gazed hopefully into her eyes. "I...I...I'm in love with you and I want to marry you."

There, I said it. He held his breath for her reply.

"Oh..." Whitney blushed and stared at the ground. "Well, uh...I feel strongly about you, too, Bob."

Bob's heart began to race. "You mean you love me?"

Whitney turned and stared out her window in silence.

"Is anything wrong?"

"Please, sit down for a moment," she said, avoiding his eyes. "I need to tell you something."

Bob released his grip on the black velvet box in his pocket. "What is it?" he asked sitting next to her. "What's the matter? I've blown it, haven't I? I'm rushing things."

"No. Please don't think that," she said with her hand on his shoulder. "I'm flattered you want me to be your wife, but I'm afraid I can't marry you. Not now."

Bob's heart sank. "But why? Is there someone else? Is it something about me you don't like?"

"There's nothing wrong with you. Oh...how can I tell you?" She looked away. "I do love you and would love to marry you, but God has revealed a new course for my life."

"What're you saying? You mean God doesn't want you to be married?"

"No, I'm not saying that. I just don't think God wants me to be involved in a serious relationship right now."

Bob grew irritated. "Whitney, you're not making sense. In one breath, you say you love me; and in the next, you say you can't be involved."

"I know it sounds crazy. I don't understand it, either. But I know I can't dive into marriage until God's will is clearer."

Bob brushed her hand off his shoulder and stood up to move toward the door. He was denied matrimony because of some strange plan from God that Whitney didn't even understand. This was too much for him to process. Maybe he'd made a mistake. Maybe this Christianity wasn't all he was led to believe. It never held his parents together. Now it was coming between him and the girl he wanted to marry.

Whitney followed him and took his hand again. "Bob, please don't leave like this. I don't mean to hurt you. I care for you. But there's something happening to me I can't ignore. Please, talk to Pastor Mitchell. He'll explain it—"

"No. I don't want to see Pastor Mitchell." He opened the door and slammed it behind him.

Whitney opened the door again and called after him, "Bob, wait! Please, don't go! There's more I need to tell you!"

"You've said enough, Whitney!" he yelled. "You *can't* marry me, you've made your point! Goodbye!"

As Bob ran down the street, Whitney began to weep. The joy of her touch by an angel was overshadowed by upsetting the man she loved. She pondered if she'd ever see him again. The loss of Bob's friendship was hard to bear. She suddenly felt very alone. "Watch over him, Lord," she prayed with uplifted eyes. Tears rolled down her cheeks. "Please open his heart to the bigger picture. Please."

CHAPTER 39

Aster had returned to his headquarters in Tel Aviv.

His stature and charisma in key circles continued to strengthen through the guidance of Satan's powerful influence. He was ready to make his next move and called a meeting with the members of the World Church council.

"Gentlemen, our situation couldn't be better," Aster said. "We've reached our objective and pulled the key nations and religions into our organization. In spite of the global devastation, the quake served as a catalyst for our cause. With the United States, Japan, and Europe on board, the formation of our ten-kingdom alliance is complete. America yielded her sovereign rights without a fight, and the constitutional convention has given birth to the ratification of a new World Constitution. We're ready now for our most strategic move."

The members of the council smiled and applauded the news.

"Mr. Chairman," one member of the council asked. "Has the recruiting for our New World Forces (NWF) been significant enough to quell the looting and other illegal activities in the aftermath of the quake?"

Aster smiled. "Yes it has. Since we've established martial

law, the numbers at our recruiting stations are exploding off the charts. The NWF grows stronger by the hour, subduing any and all disorder. Looting and anarchy have diminished by ninety percent. Because of this, reports from every nation indicate a rise in optimism for a global society. It's the first time in history that every tribe, country and nation is at peace with their neighbor. Newspapers, magazines and the networks are all proclaiming *peace* and *safety* in a New World Order."

The members of the council patted each others' back and shook hands as a messenger walked in with a note and handed it to Drakon.

His face turned pale.

"What is it, John?" Aster asked.

"Malloy is alive," Drakon whispered. "One of our intelligence officers from Washington is here to see you about it."

The mark on Aster's temple reddened as he rose from his chair. "Gentlemen, excuse us for a moment," he said and left the room with Drakon.

A stocky, well-groomed man waited for them outside in the courtyard.

"Vince, it's good to see you," Drakon said walking into the courtyard. "Reuben, I want you to meet Vince Kobrin, one of our senior officers in the WFI (World Federal Intelligence). He's been assigned to our covert operations around Washington. He knows Malloy."

Aster stared curiously at Kobrin. "You know Malloy, eh?"

"Yes, sir. We were rookies together in the CIA."

"Friends, then?"

Kobrin chuckled. "Not likely. He beat me out of an assignment we both wanted. He got it, I didn't. It opened a lot of doors for him and carried him up the ladder to the White House."

"Why did you think I'd be interested in Malloy?" Aster asked.

"I figured he might be in the way since he was a close friend of President Thomas. Dr. Drakon assigned me to kill the president. I knew about the plot he had with Malloy to take you out."

"How did you know?"

"Someone inside the CIA...a close associate of mine. When I heard Malloy was dead, I figured *you* knew about the plot and had already taken care of the situation. Since then, my team has been assigned to monitor Nathan Kelly. We tapped his phone. When he mentioned Malloy's name in a recent conversation, I figured you'd want to know about it, so I flew over to tell you. If I can help in any way..."

"And why are you so anxious to help, Mr. Kobrin?"

"I have a score to settle. Malloy busted me in a drug trafficking operation a while back. Put me behind bars for ten years."

Aster glanced at his prophet for assurance.

"He's okay, Reuben. Gets the job done on everything I've assigned him...like Samuel Thomas."

Aster turned to Kobrin. "All right, what can you tell me about Malloy? You're certain he's alive?"

"Yeah, I'm sure. A call came in two days ago to Nathan Kelly. The conversation went long enough to get a trace, but Kelly cut it off when Malloy's name was mentioned by the party on the other end."

"How are Kelly and Malloy connected in this?"

"Don't know, sir. We only know that Kelly shut down the conversation real quick. Said he'd call the party later."

"Who was the caller?"

"We traced the number back to a preacher in a college town called Canterton...somewhere in the foothills of Virginia. His name's Jack Mitchell. Our agents flew down to check on it and discovered this guy and his wife had been harboring an outsider for several months. Word got around Canterton that a strange guest was staying with them."

"Get a name on him?"

"Nobody knew it."

"Is he still there?"

"He left a week after the quake, but we're certain it was Malloy."

Aster gazed at the floor and stroked his chin. "We can't take any chances. It could be him. Only two bodies were found in the van and Malloy wasn't one of them. We've got to find him."

"That could be difficult, sir," Kobrin said. "I know Malloy. He'll have his name changed, grow hair…do anything to stay under cover. I suspect he'll avoid any and all contact with his former associates, too."

Aster leaned quietly against the wall in the courtyard and looked at Drakon. "Malloy could throw a curve into our next plan."

"He's dangerous, sir," Kobrin said. "If you tried to take him out once, he won't be careless again. Now that he knows what you're capable of he'll do everything he can to stop you. And if anyone can, Malloy will do it."

Aster sprung from the wall like a panther and grabbed Kobrin by the throat with one hand. He pressed his thumb into his windpipe and lifted him with his feet dangling six inches off the ground.

Kobrin gasped for air. He stared into the dark pools of Aster's eyes and futilely clawed to free himself from the vice-like grip.

"I don't need you telling me what he's capable of," Aster snarled.

Drakon placed his hand on Aster's arm. "Reuben, don't worry. We'll get the word out. With the right price, every bounty hunter in the country will be looking for him."

"No, I want him alive!" Aster said. He threw Kobrin to the floor. "I want him killed where I can see it. Bring him to me. This time I'll make sure the job is finished."

Kobrin picked himself off the floor and rubbed his throat.

Aster reached over and brushed the dust off of Kobrin's jacket like nothing had happened. "I want you to move your entire team to Canterton and monitor Mitchell. Don't show yourself, just watch him. Malloy may contact him. Find out everything you can about this preacher: his activity, what he says, what he teaches and how he operates his church. If he's our only lead to Malloy, I don't want anything getting by, got it?"

"Yes, sir."

"Good. Call Drakon as soon as you find out anything."

Kobrin nodded and left quickly.

Aster stared at Drakon. "We should probably advance quicker to the next phase. If Malloy's on the prowl I want to have the strategic edge."

"Right."

The members of the council grew still when Aster and Drakon returned. "Gentleman, let's continue where we left off," Aster said. "I believe we're poised for the next step."

"I agree," said a councilman. The others nodded their approval.

"Very good. I want the summit meeting held here in Tel Aviv. Contact the members of the alliance to lay the groundwork with their neighboring allies. If everyone does their job, I'm confident the World Federation will recognize the wisdom and benefits of our plan."

CHAPTER 40

College enrollment paled in comparison to the past.

The quake, coupled with serious economic conditions, reduced the world's colleges to a dream for most. Survival, above education, had become the priority.

Something else was different, too. A universal presence of soldiers from the NWF (New World Forces) canvassed colleges in every country with vigorous recruiting. It had become the gathering tool of the ever increasing might of the World Church. Aster had ingeniously married the *military* with *religion* to serve the objectives of his one-world government. The bait: promise of a secure career and income in the NWF of the World Federation.

———

As Jack Mitchell drove through the campus of Canterton University, a familiar building grabbed his attention; one he had pastored in for twenty years. His heart grieved when he saw the new sign in front of his old church:

New World Church
———

NWF Headquarters
Station 189

Jack reflected on the days when those walls could barely contain the sound of glorious celebration. Now the World Church had turned it into a *station house*; using the soldiers to bring in new or potential recruits to her so-called religious services.

Jack knew where it was going, the Bible's predictions were clear. That's why he kept his congregation abreast of the movement and activities of the World Church through his elders. He warned the people repeatedly to guard their hearts from the deceptive teachings of these soldiers, and the only way they could do that was to know their Bibles and stay close to God.

"Dear Jesus," he cried as he drove by, "Where's your Bride? When will she be manifested to the world? Have I been wrong about her? Have I believed in a fabrication of my own desires or dreams? This World Church is deceiving millions of naive saints, blinding them with her empty promises. My heart breaks for them, Lord. When...when will your Bride come and avert this godless trend?"

"The day of her wedding draws near," said an audible voice.

Startled, Jack pulled his car to the curb and slammed on the brakes. He turned to look in the back seat for the person who spoke.

Nobody's here. It had to be God.

Shaken by the encounter he bowed his head in prayer. "Dear Lord, the predictions you gave in your Word are coming to pass. But it's all happening so fast! Please...give me the wisdom to prepare the people you've given me to shepherd. If there's anything we lack, please show me. I want us to be ready to meet you when you come."

CHAPTER 41

The summit of the Federation convened in Tel Aviv.

All the members of the ten-kingdom alliance were there and formed the council of the World Federation of Nations (WFN). The ten men sat around the table buzzing with excitement over the dawning of their New World Order.

Lamar Becker, one of the ten members, stood and tapped his crystal glass of water. He had been sent by President Cane to represent the United States, and the WFN council had unanimously appointed him as their chairperson. "Welcome to our summit, gentlemen," he began. "Thank you for clearing your schedules for this historic occasion.

"As you know our fledgling government has made great strides since its conception. But the purpose of this meeting isn't to celebrate our achievements. Instead, we must address the challenges we face to secure our efforts and increase our momentum. We're still too vulnerable for the consequences of another quake or disaster, should that happen. If it did, optimism among our allied nations could return to despair, and that despair to anarchy."

The ten men nodded in agreement with Becker.

"What do you propose, Mr. Chairman?" one of them asked.

"To answer your question, I invite you to listen to the proposal of a long standing friend of the New World Order. Someone you know personally and are aware of his copious credentials. He currently chairs the council of the renown World Church; an organization who generously subsidized our cause from its vast resources.

"This man has an idea to share with you, and in my opinion, one that demands serious consideration. So without further delay, let's welcome, Dr. Reuben J. Aster."

The members of the World Federation council stood and applauded Aster as he entered the room. They were oblivious, however, to the spellbinding presence of Satan who also entered the room to seduce their minds.

Aster stepped to the podium at the other end of the conference table and held up his hands for silence. "Good morning and thank you. Please be seated."

The council sat down.

"Gentlemen," Aster began, "I bring you greetings from the World Church and stand here today as a partner with you for life. I want to share a plan with you that could secure a world filled with peace for our children, and our children's children. A world void of war and hunger. A world that will push beyond the boundaries of science and technology and bring an end to every disease and sickness known to man. I hope to inspire you to pool our strengths with the strengths of your allies. Seize the moment. Take the authority, the resources, and the opportunities at our disposal to create a new world."

As the men listened, Aster saw Satan's demonic squad at work—twenty of the creatures, swirling around the heads of each member—whispering to them, intoxicating them and seducing them to take the bait.

With Satan's operatives assisting from the nether world,

Aster continued with his own eloquence in laying out his ideas for a new government, an economic system, and a strategy for world peace. His concepts dazzled the minds of the council for the next two hours.

At the end of the presentation, Lamar Becker dismissed them for lunch, over which the dominant topic of discussion was Aster's plans and his sheer genius.

Through the suggestive powers of demons, combined with Aster's charisma and intellect, the heart of each man had been captured completely.

Aster could see it in their eyes.

CHAPTER 42

Lunch was over and the meeting resumed.

Becker quickly laid a motion on the table. "Throughout history," he said, "nations found the soul of their empires in a person who embodied their ideals and strengths. There is, and always has been, a universal principle that too many heads and no followers is sure defeat. We've tried democracy and look where it's left us; pluralistic rule, and it, too, has failed. Today we have passengers aboard a World Federation but no captain to guide us through the storms that lie ahead. Therefore, I move that we follow Dr. Aster's proposal to appoint a principal leader, a *point man*, who can take this world to greater heights than it's ever known. If this seems good to you, I also move that we add an amendment to our World Constitution that requires the appointment of an officer who will preside over our World Federation as president."

The councilmen whispered among themselves and then one of them said, "Mr. Chairman, I'd like to second that motion."

Becker smiled. "All in favor then say, Aye."

"Aye!"

"All opposed?"

Aster watched quietly at the opposite end of the table from Becker. No one opposed the motion.

Becker glanced happily at Aster and continued. "Gentlemen, since all are in favor I suggest we take a vote for the candidates of that office."

The council approved and quickly entered their nominees into a secret ballot. Becker tallied their entries.

"It's unanimous," Becker announced with a broad smile. A single name has emerged for the man who will become our world president."

The ten men stood and faced Aster, all smiling.

"Dr. Aster," Becker said cheerfully, standing with the rest, "will you accept the position of president of the World Federation of Nations?"

Aster stood as the men applauded. He returned their smiles with a nod and said, "Yes."

After a thorough exchange of congratulations, the council added an amendment to the World Constitution. It established the existence of the office and spelled out the job description; which gave Aster an exercise of power unprecedented in human history, total sovereignty over the nations. Aster's course was set. He'd reached his long-awaited fate to officially control the world, its military and its commerce through a one-world government.

Now he could secure his reign by removing the last enemies of his world and nothing could stop him.

Nothing.

CHAPTER 43

Jack Mitchell flicked the newspaper with his hand.

"Aster's popularity is a phenomenon! Newspapers, talk shows, broadcasting networks, they're all applauding this appointment."

Rhonda shook her head as she poured her husband another steaming cup of coffee. "How could every government and religion embrace him so readily?" she asked. "You'd think there'd have been more resistance to giving *one* man absolute power."

Jack took a sip of his coffee and set it down on the saucer. "The world's in denial," he said. "People are so obsessed with having peace and order they'll do anything to get it. This may be the time in Scripture when God sends a strong delusion on those so opposed to the truth, they'll allow any man like Aster to rule over them."

Rhonda stared out the window and frowned.

"What's wrong?" Jack asked.

"Oh...a thought flashed through my mind about Cliff and the letter he left us. I wonder how he's doing?"

"I'm sure he's fine. Malloy would be the last person on earth to be deceived by Aster."

"It's not him being deceived that concerns me. It's what he plans to do to Aster. I'm afraid Aster will kill him this time."

———

Vince Kobrin hated his new assignment.

To be taken out of Washington and placed in a town like Canterton was a demotion as far as he was concerned. He still had jurisdiction in Washington, but finding Malloy was top priority so he had to move.

He believed Aster was disciplining him for his presumptous remark about Malloy's ability to get even. He still couldn't get over the stranglehold Aster had on his throat. Where'd he get such inhuman strength? He was lucky to get away with his life. He certainly didn't want to go through another man-handling like that.

Since his arrival in Canterton, Kobrin had placed bugging devices in the Mitchell's home but had uncovered nothing so far. Now a courier arrived from the surveillance team with the first sign of a connection between the Mitchells and Malloy.

"Captain, sir. Malloy's name came up during the Mitchell's breakfast."

Kobrin rose behind his desk. "Did they say where he was?"

"Afraid not, sir." The courier handed Kobrin a paper. "This is the printout of their conversation. The pertinent information is highlighted."

Kobrin put on his reading glasses and scanned the print. "It appears they have some letter Malloy left them. Find it. They're on to something. Maybe the contents will reveal his whereabouts. Keep me abreast of everything they say about Malloy."

———

Cliff Malloy growled at the local news and snapped off his

walkman. He was taking a break from his ascent up the the Bitterroot Range in Idaho. "The whole world's been fooled by that cursed man!" he hissed.

"The coneys ain't gonna go for it," Grub replied. *Coney* was the nickname for militia survivalists. "They don't trust no one in government, 'specially no one-world president."

"You think I'll get into your community?" Malloy asked.

"'Taint hard, if you show Cap' you're one of us."

"How long have the coneys been here?"

"Before I got here, I reckon. Been seven years now." Grub massaged his shaved head. The tattoos on his hand led Malloy's eyes to the other markings on his arm. "The coneys don't tell me much and I don't ask much, neither," Grub said. "Less I know, the better. They likes to keep things real quiet that way."

"Where'd they come up with the name, *coney*?"

"Ain't rightly sure. Reckon it has to do with some furry critter that makes its home in rocks and caves. Like us." Malloy reached down to rub the stiffness out of his calves. "What can you tell me about Cap'?"

"I can tell you not to ask so many dadgum questions when we get there. Coneys don't like people nosing around. It's the kinda' place where you can keep to yourself. Lotsa' mean people in the coneys who hates authority and government, or anything else tries to run their lives."

This was good news to Malloy. The perfect environment to hide in; even better, to get a team to go with him to nail Aster. "So I'd have to show Cap' I'm one of you, huh? How do I do that?"

Grub seized his buttocks and scratched himself. "You'll figure it out when you get there." His coy smile revealed his two front teeth missing and the rest starting to rot.

Malloy rubbed his aching thighs as Grub glanced at the sky.

"We're burnin' daylight," Grub said. "Better get going again."

Malloy groaned. "How far before we get there?"

"About twelve miles to that peak up yonder. Should make it by sundown."

CHAPTER 44

⚬〰〰⚬

The apostles grieved over the loss of Aster.

In spite of his new identity, they still missed him.

"I'm afraid the prophecies regarding the Antichrist find their fulfillment in Reuben Aster," Nathan Kelly said. There's no second guessing it now. He has shown his hand, and according to Scripture he is the fallen star, the son of perdition, the lawless one, the little horn, the eighth king who subdues three others, and the beast who rises out of the sea in Revelation 13.

The other apostles were saddened by the reality of these words. They couldn't deny it. All were disheartened over their colleague's defection from the faith to Satan's deception.

One of the apostles spoke up. "Reuben's involvement with the World Church has rocked the faith of many Christians. Perhaps we should have told the church about this sooner."

"We didn't have anything concrete," Nathan replied. "Reuben covered himself so well he duped us all. I even doubted my own suspicions about him; that is, until he came to my apartment. By then it was too late. No, brothers, we couldn't have stopped him any more than the disciples could've stopped Judas from betraying Christ."

"Isn't there *anything* we can do?" another apostle asked.

No one responded. Everyone stared sadly at Nathan Kelly. "There is one thing we can do," he replied. "We can warn the Church that Aster *is* the predicted Antichrist and the World Church, the predicted Harlot of Revelation 17.

"We must warn them against her teachings, or any law of Aster's that demands they receive the *mark of the beast*—the number 666 on the forehead or right hand in order to buy or sell. I'm certain that'll be next on his agenda.

"Ever since cash cards came into the banking system, the culmination of a cashless economy became imminent. Cyberbanking will be the wave of the future, and Aster'll move as quickly as possible from cash cards to the bio-chip. After that, destroying the Church will be easier for him; and we'll be on the top of his list."

The men sat quietly and stared at the floor.

Nathan surveyed their faces. He could feel their despair about the future—perhaps like the disciples must have felt about their future when Judas betrayed Jesus in the garden.

"How could he do it?" a younger apostle asked. "After all we've been through the past ten years."

"He's not the same man," Nathan replied. "The man who prayed with us, cried with us, and labored to advance the gospel with us is no longer there. I saw it in his eyes. They were the eyes of a man dead in his sins, and full of the Devil. Drakon, too. He wasn't the prophet we once admired."

The apostles shifted in their seats and glanced nervously at each other.

Nathan knew their thoughts. They were his as well. "Yes, if it can happen to Aster and Drakon, it can happen to us. That's why we must pay close attention to ourselves. Don't think for a moment that we can stand up to deception any better than Aster or Drakon faced. We must cling tight to God. Be accountable to him and each other. What we taught the pastors in Amsterdam, the same applies to us. We must prepare our hearts. If our understanding of the Scriptures is accurate, Christ will come soon for his Bride and, gentlemen, we don't want to find ourselves disqualified."

—⫶⫶⫶⫶⫶—

The world loved their new president.

Order prevailed. Optimism abounded.

But the predetermined event on God's prophetic schedule had arrived. The momentum that Aster and the World Church enjoyed was about to slow down with the greatest threat they had ever encountered, the unveiling of the Bride of Christ.

CHAPTER 45

A holy hush settled over the earth.

Behind the invisible veil of the third heaven, Jesus, still holding the scroll, peeled away the *seventh* seal. For the next half hour, the citizens of heaven stood in complete silence for the long-awaited marriage of the Lamb.

The people of Canterton slumbered at the approach of the chilled, October midnight.

Shayne and Laura Taylor were asleep in their humble apartment, oblivious to the sudden appearance of two nine-foot angels standing on opposite sides of their bed.

In deep baritone voices they whispered simultaneously, as with one voice, "*The Bridegroom is coming, prepare to meet him.*"

Shayne, laying on his back, opened his eyes and kept his head still. He saw the silhouetted images of glowing figures fade away, and then sat up.

They were gone.

"Laura, Laura!" Shayne said, frantically shaking her

shoulder. "Laura, wake up!"

"What...?" she asked groggily, lifting her head.

"Did you hear them?"

"No..."

"You mean you didn't hear the voices?"

"What're you talking about?"

"Get up. We've got to get dressed. Tonight's the night. Jesus is coming for his Bride. That was their message."

Laura sat up. "Who's message?"

"Two angels. They said the Bridegroom is coming and we're supposed to prepare to meet him."

Laura rolled her eyes and flopped back down on the pillow. "Go to sleep, honey, you had a dream."

Shayne ran around the bed and knelt on the floor at her side. "Look at me. I'm serious. This was no dream."

Laura grunted and sat up to turn on her light. She rubbed her eyes and studied Shayne's face. "You're serious aren't you?"

"I've never been more serious in my life. I...just...saw...two...angels. They told us to prepare ourselves for the Bridegroom. He's coming tonight."

Laura scanned the room as she rubbed the goose bumps that had formed on her arms. "Oh my, do you think we're ready? Will it really happen like Pastor Mitchell said?"

"After seeing those angels, yeah, I believe it's going to happen."

Shayne and Laura put on their robes and knelt beside the bed, praying, confessing and repenting of everything they could think of. Then they opened their Bibles to Psalm 45, Shayne's favorite passage about the Bride and her Bridegroom.

When they finished reading the last verse, the antique clock on the fireplace began its twelve-stroke chime toward the midnight hour.

Shayne stared at Laura with bated breath. At each stroke of the clock, a heaviness wrapped him tighter and tighter. His arms and legs grew heavier until they felt like dead weight.

Suddenly his and Laura's body began to glow brighter and

brighter, until a burst of light from their bodies blinded them momentarily.

Shayne grabbed Laura and held her tight. As his vision cleared up he gazed curiously at the glow on his wife's face. "Honey, you look radiant," he whispered, but she made no response. Her eyes were staring past him at something. He followed her gaze around to a glowing man dressed in a white, full-length robe. A golden sash wrapped his chest. Rays like sunlight poured out of his face. Glittering sparkles swirled around his pure-white hair and his penetrating eyes flickered with tiny flames. His feet, too, were aglow, burning like bronze in a furnace.

No introductions were necessary.

Shayne knew in his heart it was Jesus.

Weakened by the majestic presence, Shayne found himself completely immobilized. Only his eyes could move to where he could see only the Lord, and not Laura behind him.

Suddenly a strong wind blew into the room and wrapped his flesh like static electricity. He felt his skin begin to tingle, like it was peeling away from his body.

Christ's fiery eyes penetrated his, as if he were searching through his soul to purge every sinful thought. Then something bubbled like a flood and rushed through his body. It made him feel clean, pure, holy. He began to laugh from the joy that welled up inside him. When it was over, there were no words in his language that could describe how he felt.

Then Jesus spoke to them with a voice that resounded like the roar of Niagara,

"You are my Bride, and I am your Bridegroom. As my Father and I are united in heart, thought, and purpose, you are united one with me. Tell the world that I'm coming soon. As you go, heal the maimed, the lame, the blind, and the sick in my name. In my name, raise the dead and cast out demons. I have chosen you and equipped you to bring in the harvest for the harvest is ripe.

156

"You will be persecuted for my name's sake, but have no fear. When your mission is finished, I will gather you to a safe place where your needs will be met. Then I will gather you to myself, and judge the world.

"Don't be dismayed at the hardships, nor the darkness that will soon prevail. These things must come, but are temporal, for as surely as I live, the whole earth will be filled with my glory."

When he finished speaking, Jesus disappeared as quickly as he came.

Shayne remained paralyzed and glowing from the residue of Christ's presence. He couldn't talk until a few minutes had passed and a measure of his strength returned.

"Laura," he said, light-headed, "did you see it? Did it happen to you...like your faith level made a quantum leap?"

"Yes, I saw it. I feel tingly inside, and my heart feels completely pure."

"Did you hear him call us his Bride?"

"It was incredible...and his voice..."

Shayne laughed. Then Laura.

The joy of the Lord was so full in them, they couldn't stop laughing for nearly an hour.

Finally, their strength returned completely. They could stand again, a little slowly at first, and were still light-headed.

"Do you think we'll know who the other members of the Bride will be?" Shayne asked, "I mean, when we see them?"

"If we see what I see in you," Laura said, "I'm sure of it. They'll be out there, all over the world, doing the same things Jesus just told *us* to do."

CHAPTER 46

Whitney Conner lay awake in prayer that night.

She prayed her mission would be clear about why she had received the seal on her forehead. What was this special assignment God had for her?

Pastor Mitchell didn't know. Even Nathan Kelly said it was a mystery to him when Pastor Mitchell asked him.

Only the Lord could tell her. She prayed fervently, not only to be found ready, but that she would be counted worthy to receive his answer. As she continued in prayer, a heaviness fell over her and she looked at the clock.

It was midnight.

The curtains began to move when the windows opened on their own. A strong wind blew into the room, wrapping her like a blanket. Her flesh experienced a sensation of skin peeling off her body. Then a burst of light followed, flooding her soul with a sense of purity and holiness.

Whitney was startled next by the sudden appearance of a divinely clothed man with piercing eyes and a glowing garment. His face appeared to flash like lightning.

As he approached her bed, she lay immobilized, but felt no alarm. Somehow she knew it was Jesus.

He smiled at her and gently laid his hand on her head.

He looked into her eyes and said she was his Bride. He told her she would harvest souls into his kingdom and that he'd protect her in the years of great trial. Finally, the most important thing he told her was the purpose for the seal on her forehead and the miracle that would take place in her womb.

As Whitney gazed at his glowing face, her mind was filled with questions, but she couldn't speak. Then he vanished as suddenly as he came. The room became dark except for an aura of light that radiated around her body.

CHAPTER 47

Bob Jansen sulked and stared at the bottle of wine in his hand.

He had returned to his old habits, and now twice as miserable. He never got over the rejection from Whitney, and like his previous pattern, hid himself again from his friends.

Sitting in his rusty green Cougar at the Quik Stop, he didn't see the man approaching and reach in the window to grab him.

"Oh!" Bob gasped, jumping in his seat.

"Whoa, hold on there, pal. It's just me, Tim Patterson."

Bob quickly shoved the bottle next to his right thigh. He then turned to the football jock he had met at the small group in January. "Man, why'd you sneak up on me like that? You nearly gave me a heart attack." "Sorry, I wasn't sure it was you until I got to the window. Didn't mean to frighten you. Forgive me?"

Bob looked straight ahead. "Yeah, I guess. Just thought I was getting jumped."

Tim chuckled. "Jumped? I doubt if that'll happen in Canterton with all these NWF soldiers around. Or at least not until Aster makes his move and cracks down on Christians."

"Aster?"

"Haven't you heard? The new president of the entire planet. The Federation of Nations pulled a surprise on everybody and appointed him, just like that." Tim snapped his finger.

Bob touched the bottle next to his leg. "Who cares? It's got nothing to do with me."

"But it does, Bob. Pastor Mitchell said Aster's the predicted Antichrist of Revelation 13. Ironic isn't it? How he used to be one of the twelve apostles."

"Apostles?"

Tim poked Bob's shoulder. "Where have you been, pal? Haven't you been paying attention to the information passed down by the district elders?"

"No, I haven't and I don't care. I don't agree with this end-time stuff."

"You're not serious?"

"Yeah, well I am. How do you know the World Church isn't as good as any other church? If it's so bad, why are so many people going to their services? People from your church have joined them, haven't they? I've seen them."

"They're deceived," Tim replied. "If they don't want the truth, they'll believe the lies."

Bob shrugged. "I've been talking to these soldiers myself. Around town, on campus. They seem to be a pretty decent bunch of guys. They told me they don't believe it's the last days, and they don't believe in any Antichrist."

"Of course they don't, can't you see? If they did, they'd have to admit he was Aster and condemn their own church."

"Well, I don't believe it. I think their teaching makes better sense. Better than the fairy tales you guys teach about some Bride, or an Antichrist in a world conspiracy. It's all baloney."

"Bob, be careful," Tim pleaded. "You're vulnerable right now. Satan wants to pull you in like the rest of them. Don't you know the World Church is bad news? The Bible calls her *Babylon*. She'll mess with your mind, man, stay away from her. If you get taken in, you'll wind up with the same judgment she gets when Jesus comes back."

Bob shook his head. "You're beginning to sound like Whitney Conner. She told me the same thing and I think you're both crazy. Go on. Leave me alone. I'm done talking."

Bob saw Tim glance down at the car seat where he hid the wine. "What of it?" Bob said defiantly, picking up the bottle.

Tim backed away from the car. "I can see my timing is bad." He pulled a card out of his wallet and handed it to Bob. "If you need someone to talk to, here's my number. Call me."

"Sure," Bob replied. He stared at the card. "Maybe I will. Just leave me alone now."

"Sure," Tim replied. He said goodbye and walked off.

Bob watched his old acquaintance stroll down the road. He felt ashamed for treating him so badly.

At that moment, the tower clock of the campus gonged its toll toward the midnight hour. When it struck twelve, Tim, who was a block away, fell to his knees on the sidewalk as though an invisible hand knocked him down.

"Tim!" Bob called from the car, startled by the scene. He got out and ran toward the crumpled figure. Within six feet of him, Bob's feet stuck suddenly to the ground. He fell forward from the abrupt stop.

On the ground, Bob reached out his hand. "Tim! Are you okay?"

Tim didn't answer, but stared ahead as though someone stood before him...someone invisible to Bob.

A shiver sprang up Bob's spine when Tim started to glow brighter and brighter, until a burst of light shot out of his body. When the flash occurred, Bob felt a heavy, tangible presence sweep past him. Had he been standing, it would have been powerful enough to knock him down.

Unable to budge his feet or his body, Bob kept his eyes on Tim.

Who's he talking to? Was this the event Whitney had told him about so often...when Jesus would come for his bride? He never took it seriously.

Now he wondered.

CHAPTER 48

Gamliel held tight to his assignee's feet.

Tonight he *had* to intervene. Bob Jansen nearly stepped onto holy ground. It would have killed him if Gamliel hadn't grabbed him in time. Only a consecrated heart could handle contact with Jesus. Bob's heart was in no condition to see the Lord face to face, and live through it.

While Gamliel watched Jesus talk to Tim, he wondered what was going on in Bob's head. Obviously, Bob had missed his chance for the Bride or Gamliel wouldn't have received the command to stop him.

Gamliel was Bob's guardian angel, sent from the ranks of the *elect* angels. Unlike cherubim or seraphim, they had no wings. That was man's misguided image. Were he to make himself visible, he'd look like any human—or giant human. But, he wasn't, and never had been a human. That *human-to-angel* idea came from man's fantasies. He and other angels had many a laugh over that one. Imagine, an angel formerly being a human. Why, the idea of it made Gamliel shudder. He couldn't imagine going through all the problems he'd seen these human go through because of their sins. No, God created Gamliel before he created humans. Why, he was there when Lucifer, a chief cherub, led a rebellion against the Creator. Big mistake. One Gamliel never planned to make.

Tonight, Gamliel felt sorry for Bob. He knew when the *seventh* seal was opened that his assignee wouldn't be ready for the Bride. It wasn't the man's disbelief in the concept that kept him out, it was the condition of his heart. Had his heart been right with God, Bob could've made it. But, unfortunatley, Bob was in rebellion and lukewarm about his relationship with Jesus. The guy loved *himself* more than he loved God. Gamliel could see it. He'd seen the same thing in many saints throughout his 150 generations of assignees.

So now, at this moment, Gamliel knew Bob's only opportunity to get in the Bride had passed. The Bridegroom had come and Bob Jansen, like millions of other Christians, wasn't prepared. Like the five virgins in Matthew 25 who weren't ready for the wedding.

Though many Scriptures like Matthew 25 were a mystery to Gamliel, he eventually discovered their meaning through the course of history when they came to pass. He liked it when this happened. And like all the other angels, he longed to look into these things. Now he could add another fulfilled prophecy to the list. There were two passages he knew related to this particular event. He quoted the first passage from Matthew out loud, paraphrased of course, in a way he now understood,

> "Those who were ready went in with Jesus to the wedding. Then the door was shut. When the other saints came, they cried, 'Sir! Sir! Open the door for us!' But Jesus replied, 'Truthfully, I don't know you.' So Christians keep watch, because you don't know the day or the hour when he comes."

Matthew 25 was taking place throughout the world. Jesus came looking for his Bride. Some were ready, like Tim Patterson; and others were not...like Bob.

Now how did that other scripture go about this event, the one in Revelation? Ah, he remembered.

Jesus had gone, so Gamliel let go of Bob's feet. As he did, he stood to his full height of ten feet. He looked at the cluster of stars overhead and cried, unknown to Bob,

"Rejoice! Be glad! Give glory to God! The wedding of the Lamb has come, and he found his Bride ready."

CHAPTER 49

The sun set on the mountainous terrain of Idaho, casting a red hue on the Bitterroot Range to the east.

Tired and out of shape from the months of convalescing, Malloy crested the last peak of his ascent up the mountain with Grub.

Below them lay the valley gorge of the militia community. Thirty camouflaged cabins and tents lined the banks of a crystal mountain stream. The other dwellings were flanked by a wall of the gorge where large canvas canopies extended from the mouths of several caves.

"There's our camp," Grub said, and spit out a glob of black molasses chew.

Malloy scanned the ridge. "Where are the guards?"

"They're around, but you can't see 'em. They know we're here, and so does Cap'."

The snap of a branch caused Malloy to spin around with his pistol drawn. Two men stood in camo gear, shrouded with leaves and black grease on their faces. He recognized their rifles, H&K-PSG1's...top notch sniper power.

"Drop your weapon, mister!" the guard commanded Malloy.

Grub cackled and stepped between them. "Is that you, Brad, you 'ol weasel? You pert'neer made me drop my drawers, sneaking up on us like that."

"You're getting careless old man," Brad replied. "We've had you in our sights for three miles."

"Shucks! And I thought it was only two miles you boys been stalking us."

"Two miles?" Malloy said. "You knew they were watching?"

"Yep! But Brad's right. Didn't catch him the first mile. You've gotten better, son. I'm gonna hafta' give that mile to you."

"Thanks teacher. Next time, you'll miss *every* mile we stalk you, if you're not careful. What tipped you off?"

"You were messin' with your safety."

Brad's teeth beamed from his black-greased face like a Cheshire cat. "You old horn-toad, how'd you hear that? You were a hundred yards out...down wind."

"Secrets of the trade, boy. You don't think 'ol Grub taught you everything now, did you?"

"And what *did* you teach us, old man?"

"Enough to keep yourself alive and make the enemy dead."

"Who's the slick?" Brad's partner asked, apparently impatient with the bantering.

"Name's Macully," Malloy replied and reached out his hand. He decided to play it safe by using an alias.

The soldier ignored Malloy's gesture. "Cap's waiting. You'd better have a good reason for being here, mister. Follow me."

Malloy shrugged his shoulder and smiled at Grub. They followed the men down a narrow trail until it led them along the side of the gorge and into the colony of survivalists. Malloy took note of the four guards posted strategically on the ridge. They were armed with AK 47 rifles.

At the bottom of the valley, men, women, and children milled around their humble homes. Everyone stood or sat near their campfires eating dinner. They stared warily at the uninvited guest.

With the sun behind the ridge and dusk approaching, kerosene and white gas lanterns burned brightly throughout the camp like giant fireflies.

The soldiers led Malloy to a canopy protruding from the largest cave. It served as a porch that sheltered a log-faced wall built into the cave's mouth. Brad knocked on the tent pole.

"Enter!" a raspy voice barked.

Brad motioned for Malloy to step through the canvas. Behind the flap, two wooden doors were blocked open in the log-faced wall exposing a ten-by-ten-foot entrance into the cave's thirty feet of spheric space.

Malloy stepped through the log-faced opening onto a solid rock floor, overlaid with bear and deerskin rugs. Against the rock wall stood a large metal tub, probably used for bathing. The bed and eating table had been hand-crafted from the pine in the forest. At the back of the cave, an underground stream trickled down the side of the wall into a small basin, draining into a copper conduit that ran underground.

A well-groomed officer sat in a pine rocker with a book on his lap, puffing on a corn-cob pipe. He appeared short and was about Malloy's age, early fifties. Dressed meticulously in camos, he sported an insignia on each shoulder which Malloy figured represented his rank among the members of the militia.

"Captain, sir," Brad said, saluting smartly. "We have Grub and the outsider."

"Thank you, sergeant." the Captain replied. He returned the salute with his nose still in the book. "Leave him."

"Yes, sir."

"Sergeant!" the Captain said.

"Sir."

"Aren't you forgetting something, son?"

"Sir?"

"The man's weapon, please." He held out his hand, still reading the book.

"Yes, sir." Brad pulled Malloy's pistol out of his vest. "Here you are, sir."

"Well done, men. You're dismissed."

Brad and his partner left while the captain, still reading, sniffed the air and scowled, "You, too, Grub! I don't want you staining up my rugs with that fowl tobacco juice."

Grub saluted leisurely. "Yes, sir, Cap'n, sir!" He did an about-face toward the door and winked at Malloy. "Good luck to you, that's Cap'," he said nodding at the captain and ducked through the flaps.

The Captain laid down his book and silently inspected the gun. While he removed the clip of bullets, Malloy scanned the cave once more.

A picture of President Cane hung on the wall. It was riddled with dart holes. Two of the darts remained stuck in the President's chin. The poster next to Cane's, however, made Malloy's heart sprint. It was a picture of Reuben Aster.

The captain stood up and ran his hand through his silver crew cut. He studied Malloy. "Nice pistol," he said, holding the gun up with his right index finger. "You always carry a Gloch 9mm with you?"

"Comes in handy at times."

"The only soldiers that carry one of these in this colony are ex-cops. We've got a few of them from L.A. You a cop?"

"No."

"Ex-cop?"

"Something like that."

"What's your name?"

"Cliff Macully."

"State your business, Macully, why are you here?"

"I'm a survivalist, like you. Lost confidence in the government. Too big. Even more so when it's run by one man."

Cap' followed Malloy's gaze to Aster's picture behind him and smiled. "You like darts, Macully?"

"As long as they're deadly."

Cap' went to the board and pulled four darts out of Aster's

face. He came back and held them out to Cliff. "How good's your aim?"

"Adequate," Malloy replied, taking the darts.

He threw them at Aster's poster from where he stood. One—two—three—four! Two in one eye, two in the other.

Cap' glanced at the target and grinned. "Not bad for an old guy."

"Old guys have experience," Malloy said. "We work smarter."

Cap' walked to his dresser and poured himself a shot-glass of whiskey. "Can you shoot a rifle as accurately as you throw darts?"

"Yes."

"I'd like to see that." Cap' downed the whiskey in one gulp and went to a cedar chest at the foot of his bed. He pulled out a small wooden box and turned to Malloy, "Care for a game of chess?"

"Might as well. Didn't see any bowling alleys when I arrived."

Cap' chuckled and poured the chess pieces onto the table. "No competition these days," he said, setting up his men. "I've beaten everyone in the camp. You like chess?"

Malloy nodded and set his black pieces in place.

"So..." Cap' rubbed his hands together. "What are the stakes?"

"Induction into your camp."

Cap' peered at Malloy. "And if you lose?"

"It's your call."

"You must be good."

"I love strategy," he said and stared once more at the poster behind Cap'.

Cap' glanced over his shoulder and back at Malloy. "You hate him, don't you? I can see it in your eyes."

"Passionately, Captain. It's your play. You've got the white."

CHAPTER 50

A deluge of prayers threw open heaven's gates.

The petitions from Christ's new Bride ascended out of every tribe, language and nation.

In response to the prayers, an angel with a golden censer was given incense and came to offer it on the altar before God's throne.

Laced with the prayers of the saints, the fragrant smoke of the incense rose before God from the angel's hand. The angel then took fire from the altar and placed it into the censer.

Seven other angels, with seven trumpets, stood ready before God. They watched the angel swing the censer like a sling, and hurl it to Earth. As it struck, rumbling peals of thunder and flashes of lightning broke out, and a great earthquake rippled again across every continent.

As the quake shook the planet. The seven angels with their trumpets positioned themselves to sound off.

When the first angel trumpeted, hail and fire mingled with blood, fell furiously from the sky to destroy a third of the trees and grass.

The air had been motionless for weeks over the planet's surface. But not tonight. Menacing clouds and sheets of rain pounded the earth with hail stones the size of golf balls. The ground quivered from the quake under the black raging skies, and lightning struck so frequently that the horizon glowed red from the burning vegetation.

Back in Idaho, Malloy covered his head with his coat as he returned from his visit to the latrine. The hailstones pounded him, bruising his arms and back.

Suddenly a crack and a flash of lightning, followed by a loud boom, struck above his head. Malloy instinctively ducked and then glanced up where a towering pine tree on the side of the gorge had been struck and caught fire. It groaned under the teetering weight, ten feet above the canvas porch of Cap's cave.

Malloy ducked through the flaps to check Cap's position. He was directly below the tree.

With a screeching twist, the pine gave way from the last strands of wood that held it in place.

Malloy sprang instantly and threw his body against Cap', just clearing the tree as it crashed through the canvas with an avalanche of hailstones.

Malloy peered through blazing branches at the scene outside and jumped to his feet. "The camp's on fire!"

Cap' jumped up beside him and shouted above the roaring hail, "Let's get the children into the caves!" He grabbed the metal tub and handed it to Malloy for protection. Then he grabbed a smaller basin for himself."

"What about the lightning?" Malloy shouted. "This copper will attract it!"

"Which do you prefer?! Getting struck by lightning or pounded to death by those golf balls?!"

"Good point!" Malloy replied.

They squeezed passed the tree and ran outside, going from cabin to cabin, escorting families under the tubs and into the caves.

The storm had passed.

Only a few lingering brush fires remained. The coneys had worked all night to salvage what they could and welcomed the first rays of sun now rising over the Bitterroot Mountains.

Cap' strolled up to Malloy with his face smeared from the soot of the charred cabins and vegetation. The hardships of the all-night rescue showed in the tired shuffle of his feet.

"Well, Macully, there are no casualties and everyone's safe, including me. Never had time to thank you last night." He held out his soiled hand.

Malloy smiled and shook it, "Does this mean I'm a member in the community now?"

"You won the chess game, didn't you?"

"I wish you would've told me that, before I did all this work."

Cap' smiled and saluted. "Welcome to the colony, friend. I don't think anyone here will bother you; not after you pitched in to save their lives."

"Thanks. It was an adventure, wasn't it?"

"One I don't hope to repeat," Cap' replied.

Malloy scanned the charred remains of the valley. "You think this fire will drive us out? Looks like most of the trees and vegetation are gone."

"We'll bounce back. We're trained for hardships, and conditioned ourselves for the worst."

"Looks like we'll have plenty of hardship practice then."

"Better get some rest in my quarters, Macully. You look terrible."

Malloy concurred and retired to the cave.

As he lay on the bearskin rug, his thoughts wandered back to the Mitchells. How were they faring through this? He didn't think long about it, however, because he didn't want to deal with the guilt of what he was planning to do.

173

So far, he had made it into the colony where he could recruit the expertise and fire power he needed. Now that Cap' owed him his life, it might be possible to create a strike force that could terminate Aster.

CHAPTER 51

Jack and Rhonda Mitchell didn't sleep all night.

They stayed up to pray through the hail and fire of the first trumpet that followed their midnight encounter with Jesus.

At the first rays of dawn, the sirens could be heard throughout Canterton as the new day revealed another catastrophic thrashing. Jack and Rhonda left their house to examine the damage and assist others in any way they could.

Branches and leaves covered the ground on their street with fallen limbs and trees blocking the road. The smell of smoke from scorched houses and vegetation still permeated the air. Electric wires were snapped and draping over branches, buzzing and crackling from the flying sparks.

Windows in homes and cars had been shattered or cracked by the marble-sized hailstones that still littered the ground. Cars that were parked in the streets all night were riddled with indentations like the surface of a golf ball.

"Jack, look!" Rhonda said, pointing to Mrs. Johnson's house next door. The main branch of her oak tree had fallen through the roof.

Jack stepped carefully across the widow's yard over the

hailstones and branches until he reached the porch and tried her front door. It was locked.

"Mrs. Johnson!" he yelled, banging on the door. No one answered.

He continued to pound.

"Help me, please!" cried a faint voice from the hole where the tree had punched through.

"Jack!" Rhonda called from the front yard. She pointed to the window below the leaning tree. "Up there!"

Jack located the window and returned to the door to kick it down. He was surprised at how easy it was; as though the Holy Spirit came on him like Samson of old. He bounded up the stairs with Rhonda behind him, and found the room where Mrs. Johnson lay. She was pinned in her bed by the tree.

"Help me, Reverend," the faint widow cried. "My legs, I think they're broken."

"Don't worry, we'll get you out," Jack said.

He assessed the limb and the angle of the tree, and looked at Rhonda. "The weight of the oak is pivoting on her. It'll take a crane to pull it off."

Mrs. Johnson groaned and fainted. The tree was shifting outside, grinding the limb into her legs.

"She's out," Rhonda said. "Can't we do something?"

"Pray," Jack said, taking her hand. He gazed at the sky through the hole in the roof. "Father, in the name of Jesus, I need the strength to lift this limb off her."

"*Lift it off,*" the Holy Spirit whispered.

Jack let go of his wife's hand, surprised by the voice.

"What is it," Rhonda asked.

"The answer to our prayer," he said and crawled under the limb. Part of the branch curved up which allowed him to fit under it like placing a yoke on his shoulders.

"Rhonda, as soon as I lift, pull her out fast."

"Be careful," she said as she shoved her hands under Mrs. Johnson's shoulders.

"On the count of three," Jack said. "One...two...

three...pull!" As he clenched his teeth and pushed, a surge of energy coursed through his body. The tree groaned and cracked from the shifting of its immense size, and to Jack's surprise, lifted with ease.

Rhonda snatched Mrs. Johnson off the bed, clear of the tree. Her thighs and knees were flat as a notebook. Jack lowered the branch to the bed again, and then kneeled beside the unconscious widow.

"She's in bad shape," Rhonda said.

"I know, but I believe God will heal her if we pray for her."

Rhonda stared at her hands. "Feel these. They're hot!"

Jack touched them. "It must be a sign."

The Holy Spirit whispered again, *"Pray for her."*

"Did you hear that?" Rhonda asked.

Jack nodded and smiled.

They laid their hands on the widow's legs and prayed. A cracking, gurgling sound emerged and the shattered bones beneath their hands began to move. Within seconds, the deformed, compressed flesh of her legs returned to their normal shape and size.

"This is wonderful!" Rhonda shouted and clapped. "The door blew off its hinges when you kicked it, you lifted the tree like a feather, and now the Holy Spirit speaks to us like he's sitting on our shoulders and this miracle takes place."

"Ohhhh..." Mrs. Johnson moaned, awakened by the voices of her rescuers.

"Hello," Rhonda said, grabbing the woman's hand. "You're safe now, Martha, you're going to be all right."

CHAPTER 52

Martha Johnson grinned at Jack and Rhonda.

She hadn't smiled for thirty-five years since her husband died in Vietnam. She had blamed God for her misfortune and shut herself off from the rest of the world. When the Mitchells moved in next door, she had been a recluse and ignored their repeated attempts to reach out to her.

That all changed today.

"You dears saved my life!" she said, reaching up to touch their faces. "After I've shunned you and treated you so badly all these years. Can you ever forgive this mean 'ol woman for being such a hateful neighbor?"

"Of course we forgive you, Martha." Jack took her hand.

Martha liked the affection. She hadn't gotten any like this in years. But her smile turned to sobriety when she saw the tree punching through the hole in her roof. "I guess I should ask God to forgive me, too. Look how he spared my life. If that tree had fallen another foot, my chest might have been crushed instead of my legs."

She felt for her legs and gasped.

"My legs!" she cried, putting her hand over her mouth. "What's happened to my legs?"

"You're healed," Rhonda said and smiled.

"Look at them!" Martha screamed, wiggling her toes. She pulled her knees to her chest and stretched them out again. "My God, they're completely healed!"

"Try to walk," Jack said.

"Is it possible?" she asked, rising to her feet. There was no pain, no disability. She walked freely across the room. "But this can't be. Only moments ago my legs were crushed. What happened?"

"A miracle," Rhonda said. "Jesus sent us here to find you. Then he healed you."

"Jesus healed *me*?" Her mind raced to the past. "I heard about this when I was a little girl, back when mother took me to church. The Sunday school teacher used to tell us stories about the miracles and healings. But why me? Why would Jesus do this for me after I've hated and blamed God all these years for my husband's death?"

The Mitchells didn't respond to her question, but sat there and smiled as she kept testing her legs. Suddenly, Martha felt overwhelmed by God's goodness. Pangs of conviction pricked her heart. The years of pent-up tears now broke like a breached dam. She dropped to her knees and cried, "Dear God, forgive me for hating you. I never realized how much you cared for me."

She looked desperately at Rhonda, "Tell me what to say? How can I make things right with God?"

Rhonda kneeled beside her and laid her hands on her shoulders. She gazed into Martha's eyes and said, "If you're willing to turn from your sins, believe with all your heart that Jesus Christ is God's Son and that he died and rose from the dead, you can be saved and forgiven right now."

Martha smiled gratefully. Tears streamed down her face and onto her folded hands. "Oh yes," she replied, bowing her head, "I don't ever want to hate God again. I believe Jesus *is* God and that he rose from the dead. Thank you, God, for saving my life. Thank you for healing my legs. Please help me to serve you the rest of my life, and to never be hateful to you or anyone else, again."

179

That same day after the wedding of the Bride and the first trumpet's sound, similar miracles, like Martha's, were happening all over the world. What the Mitchells experienced of God's anointing power came upon *every* member of the Bride, from every tongue, every tribe and every nation.

The great harvest of souls had begun.

CHAPTER 53

A brilliant white cloud appeared in the heavenlies, and on that cloud sat someone like the Son of God who wore a golden crown and held a sharp sickle.

An angel came out of the temple and shouted to him, "The time has come—Earth's harvest is ripe—take your sickle and reap!"

So he swung his sickle over the earth to gather the harvest of souls into God's kingdom.

Three months had passed since the Bride's debut.

Frustration over her activities came to a peak in the World Federation headquarters in Tel Aviv.

"John!" Aster screamed, crumpling the report in his hands. "Get in here!"

Drakon stuck his head through the adjoining door of their offices. "What's wrong?"

Aster held up the paper in his clenched hand. "More bad news from the World Federation Intelligence. Three months ago, we were driving back these Christians. Now we have reports of miracles, healings, and mass revivals happening in the capitals of every nation. Thousands of our members are defecting to the Christian faith. Look at these headlines from New York." He opened the crinkled paper and read,

"Old Time Pentecost is Back!
The Blind See, the Lame Walk!
AIDS Victims Are Cured!
Miracles of the Gospels Break Out!"

Aster threw the report on the floor. "Just what do these stupid journalists think they're doing? Have they forgotten whose cause they're supposed to promote? While we're busy cleaning up the mess from these global disasters, and putting things back together, *they* herald the movement of Christians for the ratings!"

"What should we do?" Drakon asked.

"If we don't stop these Christians, we'll lose the momentum we've gained, but we can't do that until we tighten the grip on our journalists. We must screen every story they give to the public. Make sure that what they print or show on TV promotes no other cause but ours."

Drakon nodded.

"I want you to deploy Intelligence to search out every journalist who secretly supports Christians and kill them. Set up a reward system for those who promote the New World Order. Tell them to do stories on me, the clean-up, and the progress of peace and order."

"And the Christians? How will we stop their revival?"

Aster sat down and stared out the window. "Get me Lamar Becker on the line. I've got a speech for him to give to President Cane."

CHAPTER 54

President George Cane faced the camera lights.

He fidgeted in his chair as the make-up crew quickly dabbed the beads of sweat and powdered his forehead.

"You ready Mr. President?" the director asked.

Cane nodded.

"Okay, cameras ready. Countdown, three...two...one..."

"We interrupt this program with a special broadcast from the president of the United States."

"Citizens of America and the World Federation," President Cane began, "what I'm about to share with you is of grave importance. The council of the World Federation of Nations concluded in a recent summit that this message be aired worldwide. I've been assigned to speak tonight, on their behalf, about a conspiracy that threatens the future of the WFN and the New World Order.

"As you know, I'm in office because the United States lost President Thomas to the bullet of an assassin last year. When sworn in, I vowed to the American people and to the world, that I would not rest until we brought those responsible for this crime to justice.

"After months of investigation and research, the World

Federation Intelligence has uncovered a plot which involves more than one lone fanatic lusting for notoriety. To our surprise, we uncovered the network of a global conspiracy.

"Samuel Thomas was loved and admired by every nation; and could have become the world president himself. However, one organization disdained him because his ideals and beliefs kept them in check. In an effort to throw off the restraining powers that the president has to protect *your* rights, they took his life.

"We have discovered that their objective has been, and always will be, to remove every official from office who opposes their ideology. No doubt, I place my own life in jeopardy tonight as I expose their conspiracy to you.

"Citizens of the World Federation, the people responsible for the assassination of Samuel Thomas are right wing extremists called Christians. As incredible as that may seem, please hear me out.

"Over the last three months, many of you have been touched in some way by a religious awakening among this sect. Obviously, no one can escape the attention they've brought to their faith, and no one can deny that good things have been happening to the people they've helped. The results have caused many to accept or even embrace the philosophies and ideologies of these gift-bearers.

"But I urge caution! Beneath the appearance of their goodwill and deeds lies a universal plot to overthrow the World Federation, and ultimately to destroy the New World Order.

"Assisting their conspiracy is an alliance of national and international militia colonies who have thrown in their fire power. By doing so, it's evident these Christians will employ any means to see their objectives carried out; even assassinating presidents, kings and high officials.

"What evidence have I to confirm such an incredible indictment, you might ask? I hold in my hands from the WFI, 1300 pages of documented proof that President Thomas was murdered by this maniacal sect.

"If you find this hard to believe, then I challenge you to

ask any Christian if they support the New World Order. Ask them if they believe in our world government or its state religion. Ask them if they support the world president, and if they're ready to back his leadership. Ask Christians any of these questions and you'll soon discover, my friends, that their answer will be a resounding, 'No!'

"Yes, they have demonstrated incredible powers. No one denies this. But the miracles they're performing serve only as decoys to win your empathy and to distract you from their hidden objectives. Once you're in their grasp, once they've captured your hearts; they'll ultimately control your minds and your freedom.

"Obviously we can't imprison them all, nor can we stoop to their level of annihilation. Therefore, to protect you and the future of the New World Order, we are commissioning our New World Forces to register every leader of the Christian movement so that we may keep them under tight surveillance. After today, every ordained minister must report to the local NWF station houses in their town or city. They must register for a state clergy license. The clergy of every religion under the umbrella of the World Church have agreed to cooperate fully in this.

"Failure to respond within thirty days will be deemed an act of treason. Such outlaws, and those who offer to help them, will be arrested and imprisoned. Also, a reward will be granted for information that leads to the arrest and conviction of any minister who refuses to register for a state license.

"I ask you tonight, citizens of the World Federation, to resist this Christian movement and see it for what it really is...a global conspiracy. Remember the martyrs who've gone before President Thomas, who died for *your* rights and freedoms for a new social order. Let's take back the ground we've lost and deny these conspirators any chance for victory. The choice is yours to help us bring down this menacing cult. They've drawn a line in the sand, now we must respond."

CHAPTER 55

"Okay...cut," the cameraman said.

President Cane sat quaking in disbelief as he finished the speech he *didn't* write.

No president in U.S. history would have done what he just did, attack the religious sect that had founded America.

But this was a new day, a different America. An America that had sold out to a World Federation of ten kingdoms, who in turn, sold their allegiance to a madman named Aster.

George Cane felt sick and left the room. What a puny little flunky he'd become; a puppet president doing Aster's dirty work. "Thanks for nothing, Aster!" he whispered vehemently, as he walked down the corridor. "Thanks for setting me up to play your hatchet man."

In the Oval Office, Cane sat at the desk of what used to be the most influential position in the world. Now he had no power, no authority to make a difference. All his ideals and political dreams had been dashed, swallowed up in the ruthless agenda of Aster's egomania.

Aster's ten-kingdom empire had become a formidable world force, a crushing terror, dominated by the World Church and her enthroned king. Anything that posed a threat, anyone who got in Aster's way, became the target of his obsession. Early in the developing stages of the alliance, he had subdued three world leaders who refused to comply to his schemes. President Thomas was one of them. All three of them mysteriously lost their lives and were replaced by puppets like himself. But rather than being a man, he succumbed like all the cowards before him. How he despised his spineless life!

Cane reached for the phone and paged his secretary.

"Yes, Mr. President?"

"Carla, please hold my calls, I don't want to be disturbed."

"Yes, sir, I'll clear your schedule."

Cane turned his chair to face the window and stared at the bleak winter sky, and then at the grounds. The once-beautiful lawn of the White House reminded him of the yard of a haunted house. The charred trees were like crippled, lifeless sentinels. Everything was dead. Cane felt dead. He was ready to check out of this miserable world.

Swiveling his chair back to his desk, he opened the right hand drawer and pulleu out a .38. He placed the muzzle against his temple and, with one last look around the office, he yelled defiantly, "I know you're listening, Aster, but I don't care! I'm through being your puppet and I won't stick around for the carnage of this personal war of yours. You can give the job to Becker! I'm sure he'll do everything you ask.

"When your sinister deeds catch up with you, Mr. World President, I'll see you in hell!"

Cane took a deep breath and squeezed the trigger.

CHAPTER 56

Back in heaven, when the *second* angel trumpeted, something like a formidable mountain was hurled toward the earth to strike the sea and destroy a third of the ocean's creatures and ships.

Then the *third* angel trumpeted, launching a great blazing star to fall on a third of the rivers and springs, and to kill those who drank from the poisoned waters.

While the White House scrambled to deal with their crisis of Cane's death, a panic-stricken NASA buzzed intensely from the discovery of a frightening phenomenon.

Orbiting three hundred and eighty-one miles above the earth, the 12.8 ton observatory of the Hubble Space Telescope transmitted images of imminent doom. On a trajectory for earth, a menacing *asteroid* the size of a large mountain was estimated to smash into the planet in three days.

But that was only *one* of the asteroids Hubble discovered.

In its wake, approximately thirty days behind, a second

asteroid, a mile in diameter, was speeding toward the earth along the same course.

The astronomers were perplexed by this sudden appearance, unable to determine their origin. These were not strays from the asteroid belt of Jupiter, but asteroids that appeared out of nowhere from an unchartered place.

———◦◦———

Bob Jansen switched off the radio after President Cane's speech. He believed what the president had said about the Christians. Now his mind swirled in a bitter pool of hate.

"He's right, Christianity's been a front all along to take over the world. What a fool I've been to let them sucker me into it. They probably use women like Whitney to bait stupid guys like me, then drop you after you're in their clutches. It all makes sense now, and here I've been feeling guilty about the whole thing."

Something, however, didn't set right in Bob's conscience. He had to be sure they were conspirators.

The questions. That's it. He'd go ask them the questions President Cane challenged them to ask. That should settle any doubts.

———◦◦———

Later that evening, Shayne Taylor answered the door and found Bob at his doorstep.

"Bob, where have you been? I was beginning to think you were killed by that last quake or the fire. Come in, come in."

"I can't," Bob replied, warily. "I'll just stand here. I need to ask you a couple of questions."

"Who is it Shayne?" Laura asked walking up to the door. "Bob!" she said reaching out to embrace him. "We thought you were hurt or dead. Come out of that cold snow and warm yourself with a cup of my hot chocolate."

Laura's congenial demeanor diffused Bob's guard. Seeing her and hearing her voice brought back memories of Whitney. "Okay, I'll come in. But only for a minute."

Bob planted his feet in the foyer as they closed the door. He didn't want to go any further.

"Come in and sit down," Shayne said.

"No thanks, I'm fine."

"What's been happening to you?" Laura asked. "Whitney's been worried about you."

Bob frowned. "I doubt that. I'd rather not bring *her* up if you don't mind."

Laura looked at Shayne. "Sure, if that's what you want."

Bob looked down and shifted his feet. "Did you guys watch that special broadcast the president gave tonight?"

"No," Shayne replied. "We've been out helping the neighbors down the street."

Bob began to sweat. He hated this. He still cared for his friends, and wrestled with his conscious. He didn't want to know if they were part of the conspiracy, but he had to find out. "Uh...I need to ask if you guys support the WFN and the World Church..."

Shayne glanced at Laura.

"...and do you support our new president, Reuben Aster?" he added quickly.

"What odd questions," Laura said. "You should know more than anyone that we can't support a one-world government...nor Aster. They're enemies of the faith."

"Didn't you know," Shayne asked, "that Aster used to be one of us—?"

"Enough," Bob said, placing his hands over his ears. "Then it's true. It's all true what the president told the nation tonight."

"Bob, what's eating you?" Laura asked.

"I'll tell you what's eating me...you guys are conspirators."

"What?" Shayne said.

"Yeah...you Christians killed President Thomas. Your people plotted the assassination, and now you're trying to take over the world...even destroy the Federation."

Laura stepped toward Bob to calm him. "What is it, Bob? There's more to this, isn't there?"

"Stay back," he said, with his hands extended. "I know how you guys work, smothering people with your smooth talk and good deeds. Working your spells to heal people."

Shayne looked Bob in the eyes. "Hey, remember me, pal? Three years...dorm mates...Canterton University? Do you really think your old friend would try to overthrow a government, let alone assassinate President Thomas?"

"Not *you* maybe, but your religion. It's you extremists who are responsible."

"Bob," Laura said. "Can't you see Aster is scared? We're having a revival and he's trying to frame us as the bad guys. I don't know what the president said tonight, but if the speech was bent on painting Christians as conspirators against the Federation, he's wrong. I'd be willing to say that Aster fabricated the whole thing and had the president give the speech."

Bob's mind spun with confusion. He wanted to believe them, but his anger at God over Whitney was deep. "Lies, lies," he said. "I can't listen to anymore of your lies. You pulled me in once, but not again."

Before Laura and Shayne could respond, Bob opened the front door and ran out. As he went, he yelled back over his shoulder, "You'd better tell your pastor to register at the station house or I'll have him arrested for breaking the law!"

CHAPTER 57

The world braced itself for the impact of the asteroid.

NASA had projected it to hit the Atlantic Ocean, about 40 degrees longitude between the coast of Portugal and New York.

When the meteor entered the earth's atmosphere, it ignited from the oxygen and friction, lighting up the sky over the Atlantic. Upon impact, it pierced the depths of the ocean floor as easily as a spear would strike the bed of a shallow river. The shock triggered oceanic quakes which opened fissures in the earth's crust. Gargantuan tidal waves crashed into the harbors of the Atlantic coastal regions and destroyed a third of the ships in port.

Then, from the finger of God, the Atlantic and the Mediterranean turned into blood, killing a third of the plant life and creatures of the deep.

Carcasses of whales, mammals and every species of fish floated above the bloody mire with a tangle of dead plant life. Even the ships at sea were immobilized, stranded by layers upon layers of dead fish and plants which jammed their propellers. Another disaster. Another setback for Aster.

After George Cane's death, Lamar Becker was sworn in to take his place by an executive order of Aster and his World Federation council, the ten-kingdom alliance. Still holding his position as chair of the council, Becker now addressed Aster and the other nine members.

"With this latest phenomena," Becker said, "our efforts to stir up a grievance against the Christians have been road-blocked by this growing *fear-of-God's-wrath* complex. These catastrophes have added momentum to their revival by giving them opportunities to either heal people or raise them from the dead."

"What can we do?" asked a council member.

"Our greatest concern right now is the media," Becker replied. "They ignorantly continue to fuel this revival by their coverage." Becker turned to Aster, "I recommend, Mr. President, that we pass a law to clamp down on all forms of news coverage. Control it with what we want the public to know or not know."

"It's that sect they call the *Bride* that started this mess," another member of the council said.

"You're right," Becker replied. "Intelligence traces it back to when the Bride first appeared. If we can discredit or destroy the Bride in some way, we can pull the plug and recapture the lead of conversions to the ranks of our World Church."

Aster cleared his throat. The ten heads of state of the Federation council shifted their attention to him. Throughout the onslaught of disasters, Aster continued to exhibit an emotionally firm grip; undaunted in his dream to subdue the world. He always managed to see these obstacles as mere opportunities to demonstrate his strengths. The chaotic conditions created and sustained a perpetual need for his skillful leadership; shackling the alliance to his exceptional wisdom, to a leader who always produced.

"Gentlemen," Aster began, "I agree with Becker. We must

control the media for the safety of our cause. We can't keep peace and deal with the problems if everyone's provoked to panic and run to these Christians for help. As I speak, a task force is researching new ways to accomplish a screening process to muzzle and channel the appropriate information that will benefit only our world government and no one else.

"This Bride society is another problem altogether. As Becker pointed out, she's effectively manipulated the phobia to her advantage."

"So how can we stop her?" one of the council members asked. "Where do we even begin to track these people down?"

Aster smiled. "Before President Cane was murdered, we passed a new law in the Federation to register every ordained minister for a state license. That license will insure pure representation of our government and the World Church. Unfortunately, the asteroid has prevented us from launching that effectively. We must renew our efforts to enforce the registration on all fronts."

"But Hubble has sighted another asteroid," another council member said. "It's scheduled for impact in three weeks. We may not be so lucky this time if this one hits land. Shouldn't we concentrate our efforts to prepare for that?"

"You have a point," Aster replied. "Preparations are necessary, but we must take extreme measures of caution to keep this from leaking to the press. Our first priority is to execute Becker's suggestion and take control of the media. Then we can buy more time to get at the Christian perpetrators and destroy their thrust during this three week window."

"How do you propose to find them, Mr. President?" Becker asked.

"With the intelligence files we have on these fanatics. I can assure you that many Christian leaders were candidates for the Bride, beginning with their apostles. If we start there, we can trace the members of this Bride society down through their ranks and into their underground network of small groups."

Murmurs of approval rose from the members of the council.

Aster continued, "Now that *former* President Cane exposed the Christians as treacherous conspirators, we can pass a law in the interest of national and world security, making it illegal to convert anyone to a religion not endorsed by the World Church."

"The World Church can assist us in manpower and finances," Becker replied.

"That's right," Aster said. "And she can inform us of any members in her organization who have defected to the Christian faith. We'll pass a law that acknowledges the World Church as the only state-approved religion throughout the World Federation. That will give her the authority to chastise defectors from her own assemblies."

"How about media assistance in this hunt?" Becker asked.

"After we chain the media down, we'll run campaigns through literature, radio and television; blaming the Christians for our problems that God has sent on the earth to judge *them*. We must paint them as the heretics, deceivers, sorcerers and witches they are. Whatever it takes to turn the tide of public opinion against them."

The council applauded Aster's proposals.

"Gentlemen," he continued, "let's not forget that *we* control the world's government and the world's military; we control the world's population; we control the largest world religious system known to man; we control the world's economic resources and we'll soon control the world's media and press. With all of that going for us, how can we possibly lose to the ragtag society of the Bride?"

CHAPTER 58

"It's Shenzar!" Drakon whispered to Aster.

The room grew cold as the billowing smoke interrupted Aster and Drakon's private meeting back in their hotel suite. The familiar outline of Shenzar appeared in the rumbling cloud, while rays of light burst forth in an energetic pulse from his dark form.

"Loyal servants," Shenzar said in a deep-throated voice,

> "A prophecy foretells of a manchild born to the society called the Bride. It predicts this child will rule the nations. Our watchers report that 144,000 women conceived at the time of the Bride's appearance, and are possibly the carriers of this child. Like the Bride, this child could represent more than one child or one out of the 144,000 born, with the other children serving as decoys. Find these 144,000 women and destroy every male child born to them or your throne could be threatened."

Shenzar said no more and quickly disappeared. Two bolts of lightning sprang from the fading cloud and encircled Aster and Drakon, creating a momentary surge of energy to flash through their bodies and then vanish.

Aster enjoyed this experience for the second time now. It left him feeling stronger, both mentally and physically.

When he regained his strength from the encounter, Aster remembered a story from the Bible. "This manchild reminds me of when Moses escaped Pharoah's edict of death for all the male Hebrew babies."

"And the Nazarene…when his parents fled with him from the hands of Herod," Drakon added.

"We can't afford to fail in our effort to kill these children like Pharoah and Herod did. We *must* be thorough."

"Pharaoh and Herod were fools," Drakon scoffed.

"Contact Intelligence and have them get on it. Find out the exact time of the Bride's appearance and locate every woman who's been pregnant since then."

"And what do we do when we find them?"

"Assign a surveillance team to each of them, but don't touch them yet. We'll monitor their activities. Perhaps they'll lead us to the *other* mothers and members of the Bride society. We'll bide our time until they deliver. Keep the teams close. As soon as those babies are born, I want them killed."

CHAPTER 59

Whitney answered the knock at her door.

When she opened it, three hard-looking men stood outside her apartment—two NWF soldiers and a bearded man dressed in a bland, wool-tweed sports coat.

"Miss Whitney Conner?" said the plain-clothes man.

"Yes," she replied warily.

"Name's Kobrin, Vince Kobrin." He flashed her his badge. "I'm from the World Federation Intelligence. Mind if I ask you a couple of questions, ma'am?"

Whitney glanced at the young soldiers and then back at Kobrin. His face showed no warmth or compassion. The deep set lines of his dark eyebrows, and the gray-streaked beard reminded her of a madman in a horror film.

"Come in," she said, backing up and carefully keeping the three men in her sight.

Kobrin entered first and looked intently at her pregnant womb. Her eyes caught his as he looked up.

"I see you're expecting," he said. "When's your baby due?"

Whitney remained silent.

"Listen lady, I know we aren't the friendliest looking guys in town. I'm just trying to break the ice. Okay?"

Whitney relaxed a little when Kobrin smiled. "I'm due in June," she said, still cautious.

"Really? I have a daughter, about your age. She's due this summer, too. She and her husband are mighty proud. It's their first child you know. It's going to be a boy."

"That's nice," Whitney replied, but didn't believe him.

"And your husband? I'm sure *he's* a happy man."

"I don't have a husband, Mr. Kobrin. I'm not married."

"Oh, I see…right…it's *Miss* Conner. Then who's the lucky father?"

Whitney saw through his feigned concern. "Mr. Kobrin," she replied sweetly, "I don't wish to be rude, but I need to leave in a few minutes for an appointment."

Kobrin pulled a small notepad from his jacket. "Okay Miss Conner," he said, clicking his pen, "I'll make this brief. We're conducting a survey for the Federation to update our files. I'd like to confirm the information we have on you. Your full name is Whitney Jean Conner?"

"Yes."

"This is your current address?"

"Yes."

"Do you plan to move in the near future?"

"No."

"Are you a member of the World Church?"

Whitney paused at this question. "No," she said.

Kobrin glanced at the soldiers. "That's odd. Most people in Canterton are members of the World Church; that is, unless they belong to that Christian sect. You know…the conspirators who arranged for the assassination of President Cane."

"I don't know any conspirators, Mr. Kobrin."

He nodded and continued. "Your child is due in June, you said?"

"Yes."

"Boy or girl?"

Whitney stared at him. "Why do you need to know all of this?"

Kobrin ran his fingers through his hair and looked at the soldiers. "Well ma'am,...with the catastrophes and all, we're developing a numbering system to create a better method of registration. This will help us assist people quicker in case of an emergency."

"Didn't you just do a census last year? Why do we need another—"

"Needs updating, ma'am. Since the quake."

"I see. But why would they send a high-ranking intelligence officer, like yourself, to ask these simple questions? Couldn't either of these soldiers do that? Doesn't that seem a little strange to you, Mr. Kobrin?"

Kobrin rubbed his face. "Miss Conner," he sighed, "are you refusing to cooperate?"

"No."

"Then just answer the questions, please. Are you carrying a boy or a girl?"

"Does it matter?"

He tapped his pen against the notepad. "It does."

Whitney knew why they came. The Holy Spirit revealed their intentions to her long before they rang the doorbell.

"It's a boy," she said finally.

"Do you have an ultrasound report to verify that?"

"No."

"Then how do you know it's a boy?"

"I know."

Kobrin sighed loudly and wrote in his notepad.

Whitney glanced at the soldiers and smiled. They stared back at her without a response.

"Thank you for your cooperation, ma'am," Kobrin said, finishing his writing. He closed the notepad and placed it back in his jacket. "I trust everything will go well for you and the baby. Please inform the WFI at the station house of any change of address you might make in the future. Good day."

He nodded at the soldiers and left the apartment with them.

Whitney closed the door and touched her protruding stomach. "They'll be back," she said, "I know they'll be back."

CHAPTER 60

Vince Kobrin shoved Jack Mitchell into the chair.

Behind the closed doors of his station house office, Kobrin rolled up his sleeves and slapped him across the face. Blood streaked down his chin and neck from the gash in his mouth.

"We don't take kindly to rebels in this town, Reverend," Kobrin said. "We've been informed that you refuse to register with the state. The Federation has made it illegal to preach without a license, yet you've been active in the neighborhoods, speaking here and there to pockets of Christians." Kobrin studied his prisoner and then placed his hands on the arms of the chair. "We also know about you healing and performing miracles on people. An enterprise one would find happening among the members of the Bride, wouldn't you say?"

Jack turned his head from Kobrin.

"So what have you got to say to these charges, Mitchell?" Silence.

Kobrin sneered and punched Jack in the stomach.

"You're wasting my time, Reverend...bring in the witness."

When Bob Jansen entered the room, Pastor Mitchell was leaning over in his chair gasping for breath. It delighted Bob to see the deceiver suffering with his hands cuffed and his face bleeding.

Kobrin walked up to Bob and laid his hand on his shoulder. "Is this the man you confronted?" he asked, pointing to his prisoner. "The one who told you he would never register with the state?"

"Yes sir, that's him."

"And is it true," Kobrin continued, "that you saw him breaking Federation law by healing people in the name of Jesus, and proceeding to convert them to Christianity?"

"That's right."

"Thank you, Mr. Jansen. That'll be all. You can pick up your money at the desk."

Bob glared at the beaten pastor. How he loathed him for deceiving the girl he loved, filling her head with nonsense. Mitchell was the reason Whitney refused to marry him. He knew it from his conversations with her. All he ever heard from her was *Pastor Mitchell said this* or *Pastor Mitchell said that*. Well, no more. He had seen to it that Mitchell was stopped for good, locked up and would get what he deserved.

"By the way, Jansen," Kobrin said glancing at Bob's clothes. "You look like you could use a job, son. That reward money won't go very far."

"Why...uh...yes sir, you're right. I do need work."

"Good. We need loyal men like you to serve in our military. The pay's good and you'll have a secure future. Why don't you come by later and talk to the recruiter. He'll tell you more about it."

"Yeah...okay. I'll look into it."

Before Bob turned to leave, Pastor Mitchell looked directly into his eyes.

Instead of hate, Bob saw compassion; as though he were pleading with him not to join the military.

Bob curled his lip and glared at him as Kobrin strolled back for more play. Maybe he could stay and watch Mitchell get hit some more. The soldiers didn't seem to mind him being there.

"All right, Reverend," Kobrin said, resting his hands again on the arms of the chair. "There's something we need to discuss. You're going to tell me where we can find an old friend of yours. Cliff Malloy."

CHAPTER 61

"Heart shot—dead center!"

Malloy lowered his binoculars and smiled at Grub. "Not bad at 900 yards."

Grub frowned and spit. "What do you mean, not bad?"

"Your turn, Macully," Cap' said. "Let's see you hit the target's head at that distance."

Malloy grabbed the H&K PSG1 rifle from Grub and walked off fifty more yards.

Grub yelled back to him, "Would you like me to get you some eyeglasses?"

Malloy chuckled. "Just watch the target, gentlemen!" he yelled from his spot. He sighted the cross hairs on the head of the life-size silhouette and squeezed the trigger.

The projectile sped 950 yards to the target...dead center. Grub and Cap' lowered their binoculars and stared at Malloy in disbelief. "Dang! He did it again," Grub said. "Where'd he learn to shoot like that?"

Cap' pulled out a pouch of tobacco and rolled himself a cigarette. He lit it and took a puff, studying Macully's face as he walked up. "This mission of yours is pretty dangerous, Cliff," he said. "I hope your aim will be as accurate when Aster's in your sights."

"That makes two of us. How soon will the team be ready?"

"Everything's packed. Operation *Falling Star* will be ready to move out at 0600 hours."

"Good. My point man in Washington has everything in place. Let's hope Aster sticks to his schedule."

———

Bob surprised Whitney that night with a visit but he watched her smile disappear when she saw his NWF uniform.

"Is this official business?" she asked.

"No…nothing official," he said, staring at her stomach. His heart grieved when he saw the protrusion from her belly. "I just thought I'd come by to see how you're doing. I heard rumors that you were pregnant."

"Yes, I am, as you can see." She placed her hand on her stomach. "Is that why you stopped? To see if I was pregnant?"

"No, uh…well…yes, it is. I guess I didn't know you had someone else in your life. Now, I'm embarrassed for even coming."

"You don't have to be embarrassed, because I have no other man in my life. In fact, I've never had another man in my life."

Bob's eyes widened. "You mean you were raped?"

Whitney laughed. "Of course not."

This confused Bob. He could feel his face turning red from his brain short-circuiting. Now he was mad.

"But the baby? How can you stand there and tell me there's been no other man? It's either that or you've been raped?"

"I tried to tell you the night you ran out. It's hard to explain without spiritual insight."

Spiritual insight! Now he was really mad! "You stand there, Miss high-an'-mighty, and tell me I need spiritual insight. And what makes you spiritual, being pregnant out of wedlock? You expect me to swallow that? Do you think I'm a fool? You're lying to me."

"But it's not like you think..."

"Ha! You said you couldn't be married. Had to keep consecrated for the Lord's work you said..." He pointed to her stomach. "...this isn't of God. This is hypocrisy. You're just like my parents and every Christian I've ever met. I thought *you* guys were different, but you're just like the rest of them...hypocrites...all of you."

Whitney reached for his arm, but he jerked it away.

"Boy, you people had me believing it for awhile. Well, my eyes are opened, Miss Conner. I've found the truth from others who make sense. They're trying to bring order to this messed up world while you Christians propagate these wild and crazy ideas that it's all coming to an end. You're all conspirators just like the president said."

Tears welled in Whitney's eyes. She said nothing and turned away.

Bob couldn't handle that and stared at her for a moment. He felt like a deflated balloon with nothing left to blow out.

With slumped shoulders and a broken heart, he turned and left the room, this time with his mind made up...he'd never see Whitney again.

CHAPTER 62

A week had passed since they arrested Pastor Mitchell.

During his time in jail, the church prayed regularly for him until they allowed him to go home.

Rhonda Mitchell met him at the door and embraced him. "Oh, Jack, look at your face," she said, examining the cuts. She led him to the couch and ran into the kitchen for a clean, damp rag. She returned and knelt beside him to wipe the caked blood from his swollen lips and bruised face. "What happened to you, dear?"

Jack winced as she applied the rag. "Bob Jansen turned me in for not registering with the state. When I refused to sign, they beat me."

"Everyone who knew of your arrest, prayed and fasted. I'm so thankful they let you go."

"I guess they got tired of trying to get me to register. Since the thirty-day grace period isn't up, yet, they could only threaten me with imprisonment. I *really* believe they sent me home to see if Cliff Malloy would contact us."

Rhonda stood up. "They know he's alive?"

"Yes, but they obviously haven't found him or they wouldn't be asking me where he's hiding?"

"Cliff would never contact us. He knows that would endanger our lives."

"Let's pray he *doesn't* contact us...for his sake."

"What'll happen now?" she asked, caressing Jack's hair.

"We can't worry about Cliff, but I'm concerned Aster will tighten the net to locate the members of the Bride. He'll probably start with the pastors to track her down."

"That would explain the mandatory registration."

"Exactly. But I overheard a disturbing conversation at the station house when they thought I was sleeping."

"What?"

"They're combing the area for all the women who've been pregnant for the past three months."

Rhonda frowned. "That explains why Whitney had an officer from the WFI visit her this week."

"Really?"

"Yes, they asked her about her pregnancy and who the father was. Then Bob Jansen showed up a couple of days later in a NWF uniform."

Jack remembered his encounter with Bob at the station house and sighed. "He must know about the child, too. Poor guy. We need to keep praying for him. He's in a bad way right now."

Rhonda walked to the mantle of the fireplace where she had placed a registered letter from the World Federation. She took it and handed it to Jack. "This came in the mail the day you were caught. They must have sent it before they arrested you."

Jack gazed curiously at the unsealed envelope, opened it, then read it:

Reverend Mitchell,

On behalf of the council of the World Federation, you are hereby notified that any and all forms of ministerial activity, herewith, will be regarded as an act of treason unless you register with the state for a certified license.

In addition, a law has been ratified which outlaws any form of converting individuals to Christianity. Please inform the members of your congregation. Failure to obey these laws will result in immediate arrest and imprisonment.

Vince Kobrin
Department of Internal Affairs
World Federation Intelligence

CHAPTER 63

It was the last day to register for a clergy license.

Instead of arrests, however, the Federation had pressing matters at hand.

The judgment of the *third* trumpet was speeding toward earth.

Throughout the regions of North America, sirens alerted the citizens to get on their internet, radio or televisions for an urgent announcement:

> "Citizens of the Federation, this is a disaster alert...repeat...a disaster alert! We have a breaking report that another asteroid is approaching the earth's atmosphere, scheduled to hit our planet at 1:40 PM, Eastern Standard Time. We urge you to get into an underground basement for cover.
>
> "NASA has calculated a land strike somewhere in the upper regions of North America. Again, this is a disaster alert! Please get into a basement and stay off the streets."

The asteroid hit sixty degrees longitude on the north Canadian border of Saskatchewan. The explosive force, estimated at three million megatons of TNT, sent a blast of intense heat across Canada and into the bordering regions of the United States. The impact left a crater fifteen miles across.

Jack Mitchell couldn't fathom the power the asteroid must have packed. Fortunately, the advanced warning helped many survive the blast on the outlying areas of its reach. Jack had learned through the underground network of churches that no Christians were injured by the blast. He believed God delivered them like Shadrach, Meshach, and Abednego when they were thrown into the fiery furnace.

Jack stared out the window at the gray sky and the faint outline of the sun. The dust from the explosion permeated the atmosphere and the temperature in Canterton had dropped 18 degrees below zero. He'd never seen it this cold in Virginia.

It amused him that NASA christened the asteroid, *Wormwood*. He knew the Revelation predicted the same name. Scientists called it Wormwood for the burning nitrogen in the atmosphere that produced a precipitation of acid rain. The heat from the blast had warmed the atmosphere long enough for the acid to penetrate the rivers and springs of water. Now, a third of the fresh water on the planet was poisoned.

As Jack drank from the pre-bottled water of their stockpile downstairs, he thanked God for the knowledge of these events beforehand. The Holy Spirit would warn them by using the Revelation as a map through the mines of God's judgments. It became the Christian's handbook for survival.

Not so, however, for the World Church who didn't believe in Bible prophecy. Aster had outlawed all Bibles from the possession of World Church members and burned every one they found. The World Church lost many lives among her members while the Christians all managed to survive the catastrophes. It made believers out of the unbelievers who defected to Christianity.

Despite the grim surroundings of a crippled planet, it was an exciting time to be alive. Jack was amazed at how open people were to the gospel. Bringing converts to Christ had never been easier. He enjoyed showing the seeking soul what was happening in the Revelation, and what God would do next. The apostles advised all the saints to do this which added credibility to their message, especially when it was accompanied with the signs and wonders performed by the Christians. The World Church couldn't offer what the Christians were offering: hope, deliverance, healing, and especially answers to the questions about the times that were upon them.

How thankful Jack felt to be a part of it, even in light of the remaining trumpets to come. But he couldn't stop thinking about Malloy. Perhaps God kept reminding him because he and Rhonda were the only two people who *could* pray for Malloy. They prayed continually for his survival, for God to keep him around long enough to get saved.

After three months of cloaked darkness, the dust from the asteroid finally settled and the sun broke through once more. But not for long.

Soon, the *fourth* angel would blow his trumpet and a third of the sun, moon and stars would turn dark. In other words, eight hours a day—every day—from now on, no light above the earth's atmosphere would be able to filter through.

CHAPTER 64

Aster's hands were tied.

His efforts to quell the fires of revival were continually frustrated by the unceasing judgments of God. His plan to frame Christians with conspiracy had little effect so far, for the world ignored the allegations to concentrate their efforts on something more critical: global chaos.

Something had to happen for Aster. Something that could help him regain the momentum. But he could only focus his energies toward the recovery of a world caught up in the mourning and burying of their dead.

This left little time for revenge in anybody's mind.

Bob Jansen waited on the steps of his barracks for his partner, Blake Harris, to join him.

Though the sun shone brightly again, it didn't shine on the same beautiful town he remembered last May; that is, before the quake. The air had grown stale since the wind stopped blowing, and the smell of death permeated the atmosphere.

The dust-like ash, from the fallout of Wormwood, still covered the ground making Canterton appear like a scene from a futuristic movie. The Roanoke River, as well—Bob's place of memories with Whitney—now reeked from the floating carcasses of fish destroyed by the acidic rain. How he ached to wake up from this nightmare. If only it were a dream.

Blake finally appeared, coming from the station house with their new assignment. He and Blake had been together through most of these duties. Their orders would show them which area of the city to cover and seek out new recruits. Bob liked this job because one of their responsibilities while recruiting, was to arrest any Christians they found praying for people, or converting them. He would handcuff them, confiscate their Bibles and then haul them to the nearest station house; joining in on the fun of knocking them around a bit when the WFI officers interrogated them.

Blake came up and waved the orders in the air. "We've got the market square today."

"Great!" Bob said with a clap of his hand. "There's a lot of action in that district. We'll bag us some Christians for sure. Let's go."

As they started for the square, something caught Bob's attention that chilled him and flashed him back to a similar experience a year ago. He stopped and grabbed his partner's elbow. "Do you see it?" he asked Blake.

Blake's eyes grew wide. "I sure do."

"I hope it's an eclipse?"

"I don't think so. We shouldn't be seeing one of those for awhile."

Bob groaned. "Then it's another judgment." The daylight gradually diminished as a supernatural darkness crept eerily over Canterton. Bob turned and ran back to their barracks for his flashlight with Blake at his heels.

"What's happening?" Blake asked as the darkness blanketed the sky.

Bob frowned. "It's another curse these Christians have brought on the earth!"

"You think it'll last as long as the darkness after the quake last year?"

"I don't know. Every time another phenomenon happens, it seems different. No telling how long it'll be. But I'm not going to let it stop me from doing my job. These Christians are going to pay..."

"Maybe it isn't their fault."

Bob placed his fists on his hips. "What?"

"Have you ever stopped to think that these judgments might be from God because of *our* sins? Why do we keep blaming the Christians for something *we* might be responsible for?"

Bob glared at Blake. "I can't believe what I'm hearing? Have you been listening to these Christians, soldier? Talking to them—"

"No way. That would be treason."

"Well be careful then what you say. Questions like that could get you hung. I say *they* brought this trouble on us, and the sooner we're rid of them the better. Come on. We've got a job to do."

After the *fourth* trumpet, darkness wrapped the planet. Another angel flew in the middle of heaven and cried with a loud voice,

"Woe, woe, woe, to those who are left on the earth! Three more angels will blow their trumpets. Disaster is on the way!"

CHAPTER 65

In a private cottage near a village in Belgium, a secret meeting took place among the twelve apostles. Aster had been replaced by another. They arrived from various international locations, strategically based to spread their ministry among the nations.

Nathan Kelly had arranged the meeting, but due to the increasingly difficult task of evading Aster's operatives, they each asked the Holy Spirit to show them the exact location, time and date to meet without contacting each other.

It worked. Aster never found out.

When they went through WFI's security at the airports no one saw them. The Holy Spirit helped each of them pass by the guards undetected.

When they arrived at the cottage, Nathan Kelly embraced his eleven colleagues and exchanged greetings. "Brothers, I have great news and I'm anxious to hear your reports as well. The flames of revival continue to spread and are stoked by the abundance of opportunities for Christians to help the lost in their needs. The reports have been incredible.

"Testimonies come in every day about supernatural feedings

among the masses, just as our Lord did when he multiplied the loaves and fishes to feed the five thousand.

"Even the rising number of deaths from the judgments have provided great opportunities. Members of the Bride are continually called on by families and relatives to raise their loved ones from the dead. Miracles of this nature have become a daily occurrence."

The men applauded and gave thanks to God.

"This kind of news," Kelly continued, "travels like wild-fire. The diseased and injured now come in droves to be healed. Nothing like it has ever been witnessed in the history of the church. The Bride and her converts have brought in a harvest of souls numbering into the billions.

"The most exciting news of all, however, is what's been happening to the new converts. There're so many of them it's impossible to follow them up, yet they require neither shepherding nor counseling. They, like us, have received the *third work of grace* that has removed the sin nature from their lives. They immediately join a small group of believers which have been multiplying daily. Brothers, we have much to thank God for!"

As the eleven men rejoiced, a tiny mantle clock in the cottage struck four in the afternoon. Kelly went to the window and drew back the curtains. The sky began to darken as it had done so the day before and the day before that, ever since the sounding of the *fourth* trumpet.

The others turned to watch him as he returned and lit the kerosene lamp on the table.

"The harvest is nearing completion," he said with his face and white-gray hair glowing in the light. "The time of the Gentiles is coming to a close, and as you can see," he pointed at the darkness outside, "we are beyond the fourth trumpet. The *fifth* angel waits to sound the next trumpet; and the star, Reuben Aster, is about to fall.

"His life now weighs in the balance, for somewhere out there, his attackers draw near to inflict the fatal wound predicted in Revelation 13."

Aster reflected over his speech to the United States in the president's cabin of the Boeing 777. He stared out the window to the left of the aircraft with a full view of the east coast.

The speech he had prepared would be aired nationwide. He planned to encourage the nation through their recovery from the aftermath of Wormwood. Today, he would meet with President Becker and the cabinet to go over the details of the next phase in the cyberbanking system. A one-world economy was imminent.

The jet descended at seven o'clock in the morning, with the sun casting its light above the shimmering blood in the Atlantic Ocean. Aster had been studying the shoreline from Boston to the Delaware Bay, a disheartening vista of stranded ships and floating masses of dead fish. How could he ever restore such a mess to the beautiful blue-green waters that once teemed with life?

The Captain spoke over the intercom, "Mr. President the Fasten-Seat-Belt light is on. We're passing 18,000 feet and we'll be touching down at Andrews Air Force Base in fourteen minutes."

Aster looked at Drakon, still asleep in his chair. If he could only sleep like that again. Unfortunately, too much activity swirled in his head twenty-four hours a day. Controlling the world wasn't easy. The challenges of the disasters, the Christian revival, all kept his mind in a constant state of turmoil. He had to find a way to turn the tide.

Somehow, some way, he would.

CHAPTER 66

"Commander, sir!"

"Yes, Grub," Malloy replied through his headset.

"Our snipers are in place and the ground team's waiting for action."

"Excellent! Tell them to say their prayers if they believe in God. We've got to take Aster out now or we'll never see this opportunity again."

"Yes, sir."

Operation *Falling Star* was in its final hour. Months of strategic planning and training had gone into Malloy's nine-man team. With Cap's help and influence, Malloy earned a place among the coneys as a high ranking officer. This enabled him to recruit the cream of the mercenaries from other militias, and three from his own camp: Cap', Grub and Brad. The other six had relocated from various nations to America. They were the best-of-the-best for a world-class terrorist assignment—take out Aster and his lethal cohort, Drakon.

Malloy sat quietly in his sniper's perch in a closed down department store across the street from the hotel where Aster and Drakon were staying. The smoke from his cigarette lingered in the air as he cradled an H&K PSG1 rifle in his arm. He checked his time piece. *It won't be long now.*

When Malloy had left Pastor Mitchell's house, he returned to Washington under an alias and contacted his best friend and associate, Kent Jones, who worked with him in their early years as rookies. Malloy had saved Kent's life on a number of on-duty assignments, including Kent's wife and children when a contract was put on them. Malloy had uncovered the plot and took the killers out in a shootout at Kent's house.

Today, Kent still worked for the CIA, but now in the shadows of the World Federation Intelligence. Ever since America had surrendered her sovereignty, Kent had refused to give his best to the new boss. He didn't want to. He had a hidden dislike for Aster and the whole idea of a World Federation. Like Malloy, Kent had come from the old school. He despised the oppressive, brutal techniques of this new Intelligence.

When Malloy showed up after he had left the Mitchells, Kent was shocked. Everyone thought he was dead! To maintain his cover, Kent helped Malloy get out of Washington and hooked him up with a contact in Idaho who had connections with the coneys. Kent gave him money for a bus ticket, a Gloch 9mm gun for protection, and a few extra bucks. The contact in Idaho then sent him to a small tavern where the coneys occasionally came down from the mountains for a drink. That's how Malloy came to meet Grub, the thirsty coney from Cap's camp.

Malloy figured it must have been destined for him to make it this far. He was ready to do his part for his murdered friend, Samuel Thomas, and his Christian friends who were now threatened by Aster's existence.

Malloy sat calmly focused at his post. He scanned Aster's suite through his binoculars again and checked his watch. It was 1500 hours. With the months of extensive research and intensive training, the day had arrived to settle the score. Kent's information was accurate and conditions were perfect; a turkey shoot for Malloy's top guns. He would signal his snipers through his voice-activated communicator when the target was in the clear. All would fire at once. Malloy and Cap' would shoot Aster, while Grub and Brad took out Drakon.

Another hour passed. It was 1600 hours. Malloy watched the sunlight disappear from the routine curse of the fourth trumpet. Every day—four hours before sunset to four hours after—a supernatural canopy of darkness blocked out the sun, moon and stars. In this situation, it was an added blessing for Malloy. It served as a cover for his team, and a clearer shot into the illumined suite of Reuben Aster.

CHAPTER 67

President Becker raved over Aster's next phase for a global, cashless economy. His cabinet members were also impressed.

"Reuben, I don't know how you do it," Becker said, as they left the conference room. "It's nearly inhuman the way you come up with these ideas."

"Thank you, Lamar. You're not doing so bad yourself in the presidency. It fits you well."

Becker smiled. "I've gotten a lot of practice after running the show for the last three presidents. The job's been a snap without having to be the middle man."

Aster glanced at his watch. "Where has the time gone? It's four in the afternoon and that cursed darkness robs us of another full day."

"Perhaps you should get some rest, Reuben," Drakon said. "With your schedule tomorrow, you'll need to be fresh for your speech."

Aster nodded and turned to Becker. "Thanks for an encouraging day, Lamar. I look forward to our meeting tomorrow. We'll go over our plans to implement the new bio-chip. Are the economists here?"

"The brightest I could find."

"Good. Their input will be timely."

With an exchange of handshakes from Becker and his cabinet members, Aster and Drakon left the White House and returned to their hotel.

When the elevator opened on the top floor, four secret service agents stood guard in the hallway. They saluted the president and unlocked the door to the suite. Two of the agents went in to check each room. All was clear and Aster and Drakon walked into the living room, removing their coats and ties.

"Everything's secure, Mr. President," the agent said, backing out of the room. "Have a pleasant evening. If you need anything, we'll be outside the door."

"Just bring us our dinner in an hour," Aster replied.

"Yes, sir."

———⛓✺⛓———

At that moment, in the third heaven, the *fifth* angel stepped forward to blew his trumpet.

———⛓✺⛓———

"They're settled in!" Malloy said, alerting the others through his headset.

His snipers were poised to lock on to their targets as soon as they were visible. Malloy listened calmly to his heart in order to time the squeeze of his trigger between beats.

———⛓✺⛓———

When Aster and Drakon sat down on the couch, hidden receivers planted by Kent Jones, signaled a device that flipped open the blinds of their balcony windows.

Drakon instinctively jumped and lunged to shield Aster as four bullets zinged through the windows, shattering the glass.

The first bullet whisked through Aster's temple and exploded out the base of his skull.

Drakon's dive toward Aster saved himself from a direct hit as two bullets grazed his scalp. Another bullet, meant for Aster, zipped past him; but his effort to save the president was too late.

The first bullet through the window had found its victim. Aster lay dead on the floor in a pool of his own blood.

CHAPTER 68

Aster's spirit hovered above his body.

He saw Drakon leaning over him and the guards rushing in to administer CPR. They soon gave up and shook their heads in disbelief. Drakon covered the dead body with a sheet.

"Nooooo!" Aster screamed. "Keep going! I can't die now!" Drakon and the guards didn't hear him. Neither could they see him above their heads.

Suddenly, Aster felt himself descending as though he were being pulled toward the ground.

Good! I'm returning to my body. But it wasn't so. Instead of entering his body, clawing hands from shadowy figures reached through the floor and grabbed him, dragging him into a dark tunnel below. He was pushed into what seemed like an elevator shaft that perilously hurled him toward the bottom. Down and down he went, spiraling past screams and moans while flames shot out of the tunnel walls.

The ride seemed endless until he came to an abrupt stop. As he checked to see if he survived the fall, he could feel someone's eyes on him. He turned around and found himself standing before a beautiful creature.

"Where am I?" he asked.

"Before the throne of the nether world," a voice cackled behind him.

Aster turned and saw no one. He heard a flurry of wings like bats in a cave, followed by echoing voices of laughter.

He turned back to the creature. "Who are you?" he asked warily.

"I am Lucifer, your Master," the creature replied. His voice bellowed like a gigantic pipe organ—melodious and majestic.

Aster blinked. *Lucifer? Can it be?* The creature looked nothing like the myths or legends he'd seen painted on the canvas of man's imagination. This Lucifer was bejeweled with precious stones of ruby, topaz, diamond, chrysolite, onyx, jasper, sapphire, carbuncle, and emerald; all set in gold.

But Aster didn't know that he only saw an illusion; a mere reflection of Lucifer's former self before he rebelled against the Creator.

"Come to me, my son," Lucifer whispered.

Aster began to shake.

"Come. There's no need to fear."

Aster took a deep breath and stepped to the foot of the throne. The glorious creature reached out and touched him to calm his quaking body. He gazed in awe at Lucifer's stature, much larger than that of the courier, Shenzar.

Enamored by Lucifer's beauty, Aster forgot his surroundings as well as the hideous creatures he had heard lurking in the shadows.

"Your place," Lucifer began, "is at the throne of the world government. Why are you here?"

"I was ambushed by terrorists. Not even Drakon detected them."

"You were careless, my son. But, I'll take the frailty of your human inadequacies into consideration. This always makes humans more vulnerable which I'll change in your situation. I'll give you powers beyond the endowments of your former self. I'll be your eyes, your ears, and will give you the secrets of the ages past. I'll make you even wiser than Daniel. Come closer. Let me embrace you."

Aster stepped forward and closed his eyes as Lucifer unfurled his wings and wrapped them around him, calling on his top ranking demons to join them.

"Take a deep breath, my son, and drink of me," he whispered. Aster inhaled, unaware of the demons that covered him like swarming bees. They rushed into his soul as he took deep breaths. Liar, seducer, blasphemer, diviner, seer, murderer, and deceiver; every hellish trait in Lucifer entered Aster's soul.

The procedure went quickly. When Aster opened his eyes he felt different, smarter, stronger and more determined than ever to fulfill what he had set out to do. Then he remembered his dead body back at the hotel.

"But I was shot," he said. "How can I go back and complete my mission?"

"You must stay with me a few days, my son. We'll talk about plans for the future. Then, I'll send you back to your body to conquer the biggest problem you face, the Bride and her manchild. We'll wipe these trespassers off my planet and make you a god among men. Together, we'll conquer the world and, in the end, dethrone the Nazarene."

CHAPTER 69

∽ↀ∾

Three days had passed since Aster's death, and the world was still in shock over the assassination of their beloved president.

The citizens of the World Federation had put aside this day, the day of his funeral, as a day of universal mourning. Drakon himself officiated the ceremony, praising Aster for his global achievements.

The cameras rolled as the whole world looked on when, suddenly, the ground began to shake below Aster's casket.

No one noticed the smile on Drakon's face who only the night before had received a visitation from Apollyon, the gatekeeper to the bottomless pit. Apollyon had informed Drakon that Lucifer gave Aster the key to open the bottomless pit and return to his body, an event that would gain the attention of the entire world.

The crowd panicked at the shaking ground and began to run. "Wait, Look!" Drakon cried after them. "It's Aster! He's come back from the dead! Your president is rising out of the grave!"

The people stopped at the prophet's announcement and stared at the trembling coffin. The ground had cracked wide enough below to keep the casket from falling in. Out of the crevice a billow of smoke emerged and darkened the sky.

"Look!" the people shouted, pointing to the coffin. The lid mysteriously began to open by the hand of an invisible demon.

The crowd gasped and Aster sat up with his eyes opened.

In stunned silence the people stared at him.

"It's a miracle!" someone shouted and the crowd went wild, cheering for their beloved president.

Aster waved at the television cameras and the people as he climbed out of the casket.

"Who is like Aster?" somebody yelled.

"He's a god!" another screamed.

Drakon winked at Aster and nodded toward the crowd. With the television cameras still running, Aster walked among the people, shaking their hands.

Drakon chuckled and started a chant which caught on and spread through the crowd, "Who is like Aster?" they shouted again and again, "He's a god among men!"

For the rest of the day, citizens of the World Federation in every nation celebrated the resurrection of their president. Rumors spread rapidly about his power and authority over death.

Overnight, Aster became a *god* as his followers proclaimed him *Messiah*. Every radio and television network repeatedly broadcast the footage of this miraculous feat, accrediting the power to Aster. There wasn't a doubt in anyone's mind that this man had indeed risen from the dead.

CHAPTER 70

The smoke continued to billow out of the pit.

After the crowds left the funeral site, a crew of workers came in to remove the casket and seal off the fissure. But a powerful entity, invisible to the naked eye, resisted them at every turn. Their equipment would either shut down or hit an invisible wall that encircled the opening.

Frustrated and spooked by the paranormal activity, the crew gave up their attempt to fill in the hole and declared it a holy site which would be better left untouched.

———

"Okay, Mr. President," the technician said, "I'll count down from five, and you're on the air."

The day after his resurrection, Aster faced the camera with a sinister gleam in his eye. His olive, chiseled face was as handsome as ever, elegantly carved like a marble statue by Michelangelo. Not a trace of disfigurement showed from the assassin's bullet. There wasn't any. He had been completely healed.

Now he was ready to address his beloved world in a live broadcast.

"…five…four…three…two…one…you're on!"

"Good evening, ladies and gentlemen," Aster began. "It is with honor and good fortune that I'm able to speak to you. Four days ago, I came to America to encourage the nation in the aftermath of Wormwood. Little did I know that my life would end by the hands of terrorists, and many have asked what can be done to avoid any future attacks. The obvious is to find the source and destroy the root.

"An all-out investigation has been launched to locate the perpetrators. Two suspects were apprehended on the day of my assassination. They were involved in an elite team of mercenaries who executed the assault.

"Since then, the investigation has led us to the leader of these terrorists, an ex-CIA official named Clifford Malloy. We have documented testimonies that tie Malloy to the Christian movement who commissioned him to assassinate Presidents Samuel Thomas and George Cane.

"While serving under Thomas's administration, Malloy mysteriously disappeared at the time of the assassination. His cover went unsuspected due to the belief he had been kidnapped and killed. Such a belief allowed him the freedom to move covertly among his associates in the agency. Several agents have testified that Malloy shot President Cane and staged it to appear like a suicide. When I conclude my message tonight, we'll show you pictures of this man. A two-million dollar reward will be secured for the person who offers any information that leads to his arrest.

"In honor of the late President Cane, I'm going to replay the message he gave the day he was murdered. In that address, he warned us about these Christian zealots. His message will remind you again of their relentless effort to overthrow our World Federation of Nations.

"I firmly believe that the actions and activities of this barbarous sect have provoked a divine wrath on our world and brought on the plagues and disasters we've been suffering.

Perhaps the gods have united to punish the Christian faith since they acknowledge no other god but their own. My hope for our planet is to appease this divine wrath through stopping these Christians. With your help, together we can put an end to their madness. We'll fight them until we rid our planet of their terrorism and the threat of further punishment from the gods. We can and will bring them to justice."

<hr />

The smoke from the crack in the ground continued to billow during Aster's speech, preparing to erupt the most frightening plague of the *fifth* trumpet on the inhabitants of the earth.

CHAPTER 71

Cap' clicked off the TV when the rerun of Cane's speech was finished and they showed the photos of Malloy. He quietly stared at the red vacancy light, blinking outside their motel room, while he pondered the new identity of his partner.

Malloy said nothing, but lay on the bed reading the paper.

"Why didn't you tell me your real name?" Cap' asked.

"It wasn't necessary," Malloy replied.

"But we've been friends for months."

"I don't always reveal everything to friends who I want to keep alive."

"Well it didn't work, did it? Now I'm a sitting duck. The whole world will be looking for you, drooling over that two million dollars they got on your head. Of all the people I had to get mixed up with, I had to pick public-enemy number one."

"That photo of me was 15 years old. No one will recognize me in my beard."

"But they'll use computer graphics, advertise you through papers and the internet; every which way you *might* look today. It's going to be hot out there with all those bounty hunters on your trail."

Malloy smiled. "Then you better go while you can."

"Nothing doing, you're not getting rid of me that easy. We still have to break Grub and Brad out."

"Forget it. They'll be too well guarded. Aster'll showcase them to the ends of the earth, use them to stir up his followers like an angry hornet's nest, and then kill them. We can only hope they get right with God."

"And Kent Jones? What about him? He buckled. He's the only one who knew about your plot."

"I don't believe that," Malloy replied. "They probably caught him and killed him on the spot. Aster's just making it up to get me."

"But what if Jones *did* trash you?"

"Even if he did, who could blame him? The man's got a family to protect. He knows I stand a better chance of protecting myself...better than he can protect his family. Kent's done a lot for me. I'm not going to lose any sleep over it if the guy had to sing to protect his own."

Cap' stared curiously at his friend. How odd for a man with Malloy's background to so readily forgive Jones for turning him in. He decided to change the subject. "How do you think Aster survived that head wound?"

"It doesn't figure, does it? But then, nothing figures these days the way everything's been happening."

"Something Aster said that's baffling me," Cap said.

"What's that?"

"You being linked to the Christians. How does he get that? I never heard you talk about religion."

"I've got no dealings with Christians. But they are a threat to Aster. He's using me to turn the world against them. You've heard what they're doing—people healed, raised from the dead. Aster can't compete with that through his World Church. He's lost a lot of followers to Christians."

Cap' shook his head. "So it's an all-out war between the Christians and Aster. Why?"

"Because Aster wants to be God and Christians can't abide by that. They have their own God."

"Interesting how people say he's a god. Doesn't that make you wonder? After all, he raised himself from the dead, didn't he?"

Malloy stared at the blinking red sign outside. He recalled the night of the explosion that nearly killed him. "I wouldn't care if Aster parted the Atlantic Ocean and walked across it on dry ground. He's nothing but a low-life con artist with the IQ of a genius."

"You siding with the Christians then?"

"Maybe."

"Why?"

"They helped me once. Never met anyone like them. They're selfless, caring. There's something in their eyes that gets to you...like they shine."

"Ever thought about being a Christian?"

"Yeah, but, I can't. Got too much blood on my hands. Innocent blood. When I worked for the CIA, I did terrible things in the name of justice; things that can't be forgiven."

"Then who can be a Christian?" Cap' asked. "We've all done unforgivable things."

"I don't know. Seems like a lot of people are joining them, though. Probably not as bad me."

"Nor I," Cap' said. "So I guess we're *both* going to hell."

"In case you haven't noticed, I think we're there already."

<hr />

Back in Washington D.C., at the site of Aster's resurrection, the sun and sky were darkened by the billows of smoke rising from the Abyss. The events of the *fifth* trumpet hadn't ended with the assassination of Aster.

Out of the pit crawled an army of locusts; hideous, horse-like creatures with breastplates of armor and scorpion tails curled over their heads. Their human faces had teeth like a lion and their coarse, long hair was adorned by a gold-colored crown. Apollyon, their king and angel over the bottomless pit, led them forth with a mission to inflict pain on men and women through the sting of their tails.

As they took to flight, their wings roared like an army of dirt bikes. Then a voice from heaven cried,

"Don't hurt the grass, the plants, or the trees, but only those without the seal of God on their foreheads. You may torture, but not kill them, for five months."

CHAPTER 72

Aster's resurrection stirred up a great deal of religious confusion among the members of his World Church. Every religious sect became divided in their loyalties to the traditions and subculture gods of their forefathers and Aster.

Under the umbrella of the World Church, the ecumenical movement had allowed a wide door of acceptance and tolerance for the religious traditions of these sects. But now, Aster wanted to narrow the gate and nudge their traditions and gods aside. His goal was to position himself as the *prominent* god above all gods.

Momentum toward this objective accelerated when neither Aster nor Drakon were stung in the demonic assault. Lucifer forbade it. This added credibility to Aster's claim of *godhood*.

Even among Christians, his resurrection created a stir; not in the Bride or her converts, but among those who had been straddling the fence between Christ and the world. The voices of false prophets and teachers emerged to endorse Aster as the Messiah. But was he the Messiah? Was he the Christ who would come back to rule the world? Many allowed themselves to believe this and embrace it. Aster *did rise* from the dead, didn't he?

Taking advantage of the confusion and the terrorizing effect of the demonic hordes, Aster offered amnesty to any Christian who was willing to leave their faith and worship him in his World Church. Many accepted this offer; including pastors abandoning their faith to serve an alternate Christ, the Antichrist.

⸻⟨⟩⸻

Bob Jansen spent the next five months in complete misery as he watched civilians and soldiers in his division suffer from the stings inflicted by the locust-like demons. Nearly every soldier in his barracks moaned and cried in their bunks from the plague. All, that is, but three of them who were never stung, including Bob.

A fellow-soldier, ran up in the barracks and grabbed his arms. "Kill me, Bob!" he screamed. "Please, you've got to kill me! I can't take it anymore! It burns so bad…like the sting of a hundred scorpions!"

"No!" Bob shoved the tormented soldier away. "Leave me alone."

"Please…take your gun and shoot me."

"No, I won't do it."

"How come you ain't been stung, Jansen?" another fever-ridden soldier asked from his bed. "You've seemed to manage to come through this unscathed. What's you're secret? Tell me!" He jumped off his bed and grabbed Bob by the shirt. "Tell me! How come they never touched *you*?"

"I told you, I don't know!" Bob yelled and broke free.

The other soldiers sat up in their bunks and glared at Bob, then at Carl Hayes sitting in the corner clutching his blanket. Carl, too, had not been stung; but the sight of the hideous creatures had frightened him so much, he had a nervous break down. Now he sat in the corner, recounting the nightmare with his eyes bugged out in a glassy stare. "Fiery-red breast-plates," he muttered, "horses with human faces. Teeth like

239

lions. Wings and scorpion tails. Flew in. Stung everybody. Go away! Go away!" he shrieked, covering himself with his blanket.

"Shut up, you moron!" a soldier yelled, "shut up or I'll knock your teeth out!"

It was nerve-racking. Day after day, Bob had to listen to Carl and the wailing agony of his comrades. He tried desperately to maintain his sanity, but thought he'd go nuts if he stayed any longer. The only thing that had kept him from leaving was his fear of the demons. Afraid they might still be around. He never understood why they left him alone, but he didn't want to take any chances. This place was probably the safest place to hide since they had already hit the barracks.

"Horses, lion's teeth—" Carl muttered.

"Shut up!" the soldier yelled.

"—Just flew in," Carl continued. "Out of nowhere..."

Bob clamped his hands over his ears. He wanted to knock the guy's lights out himself.

"...like horses," Carl said with widening eyes. "Covered everybody. Aieeeee! Don't sting me! Please don't sting me!"

"I'm going to kill you!" the soldier said, yet obviously too weak to follow through.

"That does it," Bob said, raising his hands in the air. "I'm out of here."

———

Gamliel, Bob's angel, followed his assignee out of the barracks.

Poor, confused human he thought, shaking his head. The demons were long gone. He knew that from Scripture. It said in the Revelation they'd be around for only *five* months.

They came. They went. That's it. Another prophecy fulfilled in the countdown to Christ's return. Gamliel loved it. They were getting so close! He already quoted the prophecy about the demons last night, just like he did with all the other prophecies as soon as they came to pass.

Now what was the last part of that prophecy in Revelation? Oh, yes, the first woe is past and two more to come.

It was the *other* two woes that had Gamliel concerned for Bob's sake. It might make or break that stubborn assignee of his.

"Come on, wake up," he said with his hands cupped in Bob's face. Of course Bob couldn't hear *or* see him, but he wanted so bad for Bob to turn back to God before it was too late. Guardian angels loved *all* their assignees and never enjoyed losing them to the opposition.

Many times, in his past assignments, he wished he could know the outcome of a person's life like God knew. But he always concluded that knowing might make his job more difficult.

"Come on, you can do it, buddy," Gamliel said, walking beside Bob. "Let's get back on track here. Your guardian angel's pulling for you now, let's go."

Bob heard nothing.

CHAPTER 73

Bob wandered about Canterton for two solid hours.

It depressed him to go through the downtown section. The images he saw left him with little optimism for the future. There were people lying on the streets, empty buildings, closed store signs and broken glass; all painting a picture of unalterable doom. He could only envision more devastation and nightmares ahead, never to return to the thriving economy he once knew.

Since he left the barracks, Bob had been thinking about the choices he'd made. Nothing had gone right since he left Whitney crying at the door. He missed her and all his old Christian friends. The brightest moments he'd ever had was when he hung out with them. He wasn't as sure as he used to be about turning away from it all. Now he felt helpless. Insecure. And worst of all, there was no one to talk to. No one who cared about Bob Jansen.

And how *could* anybody care? His present associates were all members of the World Church, most of whom were soldiers who were either sick or dead. Bob realized now that nothing significant had ever developed in his relationship with them. Not like it had with his Christian friends.

When he turned the corner he found Shayne and Laura Taylor across the street, comforting the victims who had been stung. He stopped abruptly and ducked behind the building, then slowly peered around the corner to see if they had spotted him. They hadn't. They were engrossed with the people suffering in the streets.

As he watched them move from person to person, some of the people they talked to spit on them. Others turned their backs. But then, there were those who responded kindly and followed the pattern of letting Shayne and Laura pray for them, then jump up all excited because they were healed. Shayne and Laura would then lead the grateful recipients into a prayer to receive Christ.

Bob used to arrest Christians for doing this. Not today. Deep in his heart, he couldn't deny the warm feeling he got when he saw the people be healed and then saved. He remembered how good it had made him feel to receive Christ. But that seemed an eternity ago.

Over time, Bob began to turn when he noticed the World Church didn't have the same goal as Christianity. They helped people, yes; but were motivated by conquest and multiplying their numbers, rather than offering simple acts of love and kindness. Whenever Christians reached out to the people's needs, they were loving and caring. There wasn't the sense of *cause* behind their deeds like the World Church.

As he watched Shayne and Laura move from victim to victim, it dawned on him that they weren't afflicted like the soldiers in his barracks. Perhaps God protected them, too, which made sense that he would. But what didn't make sense was why *he*, Bob Jansen, never got stung? Especially after he had denounced Christianity and pledged loyalty to the Federation, to Aster and to the World Church. If these demons were God's wrath on Aster's followers—"

"Hello, Bob," a calm voice said from behind. Bob turned to identify the person. It was Pastor Mitchell.

Bob stood speechless, embarrassed to stand face to face with the man he had turned in to the WFI. Remembering his position as a NWF soldier, he collected his wits and said with all the authority his voice could muster, "Who let *you* out? I thought I turned you in months ago. How'd you escape?"

"I didn't escape. They let me go."

"Why?"

"The thirty-day grace period wasn't up yet when they arrested me, so legally, they couldn't keep me. And with the invasion of the demons, other things took priority." Pastor Mitchell pointed at the victims lying in the street.

Bob stiffened and threw out his chest, avoiding eye contact. "Well those thirty days were up four months ago, so it's my duty to arrest you now." He placed his hand on his gun holster. "Are you going to come peaceably, or do I have to use this?"

"Do as you wish, brother," Pastor Mitchell replied. He held out his hands to be cuffed.

Bob stared at him. The pastor's cooperation took him by surprise. He didn't *really* want to take him in. The station house was full of suffering soldiers and WFI officers he'd rather avoid. "Don't call me, brother," he snapped, taking his hand off the holster. "I'm not your brother!"

"But obviously you're my *Christian* brother or you would've been stung like the others."

Those words stuck like a spear in Bob's heart and punched a hole in the veil that had cloaked his mind since he had walked out on Whitney. He gazed into the compassionate eyes of the pastor. "Are you saying that God protected me from those demons?"

"That's what I'm saying."

"But how can that be, after all I've done? I've cursed God, thrown his people in jail and even beat them with my own hands."

"God doesn't like what you did, Bob, but he still loves you and wants you to come back."

"And *you* don't have any hard feelings toward me after that beating from Kobrin?"

Pastor Mitchell placed his hand on Bob's shoulder. "I forgave you the minute you walked into Kobrin's office."

Bob's heart melted at this genuine demonstration of love. The walls he had erected toward God, shattered around him like broken glass. He glanced at his uniform and stared tearfully at Jack. As conviction gripped his heart, he fell to his knees and cried, "Oh Lord, I feel so ashamed. Again you've shown your love and mercy to a fool like me. You protected me from the torture of demons and sent me the pastor I've hated to show your love through him. Forgive me for my stupid pride. I've been selfish and self-centered. Help me start over, Lord, please. Show me how. I need you desperately. I'll serve you the rest of my life, even to death if I have to."

Bob put his face in his hands and wept. The love of God poured into him, sweeping his soul clean of the hate and bitterness that had cluttered his heart. When he stopped crying he looked up at Pastor Mitchell. "Please forgive me for the harm I've brought on you and your wife. I was wrong."

Jack knelt down and grabbed Bob's shoulders. "I forgive you...and the Lord forgives you, too. What do you say we go to my place now for a long talk. I need to catch you up on a few things and prepare you for what lies ahead."

Bob wiped the tears from his eyes and embraced his pastor. That load of resentment he had was all gone, and it felt good to have someone care again...really care.

"The first thing I want to do when we get to your house," Bob said, "is to get out of this uniform. Somehow it just doesn't fit my taste in clothes anymore."

Jack laughed and looked Bob over. "I think I can fit you into something, but we'll have to shorten the length of the pants a bit. Let's go see what I've got," he said, laying his arm across Bob's shoulders.

As they started toward the house, Jack turned to Bob and said, "Rhonda will be thrilled to see what I've brought home. Maybe she'll let us keep you awhile...like an adopted son."

Bob nodded and chuckled. That sounded good to him.

CHAPTER 74

Bob's future looked brighter now.

With Pastor Mitchell's help, he understood what had happened to Whitney and why she couldn't marry him. He also learned about the wedding of Christ with his Bride, the ministry he left her to accomplish, and the imminent conflict with Aster.

"So...I guess I missed my opportunity to be in the Bride?" Bob asked sadly. "Whitney warned me about this."

"Unfortunately, many Christians missed out that night," Jack replied. "I'm afraid it was the only night that door was open for those whose hearts were ready."

Bob sighed. "Well, I've got nobody to blame but myself. I just wish I could turn back the clock, knowing what I know now. I would've paid more attention, gotten more involved, spent more time with God and done more serious reading in the Bible."

"You can still do that," Pastor Mitchell replied. "Yes, you played Russian roulette with your faith, but you're still saved."

"I hope so..."

"Of course you are! You were never stung, remember? If

you weren't saved, those locust-like demons would've been all over you."

The pastor's comment triggered Bob's memory. For the first time, he thought about someone else's welfare besides his own. "The two other soldiers in my barracks—"

"Who?" Jack asked.

"Two soldiers. They weren't touched by the demons, either, like me. You think they could be backslidden Christians?"

"Can't think of another reason for their immunity."

"Then, I've got to help them. I can talk to them. Maybe bring them back to Jesus. What do you think, Pastor?"

Jack smiled and chuckled. "I think it's a great idea."

"Why are you laughing?"

"Oh, nothing really. I was just thinking how great it is to see you excited about God again."

———

As Jack shared more with Bob about the coming judgments in the Revelation, Gamliel stood in the corner with his arms folded in smug satisfaction.

What a great day it turned out to be. His assignee was back with God and he couldn't be happier. He felt confident that Bob would stay on track now since his eyes were on Jesus instead of Whitney.

Yes sir, he could tell when someone made up their mind to serve the Creator. He'd seen that look in their eyes. Bob definitely had that look. The kind that says, "I messed up my life once, and I'll never do that again."

Gamliel loved it! Another battle lost by Satan. Another victory won for his side, not to mention he'd have another new friend with him in eternity.

Let's see now, he thought, that would make 182 assigned humans that made it on his watch over six millennia. "Glory to God!" he yelled. It'll be a great time of fellowship in the coming age.

Four large angels stood leashed at the Euphrates River. But their hour had come to lead a host of demons with a mission to slay a third of the human race.

In the throne room of God, a voice from the four horns of the golden altar said to the *sixth* angel, trumpeting the *sixth* trumpet, "Release the four angels who are bound at the great river Euphrates."

Like an awakened giant, an explosion of fury shot out of the river as two million horse-like creatures flew out across the horizon toward the four corners of the earth.

The riders wore fiery breastplates with flashes of blue and yellow. Like monstrous dragons with lion's heads, they spewed smoke, fire and sulfur from their mouths to incinerate their victims.

As did the previous horde, these demonic creatures struck the inhabitants of the earth with scorpion-like tails, but with one exception: their tails had heads that bit their victims with fatal wounds.

Of all the judgments that had come on the planet, this was the most frightening.

Billions of people were slain without mercy, yet the surviving followers of Aster continued to harden their hearts and refused to repent of their sins and worship God.

CHAPTER 75

The smell of burning flesh filled the air.

Flames of fire crawled over the remains of bodies stacked twenty-feet high. There were so many dead it made burial impossible. The final count of victims in Canterton came to a third of the citizens.

None were Christians.

They had all been killed by a death squad of hideous creatures that swarmed out of the sky like locusts that stung or incinerated their victims. These demons were similar; yet differed from the other demonic horde which tormented their victims, but never killed them.

Jack Mitchell stood on the fountain wall in the middle of the square. He grieved for the survivors who were moaning and wailing for their loved ones. He came because the ensuing months of God's relentless judgment had sifted out the last of those who remained open to God. He was hoping to find that one last soul if he could.

"Jesus loves you!" he shouted from the fountain. "Come to him and he'll save you!"

A man, who stood near the fire, swore at him and yelled, "We curse your God for what he's done..."

"Yeah!" another shouted. "We're tired of listening to you Christians! Your fanaticism brought this trouble on all of us!"

Jack stared at the restless crowd, now focusing on him. His objective seemed futile. Canterton had been harvested out. Only the hateful were left to their cursing and bitterness.

"He's breaking the law!" someone cried. "He's not supposed to be preaching about the Nazarene. Get the conspirator!"

A rock flew out of the crowd and hit Jack in the head. Then a handful of angry men started toward him.

It was time to leave.

Another barrage of rocks flew at his head while he scurried out of the market square and down an alley. As he rounded the corner he glanced back to locate his pursuers and ran into someone coming from the opposite direction.

Wham!

Flat on his back, Jack gasped for breath and shook his head. He raised himself up on one elbow to see if the angry crowd was still after him. No one had followed him. He peered over his feet into the shadows to see who he hit and discovered the surprised face of Bob Jansen.

"Pastor Mitchell!" Bob shouted.

Jack held his finger to his lips to hush him. "You all right, Bob?" he asked.

"Yeah, I'll be fine." Bob got up and brushed the dust off his pants and sleeves. "How about you?"

"I'll be okay, when I can breathe again."

"Hey, did I do that?" Bob asked, pointing to a streak of blood running down the side of Jack's face.

"No, it wasn't you. My message wasn't received very well back at the square. They decided to change the channel with rocks instead of the remote."

Bob chuckled.

"So. What're you doing down here?" Jack asked.

"I was taking a shortcut home from the barracks. I went to see those two soldiers I told you about."

"How'd it go?"

"One guy is completely bonkers. I couldn't talk to him. But the other showed promise. We were partners on a number of assignments. Every now and then he'd ask questions that made me believe he was interested in God. He never liked it when we arrested Christians."

"Did you talk to him?"

"We were just getting into a conversation when a handful of soldiers came in and saw me out of uniform. They went wild and started interrogating me. It got so intense I thought they were going to tear me apart, so I left and here I am."

"Too bad, maybe you can talk to your friend, later. Take Shayne Taylor with you next time?"

"Now there's an idea." Bob eyed the gash on Jack's head. "Hey, you took a nasty hit there. Let me pray for you." Bob softly touched the wound and closed his eyes in prayer. Within seconds the bleeding stopped. Jack felt the bump disappear under Bob's hand.

"Whoa," Bob said looking at the healed area. "It really works!"

"Get used to it," Jack replied. "God will keep using you this way."

CHAPTER 76

Bob put on his NWF uniform again.

He didn't want to repeat the last altercation he had with the soldiers, and this time he brought Shayne Taylor along.

When he and Shayne arrived, they found Blake Harris near the station house gathering up the dead in the aftermath of the demonic attack. "There he is," Bob whispered, "over there." They casually strolled over to the soldier and came up beside him. "Blake," Bob said, tapping him on the shoulder.

Blake gasped and put his hand on his chest. "Bob, you scared me. I didn't see you coming. With all these dead bodies around, I thought you were a demon jumping on me."

"Not a demon," Bob said, and introduced Blake to Shayne.

Blake nodded and the two exchanged handshakes.

"Shayne and I came by to talk to you about something. Something you and I discussed a while back."

"What's that?".

"Remember when you asked if the problems we were having may not be about the Christians, but our own sins?"

"Yeah, I remember."

"Do you remember how angry I got with you for asking that?"

"Uh-huh."

"Well, I was wrong."

Blake smiled. "I knew you were wrong."

"You did?"

"Sure. I used to be a Christian. I could tell you were running from God."

"You were right. I was running from God, but not now. How about you? Given any thought to coming back?"

Blake nodded. "Been giving a lot of thought to it, but I can't."

"Why not?"

"Because I've blasphemed God and joined the World Church. I've committed the unpardonable sin."

"But I did the same thing you did and God took me back." Bob glanced at Shayne for help.

"Look, brother," Shayne said, "I can assure you, you haven't committed the unpardonable sin."

"How can you know that?"

"Would you come back to God if you could?"

"I'd do it in a heart beat."

"Then if you really *had* committed the unpardonable sin, your answer would be different."

"What do you mean?"

"The unpardonable sin happens to those who've reached a point where they no longer feel any conviction for their sins. If you were at that point, you wouldn't have the least desire to come back to God. The fact that you *want* to come back is a clear indication that the door hasn't been locked behind you."

"So I'm still saved, because I want to come back?"

"That's right. All you've got to do is repent and ask God to forgive you. He's waiting for you to come home, just like the father who waited for the return of his prodigal son."

Blake smiled and glanced at the barracks. "Let's go in there," he said cheerfully, "and I'll pray."

"Hey, great!" Bob said. He smiled at Shayne and patted Blake on the back. "Let's go."

When they entered the barracks it smelled like rotting meat inside from a few grisly bodies incinerated by the demons. The rest of the beds were empty and stripped of the sheets that were used to carry out the corpses.

Suddenly a shuffle in the corner caught their attention. Blake switched on the lights. "Who's there?" he asked.

Bob saw a frail, terrified soldier, huddled and shivering in a wool blanket. "Smoke! Fire!" he muttered. "Don't sting me! Don't sting me! Noooooo!"

"Who is that?" Shayne asked.

"It's Carl," Bob replied, recognizing the voice of the man who nearly drove him crazy for five months. "The poor guy is still out of it."

"The first demonic attack got to him and he snapped," Blake said. "He was just starting to pull out of it when this second horde came and started killing everybody. It sent him back over the edge and he's been that way ever since."

Bob felt compassion for the emaciated man as they walked up to him. His face was thin and pale, and his bones protruded from his body like the ribs on a washboard. His fingernails had grown into long claws which accounted for the numerous bloody scratches on his face and arms.

Shayne knelt before Carl and reached out his hands.

"Back! Back!" Carl screamed, pulling the blanket over his head. "Don't hurt me! Don't hurt me!"

Shayne pulled the blanket away and placed his hands under Carl's chin. He gently lifted the bleeding face to his. "Carl," he said with a calm voice. "Carl...open your eyes and look at me."

Trembling, Carl opened one eye and then the other. "Carl, listen to me," Shayne said softly. "Jesus Christ of Nazareth heals you. You're free from this prison of fear. Be released now, in the name of Jesus."

Immediately, Shayne's hands grew hot and jerked from a surge of power which sprawled Carl out on the floor.

"Don't be afraid," Shayne assured the others as they stared at the still figure. "The Holy Spirit came on him. Bob and Blake nodded and gazed at the miracle taking place before them. A robust color returned to Carl's ghostly pale face. The bleeding scratches on his body disappeared and were replaced by new skin. Then, his emaciated frame of skin and bones began to fill out until the soldier looked whole again. It was a creative phenomenon.

"Let him lie there for awhile," Shayne said. "The Holy Spirit is restoring his mind. He should be normal again when he wakes up. I've seen God do this to a lot of Christians who were in the same condition."

Blake anxiously jumped in after what he saw and said, "Let's finish what we came in here for. I'm ready to give my life back to God."

Shayne and Bob smiled and the three knelt together on the floor to pray.

Bob laid his arm across Blake's shoulders and said, "Let's do it, brother."

CHAPTER 77

While the world mourned over their dead from the massive invasion of demons, the second woe had come and gone, giving way to the third.

In the throne room of God, while the seventh angel prepared to sound, the command went forth to ban the accuser of the saints from heaven.

Under the direction of Michael the archangel, a host of God's elect angels prepared themselves for the confrontation against the great red dragon and serpent, Satan.

Lucifer's great wings carried him across the span of the first two heavens toward the throne of God in paradise. He had come for his customary routine of slandering the sons and daughters of God, unaware that this would be his last trip to the third heaven.

Michael stood alone at the gate to block Satan's path. "Halt," he shouted, "The Lord rebukes you."

"What's this?" Lucifer hissed.

"Jehovah God forbids you to enter. Leave and return no more."

Lucifer coiled and reared. "Get out of my way!" he screamed. A host of the princes of darkness appeared at his side with their swords drawn.

"The Lord God rebukes you!" Michael repeated. "Go back! You are banned from entering!"

Lucifer glowered at Michael and spread his cherubic wings to their full span. His chest expanded and heaved furiously. "Stand down!" he screamed again, "I'm coming through!"

Michael braced himself and drew his sword as Lucifer cautiously advanced with his fallen angels. "The great God Jehovah rebukes you, Satan!" Michael said again. "Be gone!"

Lucifer halted and blinked. He glanced at his army and nodded. Then he looked back at the lone figure before him. "Never!" he shouted and stepped toward Michael.

Michael stood fearless, yet hopelessly outnumbered.

Lucifer sneered, he could taste the victory.

His arrogant confidence was shattered, however, as a myriad of angels appeared behind Michael, brandishing their golden swords. With a shout, they charged into the fray.

Lucifer roared furiously, thrashing his great wings to dodge the onslaught of the fierce celestial warriors. His princes were outnumbered five-to-one, and the battle was over within minutes.

"Throw them back where they came from," Michael shouted.

The powerful hands of the victors rounded up their enemies and hurled them to Earth with an unseen power greater than their own—the omnipotence of their Creator.

After tumbling to Earth like a rock, Lucifer glared back at the stars above. For the first time since his rebellion, the third heaven was off limits to him. Never again would he enter that gate.

As he crawled back to the throne of his nether world, he could hear a loud voice in the heavens cry,

"It's happened at last! Salvation! Power! The kingdom of our God! The authority of his Christ! It's all established now. For he who accused our brothers and sisters—day and night before God—has been thrown out.

"Rejoice all you heavens, and you who live there! But woe to the earth and sea, because the devil—raging and furious—is confined to you, and knows that his days are numbered!"

CHAPTER 78

"All rise for the President of the World Federation!"

The largest gathering of world representatives ever conceived in the annals of history stood before Aster.

Every religious and government official was present: the chief council to Aster, John Drakon; the ten-membered council of the Federation with their allied nations of kings, presidents and governors; and the twelve-member council of the World Church with her archbishops and bishops.

Lucifer as well had come, still smarting from the humiliating defeat and ousting from the third heaven. With him were myriads of seducing and deceiving demons, brought to spellbind the audience who would listen to Aster's speech.

With the restraining force of the Holy Spirit gone, nothing could block Lucifer's plan to make Aster the king and god of his world. He watched the humans at his mercy from his invisible perch. How he had longed for this day. A moment he had waited for, for six thousand years.

Aster silenced the crowd who applauded him.

"Thank you," he said, "Thank you for attending this great and glorious banquet we've hosted for you tonight. I trust the meal has provided you with a little pleasure in the midst of a very dark hour...an hour I must address.

"If you were to view our beloved planet through the eyes of our satellites, you would see a maimed and desolate mire, a sad contrast to the former shades of greens, blues and browns.

"In place of the swirls of billowing white clouds, we see a thinly veiled haze of gray smog. In the Atlantic, from north to south, the discolored waters of blood are mixed with vast pockets of oil spills and carnage from the ocean life. In the upper regions of Canada, blotches of gray appear from the devastation of the asteroid, Wormwood.

"Our streams are polluted and the crops and vegetation are stripped bare. The ravaging jaws of famine perpetually consumes every continent with an endless wake of disease.

"Every one of you has been touched in some way by the death of a loved one through these relentless calamities. We live in a dying world. Tears stain our pillows at night, shed for the days of yesteryear when we remember how life used to be.

"All of this discourages the optimism we so desperately try to cling to. But we must not succumb to despair, nor the urge to lie down and quit. To accept defeat is not an option."

The audience mumbled in agreement.

"The history of our planet has always been riddled with mayhem and setbacks. Yet, we've seen it rise again and again to conquer its enemies through heroic leaders and those who followed them. The human spirit is strong. It has always risen to the challenge, and today, it will rise again!"

Aster paused for effect as the audience applauded. He smiled with smug confidence and waved his hands for silence.

"How can I be so sure? You might ask? I'm sure because history has never recorded the measure of unity represented tonight in this room. And *with* such unity, nothing is impossible for a world that is united on the three fronts of commerce, religion and politics. The only thing that can stop us, my friends, is the limit of our imaginations."

Again applause.

Aster smiled and appealed again for silence. "I have been to a place on the other side of life for three days and three nights. During that time, I talked with the god of this world who gave me a mission and sent me back to fulfill it.

"I stand here tonight as one who was dead and now lives. I have returned so that *you* might have life in a new world...a world of bliss for you, your children and their children's children."

A man shouted from the audience, "A curse be on you, you son of the devil! You're no more a god than I! If you're really a god, prove it! Prove it, right now, before these witnesses!"

The audience booed at the outburst.

Aster motioned to the crowd to calm down. "Dear, sir," he replied, "believe me when I say I can offer you a new life. I rose from the dead, what more proof do you need? I have no desire to stand before you as a magician. Accept what I offer, to serve you as the President of the World Federation. Now please take your seat and enjoy the rest of the evening with us—"

"I say you're a liar!" the man screamed and scanned the audience. "You're all fools if you believe him! Get out while you can! Death to Aster!"

The audience gasped as a pillar of fire dropped suddenly from the ceiling and consumed the man; reducing him instantly to a pile of foul, smoldering ashes. Then Satan shook the room with a deep booming voice and said,

This day I exalt my son and have made him a god before you. Listen to him! He will take this broken world of yours and restore it.

A terrified hush fell over the audience, and a woman ran up and fell to her knees before Aster. "Long live Aster," she shouted, "the god of this world! Long live our president and the New World Order!"

One by one, everyone left their chairs and bowed before Aster, saying over and over, *"Long live Aster, the god of this world!"*

Aster looked at Drakon and grinned. How he savored this moment. Today he had become more than the president of the Federation. His claim to godhood was confirmed by Lucifer himself. Aster was now *the* god and chief sovereign of the world.

CHAPTER 79

Aster moved his headquarters from Tel Aviv to Jerusalem, the principal capital of the world. He then made New York, London, Tokyo and Rome as his secondary capitals.

Things were going well for him.

Every tribe, tongue and nation had been swept into the delusion of worshiping Aster as a god under Lucifer. Even the coneys joined in, unable to resist the deception.

The survivors of the human race had been reduced to three categories: Christians, God-fearing Jews and the World Church. This made Aster's job much easier. With the gray areas removed, his primary objective could be carried out: terminate the Bride and her Manchild.

Vince Kobrin paced nervously downstairs in the home of Jack and Rhonda Mitchell. He wasn't particularly fond of his new assignment, but had strict orders to confiscate the baby as soon as it was born.

Never in his bloody career had he ever killed an infant.

Yes, he was calloused and cold-blooded; but a baby was different.

Kobrin jumped when he heard the scream of the newborn. He wiped the sweat off his brow and motioned to the soldiers to guard the windows and exits. He pulled out his gun, took a deep breath and ran up the stairs.

"What is it?" he asked, as he walked into the room uninvited.

Rhonda stepped calmly between them. "It's a boy, Mr. Kobrin," she said. "Would you like to see him?"

Kobrin pushed her aside and went to the bed where Whitney held the newborn.

He glanced across the bed at Jack Mitchell and then at Whitney. A faint glow covered her face. Her cheeks were still flushed with color from childbirth.

Kobrin turned and impassively addressed the group.

"This child belongs to the state. I'm here under the orders of the president to arrest all of you for treason. You Mitchells will come with me to the station house. The guards will stay with Miss Conner." He had given the guards downstairs their orders. They were to kill the mother after the baby was born.

Kobrin stared at the Christians when he finished his statement. Their calm response unnerved him, even more so when they held out their hands to be cuffed. He expected resistance, especially from Whitney Conner. *What's wrong with these people? Don't they care?*

"Corporal!" he barked to the guard outside the door.

The guard entered the room. "Sir!"

"Escort the Mitchells to the station house. I'll meet you there, later."

"Yes, sir...and the baby, sir?"

"I'll bring it myself," Kobrin said.

He reached down and took the newborn, avoiding eye contact with the mother. Her calm demeanor baffled him.

He quickly left the room and walked down the steps,

refusing to look at the child. He carried the boy to the car, surprised at how quiet he was.

He hated this assignment. He wasn't a baby killer. Yet in his arms was some kind of…maybe…prince among a number of princes, predicted to rule the nations. This kid was supposed to be a threat to Aster's throne. If he failed to kill the baby, he'd have to answer for it; something he didn't relish repeating with Aster.

Kobrin got into his car alone and stared at the helpless child. He clenched his teeth, took a deep breath, closed his eyes, and with his broad hand covered the baby's mouth and nose. The child struggled to breathe in his powerful grip.

"Die, kid. Please, die quick," he muttered.

Suddenly the car tipped on its side as if held in the air by an invisible hand. The door next to Kobrin was ripped off its hinges like a toy.

"What!" Kobrin shouted, finding himself face to face with a towering angel. He reached for the gun in his holster to shoot the child, but his hand was grabbed and held fast by the vice-like grip of the divine rescuer.

Kobrin dropped the baby on the floor of the car and used his free hand to swing at his assailant. The angel snatched him up like a paper bag and hurled him twenty feet through the air across the street. When he landed on his back at the curb, the wind was knocked out of him. While he gasped for breath, Kobrin watched the angel cradle the child out of the car and into his arms. The creature glanced at Kobrin with a frown, and then whisked toward the sky through the smog-covered veil.

Throughout the world that day, the same divine rescue took place for a hundred and forty-four thousand infants, snatched from the jaws of death by a dispatch of angels and carried to the throne room of God.

CHAPTER 80

"What do you mean they just disappeared!?" Kobrin screamed, staring in disbelief at the unlocked cell. "How is that possible?"

"I...I don't know, sir," the trembling guard replied. "I remember locking them in and then I must have fainted. When I woke up, I found the door open."

"I'll have your head for this, corporal, if you don't find them and find them quick!"

"Yes, sir!"

As the guard dashed out, the phone buzzed at Kobrin's desk. "Kobrin, here."

"Commander, sir?"

"What is it, soldier?"

"Me and, uh, two other guys were assigned to Miss Conner and—"

"And?"

"Well, uh...she's gone, sir. Just vanished before we could kill her."

Jack Mitchell gazed at the bloody waters of the Atlantic Ocean below. It reminded him of the story in Exodus when Moses had turned the Nile River into blood. He also thought of the story in Acts where Philip the evangelist had been whisked into the air by the Holy Spirit and taken from Gaza to Azotus.

Like Philip, Jack now flew with the wind in his face and his hair blown back, thousands of feet above ground.

Rhonda flew beside him.

"Look behind us, Jack!" she yelled, pointing toward the horizon. "We're not alone!"

Jack glanced back at the sky now lined with thousands of people in flight. They dotted the horizon for miles, like layers upon layers of migratory birds. Below them he saw the faint images of other saints, still ascending through the air.

The experience sent a chill of excitement through him. The awesome display of God's power was overwhelming. He knew from Scripture these saints were members of the Bride, snatched from the clutches of Aster's soldiers, and safe on the wings of the Holy Spirit.

"It's happening, dear!" he shouted. "Just like it says in the Revelation: *The woman was given two wings of a great eagle, to fly to the place prepared for her in the desert.*"

Rhonda quoted a similar verse in Exodus, "*I carried you on eagle's wings, and brought you to myself.*"

Jack smiled and glanced back down at the planet's terrain. They were passing over the west coast of Africa. It amazed him how fast they were moving, faster than he could imagine. It wasn't long before they crossed the African continent and found themselves descending over the blue-green waters of the Red Sea. On the eastern horizon, beyond the ridge of the Tihama mountains, he could see the vast expanse of the deserts of Saudi Arabia.

When they approached the Rub' al Khali, in the southeast region of Arabia, an amazing sight took Jack's breath. From every direction along the horizon, the sky was darkened by millions of saints converging onto the same location like a cloud of locusts.

Below were other members of the Bride who had already landed on the ground. From this height, they looked like tiny ants in a sand box.

As he and Rhonda descended with the other new arrivals, they gently touched down among a sea of faces; and to their delight, familiar faces. Members from their former congregation.

Whitney Conner, Shayne and Laura Taylor, and Tim Patterson were all there, running up to greet them and wearing fine linen garments, radiantly white. Jack looked at his own attire for the first time and discovered that he, too, wore the same type of clothing.

"Pastor Mitchell's here!" was the constant reaction of Jack's former flock. One by one, they came to greet him. The wonderful reunion blessed him when he realized he hadn't seen many of these faces for the last nine months. Most of them had left Canterton to spread revival in other parts of the world. Some, he learned, had gone to neighboring countries like Canada and Mexico, while others had gone as far as Africa, South America and Asia.

Suddenly, one former member came running up and shouted, "They're here, Pastor Mitchell, they're here!"

"Who's here?" he asked.

"The Twelve. They're all here. Nathan Kelly's been looking for you. He wants all the pastors to join them to thank God for a safe journey and to pray for those who were left behind."

"When did you last seem him?" Jack asked, scanning the wall of faces.

"About an hour ago, in that direction."

Jack's heart pounded with excitement. Now he could talk with his friend and mentor freely, uninhibited by any bugging device from Aster's secret operatives.

He grabbed Rhonda's hand, and said, "Come on dear, let's go find Nathan Kelly."

—⊸⫘∿⫘⊶—

For several days the members of the Bride exchanged stories of revival, miracles and healing. There were so many accounts to tell, all the libraries in the world couldn't contain the books required to hold all the experiences.

The fellowship they enjoyed was inspiring, and the peace and safety, sublime. There was no sin nature, no envy, no jealousy and no sickness; nothing but freedom to celebrate and worship God. If it weren't for the reminder of their desert surroundings, it would've felt like heaven had come to Earth.

Every day they were fed by angels who appeared with a cake of baked bread and a jar of water. During the day, a cloud covered the camp to protect them from the sun. At night, a pillar of fire lit up the sky to provide them with heat in the cool desert nights. They had nothing to fear or need. God was their sole provider.

Whenever stories were exchanged about the goodness and deliverance of God, celebration and praise would break out in pockets around the camp.

The teachers of God's Word continued to receive further revelation about the events they had experienced, and went from group to group teaching the people and shedding light on the Scriptures.

As the days went by, everyone came to the understanding that they were brought there for protection. Their stay would last until the remaining judgments had passed, a total of three and one-half years.

That time would pass quickly, however, with the abundance of truth they would learn and the time they would spend in prayer. Mindful of their brothers and sisters in Christ who would live or die under the wrath of a frustrated dictator, the Bride spent hours on her knees interceding for the remnant of Christians.

Whitney, Shayne and Laura never missed a day to pray for those *they* had led to Christ and who would have serious hardships to face in the future...especially their beloved friend, Bob Jansen.

CHAPTER 81

Malloy laid low in Washington for four weeks.

He decided to wait until the furor over the assassination had died down.

Sadly, Grub and Brad had been captured and were executed in the same fashion they attempted to eliminate the president. They were shot through the head. Malloy would miss them. They were good men. He had a twinge of concern, however, for where they were now...heaven or hell? His interest in this surprised him.

With the road blocks all cleared, Malloy and Cap' left Washington under the cover of the dark canopy that started each day at four in the afternoon and lifted at midnight.

They were heading for Canterton, Virginia.

"What are these people like?" Cap' asked in the car.

"You mean the preacher and his wife?"

"Yeah."

Malloy smiled. "The kindest people you'll ever meet."

"You seem pretty fond of them."

"They saved my life and kept me until I was strong enough to be on my way."

"You sure they were Christians?"

"That's what made the difference. You ever meet a real Christian, Cap'?"

"Nope, I grew up in the army. Mom was a major and Dad was a colonel. We never had time for religion. Too busy moving around from base to base, defending the country, trying to keep peace in the world. During that time, I only heard that Christians were always against this or against that—"

"It all depends on *what* they're against. I served under three presidents while I observed their political involvement. No one in Washington liked them and neither did I until I wound up on their doorstep by accident. The stereotypes about them were wrong, Cap'."

"So what did you find out?"

"That they're not the militant extremists they're made out to be, at least not the Mitchells. They're loving, compassionate, and really believe in their God."

"And?" Cap' prodded.

"Well…this may sound weird, but they have this strange ability to understand everything that's been happening in the world. Their Bible appears to have all these predictions in it—and I mean *specific* predictions—about Aster, the world government and these incredible disasters. They even knew about the blood in the Atlantic Ocean before it happened. The preacher told me about the things that would happen next, and it all happened just like he said."

"What things?"

"Well, there's the hail storm we had in Idaho, the asteroid that hit Canada, and this crazy darkness we get every day that covers the sun and the stars. It's all there in the Bible."

"Go on," Cap' urged.

"After the big quake, Pastor Mitchell showed me some incredible things about Aster and Drakon."

"Like what?"

"They're mentioned in the Bible. You wouldn't believe how many predictions there are about them. The preacher showed them to me."

"You think this Bible of theirs says anything about Aster rising from the dead?"

"Maybe. I can't remember, but I'm sure it's in there. There was so much to absorb I couldn't get it all, and I was in a hurry to leave."

"So that's why we're going back, isn't it? To see what'll happen next?"

"There's no where else to go, and I've got to know if our effort to kill Aster was all in vain. Jack Mitchell is the only man who can tell me."

———

Bob Jansen was wearing his NWF uniform on the other side of the campus. He was with Carl and Blake on a covert mission, witnessing to a few soldiers whom Blake knew to be backslidden Christians.

While they were talking, another soldier ran up and hailed them. "Did you hear the news?" he asked, trying to catch his breath.

"What news?" Blake asked.

"The members from that Bride cult we've been watching have disappeared. It happened two hours ago. We arrested some of them today and took them to jail. They just vanished like a mist."

Bob groaned. "Are you sure?"

"I'm sure all right. My friend, Lance, and another soldier were guarding this woman who had given birth to a little boy. Vince Kobrin was there and took the baby. He told Lance and the other two guys to guard her until everyone left and then kill her. Somehow they fell asleep without realizing it, and when they woke up she was gone."

Bob's heart began to pound. "Who was your friend guarding?"

"Some chick named Whitney Conner."

CHAPTER 82

"Whitney!…Whitney! Where are you?"

No one answered. It was the same at Shayne and Laura's apartment. The only place for Bob to go now was the Mitchells' house.

He ran as fast as he could, praying along the way that it hadn't come—the time when the Bride would depart.

It never dawned on him that the stepped-up monitoring of the World Federation Intelligence might have been the prelude to her being taken away and protected from Aster. But he didn't want to accept that. Not yet. Not until he was sure. Perhaps they were all at the Mitchells' for a meeting, or with Whitney while she was having her baby.

That's it! Whitney could be having the baby at the Mitchells' and they're all over there to assist her. With renewed hope he headed toward the familiar road of his pastor, but moved cautiously to avoid soldiers or intelligence officers who might recognize him. He was a deserter now, wanted by the law.

As he approached the Mitchells' street, he found the neighborhood swarming with WFI agents, many accompanied by soldiers. They were at the door of every home on the street. There was no way he could get close enough to find his friends.

Bob retreated behind a parked truck where he could safely observe. He noticed a couple of men walking out of the widow Johnson's house, next door to the Mitchells'. Maybe he could sneak to her place and find out what was happening.

He doubled back and ran around to the alley which divided the back yards through the middle of the block. The path was clear all the way to her yard. He approached cautiously and snuck into the bushes near the widow's back porch.

⸻⁂⸻

Martha Johnson peered through her front curtains, watching the agents and soldiers continue their search for Jack and Rhonda Mitchell.

They had just been through her house.

Suddenly, she heard a clicking noise from her kitchen. "What's all that racket about?" she said aloud. Living alone, she talked to herself often.

As she entered the kitchen, Martha saw a pebble strike her window. "Land's sakes!" she said, peering into the backyard to locate the prankster. She spotted no one until she saw the bushes move. She stared at the foliage a while until a familiar face appeared, peeking through the branches. Their eyes connected and he smiled at her.

"Why it's that young Jansen fellow I met at the Mitchells'."

He waved and she waved back.

He stepped out of the bushes and signed to her with his hands for her to open the back door.

She motioned him toward the house and went to the kitchen door to unlock it.

"Come in, boy, come in!" she whispered, holding the door open. Bob darted across the yard from his cover and stepped inside.

Martha quickly locked the door behind him and pulled the blinds shut.

"Dear boy, what are you doing here?" she asked, giving him a hug.

"I need a place to hide, Mrs. Johnson."

"Child, I thought you'd be out of the state by now. They've got an APB out on you for desertion."

"I know, but I couldn't leave, not until Whitney's baby was born. I wanted to say goodbye to her and the Mitchells before I left. Do you know where they are? I've got to find them."

"I'm afraid you're too late. Aster's men have been crawling around here like ants on a drop of honey. They've been looking for the Mitchells ever since the Lord came and swept them off somewhere."

Bob groaned, "You mean it's happened? They're really gone?"

"That's right, child."

"But, Whitney...what about Whitney? She was due to have that baby any day now."

"She did have it, right there in the Reverend's house. But that wicked Kobrin came with his soldiers and took the child as soon as it was born. I saw him walk out of the house with it. Then the Mitchells were taken away in handcuffs by the soldiers."

"And Whitney? What'd they do with her?"

"I only saw two soldiers leave the house, but no Whitney. I was afraid they'd done something awful to her, but when I went over to see, there wasn't a soul in the house anywhere."

Bob plopped on the floor with tears in his eyes. "Oh, Mrs. Johnson, if only I had paid attention when Whitney tried to tell me about this. I was a stubborn fool. If I could do it over again, if the clock could turn back, I would serve God like they did. But, here I sit...without Whitney, without the Mitchells, and without Shayne and Laura. If I had listened, I'd be with them now...out there."

Martha laid her hand on Bob's shoulder to comfort him. "That makes two of us, child. If I had responded to the

Mitchells' attempts to be neighborly, I might have been saved early enough to be ready for the wedding with Jesus."

Bob smiled at Martha and wiped the tears off his cheeks. He stared at the old clock on her mantle as it chimed three o'clock in the afternoon. "I know Pastor Mitchell told me this would come," he said, "but I'm not prepared for it. I guess I'll just have to accept the responsibility for my own folly and go on. There's so much coming yet to deal with, I can't look back now."

He gazed up at Martha from the floor and stood up.

"From now on," he said, taking her soft wrinkled hands, "I'll spend the rest of my life encouraging others to hang in with their faith. Before Pastor Mitchell left, he told me the trials and the judgments will only get worse, and the temptation to quit would be our greatest temptation."

"But he also told me," Martha added, "that God wouldn't let us be tested beyond anything we couldn't handle. Besides, we still have each other."

"You're right, we do. And I have *other* friends, too, that need us now. You up for taking in some boarders?"

"Why of course, child. I've got plenty of room in this old house."

Bob gave her a hug.

Martha liked this young man.

CHAPTER 83

Later that night, after the neighborhood search had ended, Martha and Bob had just finished eating in the kitchen when a knock came at the front door.

Bob jumped from his chair, "Someone's here!"

"Sit down, child, I'll see who it is. If it's Kobrin, hide in that pantry over there."

Martha went to the darkened front end of the house and peeked through the curtains of her dining room. She could barely make out the two figures, silhouetted against the faint glow of the street light.

A gray-bearded man paced the floor of her porch, watching the street. The shorter man continued to knock on the door.

The Holy Spirit gently whispered to Martha, *"Let them in."*

She turned on the porch light and opened the door with the security chain in place. "May I help you, boys?"

The gray-bearded man stepped from the edge of the porch and into the light. "Pardon me ma'am," he said, "I'm a friend of the Mitchells, next door. I rang their doorbell twice and no one answered. Could you tell me, please, if they still live there?"

"No sir, I'm afraid they don't. They left town."

"Could you tell me where I might find them, ma'am? Did they leave a forwarding address?...a phone number?"

"Before I answer any of your questions, mister, might I ask you one?"

"Sure."

"Do you work for the WFI?"

"No, ma'am," he replied, "I assure you, I don't work for the government. We're just passing through and stopped to see a couple of old friends. They helped me a year ago when I was down on my luck. Took care of me for several months. I just wanted to see them again."

Martha smiled. "Sounds like something the Mitchells would do." She closed the door, unhooked the chain and opened it again to let them in.

"You boys look tired," she said, closing the door behind them. "Have you eaten anything yet, uh, Mr...."

"Malloy's the name ma'am."

"Cliff!" Bob shouted, walking out from the kitchen.

"Bob!" Malloy said. "Thank God there's someone here that I know. I was beginning to think I'd never see any of you guys again."

Martha looked on with delight and thanked the Holy Spirit for not letting her turn these men away.

"Martha," Bob said, "Cliff is on *our* side. I remember when Pastor Mitchell was keeping him in his home. You were recovering from some serious injuries weren't you, Cliff?"

"That's right. I owe the Mitchells my life."

"You and a hundred other people in Canterton," Martha said. She looked past Malloy at the man standing behind him. "And who might you be, young man?" she asked warmly.

"Oh!" Cliff said, "Where are my manners? Bob, Mrs. Johnson, this is Cap'."

"Nice to meet you, son," Martha said, "Why don't you all have a seat, please." She herded the men into the living room. "Let me get some lights on in here, and I'll fix you a plate of leftovers."

"If it's not too much trouble, ma'am?" Cap' said.

"Not at all, child, not at all."

"So Cliff," Bob began, as Martha went to the kitchen, "Where have you been? Jack and Rhonda were worried about you when you disappeared. Even more when they heard you shot Aster."

Malloy looked at the floor, "I was a jerk for leaving like that. And, yeah, I shot Aster, but it didn't stop him did it?"

"It had to happen according to Scripture," Bob said. "It's just weird that you're the one who did it."

Malloy scooted forward in his chair. "I need your help, Bob. The Mitchells are the first people that made sense to me. Do you know where they are?"

Mrs. Johnson entered the room with a plate of cookies. "Well," Bob said, grabbing two cookies off the tray, "it's kind of a long story. It'll take some explaining. Do you have to be anywhere soon?"

Malloy cast a smile at Cap', and then at Bob. "Kid, you're looking at a couple of world-class fugitives here. We've got all the time in the world."

CHAPTER 84

It was two days after the Bride and her manchild disappeared.

The staff of the World Federation Headquarters in Jerusalem still smarted over the failed assignment. Aster had finally cooled down and decided to forego any disciplinarian action since every agent reported the sighting of an angelic abduction. Obviously, circumstances beyond their control.

Today, however, his hope was renewed by a discovery made from one of their orbiting satellites.

Aster summoned a meeting with his chief military advisers.

The Air Force chief of staff began the meeting pointing to a large map. "Mr. President, our satellites have picked up activity in a deserted quarter of the Arabian Peninsula, the Rub' al Khali. It's located at the crossline sector of twenty degrees latitude and fifty degrees longitude.

"What type of activity, General?"

He handed Aster a file of photographs. "These are satellite pictures of the first day these people appeared in that region."

"People?" Aster replied.

"They number in the millions. We've never seen a population of this magnitude, not in any city."

"Are they armed?" Aster asked, as he studied the photos.

"No sir, not a trace of weaponry."

"This *all* desert, General?"

"All of it."

"How're they surviving?"

"We don't know, sir. After those pictures were taken, a large cloud formation appeared covering a hundred square miles." He pointed to another enlarged photograph beside the map. "As you look at these pictures, those same clouds appear to be glowing at night...like they're on fire."

Aster sat back and rubbed his chin. "If any of you planned to strategically hide a population that size from a military invasion, where on this planet would you put them?"

The officers looked at each other and then at the world map. "Well, sir," the army general replied, "if you had the provisions and equipment to accomplish such a feat, that location would be as good as any. The conditions are extremely hot and arid, but with this unusual cloud formation it could be tolerable. Temperatures at night can drop as low as twenty degrees below zero, but if that really is fire in those clouds, it might be enough to keep them warm. There's one thing that baffles me though..."

"What's that, General?"

"How so many people could survive without livestock or crops in a non-agricultural environment."

Aster rose from his chair with the photos in his hands. "Gentlemen, these people are from the Bride society we arrested two days ago and then disappeared. They probably have the babies, too. I don't know how they got there, but they've managed to get provisions through some mysterious power they must have."

"What do we do, sir?" the naval Chief asked.

"They've done us a favor, Admiral. Now that we have them in one place, it makes our job easier to eliminate them."

"But how?" the army chief asked. "Under the new laws of the world constitution, the World Federation Council had every nuclear and chemical weapon on the planet, banned and deactivated. Without bombs or aerial artillery, an air strike is out of the question. Even our naval power has been reduced to carrying conventional weapons with jeeps and tanks. We can't even use the fire power of the ship's big guns."

"We'll just have to work with the conventional weapons we have, and send in our ground troops," Aster replied. "Can we drop them in from the air?"

The Air Force chief of staff leaned forward, "We could if we had that kind of air power at our disposal. Unfortunately, our bases and runways are still being repaired. Most of our planes have been grounded."

"How about choppers?"

"Bludgeoned by the hail, sir. We haven't had time to replace the blades. To attack a number of people that size would require an army of ground troops, but our ability to transport them is limited by what's available to fly, and from where."

"Mr. President," the admiral said, pointing to the map. "We still have enough vessels in the Pacific and Indian Ocean ports to carry some of our troops to that area. We can take them to the closest strategic drop-off point in the Persian Gulf. One located here at Abu Dhabi and the other off the coast of Oman, near the Kuria Muria Islands."

"Can we use some of our planes to fly more troops into the Pacific and Indian Ocean ports?" Aster inquired.

"It can be done, sir," the Air Force general replied.

"Then let's do it! Send every available soldier you can. Since the Bride has no weaponry, we won't have to match their numbers with soldiers to eliminate them. A relatively simple assignment, wouldn't you agree?"

"It'll happen, sir," the marine chief said.

Aster nodded and said in a stern voice, "I want no excuses this time. Let's finish the job we should've finished the first time."

CHAPTER 85

The sand trembled beneath the members of the Bride. "Look!" someone shouted from a nearby group of saints.

Across the desert of the Rub' al Khali, a cloud of dust covered the horizon from every direction heading for the camp of the Bride.

"It's okay, don't worry!" Jack Mitchell called to the people around him.

Shouts of encouragement rippled through every quarter as the apostles cried out, "God is our Banner! Stand and watch the hand of the Lord who is mighty to save!"

Out of the clouds of dust, an army of World Federation troops descended on them like a flood. They had come from the north and southeast regions of the Rub' al Khali with tanks, trucks, jeeps and desert vehicles.

To the reasoning mind, it looked hopeless. But an amazing calm permeated the mass of saints as words of assurance continued to spread throughout the camp.

"What's going to happen now?" Whitney asked Pastor Mitchell. "What do the prophecies say?"

"We'll be safe," he replied, as he watched the tanks roll toward them. "Revelation 12 says that Satan will spew water from his mouth like a river to overtake us, but the earth will deliver us by swallowing that river. Watch the ground and you'll see."

As Jack looked across the desert sands he could begin to distinguish the soldier's faces. Any time now, he thought.

He was right. The ground suddenly rumbled above the clatter of approaching vehicles, while the cloud above the camp grew pitch black and clapped with sporadic bursts of thunder.

"What's happening?" Whitney asked, as she grabbed Jack's arm to steady herself.

"Don't be concerned," he said, gazing up at the lightning, "it's not for us but for them." He pointed at the troops.

The army continued to advance, ignoring the menacing cloud, until they stopped to level their rifles at the saints.

Suddenly, bolts of lightning struck the ground around the entire perimeter of the camp and blinded the soldiers. Before a shot could be fired, the earth split open with a crevice that encircled the hundred square miles of the Bride company.

The fissure grew wider, spreading out away from the saints toward the line of soldiers. The screams of the soldiers were muffled by the screeching vehicles tumbling over the edge into a chasm of molten, burning rock below.

The widening mouth of the circling fissure caught up to every soldier who had turned to run. Alive, they fell into the steaming, burning pit where the jaws of hell waited hungrily for them.

God's judgment was swift and complete. There wasn't a soldier in sight. The earth closed her mouth on its victims and left no trace of their existence.

The churning black cloud above stopped thundering and dropped a light shower on the cloud of dust, leaving a wet, fresh scent in the air.

Jack dropped to his knees with uplifted hands. The sea of faces behind him followed like a stack of dominoes, all praising their great God who delivered them.

The chiefs of staff sat in stunned silence as they watched their army blip off the screen of their tactical satellite monitors. They were gone, machinery and all, without a trace.

They summoned Aster and Drakon to inform them of the outcome.

"We're not going to waste any more time or soldiers on these people," Aster snarled. "They can just stay in that desert until they rot and their bones bleach white."

"Do you want us to keep monitoring them, sir?" the Admiral asked.

"Yes. In case they decide to come back."

Aster angrily paced the floor and then turned to the group. "The remnant of Christians on our soil are cut off from the Bride's influence. With their numbers diminished and their power hitters gone, we can hunt them down before they have a chance to regroup. We need a vehicle, however, to flush them out and I have a plan that can achieve that goal. Drakon...?"

"Yes, sir."

"I want you to locate the best sculptors we have. We're going to build a statue for the New World Order."

Drakon nodded and smiled.

"Gentlemen," he said to his chiefs of staff, "we've lost a battle today, but not the war. Join me for dinner and I'll show you a plan that will force every Christian and Jew into a trap they can't escape."

CHAPTER 86

While the effects of the judgments still lingered, the brief reprieve from new catastrophes enabled Aster's empire to regain control and get the machinery of progress in motion.

Drakon, now Chief Director of Commerce and head of the World Church, ordered a statue of Aster to be made in his honor.

"Your image on Mount Tabor nears completion, Reuben," Drakon said as he entered the office.

"It looks great, John. The way it towers above the valley of Jezreel is stunning."

"It was clever of you to select the site of the Transfiguration. An excellent way to trod on the name of the Nazarene."

"I'm destined to dethrone him," Aster replied. "There can be only one god and that's me. But I have another reason for picking that site. Tabor was likened by a prophet to my favorite king in history, Nebuchadnezzar. I had a plaque of that prophecy made for my wall, which says:

> *One will come who is like Tabor among the mountains...*

"Many times in the past, I've felt a bond with this Babylonian king. Since the prophecy is about him, I thought Mount Tabor would be an appropriate location for the Nebuchadnezzar of the twenty-first century."

"Appropriate indeed. I like the concept."

"How are the ceremonial preparations coming?"

"The committee informed me that personal invitations went out yesterday to every government official."

Aster nodded and walked to the window of his Jerusalem suite. He stared at the northern horizon. "This statue will become the holiest of all other images among the gods of men. We'll make it the only recognized symbol to embody the ideologies of our New World Order. Once we unveil it and the role it plays, we'll have every Christian at our mercy."

———

The day of the dedication arrived with the largest gathering in the history of man. Hundreds of thousands of people had come to witness the event in honor of their world president. They covered Tabor like ants down the sides of the mountain and out through the plains of Jezreel—also known as Megiddo.

Government and religious officials on every level, from the top down, were present. The people who couldn't make it gathered around the nearest radio or television, wherever they could be found. The government-controlled networks showed nothing else but this historical occasion—*live*.

In the third world, for those too poor to afford such equipment, regional receivers were set up on giant screens for the masses to watch via satellite.

Speakers and giant screens were set up down the mountainside of Tabor and throughout the valley so that everyone who attended could see and hear what was happening on top, at the foot of the statue.

Security choppers swept the area with floodlights as they flew past the towering monstrosity wrapped with canvas and cable wires. Aster arrived on his own helicopter which touched down on Tabor near the statue. As he stepped out and waved at the cameras, the crowds roared, many wept, and others bowed down in adoring worship.

"This is inspiring, John," Aster said, as he gazed over the valley. Everywhere his eyes could see, the horizon was dotted with a rainbow of colors in a sea of faces.

"They've come to honor you, Reuben," Drakon smiled. "Even Lucifer will be here."

Aster looked up for visible signs of his master. Already Lucifer's presence had darkened the skies with a concentrated force of his high-ranking principalities from the nether world. The kingdom of darkness controlled the air freely with the Holy Spirit no longer restraining them. Nothing hindered the permeating doses of deception they could unleash on the unsuspecting minds of a gullible world.

Aster and Drakon stepped up to the special platform built at the base of the statue. The veiled image dwarfed them in size like two mice at the foot of a man.

"It's time," Aster said, sitting down on his elevated throne. "Let the ceremony begin."

Drakon smiled and walked to the mike.

"Citizens of the New World Order!" he shouted, "Thank you for coming, and welcome to the unveiling!"

The crowd roared with an applause that echoed off the mountains and through the expanse of the valley below. Drakon raised his hand and a wave of silence fell over the masses.

"Never in the history of man," he continued, "have so many people witnessed the incredible miracle of a resurrection. Our beloved world president, Reuben Aster, stands before you as one who has died and returned from the dead."

Again the crowd roared. Aster stood and took a bow before his admirers.

Drakon raised his hand to silence them. "On behalf of our beloved president, we proudly present to you, the new symbol and icon of our Federation! Release the veil!"

The orchestra began to play with a hypnotic beat that echoed throughout the valley and on every television and radio in the world.

The cables surrounding the statue were snapped by strategically placed explosives; and the canvas was lifted with wires by four helicopters.

The crowd gasped as the search lights lit up the shimmering gold-plated giant. It was a masterpiece, towering on top of the mountain at a height of one hundred and fifty feet. The resemblance it bore of Aster was remarkable; and the number 666 was engraved on its forehead.

As it faced the south with outstretched arms toward the capital throne in Jerusalem, the computerized beams of stage lights bounced off the image, casting mirror-like reflections into the valley below.

People from every tribe, tongue and nation who witnessed the event, fell down and worshiped the image of gold that Drakon had created. Even those who watched or listened to the ceremony from their homes, bowed and worshiped the image; everyone, that is, but Christians and God-fearing Jews.

Drakon called again for silence from the worshiping crowd and continued his speech. "As you know, we have seen undisputable proof that Reuben Aster is a god and the ruling king of this world. Who is like Aster? Who can make war with him? Search the planet and you'll find no one his equal. Therefore, worship *him* and Lucifer who gave him his authority and power!"

A rumble of whispers rolled through the masses. Drakon expected it.

"I know," he continued, "that the traditions and gods of your fathers may bring conflict to your hearts. But I'm prepared to demonstrate that Aster is a god above all the gods of your ancestors. Watch and behold the power of your president and of Lucifer."

Drakon raised his hands and gazed into the dark sky. "Lucifer, Oh Radiant One and god of this world," he said, "glorify your servant this day. Forever seal in the minds of the skeptics that Aster is the chosen one, the Messiah of the New World Order."

CHAPTER 87

Lucifer answered Drakon by fire.

A swirling pillar blazed into full view out of the smog-hazed air before the golden image.

The crowd gasped, and everyone whose eyes had been glued to the television sat forward in their seats.

The fiery pillar hovered above the people on Mount Tabor until a funnel dropped like a tornado, and touched down at the foot of the mountain. The swirling fire lingered several minutes while flashes of cameras pulsated across the sea of faces. Then, it retreated back to the sky and disappeared.

Drakon called again for everyone's attention. "There's more!" he declared. "From this day forward you must know that Aster rules supreme as sovereign over all peoples, tongues and nations! There can be no doubt in your minds that he is the true god of this world, the son of Lucifer."

Drakon sensed the crowd hanging on every word and continued. "For centuries your fathers have fashioned idols after the images of their gods; but I ask you today, have any of those images ever breathed the breath of life or seen with their eyes, spoke with their tongues or heard with their ears?

Who among you has ever seen, in person, the very god *your* idols represent?

"Today, I testify that the god whom I serve stands before you in *flesh* and *blood*, and has been resurrected from the dead. He was and was not, and now is. Not only do we see him in person, but this image, unveiled before you tonight, has been fashioned in his likeness and will be greater than the images of the gods your fathers have made that neither speak, nor see, nor hear!"

Drakon turned and faced the towering image with outstretched arms and shouted, "Behold and observe! Image of Aster...*live!*"

As Drakon blew on the statue, hordes of demons—invisible to the eyes of the people—covered the image like a swarm of bats. The sound of stretching and shrieking metal echoed through the valley below.

A gasp of terror rippled across the masses. Today, something only thought possible through the special effects of movies was happening before their eyes. On the top of Tabor, an inanimate object had come to life!

A ghostly red hue of light appeared in the image's eyes. The one-hundred-and-fifty foot giant lifted its legs and moved its arms. Its head turned, like it was scanning the valley, and its chest began to expand and deflate. It took a deep breath and then said in a deep roaring voice,

"I am the image of Aster who is the servant of Lucifer. Worship me and you worship Aster. Worship Aster and you worship Lucifer who sent him, and gave him his throne and his power. Kneel before your king and your god. Worship him."

CHAPTER 88

The image on Mount Tabor generated an awe-inspiring fear of Aster throughout the viewing, listening world; all except the Christians and Jews who worshiped the God of Abraham. They had refused to attend the ceremony since their beliefs forbade the worship of idols.

They were, however, tuned into their radios or watching the televised broadcast to see what Aster was up to.

Aster savored this moment as the masses remained on their knees before him. He thought of the two objectives being accomplished right now through this demonstration of power.

First, his godhood would create a universal unity by securing every religion under one. People inherently needed a god to worship and he knew that. But the myriads of gods and religious belief systems pervading the world were at the heart of so many factions and wars. By bringing all these religions into the worship of his image, it would become easier to keep peace in the world and focus their energies on the recovery and agenda of the New World Order.

Second, he knew that as long as there were monotheistic Christians and Jews, they would never yield to worshiping any God but their own. That would undermine his plans for religious unity. To remove this threat he would make a universal law that no man could worship or serve any other god but himself through this image. This would force the Christians and Jews to commit treason and sacrilege against his very throne and godhood. Not only would his law chase them out of hiding, his economic plan would nail the lid on their coffins.

Aster now walked to the mike to address the people himself. When the crowd saw him, they remained on their knees in worship.

"Citizens and comrades of the World Federation, please rise." As he raised his arms, the statue towering behind him matched his every move in speech as well as physical motion. The people gawked in awe at this phenomenon, dazzled even more by this feat than the earlier display of fire. It appeared that the image and Aster were one.

"I have special guests with me," Aster continued, "that I wish to introduce. On my left, the ten-member council of the World Federation to whom I am indebted for this great moment in history. They have made me their king and I, in turn, appoint them to be the ten most prominent world kings before you."

The crowd applauded.

"To my right, the twelve-member council and archbishops of the World Church. They're here to endorse this event and to confirm the authority Lucifer bestowed on me. I am also indebted to them for this day. They have courageously stepped forward in a world of diverse religions and believed in me, and in Lucifer who sent me. These twelve men, I bless and appoint as messengers of my doctrine and the World Church."

Again applause.

"Finally, the head of the World Church, John Drakon. I appoint him before you as the prophet and right hand of my authority. There will be no other like him who is closer to me in rank and authority. Only I will be greater. Please honor him today."

Again applause.

"Receive each of these men in the way that I have ordained them. Honor them and you'll honor me. Receive them and you'll receive me."

Aster raised his right fist, as did the image, and shouted, "To our future and the New World Order!"

The crowd exploded with cheers. The bait was taken, and the hook was set. Satan's hour and the power of darkness had come into full play.

"I promise you," Aster continued, "as your king and your god, that I will restore love, peace, and harmony from the ashes of this broken world. This image that moves before you is not for me. It was created to help *me* serve *you*, the people; and will be the icon of a free world. A world free of war, free of factions, and soon…free of Christians and Jews who have been the cause for our suffering."

The people applauded, accepting it all; intoxicated by the deception controlling their minds as the web-weaving influence of Satan wound them tighter and tighter into his net.

Aster smiled at Drakon and raised his hand for a final word at this phase of the ceremony. "I have been granted godhood by Lucifer who has raised me from the dead. But I am only the firstfruits of that godhood. You, too, can have eternal life and become gods yourself. I have returned from the dead to teach you how to acquire this. Then you may come to know and serve my god, the Radiant One, whose name is Lucifer."

At this, the orchestra began to play. The crowd cheered and celebrated as Aster, swelling with pride and arrogance, stood with his arms outstretched in victory. He smiled upon the masses that covered Tabor and the valley below. Behind him, the golden image moved simultaneously, duplicating every motion he made, down to every minute expression of face and speech.

Everything had come together for Aster. The tide had been turned to his favor. What could possibly stop him now? He held the whole world in his hands.

CHAPTER 89

Aster gave the mike back to Drakon and sat down.

The image stood motionless when Drakon addressed the people. "On behalf of our president, the ten-kingdom alliance of the World Federation, and the World Church, I now bring you the laws of the New World Order."

A murmur ran through the crowd. Drakon continued. "To lead a broken world into a better future will require extreme measures and tough decisions. You must understand that we face insurmountable odds to save our planet. The worst is not over. Fierce storms remain on the horizon that could send us back into the dark ages, and possibly extinction. We must pull together as one voice, one force and one strength, tolerating no gray areas or division. Who among you wishes to rise above this rubble and build an empire that will extend for generations to come?"

The crowd responded in favor of survival.

"Then," Drakon continued, "we must be serious about implementing laws to accomplish that objective. Therefore, the laws of the World Federation are as follows:

"At nine in the morning, twelve noon and three in the afternoon, everyone must bow and worship the golden image. Since our survival relies on the favor and blessing of Lucifer and Aster, we must pay homage to them through the image and pray for help. Our cameras will be permanently stationed to televise the image. A brief teaching of our doctrine and ideology will be aired every half hour, 24 hours a day. Aster's image will teach you these truths. Each day there will be a new doctrine. You must listen to this half-hour presentation by television, radio or internet and observe these teachings, once they've been taught.

"Every synagogue, church and temple in the world is now owned by the World Church and will be used as permanent station houses for our New World Forces. Able-bodied men and women, from the ages of sixteen to forty, must register at the nearest station house for induction into the military.

"We will also recruit and train men and women for a priesthood in the World Church. To apply, you must go to the nearest station house for an interview. All priests or clergy from the old order of other gods or sects must cross-train into the priesthood of the World Church.

"Next, as chief economist and director of Commerce, I have supervised the creation of a numerical system that will serve us in our domestic needs. As you know, disasters have ravaged our planet and contributed to the escalating problem of famine and starvation. To curtail this problem, we are refining the cashless economy to include a structure of socialized medicine and world distribution of food and trade goods. No more will any nation, country or race be allowed to prosper above another. We have devised a new technology through cyberbanking that will allow us to monitor any and all transactions of trade and purchases.

"To do this requires every man, woman and child to receive the insertion of a bio-chip under the skin of their right hand or forehead. It is a microchip used to access every individual's financial data for debiting or crediting. Receiving this chip will be an easy one-step process that is no more complicated than getting a shot. Once inserted, the chip is invisible to the naked eye. In every store, scanners will access your assigned numeric code that is stored in the chip."

Drakon pointed up at the statue behind him. "Notice the visible marking of the number 666 on the forehead of the image. That number represents three sets of six-digit numbers that will become your personal identification number—or PIN. For example your number could be something like 279503...dash...302375...dash...450068.

"Due to the decreasing size of the world's population, we can assign this numeric equation to every person. This number and chip will replace all cash debit cards. Every monetary transaction you make in the future will be processed through this chip. No one will be able to buy or sell without it."

A rumble of murmurs rose through the crowd as Drakon continued.

"Hear me out! We have no other choice if we want to survive. We *must* streamline the banking and trade system. There will be a transition period of three-months to implement this. Everyone must go to the nearest station house to receive their chip and PIN. When three months expires, anyone without the chip will be suspected of treason and, if convicted, executed immediately.

"Due to the shortage of food and supplies, we're also calling for a moratorium on all childbirth. We can allow no more pregnancies until supply moves ahead of demand. When domestic production supersedes consuming at a comfortable lead, we'll reevaluate our conditions to see if we can lift the ban. Until then, birth control is law. Accidental pregnancy will require mandatory abortion.

"Finally, if you know of, or discover anyone who prays to or worships any other god other than our president, Reuben Aster, you must submit their names to the WFI office at the station houses in your local communities. It is the law. If you're found guilty of ignoring this law, you will be regarded as an accomplice to aiding and abetting the enemy. The punishment for this crime is death.

"Again, let me remind you, significant progress requires significant laws and strict compliance to those laws. Disregard for the law will be met with swift judgment."

CHAPTER 90

They came out of nowhere!

Two men in sackcloth and ashes appeared on the platform before Drakon.

Satan hissed.

The cameramen aimed their cameras.

And Drakon stared in bewilderment.

Suddenly an angel appeared in midair, circling the image of Aster. He shouted in a thunderous voice to the people below,

> "Fear God and exalt him! For now is his hour
> of judgment! Worship the Maker of heaven and earth,
> the sea and the fountains of water."

Aster snarled at the angel's intrusion as it flew off repeating the warning. He turned and glared at the two strangers. "Who are you?" he asked.

Malloy and Cap' stared at the TV with Bob and Martha.

"It's unbelievable!" Cap' said, shaking his head. "How could anyone follow this guy? Isn't it obvious to these people what Aster's doing?"

"No bona fide Christian would ever succumb to these laws," Malloy said, "and that bio-chip...isn't that the mark of the beast?"

"Wait!" Martha said pointing to the television. "Look! Two men just appeared in front of Drakon!"

"Hey!" Bob said. "Where'd they come from?"

"It's them!" Martha shouted.

"Who?" Malloy asked.

"The witnesses!" she said. "Pastor Mitchell taught us from Revelation that two prophets would come to oppose the Antichrist."

"But that's suicide!" Malloy said, staring at the screen. "Drakon will cut those guys down with that fire trick of his."

"Don't worry," Martha said. "Drakon can't stop them. Pastor Mitchell told me they'll be around until Jesus comes back."

"Uh, oh," Bob said, "Drakon looks mad..."

Malloy jumped up and pointed at the TV. "See there, I told you he'd fry them."

Satan came beside Drakon and whispered in his ear, *"Destroy these men. They're prophets of the Nazarene!"*

Drakon nodded and raised his hand in the air. He called down fire from the sky.

The two men stood calmly as the fire struck and engulfed them in flames. When the fire dissolved not a hair on their bodies was singed.

CHAPTER 91

The two prophets ignored Drakon's fire and calmly faced the valley of Jezreel.

The TV cameras were running as they addressed the crowd. "We are servants of the Most High God who have witnessed the death, burial and resurrection of his son, Jesus Christ. Aster has blasphemed the name of our God, and declared death upon his saints. We call on you to renounce Aster, refuse the number of his name, and repent of your sins—"

Aster motioned to the guards and shouted, "Seize them!"

A squad of security men rushed up to grab the intruders, but before they got within reach, fire from the mouths of the prophets consumed them all. Their blackened, smoldering bodies crumbled to the ground.

Drakon and Aster gasped at this astonishing turn of events. "Shut those cameras off you idiots!" Aster screamed. He approached the prophets cautiously.

"Who are you!" he demanded. "What do you want!?"

"We want nothing, you son of perdition! We've come to bring light and our testimony through this hour of darkness for 1,260 days. We will predict your demise and remind you of the short duration of your reign."

Aster squinted and glared at the prophets. He glanced again at the smoking bodies around their feet.

"Two thousand years ago," they continued, "we stood on this very mountain and talked with the Lord concerning his death in Jerusalem. Though you have defiled this mountain with your image, Jesus Christ is still Lord. He will come with clouds for every eye to see and will put an end to your reign."

"It'll never happen!" Aster sneered, "now tell me...who are you?"

Drakon walked up behind Aster and whispered into his ear, "They're Moses and Elijah. Lucifer recognized them. The Nazarene must have sent them."

Aster winced. "Moses and Elijah?" he said aloud to the prophets. "Well, you weren't invited to this party, so leave us. Now!"

"We'll leave for the moment," Elijah replied, "but as surely as the Lord God of Israel lives, there will be no dew or rain except at our word."

Aster started to rebut them when they vanished from the mountain. He looked around and decided their visit was over. Before he regained control, however, another angel descended from heaven and flooded the valley with light.

The masses shielded their eyes as they watched it circle above the image, shouting,

"Fallen! Babylon the Great is fallen! For she seduced all the nations with the wine of her immorality!"

The angel left quickly and darkness cloaked the valley once more. Only the light of the image remained, still lit by the spotlights on Tabor.

Aster surveyed the sky and then motioned to the cameraman to turn their cameras back on.

He picked up the microphone, but was interrupted again.

The crowd gasped at another bright light in the sky flooding the valley. A third angel glowed and circled above them, shouting,

"Whoever worships Aster and his image or receives his chip, will drink of the wine of God's fury, poured full strength into the cup of his wrath. You will be tormented with burning sulfur before the holy angels, in the presence of the Lamb. And the smoke of your torment will rise eternally. You will have no relief day or night, for you worshiped the beast and his image, and received the number of his name."

Under his breath, Aster cursed God and the Church as the angel faded away toward the horizon. The valley grew dark once again.

This time the people buzzed with concern over the chain of warnings announced by the prophets and angels.

Aster quickly took charge to calm the crowds.

"Turn those cameras on again," he ordered.

"They've been on, sir," a cameraman replied.

Aster growled, but there wasn't time to vent. He had to pull it back, quick!

"Citizens of the World Federation, don't be alarmed by these sorcerers and their witchcraft. They're nothing more than glorified magicians. The angels were merely an illusion of their magic, sent to confuse you.

"I have sent them on their way, so stand fast in the promises we've shown you and abide by the new laws Drakon gave you tonight."

"We must rally together in purpose and heart, and I assure you…we *will* win and we will prosper. Now go in peace and be blessed. Long live the New World Order!"

———

As the ceremony ended on this dampened note, Lucifer quickly dispatched his demons to snatch away every seed of thought that had been planted by the two witnesses and angels. By the time the people returned to their homes and countries, they forgot the divine warnings and retained only what Lucifer wanted them to retain: belief in the awe-inspiring power and message of his servant, Aster.

CHAPTER 92

Aster's new laws became ratified and enforced.

Within the next two months, everyone had gone to their local station houses to receive the implanted bio-chip and their PIN number. Everyone, that is, but the Christians and the God-fearing Jews.

Cap' and Martha returned to the house from their walk downtown. They had gone to purchase more food on the last day of the three-month transition. Tomorrow they would be outlaws.

"It's spooky out there," Cap' said to Malloy and Bob as they entered the house. "The store was crawling with NWF soldiers. They watched how everyone bought their food. Most everyone had their hands or foreheads scanned for their bio-chips—"

"They stopped *us* at the door and asked us why we used cash," Martha said.

"What did you tell them?" Bob asked Cap'.

"I told them that my aunt here was sentimental about the old way and just wanted to do it for one last time."

"Aunt?" Malloy asked.

Martha jumped to Cap's defense. "Well, I *do* like the old way better."

"But, Aunt?" Malloy persisted.

"So I lied," Cap' said. "I'm not a Christian *yet*, you know?"

Bob smiled. "Hey, he said yet."

"Well, I'm thinking about it."

Martha gave Cap' a hug. "That's great, child."

Malloy had been confined to the house since he arrived. He was curious about the development of things in Aster's new world. "Anything else happen out there?" he asked.

"Well, I saw Mrs. Pritchard from down the street," Martha replied. "She was in front of us at the line in the store. Had her hand scanned, too. We were good friends in the past, but she never took to the revival and avoided me after I got saved and came out of hiding. I'm afraid she's been taken in by Aster like everyone else. When I tried to talk to her, she looked at me like I was a stranger. Her eyes were dark. We talked for a while, but I tell you, I wasn't talking to the Mrs. Pritchard I knew. It was spooky! It was her, but it wasn't her. The hardest part was she couldn't stop talking about Aster and how much she adored him."

"I noticed the same thing," Cap' said. "Anyone who used the chip to purchase their food was different from the others who still used their cash cards."

"There were *other* people that didn't use the chip?" Bob asked.

"A lot of them," Martha replied. "They must be Christians. I could tell from the gleam in their eyes."

"What about the soldiers?" Bob asked.

"Just like Mrs. Pritchard," Cap' replied, "darkness in their eyes. Very dark. Like one big pupil with no iris."

"Except the two young soldiers that stood behind us," Martha said. "I know *they* were Christians."

"Soldiers?" Bob perked up.

"Yes, two nice looking young men."

"It could be Blake and Carl," Bob said. "They rededicated their lives to Christ with me and Shayne Taylor. I wonder how they managed to keep from taking the chips?"

"Good question," Malloy said. "Maybe we should contact them and see how they're doing."

"And *soon* if today is the last day for cash cards. They can't possibly hide their identity in the heart of the enemy's camp. They'll have to take the chip or die."

"Maybe we can help," Cap' said. "Do they have any place to go?"

"I don't think so," Bob replied. "Their parents are dead and they have no family."

"We'll be their family," Martha said. "You boys go get them and bring them back here where it's safe."

"No place will be safe for long," Bob said. "But at least we can provide them with a home until we think of a way out. It won't be long before the soldiers start breaking down every door to find those who haven't received the chip."

"Let's wait until four when the darkness cloaks the sun," Malloy said. He looked at Bob. "Do you know where their quarters are?"

"Sure do."

Malloy glanced at Cap'. "You up for a little covert operation tonight?"

"Are you kidding? Let's go!"

CHAPTER 93

Whitney prayed in her tent for Bob.

She prayed mainly for him to hold up under the pressure to receive the mark of the beast. When she finished, she decided to locate Jack Mitchell to answer some questions for her.

She found him just finishing a conversation with a former member of the congregation. "Good morning, Pastor," she said.

"Morning Whitney, what can I do for you?"

"I suspect Aster is starting to make people take the mark, the number 666."

"You're probably right. We've been here for three months now and it's certainly within the timetable of prophecy. The technology for this mark was in place fifteen years ago. Nathan Kelly told us about it when cyberbanking gave birth to the cashless economy."

"What kind of technology?" she asked.

"A bio-chip as small as the lead tip on a pencil. They insert it under your skin where you can't see it. With the aid of scanners, every transaction can be processed through it. Nathan Kelly believed that the Antichrist would use that technology for his 666 system. "

"What would happen to a Christian if they buckled under the pressure to take it?" Whitney asked. "Doesn't the Bible say that no one can buy or sell without it?"

"Yes, it does."

"Then Christians will have no choice. They'll have to take it or die, right?"

"They'll die as a martyr for Jesus."

"But what if they receive the chip?"

"If a Christian did that, they'd have to denounce their allegiance to Christ and make Aster their lord and god."

"Like divorcing Jesus and marrying Aster?"

"That's essentially what antichrist means, *in the place of Christ*. And to replace Christ with Aster is to unite with the devil himself. Any man or woman who takes that chip, Christian or not, will open the door to demonic spirits that will gain access to their soul."

"So if a Christian buckles under the pressure and takes it, they'll disown Christ and forfeit their salvation for the right to buy and sell?"

"I'm afraid so."

Whitney frowned. "Then there's no turning back for them is there?"

"No turning back. Once they've sold out to the devil, they'll lose their capacity for conviction by the Holy Spirit. The only thing left for them will be the same judgment Aster gets in the end."

Whitney stared across the desert at the rays of the sun breaking through the clouds on the horizon.

"You're concerned about Bob, aren't you?" Jack asked.

"Yes. I tried so hard to tell him…"

"But, it was his own choices that left him behind."

"Yeah, I know. I guess I can only pray he'll tough it out."

"Then keep praying, Whitney. Your burden may be the Holy Spirit prompting you to intercede for him. I wouldn't be too concerned, though. The Bob Jansen I spent a few days with was a very determined young man who planned to serve Jesus, even to his death."

CHAPTER 94

Moses and Elijah went from continent to continent, prophesying doom and destruction on those who received the bio-chip.

In their journeys, they frequently struck the earth with plagues and turned water to blood. Whenever mobs of demon-possessed souls attacked them, they were met with the same fate as Aster's security guards—incinerated by fire from the mouth of the prophets.

With the Christians now forced to go underground, revival among the Gentile nations had all but come to a close. The two prophets were the only remaining light-bearers of the gospel who freely roamed the earth.

No one could touch them. Few dared to even try.

Their mission, however, went beyond just predictions of doom and destruction. These were time-honored prophets out of Israel's history. Their reputation from Scripture gave them influence over the lives of God-fearing Jews who, like the Christians, refused to worship Aster and take his chip.

Moses and Elijah had eyewitness credentials to proclaim that Jesus of Nazareth was truly the Jews' Messiah. Eyewitnesses because they had been with Jesus on the Mount of Transfiguration. They were with him when he rose from the dead in the garden tomb, and had announced his resurrection to the women who had brought spices for his body. They were there, on the Mount of Olives, when Christ ascended. And they told the disciples that this same Jesus would come back the way they saw him ascend.

Their claim as God's prophets was authenticated by the *signs* and *wonders* they performed, similar to those they had performed in the Old Testament. This opened the hearts of many Jews to their message.

Moses and Elijah were constantly on the move, nation to nation and city to city, encouraging all Christians to be faithful to the end. After they completed their mission around the world, they spent the remainder of their days among the Jews in Israel. They went from town to town, kibbutz to kibbutz and city to city, baptizing those who believed into the name of the Lord Jesus Christ. But not every Jew believed the good news of Christ. Those who rejected the prophet's message informed the WFI of the conversions among their fellow Jews, even turning in their relatives. Jesus predicted this would happen when he said,

> "A father will turn against his son and son against his father, a mother against her daughter and daughter against her mother, a mother-in-law against her daughter-in-law and daughter-in-law against her mother-in-law. A brother will betray his brother to death, and a father his child. Even children will rebel against their own parents and have them be put to death."

CHAPTER 95

The earth was dying.

Food and water had grown scarce as famine continued to plunder the world.

Along with these hardships, the starving inhabitants of a ravaged planet grew increasingly bitter and angry. Consequently, their love grew cold and turned into hardened, calloused hearts.

They blamed the Christians for their woes who now had become the primary object of their wrath. A price had been put on their heads—a Christian for a loaf of bread—which accelerated Aster's plan to wipe them out.

Hiding became impossible for those who refused to bow to the image or receive the chip. Without the mark to buy goods, their supplies diminished quickly, forcing them to leave their hideouts in search of food. This made them easy prey for the bounty hunters; unless family, neighbors or old friends turned them in first.

The World Church profited the most from the world-scale hunt. She had ingenuously turned the execution of Christians into a sport and marketed it. By now, all the games of the past had become extinct. Games like football, soccer, baseball, basketball, hockey, even the Olympics all faded into history's past.

Cable TV movies and theaters, too, were gone; replaced by round-the-clock, half-hour teachings of Aster from the image on Tabor.

Entertainment had been reduced to the days of the Roman Coliseums, where pleasures came exclusively from the daily and nightly exhibitions of executions sponsored by the World Church.

In every city, arenas had been built near the station houses where bloodthirsty crowds cheered for the grisly deaths of martyrs. The World Church kept the crowds drunk on the blood of the saints through a variety of ways of beheading their victims: machines, tools, swords, axes, even modern day guillotines with sophisticated laser beams.

<hr />

The rescue attempt was on for Blake and Carl.

The streets were mostly deserted, but an occasional shot and a command to halt could be heard in the distance where some poor saint had been caught rummaging for food. "Cap'?" Malloy whispered into his headset, "How's it look?"

"All clear," Cap' replied from his perch in a large dead tree near the barracks. He was the lookout to warn them of bounty hunters on the prowl.

Malloy glanced at Bob and nodded for them to proceed. They darted across the street to the side of the building and under the barrack's window.

"We're at the window," Malloy said to Cap'.

Cap' scanned the area for any movement in the surrounding shadows. "Still clear," he whispered.

Malloy pointed to the window for Bob to locate Blake and Carl.

As Bob peered inside, the silence erupted into shouting and screaming. He ducked for a moment and then looked in the window again.

A group of soldiers were arguing inside with each other. Three of them were pointing angrily at the corner to Bob's right. He crouched back down near Malloy. "I don't see them," he whispered. "Let's sneak around to the other side so I can see what's over in this corner."

"Right," Malloy said. He looked over his shoulder at Cap'. "Still clear?"

"All clear."

Bob and Malloy snuck quietly to the other side, out of Cap's view. Bob peered into the barracks again. This time he could see what was in the corner.

He slid down next to Malloy. "It's Blake and Carl," he whispered. "They're tied up."

"Then they've been discovered," Malloy said. He paused to think. "Are you fast on your feet, kid?"

"Not with an empty stomach, but I'll do what I can."

"Cap'?" Malloy whispered.

"Yeah?"

"We've spotted the boys. They're in trouble. I'm going to have Bob go through the front door and draw the soldiers out of the barracks. I'll go through the back door and cut the boys loose. If Bob gets into trouble, distract his assailants somehow and give him a lead."

"Got it."

"You okay with that, kid?" Malloy asked.

Bob nodded. The shouts grew louder inside.

"Okay, let's do it." Malloy said. "Move out!"

Bob took off and rounded the corner.

—◦▥▥ᘓᘔ▥▥◦—

Malloy went to the rear and peered through the window. He saw the soldiers still arguing, about eight of them.

Then he saw Bob burst through the front door and shout, "Hey!"

The startled soldiers turned their heads at Bob.

"It's Jansen!" a soldier shouted. "Let's get him!"

Bob turned and sprang out the door into the cover of the night. Every soldier in the barracks ran after him.

Malloy quietly slipped through the back door and knelt beside the two surprised men. "Carl, Blake," he said, "it's okay. I'm a friend of Bob's. We're getting you out of here."

"Praise God!" Blake sighed.

Malloy pulled out his pocket knife and cut the ropes that bound their hands and feet.

"Can you run?" he asked.

Carl and Blake nodded. They rubbed their sore wrists and ankles, and stood up.

"Follow me!" Malloy said and darted out the back door.

Bob ducked into the shadows of an alley as the soldiers ran by. They never saw him so he backtracked to the tree where Cap' was just climbing down.

"The job's done," Cap' said, pulling off his headset. "Cliff's got the boys. Let's get back to the house."

Bob nodded and looked back over his shoulder. He could hear the commotion of eight angry soldiers in the distance and smiled. He gazed up at the pitch black darkness and said, "Thank you, Lord, for helping us tonight."

CHAPTER 96

Martha met the men at the back door.

She had been waiting in the dark, watching and praying until they all returned safely. She embraced each one, even Blake and Carl, as they entered the kitchen and then ushered them down to the basement.

Every light in the house was turned off to give the appearance of a deserted home. They stayed in the basement at night where there were no windows for the light to shine out and reveal their presence.

With everyone back, they sat in the light of the candles going over the events of the night.

"So," Martha said, pouring the two soldiers a cup of hot soup, "our rescue attempt was a great success."

Carl and Blake smiled, weak and frail from the beating they took from the soldiers.

"We knew it would happen, sooner or later," Blake said. "Carl and I never took the chip, so the soldiers found out, tied us up and planned to kill us. That's when they started to argue—"

321

"Yeah," Carl said, "Half wanted to turn us in for the bread, the others wanted to execute us in the barracks."

Cap' shook his head. "Man, I would have probably chewed the ropes off. Why didn't you try to escape?"

"They beat us so bad we were too weak," Carl replied. "And we wouldn't have been able to run, either," Blake said, "but God provided us the strength when you guys showed up."

"Yeah, that was a miracle," Carl said.

Cap' sat with a gnawing war inside him. The faith of these soldiers had stirred him.

"So how long have you guys been saved?" Carl asked Malloy and Cap'.

"We're not saved, kid," Malloy said.

"Have you taken the chip, yet?" Blake asked.

"Not after what I've seen it do to those zombies out there," Cap' replied.

"Then what hope do you have?" Carl asked. "They'll eventually catch us. Are you ready to face God when they execute you?"

"I never gave it a thought," Cap' lied and added nonchalantly, "I guess I'll just have go to hell with the rest of my friends."

Blake frowned. "Do you like what you see out there?"

"Of course not. What kind of question is that?"

"Are *they* your friends out there?" Blake continued.

"My friends are coneys. They'd never join up with Aster."

"Coneys, huh." Blake shook his head. "Are you sure there aren't any *ex*-coneys trying to hunt us down?"

Cap' looked at Malloy for support.

Malloy shrugged his shoulders.

"It appears you've been out of the info-track for awhile," Blake said. "Being in the military, Carl and I saw NWF recruits pour in everyday. Two of the soldiers who wanted to kill us back at the barracks were coneys. Their leader was killed in Montana. They ran back to Virginia, got caught, and buckled under the pressure. Word's out through the NWF bulletins that coneys are joining Aster from every militia in America. A lot of them are professional bounty hunters now, the same people you call *friends*."

Cap' fidgeted in his chair. He felt his heart pounding.

"If you don't like the way things are now," Blake said, "and if you don't care for the company of the damned out there, then how can you sit here and tell me you would prefer to be with your friends in hell? Hell makes what you see out there look like a walk in the park. So if you don't want that *or* the people, what makes you think you'll enjoy living in hell for an eternity?"

The air was thick with the Holy Spirit as Blake and Carl told them what God had done in their lives. When Carl concluded sharing his story about how God had delivered him from near insanity, every excuse for rejecting Christ crumbled at Cap's feet.

"So what do I need to do to be saved from this hell?" Cap' asked.

Bob leaned forward. "If you believe that Jesus Christ is God come to Earth in the flesh and that he rose from the dead, you can be saved."

"Is that it?" Cap' asked.

Malloy jumped in. "Not quite," he said. "When I stayed with Pastor Mitchell, I asked him the same question. He told me I needed to be willing to give Jesus *complete* control of my life, that I had to *want* to line up with the ways of Christ. Am I correct?"

"You are," Bob replied and smiled. "It's called repentance, changing your heart to turn from *your* thing to doing God's thing. You put him in charge. Unfortunately, I'm still here because I fought that part for a long time. Since then, I've realized how important it was for Jesus to be Lord. You aren't really saved if there's no evidence of that in your life. Faith in Jesus Christ without evidence of *his* life in yours, is dead faith. That's why there're so many ex-Christians out there with Aster's number on their foreheads or hands. They either *hadn't* made Jesus, Lord, or they dethroned him out of their lives. I came real close to that happening to me and could've been one of Aster's zombies if I hadn't turned around. You remember how I was, Blake..."

"Yeah, you were in bad shape."

"And that's why I gave everything over to Jesus," Bob continued, looking again at Malloy.

"Well if I'm going to do this, I'm going all the way," Malloy said. "There's nothing else for me here. I'd rather be with friends like you and the Mitchells, than with the friends in hell or out there among the living dead. Not the kind of company I fancy to keep for eternity."

"Me neither," Cap' said. "I'm ready to change and make Jesus, Lord."

Martha clapped her hands and raised them in the air. "Thank you, Jesus!" she cried, and laid her soft, wrinkled hands on the shoulders of the two men. "Let's pray, boys."

CHAPTER 97

Three dreary months had passed since Blake and Carl arrived. The highlight of each day was when Martha and Cap' had returned with some tiny morsel of food or drink. Some days they hit the jackpot and everyone ate. But most of the time Martha and Cap' would return empty-handed.

Whenever there was food, it was usually given to the weakest among them while the strongest held out for another day. They always gave Martha and Cap' something to eat, however, because they were the designated food hunters and the only two who could leave the house. The rest were wanted for desertion, and Malloy was an assassin who's face had been plastered on every tree and pole for allegedly murdering three presidents.

Today the men were wondering if Martha and Cap' would return at all. They had been gone all morning to find food. Now they were getting concerned. Martha and Cap' were supposed to have been back an hour ago. Either they had been captured or were detained for questioning at the station house.

The door bell rang.

Bob peeked cautiously through the curtain at a plain-clothes intelligence officer waiting outside. He was flanked by two soldiers.

It's Vince Kobrin!

Bob backed quietly away from the window, hoping they would think the house was deserted and leave. He then darted downstairs into the basement and went to a small trap door they had cut from the basement into the living room. They placed it, and the furniture, so they could lift the door and see every movement from the front door of the house to the kitchen door.

Suddenly, the back door exploded off its hinges and five large men rushed in with their guns and pistols cocked. Two of them walked cautiously through the hallway to the front door and unlocked it.

"Good job, sergeant."

Bob recognized the voice. It was Vince Kobrin. He could see him walk in and light a cigarette.

Kobrin took a long draw and exhaled the smoke as he scanned the living room. "Search it!" he said.

Bob softly lowered the trap door and turned to the others. "Go to the coal bin," he whispered. "We've got to escape through the loading door out the back."

They ran into the candlelit room and carefully pushed against the two-leaved door. Malloy raised it high enough to peek outside into the backyard.

"It's clear!" he said. "They must all be inside."

"What about Cap' and Martha?" Carl whispered.

"We can't help them if *we're* caught, kid," Malloy said. "We'll come back for them later."

With no one in sight, they rushed through the backyard and scrambled over the fence into the alley.

Bob glanced back and saw a soldier staring at them through a broken window upstairs.

"Chief!" the soldier shouted out the window. "They're in the alley!"

"Go get 'em!" Kobrin shouted, thrilled at the idea of a new chase. How he loved this sport! It had been three weeks since the last hunt. The soldiers with him were highly skilled trackers, best of the best among the bounty hunters. They, too, were starving for a good chase. Christians had grown sparse since the purge began and their numbers had diminished near the point of extinction. With so few left in Canterton, the bounties had increased to a lucrative sum. With no where to go and no one to turn to, the odds on a Christian escaping were next to impossible.

—◅◆▻—

They were caught on the banks of the Roanoke River.

Exhausted from malnutrition, the energy of the four men had dissipated and were easily overtaken.

"Well, well!" Kobrin said, climbing down the embankment. "What have we here?"

The fugitives lay on the ground, gasping for breath. There was nothing more they could do.

Kobrin sat down on the grassy slope above them while his soldiers held them at gunpoint. He lit up a cigarette and smiled at the closest man to him. "What's your name?" he asked.

"Bob Jansen."

"Jansen?...Jansen?" Kobrin said. He remembered the three month old APB on his desk. "We've been looking all over for you, son. You're a deserter. Didn't recognize you behind that prickly beard. Mrs. Pritchard, on your street, tipped us off. Said Mrs. Johnson had been harboring a couple of suspicious characters in her home."

"What have you done with Martha?" Bob asked.

Kobrin chuckled. "The ol' lady? She'll be in hell tonight with her friend. I believe his name is Cap'. Looks like a coney to me."

Kobrin glanced at the other three men who lay quietly on the slope.

"So, Jansen...you ready to put on your uniform and join your old pals?"

"No."

Kobrin grabbed Bob's face with his hand. "Fine," he sneered, "be a fool like the rest of them.". He released his grip and shifted his attention to the gray-bearded man. "And who might you be, old fellow?"

"A friend of Bob's," he replied, looking away.

Kobrin studied the man. "Haven't we met somewhere?"

Silence.

"No...," Kobrin shook his head, "you don't look familiar and you're too old to recruit. Let me see your right hand."

The soldiers grabbed the man's hand and held it up. Kobrin took out a portable scanner and passed it over the top of his hand and forehead. "Where's your chip old man?"

"Never got one."

Kobrin slapped him across the face and broke open the flesh around his mouth. "Why not?"

"I belong to Jesus," he replied, wiping the blood from his lips.

Kobrin jerked from a demon's reaction inside.

He said the Nazarene's name!

The demon flew into a rage and had Kobrin pounce on the old man. Demons inside the soldiers reacted as well and had one of the soldiers hold the man's hand, while another cracked it with the butt of his rifle. They pounded him sorely with their fists until he was knocked out cold.

Kobrin finally pulled himself together and regained control. He glared at Jansen and the other two who remained too weak to break free of the guards. "Take these Nazarene lovers to the station house!" he said as he straightened his jacket and brushed back his hair. "They'll bring us a good price for the arena tonight."

CHAPTER 98

Malloy woke up on a cold damp floor.

A room full of soiled faces stared at him.

As he lifted himself to a sitting position, someone touched him gently on the shoulder. "Are you all right, child?"

He turned quickly toward the familiar voice of the widow Johnson. "Martha, are you okay?"

"I'll be fine," she replied cheerfully.

"Where are we?"

"In the station house."

Malloy scanned the faces. "Where's Cap'?"

"He isn't here," Martha replied sadly. "They took him to the arena."

Malloy stared at her in disbelief. His eyes teared up.

"It's okay, child," she said, placing her hand on his head. "Cap's with the Lord, by now. We'll *all* be joining him soon."

Martha's words pierced Malloy's heart, but not with fear. Before he was saved, such words would have disheartened him. Instead, they brought peace to his soul. What joy to think he may soon be out of this dark world to join his friends in heaven.

Suddenly, he remembered the others and searched among the faces for Bob, Carl and Blake. Bob lay on the floor beside him, out cold. He looked again into Martha's eyes. She offered the same look she gave when he asked about Cap'. Carl and Blake were gone, too—taken to the arena.

The door flew open and a burly station guard walked in cradling an HK54 machine gun. He had a large, square jaw with a jagged scar from his left ear to his chin. His jet-black eyes, void of compassion, browsed the room, apparently for the next victim.

One of the emaciated prisoners screamed out, blubbering like a baby, "I can't take it anymore. Give me the chip. I'll serve Aster. I'll make him my god."

"Well," grinned the guard. "Here's a bright man for you. And a coney at that. Apparently he's seen the error of his ways. The rest of you should take note of this. Aster is a forgiving god. He'll give you a chance to make peace. Anyone else want to wise up?"

Silence.

"Suit yourself," he snarled, grabbing the coney by the collar. But before he turned to leave, he glanced at Martha who was praying next to Malloy. "You there...old woman."

"Me?" Martha asked calmly.

"Yeah, you. You've been here long enough. We don't want you taking up residence now, do we old woman? Come with me."

Martha rose to her feet before the others and looked into Malloy's tearing eyes. "Look after my boy, Bob," she said, pointing to the still form on the floor. "I'll see you shortly, child." She lovingly laid her hand on Malloy's head and then followed the guard and the coney out the door.

Malloy stared after her, praying for strength. "Dear Lord," he whispered, "please help me to be as strong as that saintly woman. Goodbye, dear friend. I'll see you soon."

CHAPTER 99

Bob woke up on a cold, tile floor.

As he moved, his body ached from the beating he had received from the soldiers.

Slowly he sat up and looked around the room through the slits of his swollen face. The other occupants of the room were staring at him.

Malloy leaned over to him. "You okay, kid?"

Bob nodded and placed his hand on his blood-caked hair. "How long have I been out?"

"About two hours."

"Man, my head is pounding. Feels like an elephant sat on it."

"Looks like it, too." Malloy chuckled.

"Very funny," Bob said. He looked at Malloy's swollen hand. "They hit you pretty hard with that rifle. Anything broken?"

"Only my ring finger."

Bob reached over and squeezed Malloy's arm, then he turned to assess the pitiful scene around him. Beneath the cracked, plastered ceiling, one lone bulb spread its 40 watts over the 20x20 foot room. The place reeked of accumulated sweat and filth from the prisoners. The tattered clothes they wore barely covered their emaciated bodies. It evoked images of the Holocaust of World War II. He searched among the faces for his friends. "What happened to Martha and the others?" he asked.

"In heaven by now," Malloy replied sadly. Took them to the arena while you were out."

Bob hung his head and recalled his last three months with them. He wiped the tears from his face with his dirt-stained sleeve. *Dear Lord, give me the strength to see this through.*

Malloy stretched out his broken hand and held it in the air to lessen the throbbing. "Think we'll get out of this alive, kid?" he said, patting him on the shoulder with his good hand.

"Don't know," Bob said as he rose slowly to his feet. "Keep praying though." He stepped over the other prisoners to examine the boarded windows and pushed against them.

"Already checked it," Malloy said. "There's no way out."

Bob sighed and stared at the disfigured cross on the door that someone had chipped at. Suddenly the room began to spin and his legs buckled under him.

Malloy rose from the floor and reached out to steady Bob with his good hand. "Whoa there! You better sit down and take it easy. You took a serious hit on that head of yours."

Bob sat down and pressed the palms of his hands against his eyes, trying to stop the spinning sensation. In a few seconds, the throbbing in his head subsided and he could see normally again. Several of the prisoners smiled at him, empathetic to his condition.

At the sound of approaching footsteps, the prisoners turned their eyes toward the door. The key turned in the lock and a burly station guard with a jagged scar across his cheek walked in with a machine gun cradled in his arm.

His jet-black eyes browsed the room. "Listen up," he said mechanically, "if you want to live: renounce Jesus, receive the chip implant and join the World Church."

CHAPTER 100

No one responded to the guard's invitation.

Malloy leaned over and whispered to Bob, "Heard that line three times today, kid. You'd think they get more creative." Bob had to chuckle and managed a painful smile behind his puffy, battered face.

"You there! Pretty boy...with the fat lip. What's so funny?"

Silence.

"Not going to tell me, huh? What's your name?"

"Jansen."

"All right, Jansen, I've got a proposition for you. You want out of here?"

Silence.

Undaunted, the guard reached into his pocket for a bar of candy and slowly unwrapped it. He took one bite and stepped over a few frail prisoners toward Bob.

Bob sniffed the sweet aroma of the candy. He couldn't remember the last time he smelled something so divine. His stomach erupted for satisfaction after weeks without food.

"Would you like a bite?" the guard asked chewing on the candy while he held the rest in Bob's face.

Bob turned away, determined to resist.

"I'll give you what's left if you show these folks how easy it is to join the World Church. What do you say?"

Voices clashed in Bob's head, battling over the temptation to appease the pangs of hunger. *Take it! You're tired of starving and running like an animal.*

Malloy draped his arm over his friend's shoulder. "Don't do it, kid."

"Shut up, old man!" the guard said, shoving his gun in Malloy's face. "I'm talking to Jansen."

Bob placed his hand on Malloy to steady himself and slowly stood to face the guard. "I can speak for myself."

The guard lowered his gun. "All right. You want the candy?"

"Keep your candy, I'm not joining."

The guard shook his head with feigned sympathy. "Where're your brains, Jansen? Your devotion to a dead Nazarene has given you nothing but hunger and death. Not much of a life is it?" He glared around the room at the other prisoners. "Wake up, people," he said, holding up the candy bar. "*This* is reality, who wants it?"

Again, no one responded.

The guard curled his upper lip. "What's the use!" he snarled, dropping the wrapper on the floor. "I'm talking to the wall!" He stepped back over the prisoners, slammed the door behind him and locked it.

The inmates sat quietly until his footsteps echoed far down the corridor. Everyone stared at the wrapper, but no one picked it up.

Malloy broke the silence. "I'm proud of you, kid," he said, "You did it! You passed the test."

The others concurred excitedly over his victory.

Bob enjoyed their encouragement and the good feeling he had from doing the right thing. But the celebration didn't last long before the key turned again in the lock.

Everyone grew still. The same guard walked in and looked straight at Bob.

"You...Jansen," he said. "It's showtime. You're going to be our first act tonight."

"You can do this, Bob," Malloy said, grabbing his friend's shoulder. "We'll be praying."

Bob swallowed hard and hugged Malloy. "Guess I'll see you in heaven."

"Count on it, kid. I'll be right behind you."

"Very touching," the guard mocked, and took Bob by the shirt.

Some of the prisoners broke into prayer, while others tried to bolster Bob's faith through quoting Scriptures to him. A four-year-old girl quickly snuck up behind him and took his hand. "Mommy told me to give this to you," she whispered, holding up a crumpled piece of paper. Bob took it and glanced at the pale woman the little girl pointed to in the corner. He nodded gratefully toward her.

The guard clutched Bob's shirt and yanked him toward the door. "Let's go, Jansen. The fans are waiting." He shoved him out of the room and locked the door behind them.

As they walked down the corridor, Bob could still hear a rumble of prayers echoing through the hall behind him. They then turned the corner and ascended the stairs to the upper level.

CHAPTER 101

When they entered the sanctuary, Bob Jansen gazed sadly at the wanton destruction before him.

The light of the courtyard shone through broken, stained-glass windows which admitted a glimmering splash of color through the shadows. Graffiti, mostly profanity, covered the walls and mahogany pews. Every picture and religious symbol had been defaced or lay broken on the cluttered floor of shredded carpet.

As they moved down the aisle toward the foyer, Bob heard the gasp of a frail voice behind him. He turned and inspected the shadows surrounding an assortment of whips and chains that lay across the pulpit.

Behind the altar, two husky men leaned over a small, crumpled body. Bob recognized them as the bounty hunters who had brought him in.

"A new arrival," one of the men said, pointing to the lifeless form at his feet.

Bob's guard laughed and said to them, "Getting the kid ready for bed I see."

A child!

When Bob saw the small beaten boy, a spurt of adrenaline surged through his body and he lunged toward the men.

The butt of the guard's gun caught him in the back and knocked him to the floor. "Try that again," he said, "and I'll kill you for my own entertainment."

Bob slowly picked himself off the floor and spotted the boy's peaceful smile. "You've got it, kid," he whispered. "God's grace is all over you."

The boy tried to speak, but another punishing blow from his captors threw his face into the railing.

Bob winced at the insanity.

The guard waved his gun in Bob's face. "Move it, Jansen!" he said, as he shoved him through the wood-carved doors of the foyer and out into the cold, night air.

Outside, a blanket of smog slapped across Bob's face with the nauseating stench of road kill. He gagged at the sight and smell of the cadaverous flesh of martyrs stacked eight feet high to the left of the church. When he realized their heads were all missing a chill ran up his spine.

"Quit dragging your feet!" the station guard said with his gun in Bob's back. He pushed him ahead toward the noisy crowd seated in the stands of a small arena. As he walked into the spotlight he felt the crowd staring at him like starve-crazed beasts. He surveyed their faces and followed their eyes to a raised wooden platform, fifteen feet high. It was lit up by a light from the steeple tower of the old church.

At the top of the platform, a bloodstained block lay below the mechanical arm of a twenty-first century guillotine. A laser gun protruded from the arm, designed to move laterally across the neck of its victims and then retract to its former position. Bob had heard about this machine from the stories Martha and Cap' used to bring back from their food hunts. A queasiness stirred in his stomach. He began to sweat.

"Death to the rebel!" someone shouted from the crowd.

"Kill the dog!" another yelled.

The crowd began to scream profanities to the rhythm of their stomping feet and rattled the stands beneath them.

With a sharp poke of his gun the guard shouted at Bob above the clatter, "Climb, Christian!"

Bob's body ached so much he barely felt the abusive jab. He stepped up to the platform, wiped the sweat off his brow, and grabbed the railing of the stairs. Exhausted from the day's events, his trembling foot could hardly make the first step.

When he reached the fifth step, a dizziness forced him to pause and cling to the rails. As he closed his eyes, the image of the little girl in the prison cell came to mind.

The note. He remembered the note she gave him.

Supporting his weight with one hand, he reached into his pocket for the crumpled piece of paper. It read:

> They overcame Satan by the blood of the Lamb and by their bold witness. Because they loved Jesus more than their own lives, they were willing to die for him.

Bob clutched the note to his chest and gazed at the dark sky. "Please, Lord," he whispered. "Help me through this."

As soon as he prayed, a tingling sensation rippled across his skin until a numbness, nearly intoxicating, cloaked his quaking body like an invisible blanket.

"Move it, Jansen!" the guard screamed below.

Bob stared at the last eight steps and, with renewed hope, completed his climb up the ladder.

An executioner waited for him on top, beside the electronic guillotine. He pointed impatiently to a white painted X in front of the bloodstained block. "Kneel here!" he shouted above the rumbling stands.

Bob stared at the laser and prayed.

Not my will, but yours, Lord.

The chants and stomps of the crowd grew louder—nearly deafening—as Bob walked calmly to the block and knelt down.

The executioner slapped his hand on the mechanical arm of the laser and shouted, "Any last words?"

"Yes," Bob shouted above the clamor, "I forgive you."

CHAPTER 102

Bob hovered above his body on the platform.

He gazed at the lifeless form which, only seconds ago, had housed his spirit.

How strange it was to watch the executioner dump the remains of his body over the side of the platform.

The crowd roared with delight when another prisoner walked out of the church doors. Bob immediately recognized the next victim. It was Cliff Malloy.

The crowd went wild with a blood-crazed frenzy as Malloy entered the arena. When the guard pushed him up the steps toward the platform, Bob shouted, "Cliff!"

"He can't hear you," came a voice beside him.

Startled, Bob turned his head to discover a nine-foot angel in a brilliant white garment with a sash around his waist.

"Who are you?" Bob asked.

The divine creature flashed a warm smile and said, "I'm Gamliel, your guardian. Don't be afraid, I'm here to take you home."

Bob was speechless. He found it difficult to process this picture. He must be dreaming. He looked down on the scene below for a reality check, but only found himself higher above the ground than before. He felt conspicuous floating above the crowd in midair.

"They can't see you," Gamliel said.

Bob stared at his celestial chauffeur. "How'd you know what I was thinking?"

"I can hear your thoughts in this world, but not down there," he pointed to the arena.

"You couldn't hear what I was thinking while I was alive?"

"No."

"But you can now?"

Gamliel nodded and smiled.

Bob realized they were ascending higher off the ground, but forgot about it when he discovered the hunger pangs he had earlier were gone.

He remembered the beating and checked his eyes and face. There wasn't a trace of swelling, cuts or bruises. He felt strong again, healthy.

"There's no sickness on this side," Gamliel said.

Before Bob could reply, he began to rotate upward toward the black sky as though a giant hand cradled him, turning him in that direction.

"You're dead," Gamliel said simply.

"I'm beginning to believe it, now," Bob said.

When Gamliel took Bob's hand, a flash of light burst before their eyes and off they went, hurling dizzily through a winding, translucent funnel.

In the lightning-speed journey Bob saw blurring images of his past flash by him. They were scenes as far back as the earliest days of his childhood to the time when Malloy and Cap' prayed to receive Christ. Images of every occasion where he did something good, no matter how great or small. They all went by like a fast-forward video, yet everything he saw was clear. Nothing ugly or sinful ever showed up during this playback. His sins had been erased by the blood of Jesus.

The trip was over and Bob felt himself slowing down and descending. Gamliel still held his hand as they stepped into the breathtaking panorama of another world.

Bob couldn't believe what he saw before him. There was no sun, yet light appeared everywhere illuminating flowers and trees, and the grasses of vast fields. Everything was transparent with light shining in and through everything, from every direction. It was bright, but not blinding, and there were no shadows anywhere. Everything was defined by a rainbow of brilliant, pastel-like colors.

"Look, over there," Gamliel said, pointing to a multitude of people on the horizon all dressed in white robes. Many carried palm branches.

Bob wanted to go to them and, surprisingly, found himself there the second he thought about it; lost in a sea of faces, all heading in one direction. There were so many people, no one could count their number. Every race Bob could imagine was there, and then some. Gamliel said they were from every tribe, people and nation.

Bob looked up at Gamliel, "Who are all these people?"

"These are the saints who came out of the great tribulation you left behind. Their clothes have been washed and their robes made white by the blood of the Lamb."

Suddenly a voice could be heard from the city ahead saying, *"Blessed are the dead who die in the Lord after this."*

Then a wind blew softly across Bob's face and the Holy Spirit whispered to him, *"They will rest from their labor, because their deeds will follow them here."*

Bob felt a chill from the experience, excited that his rest had finally come. But he wondered how his parting friend, Malloy was doing...and Martha...and Blake...and Carl? "They're all fine," Gamliel said, pointing into the crowd.

Bob looked at the spot Gamliel pointed toward and saw four familiar faces approaching him in white garments. "Martha! Blake! Cap'! Carl!" he cried. "Praise God! You're all here!"

Gamliel loved these reunions and shouted, "Glory to God in the highest!"

Bob and the others looked at him and laughed. Then they embraced each other, including Gamliel.

After Bob hugged everyone sufficiently, he noticed Cap' scanning the crowd.

"Looking for Cliff?" Bob asked him.

"Yeah."

"He was just getting on the elevator behind me. He should be here any minute now."

Cap' smiled and glanced past Bob at something.

Bob turned, expecting to see Malloy, but instead a couple walked up and embraced him.

Martha and the others started to cry for joy. They knew, like everyone else in heaven, anybody they wanted to know without asking.

Bob stepped back to look at the couple and jumped. "Mom! Dad! You're here!"

"Hallelujah!" Gamliel shouted.

Bob embraced his parents for a *very* long time and wept joyously over the sweet reunion. There were no more walls of bitterness between them, not even between his Mom and Dad.

His prayers, and theirs, had been answered.

CHAPTER 103

Gamliel tapped Bob on the shoulder.

"There's more to see," he said, nodding in the direction the multitudes were heading.

Bob said goodbye to his parents and friends and turned with Gamliel into the flowing stream of the crowd. "Where are we going now?" he asked.

"To the city," Gamliel said, pointing ahead.

The city shone on the horizon with a brilliance that resembled a rare and precious jewel, like jasper. In front of them, an endless sea of heads stretched out on every side. Those who were carrying palm branches shouted in unison,

"Salvation comes from God, who sits on the throne, and from the Lamb."

Off in the distance from the beautiful city, a reply to their chorus resounded across the great multitude like a sound wave,

"So be it! Let praise and glory and wisdom and thanks and honor and power and strength be given to our God for ever and ever and ever. Amen!"

Wow! Bob thought. That was a rush. He liked that.

As they drew near the city, Bob was fascinated by its size and beauty. Its wall spread as far toward the east as it did to the west, and appeared to be made of jasper. It was so tall, it disappeared in the sky into the bright haze that surrounded it.

The gate they entered was made of pearl, with a stately angel beside it smiling down at the happy saints. Inscribed on the gate was the name of one of the twelve tribes of Israel. The name on this particular gate was *Judah*.

Upon entering, Bob noticed the light was as brilliant inside as it was outside. The main street was made of pure transparent gold, as clear as glass. The largeness of everything astounded him. Like the vast ocean, it went on and on and on.

Suddenly, everyone ahead of them bowed their knees, and Bob glanced inquisitively at his angelic host.

"Jesus is coming," Gamliel said reverently.

Bob kneeled and stared with breathless anticipation in the direction of everyone's focus.

Walking through the adoring crowds came a man dressed in a full length robe with a golden sash around his chest. As he drew near, Bob saw an aura-like rainbow circling his head. Up close, his eyes flickered like tiny flames of fire and his hair was white as cotton. A glittering sparkle floated about his head.

Everyone reached out to touch him as he walked by, and sometimes he stopped to talk to specific individuals.

"It's him," Martha whispered, coming up beside Bob. "It's the Lord!"

Bob felt overwhelmed by the reality of his first glimpse of the Son of God. When Jesus came within a few feet of him, he stopped. Bob lowered his eyes from the gaze of Christ's fiery eyes and held his breath. He was quickly consumed by the love that burst in his heart for Jesus, a love he felt returned by the Lord without even looking at him.

"Bob," Jesus said in a voice like a waterfall, raising his arms toward him.

Bob glanced up and saw a large hole in the wrists of Christ's outstretched hands. Then the Lord said with a love that melted his heart, "Well done, good and faithful servant."

Bob bowed again and then raised his eyes to watch Jesus continue through the crowd, stopping again and again to speak to others.

"I think he does that to all the new arrivals," Martha said excitedly. "He said the same thing to me when I first came."

Bob smiled from the warm feeling her words gave him and continued to watch the procession. Then he noticed something strange about the entourage that followed Jesus. It was a steady stream of young men who each carried a royal-like scepter of iron. They were dressed differently from the other saints with garments of a brighter splendor.

"They follow the Lord wherever he goes," Gamliel said.

Suddenly, one of the young men stopped at the same place Jesus had, and stared directly at Bob. The others continued to pass as the man left the procession and made his way through the crowd. He came up to him, majestic and princely, and said, "You're Bob Jansen. Whitney will be delighted to know you made it, that is, when her time is completed on earth."

What, did he say? He knows Whitney! Before Bob could reply, the young man lovingly touched his shoulder and looked back at the procession. "I must join my brothers," he said. "We'll talk another time."

As he walked away, Bob turned to Gamliel, who of course knew his question already. "These are the pure and undefiled virgins who were consecrated as firstfruits to God and the Lamb."

Bob wasn't sure what that meant, but he knew there was an obvious connection to Whitney. He watched as more young men with the same iron scepters passed by.

"There are so many of them," he remarked.

"Yes," Gamliel replied. "144,000 to be exact."

CHAPTER 104

It was Aster's world now.

He had killed every saint on earth, except for the Bride in the desert and the two prophets completing the 1260 days of their testimony. The saints who died in Christ had triumphed over Aster, his image and the number of his name.

Now, everyone who could be saved had been saved, of both Jew and Gentile alike. There was no more left on earth who *wanted* to be saved. Everyone who was left had taken the mark of Aster.

Bob now stood with the martyred saints beside what looked like a sea of glass shot through with fire.

How beautiful it was as he watched the flames flicker through the sea like flashes of lightning. Suddenly a harp appeared in his hand and he looked around at the other saints. They had all received one.

Bob glanced at Gamliel.

"I know," he said, "you never played one before."

"So what do I do with it?" Bob asked.

"Play."

"But—"

"Just play. You're not on earth anymore, remember?"

Bob stared reticently at the harp when, on the wings of a breeze, a wave of music swept across the field of saints. A melody entered their hearts and everyone began to strum on their instruments.

Gamliel raised an eyebrow at Bob.

"Okay, I'll play," Bob said and picked at a string.

To his surprise, the skill to play flowed through his fingers as he strummed in unison with the rest. A tune filled his heart and they all sang, in one voice, a praise called *The Song of Moses*.

When they finished singing, Bob shook his head in wonder and looked at Gamliel to ask, "How did I do that?" But before he could answer, the attention of all heaven turned toward the temple in the beautiful city.

Bob looked at the glass sea one more time, but found himself with the others, quickly transported to the city for a momentous occasion.

How he loved heaven! Every second was filled with a new adventure, new scenery, another insight, a new discovery or another event like the one about to unfold. *What is God doing now?* was the constant theme of his questions.

As he watched the temple, the Most Holy Place of the Tent of Witness opened and he could see the Ark of the Covenant. It thrilled Bob that he recognized some of these things without prior instruction.

"Look!" Gamliel said, pointing to the inside of the opened temple.

Seven angels came out dressed in brilliant white linen with gold sashes wrapped around their chests. One of the four living creatures near the throne handed them each a golden bowl that carried a terrible plague. The temple then filled with smoke from the power and glory of God, a power so awesome that no one could enter until after the seven bowls were poured out.

As Bob and his companions looked on, a loud voice said to the seven angels, *"Now go! Pour out the seven bowls of God's wrath on the earth."*

It comforted Bob to know that none of these plagues would affect the saints, since they were all either in heaven, or in the Bride company, protected somewhere in the desert by God. Gamliel told him this.

—⚬ஜ۩۞۩ஜ⚬—

The *first* angel left the temple and poured out his bowl on the land. This plague caused a horrible, malignant and painful sore to break out on everyone who had Aster's chip and worshiped the image.

—⚬ஜ۩۞۩ஜ⚬—

The *second* angel left and poured out his bowl on the oceans of the earth. This plague turned the seas into the curdling blood of a corpse with a foul, disgusting smell. It killed every living thing in the sea: plant-life, crustaceans, fish, sea urchins, and mammals—all from the thick, bloody waters.

—⚬ஜ۩۞۩ஜ⚬—

The *third* angel poured out his bowl on all the rivers and springs. Like the plague on the oceans, this plague turned all fresh water into blood. After the angel poured out his bowl, he shouted to God,

> *"You, the eternal I Am, are righteous in this and just in this judgment. Since they shed the blood of your saints and the blood of your prophets, you've given them what they deserve—blood to drink in the place of water."*

A voice from the altar seconded that statement with,

"*Yes, Lord God Almighty! Your judgments are true and just.*"

———⬥———

The *fourth* angel left the temple with his bowl and poured it out on the sun. His plague caused a blast of heat to erupt from the sun's surface so intense, that it burned the people on the earth with fire. The broiled and blistered citizens of Aster's world cursed God for sending the plagues, and refused to change their minds and worship him.

———⬥———

The *fifth* angel poured out his bowl on Aster's capital seat in Jerusalem. This plague plunged his kingdom into total darkness. In the darkness, the citizens of Aster's world chewed on their tongues in anguish, cursing God again for their troubles and sores. But in spite of the rapid succession of judgments from the five bowls, they still refused to admit they were wrong and needed God's forgiveness.

CHAPTER 105

❧

Jack Mitchell shaded his eyes from the flash of light that burst above the clouds.

"The Lord continues to protect us," he said.

"What is it, Jack, what's happening?" Rhonda asked.

"The *fourth* bowl," he replied.

"Which one is that?"

"The blast of heat from the sun."

"And it won't hurt us?"

"No. God is protecting us like he protected the children of Israel from the plagues in Egypt."

Rhonda hugged Jack's arm. "And we stand here to enjoy a calm, peaceful life in the desert through it all. When the plague of sores came, we weren't touched. When the waters and springs turned to blood, we still had fresh water. And now, while the heat blast from the sun burns the skin of God's enemies, we remain protected and cool."

"And while Aster gropes about in darkness all day," Nathan Kelly said walking up, "our desert remains full of light."

The three broke into laughter, and others nearby joined in a celebration of praise to God's greatness.

"Thank God for his holy angels who daily attend our needs and provide us with food and fresh water," one saint shouted.

"Thank God that the end of our stay draws near," another proclaimed.

Rhonda raised her hands and said, "Thank you Father that Jesus is coming soon, to unite us with our loved ones and friends."

⸺⫷⫸⸺

Two bowls of wrath were left. Aster and Drakon knew it, but lived in denial hoping they had seen the last of it while they scrambled to hold their shattered kingdom together.

"I've had it with these prophets and their message!" Aster scowled. "We haven't seen rain for three and a half years, and we have no sun. Now these blasted magicians have come to Jerusalem to taunt me with their incessant rhetoric of doom."

"Let's kill them," Drakon said. "We can ambush them."

"You're right. They can't blow fire from their mouths at someone they can't see. We'll cut them down with as many shots as we can before they have a chance to react."

"We can do that."

"Round up our best team of snipers. I want those prophets dead, today."

"Done," Drakon said and left the room. He summoned six of his professional mercenaries and sent them out to the streets.

⸺⫷⫸⸺

Moses and Elijah were on the Via Dolorosa, preaching to a crowd of hecklers under the light of torches. The snipers got into position and lined the prophets in their sights; three of them on Moses, the other three on Elijah.

351

Suddenly, the crack of six shots echoed through the streets. The prophets were instantly cut down.

The panic-stricken crowds screamed and ran for cover until they heard no more firing. Peering from their hiding places, the people scanned the surrounding buildings and stared at the two men lying dead in the street.

When they realized what had happened, they knew they were safe. The bullets weren't meant for them. They were meant for the prophets who had tormented the world for three and a half years.

Word spread fast through the city and all Jerusalem joined in the celebration. They even sent gifts to each other.

No one dared touch the bodies, but left them lying on the street where they had fallen. The longer they lay there, the more real it seemed they were dead.

Aster and Drakon rejoiced with the rest of the city, and sent word throughout the World Federation to join them in the festivities. All their enemies were finally defeated—the last they would see of any saints of God.

While Jerusalem and the world partied over the death of the two witnesses, the *sixth* angel advanced from the temple and poured out his bowl on the Euphrates River. Its waters were dried up so that the kings from the East could travel across it to the valley of Megiddo.

It would be their last trip to a battle called *Armageddon*.

CHAPTER 106

One day had passed since the death of the prophets. In the midst of the celebration, Aster and Drakon still worked around the clock to deal with the domino effect of the first five bowls of God's judgments. The reports coming in of the devastation were worse than all previous judgments combined.

Instead of a third of the springs and rivers being bitter, now *all* the fresh water had turned into blood.

Instead of the Atlantic and Mediterranean, *every* ocean body on the planet had turned into blood.

Life had become intolerable for the survivors. People were afflicted with painful sores, others were blistered from the heat blast of the sun.

There was simply no relief in sight.

The next day, the *second* day since the prophets were shot, Aster and Drakon waited for Lucifer at the foot of the image. Shenzar had brought word that their master wanted to meet them.

Aster gazed at the desolate valley below and reminisced over the last three years to the time when they first celebrated the unveiling of his image. He could still see the masses of people, cheering and worshiping at his feet. That glory was short-lived.

Nothing turned out as he had hoped. The world he wanted to control was completely in shambles.

Suddenly, a billowing cloud of smoke rumbled before them and a horde of beady-eyed creatures appeared, circling like bats on the prowl. A shadowy figure materialized in the smoke.

Aster and Drakon watched as the great creature's wings unfurled, nearly spanning the base of the image. Aster felt very small. They reverently bowed their knees to pay homage.

"Welcome, Radiant One!" Aster said with his face to the ground, "we're here at your request."

Lucifer spoke urgently. "Prepare for battle," he said, "the Nazarene is coming. Have every king and nation rally their armies."

"But master, most of our forces have been disabled by the plagues. Our numbers are extremely reduced."

"Get every able body you can, then. Civilians if you have to. We must fight with everything we've got. Tell them to rendezvous here at Megiddo. There isn't much time. Go now and give the order. Your future is at stake."

Lucifer and his entourage of demons disappeared, leaving Aster and Drakon alone.

"Contact the archbishops," Aster said soberly. "I'll call the World Federation council and the chiefs of staff." He glanced up at the towering giant. "We'll have the image inform the citizens tomorrow, and call on every abled survivor to join us. I don't care what objections they have or barriers to climb, tell them this is a battle for survival. Tell them the Nazarene is coming."

The *third* day after the death of the prophets, every nation in Aster's military machine advanced as rapidly as possible toward Israel, including every available civiliah.

Though much of the population on the sea-bound continents were isolated by the bloody waters, every operable plane or jet flew around the clock to transport the troops to Israel.

Those from the land-connected countries came on horses, vehicles, buses and any other form of transportation at their disposal. All at the expense of the World Federation and the World Church.

In the meantime, in the desert of the Rub' al Khali, the preachers and teachers of God prepared the saints of the Bride for Christ's second advent.

"Pastor Mitchell," Shayne Taylor said, "I remember you teaching us about Armageddon, and I've often wondered how the entire armies of the world could fit into the valley of Jezreel."

"Most of the world's population has been down-sized through four years of judgments," Jack replied. "There's probably not much of an army left. It's also possible that not all the armies will make it due to the obstacles they must face to get there. Transportation will be greatly hampered and many of the troops could still be enroute to Megiddo when the battle begins. That would make them vulnerable to the *seventh* bowl of God's wrath."

"Which is...?" Shayne asked.

"The granddaddy earthquake of all time."

Jay Zinn

On the *fourth* day after the death of the prophets, the New World Forces drew closer to the valley of Jezreel.

As the *seventh* angel left the temple to pour out his bowl into the air, a shout came from the throne, saying,

"It is finished!"

CHAPTER 107

The bodies of Moses and Elijah still laid in the street by the *fourth* day. That morning, Aster ordered the media to showcase his trophies to boost the morale of his armies, now enroute to the biggest battle of the century.

—————

Drakon found Aster deep in thought, gazing out the window of his office at the flickering torches of the city.

"It's 11:30 in the morning," Aster said, turning his chair toward Drakon, "and this cursed darkness still lingers."

"Kind of takes the fun out of our victory over the prophets, doesn't it?" Drakon replied. "Why don't we go down and take another look."

"Yes," Aster said, rising wearily from his chair. "I could use a shot of optimism."

They left the office and went to the Via Dolorosa where many still gathered to gawk at the dead prophets.

Aster felt better when he saw the bodies and reminded

himself of his enemy's mortality. If they could do this to Moses and Elijah, they could do it to the Nazarene.

But while he gloated over the speed in which they terminated the prophets, a strong gust of wind blew through the crowd, and the corpses quivered and jerked.

A gasp rippled through the people at the chilling scene. Moses and Elijah stood up.

Aster turned to Drakon and remembered the media. The cameras were televising it—*live!* Before he could order them turned off, however, a voice shouted from heaven and said,

"Come up here!"

Moses and Elijah opened their eyes at the thunderous command and ascended into a bright, glowing cloud that descended and wrapped them like a blanket of cotton.

Everyone in the crowd and those monitoring their televisions, trembled in terror as they watched the prophets vanish through the smog-layered sky.

Aster and Drakon stared at the place where the prophets had lain. Suddenly a clap of thunder peeled overhead with a flash of lightning. The darkness that had covered the city rolled back like a scroll and the sky receded above. Those who had cursed the darkness rejoiced at the sunlight breaking through, but their budding excitement vanished when the streets began to tremble and break open beneath their feet.

The earth shifted and swayed like a drunkard.

All previous earthquakes were mere tremors compared to this, the *last* plague of the seven bowls of wrath. As the planet reeled in its orbit, widespread terror struck the hearts of every survivor. They ran for the hills and caves for cover, pleading to the mountains and rocks to hide them from an angry God.

The earth shook so violently the sea ate the islands and

the earth swallowed the mountains along with the armies enroute through the mountain passes.

Aster's image on Tabor twisted and shrieked into shredded metal as it toppled into the open jaws of the fissures below.

Then a deluge of hailstones, over a hundred pounds each, fell from the sky crushing vehicles and planes and demolishing buildings. Many struck by the hailstones were killed instantly. Those who survived *still* cursed God and refused to repent for their evil.

CHAPTER 108

Mount Zion was the only mountain left standing.

Yet the great city of Jerusalem travailed as it split into three parts. A tenth of the city collapsed, killing seven thousand people.

Aster and Drakon rolled helplessly in the street of the Via Dolorosa as the ground convulsed beneath them. Neither could cling to a fixed object since everything rocked at the mercy of the earth.

"It's the wrath of God!" cried a survivor rolling by, but before he could pass, Aster reached out and caught him by the throat. "You," he sneered, "will suffer the wrath of your king if you don't stop your foolish prattle!"

Aster was on the edge. Even now he refused to acknowledge that any god existed but himself. He certainly wouldn't allow this puny citizen to acknowledge another.

His eyes swirled with rage at the man he held. The crimson mark on his temple turned a purplish-red.

"The God of heaven is angry with us," the hysterical man still cried.

Aster thrust his fingers into his throat to shut him up, watching him squirm until he squirmed no more.

With a snarl he dropped the dead man to the ground and screamed, with his fists clenched, "I am the god of this world! There is no other!"

———✦———

Vince Kobrin staggered desperately through his crumbling apartment to get outside. The noise of cracking lumber and squealing nails muffled his scream of terror.

Like the last breath of a dying man, the building shook and plummeted with Kobrin into the gaping jaws of the crevice below.

The same fissure opened along the ground for another mile, engulfing the entire neighborhood until the shaking beneath Canterton leveled the city and campus upon the shrieks of the damned.

———✦———

The skyline of every city disappeared, never to rise again. Building upon building, skyscraper upon skyscraper fell like dominoes, crushing millions of souls under the rubble.

To and fro the earth reeled on its axis. The ocean floor heaved like a ship on the sea, swallowing range after range of mountains into the steaming fissures below. Tidal waves roared as continents drifted like icebergs into a single mass of land. North and South America connected against the shores of Europe and Africa, Australia connected with Asia. So great was the quake, every continent on earth drifted together like pieces of a jigsaw puzzle.

Never in the history of man had the planet ruptured like

it had today— when the *sixth* seal completed its cycle, the *seventh* trumpet continued to sound, and the seventh angel poured out the *seventh* bowl of God's wrath.

Haggai the prophet foresaw this when he wrote, "This is what the Lord of Hosts says,

'Soon I will shake the heavens and the earth, as well as the sea and the dry land. I will shake every nation—then the Desire of all nations will come...'"

CHAPTER 109

While Bob and his friends were safe in the arms of their celestial surroundings, a second angel, carrying a sharp sickle, came out of the temple.

Then another angel in charge over the fire of the altar, came out of the temple and cried to the angel with the sharp sickle,

"The grapes of wrath are ripe! Take your sickle and harvest the earth's vineyard."

The day after, Jerusalem stood intact on Mt. Zion, though split into three parts by the quake. The panic-stricken remnant of survivors threw the blame for the hardships at the feet of Aster. But in his usual style, he found a scapegoat for them to unleash their fury upon.

"The World Church?" Drakon gasped. Aster's suggestion surprised him.

"Yes, don't you see? The Christians and the station houses are gone now. That makes the function of the World Church obsolete, and another mouth to feed. Without the Christians to blame for these catastrophes, the people will turn on us; unless we offer them *another* sacrifice."

Drakon rubbed his chin and smiled. "You're right. Only our armies and the alliance of the World Federation are necessary to go into battle. Besides, there are a few archbishops who still want revenge for us taking their power from them. They would give anything to unseat you and regain control, especially now when were the most vulnerable."

"Precisely," Aster said. "Summon the ten kings of the alliance. We can't waste any time on this one. They should be in Jerusalem for the gathering."

The ten kings of the alliance each survived the quake and attended Aster's secret meeting. They immediately favored the downsizing, an obvious choice if they wanted to rise from the rubble of a devastated planet. They threw their authority completely behind the president and within the hour, under the pretense of mutiny, Aster ordered the execution of the twelve archbishops and the entire clergy of priests in the World Church.

Word traveled fast and the same members of the World Church who had bathed in the blood of the saints, now turned on her like a feeding frenzy of sharks.

Though Aster believed this to be his own divine scheme, God used it to judge this Mother of Harlots in order to fulfill what was written in Revelation 17 and 18.

As the empire of the World Church crumbled, another angel came down from heaven and lit up the earth with his splendor, saying,

"Fallen! Babylon the Great is fallen! She's been a den for demons, a retreat for evil spirits, and a cage for every detestable carrion bird. For all the nations were made drunk with the wine of her immoral deeds. The rulers of the earth have whored with her, and the merchants grew rich from her extravagant wealth."

In Jerusalem and every surviving nation, tribe and language, the priests of the world church were turned on and cannibalized by the starving masses. Their remains were piled high and ignited, until the air became filled with the stench and smoke of burning flesh.

All the world's leaders who had slept with her and shared in her luxuries watched the smoke rise from her charred remains. With their bellies full of human flesh they began to weep and mourn, while others stood back and trembled with fear, saying, "Woe to you Babylon, city of power, for in one hour your doom has come!"

The merchants of the earth wept also, knowing their best customer was gone and that no one like her remained to buy from them. They stood back in fear and cried over her wealth that had been brought to ruin in one hour.

Truck drivers, engineers, sea captains, pilots, all who traveled by air, land or sea, and all who earned their living from the sea trembled and threw dust on their heads in grief over their loss. As they witnessed the smoke of her burning, they cried, "Was there ever a city like this?"

Then a powerful angel flew down and picked up a large boulder, four to five feet in diameter, and flung it into the sea saying,

"With violence you're thrown down, great city of Babylon, and you shall never be found again. Never will harpists, musicians, flute players, and trumpeters be heard in you again. No tradesman and no sound of work will ever be in you again. There'll be no lamp shining, no bridegroom and bride. Your merchants were the best. By magic you spellbound the nations. But your hands are stained with the blood of prophets and saints, and of everyone you murdered on earth."

While the remnant of the ungodly survived in the final hour, another people—long forgotten by Aster—were safe in the desert of the Rub' al Khali.

Jack and Rhonda Mitchell huddled close with their friends during the continental drift of the earth. Unharmed and unafraid, they knew the great quake would come as the prelude to the return of Christ.

When the trembling and rolling subsided, Pastor Mitchell addressed the saints around him. "It won't be long before Aster gathers the remnant of survivors into the valley of Megiddo. Look up everyone, our redemption draws near...very near!"

"What will happen then?" Whitney asked.

Pastor Mitchell smiled and surveyed the faces of all who listened.

"Did you enjoy your flight to the desert?" he asked, pointing to the sky.

CHAPTER 110

Good news in heaven!

The sweet fellowship of Bob and his companions was interrupted by the announcement that the World Church had been destroyed.

> "Oh heaven, rejoice! Celebrate all you apostles, prophets, and saints! For God has returned on her the treatment she bestowed on you."

Upon hearing this, Malloy leaped for joy and the multitudes of tribulation saints shouted in unison,

> "Hallelujah! Salvation and glory and power are God's, for his judgments are true and just. He has judged the Great Harlot who corrupted the earth with her fornication. Now he's avenged the murder of his servants by her hand."

Malloy was thrilled that justice had finally prevailed over the World Church. He shouted with the multitude of saints again and again, "Hallelujah! The smoke from her burning ascends for ever!"

—◦▰▰◦▰▰◦—

Aster and Drakon were on horseback in the plain of Jezreel where Mount Tabor and the image once towered over the valley. Beside them sat the ten kings of the alliance, also on horses.

The plain spread for miles before them, this time without Tabor, Carmel or Ebal. The quake had swallowed every mountain in Israel but Mount Zion, 80 miles south of Jezreel.

Aster surveyed the sizable remnant of troops that had arrived either on horseback or foot. No one came by vehicles for they were either destroyed by hundred-pound hail stones, swallowed by the earthquake or blocked by barriers of stone and rubble.

As the army prepared for battle, an endless sea of glittering helmets, rattling swords and flashing guns stretched across the vast plain. An impressive sight to behold indeed.

For the first time, however, in his forty-two months of ruling, Aster felt helpless. His cities were gone, his resources depleted, and his communication systems were all but destroyed. To envision a future beyond this day seemed impossible.

"Reuben, look!" Drakon said, pointing at the sky. Aster glanced up at the menacing sight and gasped. A black cloud of birds from every direction on the horizon was heading toward them.

Where did they come from?

Aster gawked at the shadow of their flight as it marched across the plains. The ear-piercing noise of their screeches frightened him.

Soon they blocked the sun, flying in elevated layers of circling patterns, until one gaping hole was all that could be seen of the sky directly above their heads.

Every kind of scavenger with wings had been invited to dinner, appearing to outnumber Aster's army by ten-to-one. He couldn't imagine things getting any worse. Then an angel appeared and stood in the path of the sun in the middle of the gaping hole. He shouted to the birds,

> "Gather yourselves to the great supper of God. Eat the flesh of kings, generals, champions, horses and their riders. Gorge yourselves on them all—free and slave, small and great."

When the angel disappeared, a gasp from the army rippled across the plain. Every eye was fixed on the large hole in the middle of the circling flocks.

What is it now? Aster sighed, straining to see through the rays of light overhead.

The birds enlarged their circling pattern until the hole expanded. Then the sky above the flocks began to peel back like the opening scene in a play.

Where the blue sky rolled back to meet with the space beyond, a majestic rider, radiant and glistening, sat mounted on a white horse that pawed at the air.

CHAPTER 111

Heaven's activities had come to a halt. Every eye was on Jesus, the Word of God, who is called Faithful and True. With justice, he was prepared to judge and make war.

He sat majestically crowned, with fire in his eyes, on a gleaming white stallion. The robe he wore had been dipped in blood. From his mouth he spoke judgment by the Word of God, sharper than any double-edged sword.

By the standard of the Word he would judge and strike down the nations, trampling them in the winepress of God's full wrath.

On his robe and thigh was written the title,

KING OF KINGS AND LORD OF LORDS.

Aster, Drakon and the ten kings turned pale and trembled at the sight of the rider and the angelic host surrounding him. The panic-stricken army shot frantically at the rider and into the circling flocks of birds. Then the blast of a trumpet sounded from heaven.

The *seventh* angel, who began to sound at the beginning of Aster's reign, sounded the last trump at the command of Jesus, and a cry of voices from heaven shouted,

> *"The kingdoms of this world have become the kingdom of our Lord and of his Christ, and he shall reign for ever and ever."*

Then the twenty four elders who sat on their thrones before God, fell on their faces and said,

> "We thank you, Lord God Almighty, the One who is and who was, because you've taken control by your great power, and assumed your rightful place. Yes, the nations are angry, but now they'll experience your wrath. For it's time to judge the dead and reward your servants who are the prophets and saints, and those who reverence your name, both small and great. And it's time to destroy those who corrupted the earth."

With the blast of the *last* trump and the elders proclaiming their thanks, every saint in heaven from Adam to the last martyr found themselves back in the funnel of light...speeding to earth.

CHAPTER 112

"Whooaaa!" Bob shouted, startled by the same pulling sensation he experienced at death.

In a flash, like the blink of an eye, he and his friends were back into the speeding tunnel of light, instantly transported to Earth where their bodies had been laid in a grave.

Bob opened his eyes underground, surrounded by rocks and dirt. He found himself lying on a pile of squirming bodies of martyrs who had been formerly dumped in the same location and buried.

Unlike the feather-weight feeling of his heavenly existence, Bob could feel once again the physical weight of his former body.

Though he was able to breathe, he had little time to think about his new surroundings before the ground shook and something pushed him up through the gravel and dirt.

As he broke through the surface, he scanned the area. Canterton was gone, replaced by flattened plains of rubble and charred ground. Before he could give it much thought, however, hundreds of bodies broke through the ground around him. Carl and Blake came up beside him. A younger version of Martha Johnson, a younger Cap' and a younger

Malloy also came up through the ground. Not one saint looked any older than a healthy thirty-three-year-old, the same age as Christ when he ascended in his resurrected body.

Hundreds upon hundreds of bodies popped through the ground dressed in white fine linen, and surprisingly unsoiled by the dirt.

Before anyone engaged in an expression of surprise, they were instantly pulled bodily toward the sky.

Here we go again, Bob thought.

As he ascended, he studied the earth below. Nothing looked familiar. There were no trees, no vegetation, no mountains, no hills and no cities. It was an entirely different planet. Even more incredible was the peculiar absence of the Atlantic Ocean and that the continents had merged into one large continent.

These images were soon overshadowed when Bob turned his attention to the glorious sight around him. He was one among millions of saints, streaking rapidly through the air toward the rider above on the white horse.

As he rose to the place where the sky hazes with the darkness of space, a myriad of white horses appeared before him, majestically pawing at the air.

He watched the saints ahead land gently on the backs of their mounts.

Soon he found himself placed by an invisible hand on the powerful back of a shimmering, white stallion.

It was the most awesome display of divine power Bob had ever witnessed. The saints of all ages were there, all on horses; and the host of heaven's angels appeared, as far as the eye could see.

Bob located his friends—Malloy, Martha and the others—nearby. They all giggled like kids in their first ride on a carousel. The scene was so fantastic, Bob couldn't describe the exhilaration he felt.

Suddenly, Gamliel appeared beside him and pointed to the illumined earth below. "Look!" he said. "The Bride is coming!"

Chapter 113

A large opening appeared in the cloud in the desert.

For forty-two months, in the Rub' al Khali, the same cloud had sheltered the Bride from the heat and the cold.

Today it was different.

Jack and Rhonda Mitchell knew the opening marked the end of their long-awaited reunion with Jesus.

So did the others.

The entire population of saints stood outside their tents with their eyes fixed on the blue sky, each waiting anxiously for the unveiling of their Bridegroom, Jesus.

As Whitney watched the sky intently, she glanced at the Mitchells and Nathan Kelly. Their faces were brighter than usual. Then it dawned on her that they looked young again, about the age of someone in their prime early-thirties.

Before she could comment, however, she was immediately snatched off the ground with the others in one swift motion.

Like a flock of white doves, the Bride rose through the opening in the cloud and streaked rapidly toward the heavenly army, waiting and ready for battle. As they approached their destination directly behind the King of kings, beautiful white stallions waited to receive her company.

————◦⸫⸫⸫⸫◦————

Bob Jansen stared at the glorious sight, as the saints of the Bride mounted their steeds. He noticed they had a splendor brighter than that of the others, and while he gazed on her beauty, the 144,000 virgin men with their iron scepters appeared in her midst and mounted their own white horses.

Though much had transpired in this resurrection of saints, the rallying of the angels and the rapture of the Bride from the desert, the gathering around Jesus took place in the timeless seconds of eternity invisible to the naked eye, inconceivable to the natural mind.

Bob was glad he had been given an immortal body to handle such an experience. He was breathing in space and sitting on a white horse in midair.

————◦⸫⸫⸫⸫◦————

Lightning flashed from the east to the west over the massive army in the plains of Jezreel.

At the roar of the first thunder in the valley of Jezreel, Aster and Drakon felt something grab them by their throats.

Aster stared at Drakon with bulging eyes, begging for help. Drakon was as powerless as his colleague, however—snatched from his horse, kicking and screaming in terror!

In the blink of an eye they were taken to a massive crevice, dangling perilously above the inferno by an invisible grip. Out of the mouth of the chasm spewed smoke and intense heat. Drops of sweat broke out on Aster's forehead which ran down his face like a waterfall.

"Noooo!" he screamed as the unseen hand released him to plummet alive into the fiery lake below with Drakon beside him.

Headlong they fell into a sulfurous, boiling stew of liquid fire. When their heads bobbed back to the surface, they desperately thrashed about to escape the intolerable pain.

Aster cried out for death to deliver him. Drakon howled the same. But death eluded their immortalized bodies, doomed to suffer *eternal* judgment.

Their flesh burned and peeled, replaced only by new flesh to burn and peel again. Flesh that could feel the relentless insufferable sting of the fire.

Their burning lips and swollen tongues thirsted for water, but could not be quenched.

Their burning nostrils begged for fresh air, but could only sting from the eye-watering stench of their burning flesh and the putrid, sulfurous fumes of the lake which reeked like spoiled eggs.

For all their cursing and swearing in the lake of liquid fire, no one paid attention to their cries.

No one.

CHAPTER 114

The army went into shock.

Aster and Drakon had been carried through the air by an unseen hand, leaving them alone to face the rider on the white horse.

In an act of desperation, those who had guns fired futilely into the air while the rest rattled their sabers and swords.

Then a flash of light from the Son of God burst over their heads.

Their flesh rotted off their bones.

Their eyes dissolved in their sockets.

Their tongues dissolved in their mouths, and the entire army collapsed to the ground in the plain of Jezreel.

The battle of Armageddon was over.

But not only did Christ judge the army, his blazing splendor swept across the earth to punish every living soul who refused to obey his gospel or heed the warnings against taking the mark of the beast.

In the wake of his judgment, the circling birds of prey swept down on the carcasses to gorge themselves on the grilled flesh. From the plain of Jezreel to Jerusalem and

Egypt, the blood of the slain flowed two hundred miles long, as deep as a horse's bridle.

When the judgment on the ungodly was finished, Jesus came down on the Mount of Olives fulfilling what Zechariah the prophet had said,

> "The Lord will go fight against those nations, as he fights in the day of battle. That day his feet will stand on the Mount of Olives. . ."

As his feet touched the ground, the mountain split from the east to the west and formed a great valley.

⸺⧓⸺

"Would you look over there!" Martha said, pointing at a slinking, skittish creature.

"It's Satan," Malloy said. "With his two puppets gone and his demons all scattered, he's all alone."

"You're right!" Bob replied. "This is great!"

"Look!" Martha said. "Here comes Jesus!"

"What's that in his hand?" Cap' asked.

"It's a chain!" Blake said.

It was the most beautiful sight imaginable: Satan frozen in midair and Jesus galloping toward him on his glistening white steed to grab the devil by the throat like a rag doll. Without breaking stride the horse continued to run as the Lord held Satan in one hand and carried a great chain in the other.

⸺⧓⸺

Jesus took the devil to a canyon where the earth had opened her mouth. He descended to the lowest level of the Abyss.

At the entrance of a tomb-like cave, Jesus snapped an iron yoke around Satan's neck and fastened it to the chain he held in his hand.

"I'll get you," Lucifer hissed. "I've done it before and I'll do it again! I'll come back and I'll beat you!"

Jesus carried him into the cave kicking and screaming, and fastened the chain to the wall.

Without a reply to Lucifer's petty threats and curses, Jesus walked out of the cave to the entrance of the Abyss and locked the gate. It would remain that way for a thousand years.

⬥⬥⬥

While Aster, Drakon and Satan were cooking in a sulfurous stew, the ungodly were banished to hell where every demon and fallen angel was bound. Never again would the earth groan under the burden of these loathsome creatures or the corruption of sin. Only the residue still cluttered the ground like broken tombstones in a graveyard; grim reminders of the greed, lust and power that once ravaged the world.

Jesus changed that, however, and purged the earth with fire so intense, it burned up all the elements. Not a trace of civilization, not a relic of history's past remained.

The old was gone.

He had made everything new.

CHAPTER 115

God restored the earth back to a paradise.

Out of the ashes he created a new landscape of foliage and fruit-bearing trees. The continents, having merged into one, displayed a beautiful vista of lakes and streams filled with sparkling water. On Mount Zion, a magnificent stream flowed out of the city and down the east and west sides of the mountain. It emptied into an ocean body that teemed with fish and great creatures of the deep in turquoise-green waters.

Majestic and colorful birds of every species filled the air with their boundless variety of songs. Animals of every class roamed the earth freely. Those which once ate flesh were tamed and ate of the lush green vegetation and fruit.

In the sky above, an expanse of water covered the globe like translucent glass. The rays of the sun heated the crystalline canopy which created a terrarium effect. The atmosphere was sustained at a perfect even temperature of seventy degrees Fahrenheit. The brilliance of the sun went undetected above the watery expanse, lost in the glory of God's light which now permeated the earth. The planet glowed everywhere. Not a trace of shadows could be found. Even the homes of the saints were lit up; not with electricity, but by the Shekinah glory of God.

There were no deserts, no wastelands, no wars.

There was no pain, no crying, no poverty.

There was no sinner, no sin, no demons and *no* devil!

———

After Jesus renewed the earth, he rewarded the saints according to the works they had done.

He gave everyone lands and houses uniquely designed and created for their individual tastes and interests. He placed them in various levels of authority so that they might serve God and his people.

Over each of the twelve tribes of Israel, he placed one of the twelve apostles from the first century church to govern and serve them.

Under the twelve apostles he set up kings to govern and serve in the regions allotted to each tribe.

Under the kings, he set up officials to govern and serve in the cities of their allotted inheritance. Some governed five cities while others governed ten, according to the fruit of their walk before God in their former lives.

Positions in each city were given to the saints in every category of service, each according to the fruit of their walk before God in their former lives.

Everyone served with their God-given talents, graces and gifts happy and at rest in their allotted roles.

———

After Jesus set up his millennial kingdom, he gave a wedding feast for his Bride. Every saint came from the east and the west to take their place at the table.

Among the guests were such men as Abraham, Isaac, and

Jacob. The prophets and saints of old were there, too—great ones like Ruth and Deborah, Joseph and Daniel, Moses and Joshua, and so forth.

John the Baptist was there as the friend of the bridegroom, speaking of the day when he saw the dove descending on the Savior.

Everyone, from the least to the greatest, was there and waited upon by angels.

With gladdened hearts they drank of the fruit of the vine with Christ just as he promised his disciples at the last supper.

Truly a great feast and a great day it was to usher in the millennial order of the King of kings and Lord of lords.

The government, indeed, was now upon Christ's shoulders.

CHAPTER 116

Bob completed his tireless ascent to the top of Mount Zion. He could've been transported if he wanted, but he chose to climb instead for the scenery.

At the top he scanned the lush, vast horizon and let his eyes follow the river that flowed down the mountain on the west side toward the sea. He then turned to admire the Great City that had replaced the old Jerusalem. Suddenly, Gamliel appeared beside him.

"Hail friend!" Gamliel said. "What brings you here?"

"I've come for my shift in the temple," Bob replied.

"First time?"

"Yeah."

"Exciting, eh...?"

"I can't wait. You wouldn't believe the things Cliff Malloy told me about his first shift." Bob stopped. "Oh, yeah...I keep forgetting. You know these things."

"That's okay. I love hearing about it through the eyes of

you humans. It intrigues me. So what other new discoveries have you made since I last saw you?"

"Well, when I talked with the prophet Hosea we got on the subject of our clothes. I noticed his garments had a brighter intensity than mine, so I asked him why. He told me his responsibilities probably accounted for that and his position had a different measure of grace. Fascinating, huh?"

"Yes, fascinating." Nothing new to Gamliel, however. Angels have always had distinguishing splendors in rank.

"Then I got to thinking about Jack Mitchell," Bob continued, "because I was sure he had more responsibility than I did. So I told Hosea about him and what a great pastor he'd been. When we finished our conversation, I left and got to thinking about seeing Jack. So I transported to the front lawn of his estate."

"Great! Which tribe?"

"Benjamin."

"I've been there. Pretty country."

"And you should see all the cities he serves…"

"How many?"

"At least ten. They're beautiful."

"So how's he doing?"

"Oh, I found him excited over some new truths he discovered. He had just returned from a great time of fellowship with Jesus."

"Awesome."

"Yeah, and he shared some amazing insights with me that the Lord told him about the Father's love. Made me burst into praise and so did Jack. A few angels nearby heard us and they joined in, too. We were so filled with joy I thought I was going to explode."

"Then what happened?"

"Well, Rhonda, Jack's wife from the Pre-Millennial Age, heard I was in the area and came over to see us. We all sat down to a great meal and had the best time catching up on what everybody was doing…"

Gamliel enjoyed hearing about the glory and love of God

at work in Bob's life just like he did his other former assignees. As a celestial being unlike his human counterparts, it was difficult for him to grasp the significance of the Cross and the eternal impact it had on humans. Only the saved and redeemed could fully appreciate the suffering Jesus went through for them. Gamliel couldn't.

As Bob continued to share his experiences, the two of them walked along the road to the Great City. When they entered the gate, someone called them by name. Bob turned to a woman who was dressed like a queen, wearing a crown.

"Whitney!" he shouted.

"Hello, Bob, it's good to see you."

Bob gave her a hug. "Finally we meet. I've been looking forward to seeing you so that I could thank you."

"Thank me?"

"Of course. If you and your friends hadn't shown me God's love through your lives, I wouldn't be here. I'm eternally grateful."

Whitney smiled. "Well, thank you, Bob. That's kind of you."

"So what are you doing now?" he asked.

"Oh, I've been busy teaching my son whenever I see him. He wasn't on Earth long enough to comprehend the tragedies of sin or how much Jesus means to the rest of us who lived through it. So I'm telling him what I can to help him understand."

"That's great. I've seen others being taught about that in the city squares. You know, those who were aborted or died as small children before they were aware of sin. I loved seeing their fascination with the stories about Jesus. Your son must feel the same way."

"Yes, he does."

As Gamliel stood and listened to their conversation, he noticed a princely young man with an iron scepter making his way through the crowd toward Whitney.

"Hey," Bob said to the young man as he walked up, "aren't you the one who met me back in heaven?"

"Yes, I am," he replied as he embraced Whitney.

"I remember," Bob continued, "when you stepped out of a large procession behind Jesus and told me Whitney will be delighted to see me when she arrives."

"That's right."

Bob stared at the two for a moment. "Then you knew about Whitney because she carried you in her womb?"

"Right again. After I was born, I was snatched up to heaven by an angel. He told me about Whitney and her other friends. That's how I found out about you."

"I was told about you after the wedding feast," Whitney said, "I knew it was only a matter of time before we bumped into each other."

Bob smiled. Then a puzzled look came over his face. "How did it happen, Whitney?" he asked with innocent curiosity about her conception. "I never really understood that part."

"I don't really know. I guess it's one of those *mysteries* God reserves for himself. I only know that he chose me to carry this boy in my body. Now here he is, a prince of King Jesus."

"With 143,999 other half-brothers," Gamliel added.

"Well, I may not understand it," Bob said, "but I sure love how God puts everything together. I've never been so happy, and to think this joy will go on forever."

"So, where do you live and what are you doing?" Whitney asked.

"Hey...let me tell you...I've been assigned to the hottest spot on this planet."

"And where's that?"

"Before the very throne of God, can you believe it? I'm going to my first shift right now. I guess they put me there because I was a martyr in the great tribulation. They've got me serving as a priest, you know. Man, I can't wait. I get to see Jesus right there with the Father."

"Wonderful! You'll enjoy that."

"Yeah, and you remember Cliff Malloy, who stayed with the Mitchells? He's here, too. Died right after me. He just came off his shift and said he'd never seen or learned so much in his life. Jesus preached to everyone. Then the twenty-four elders preached, too. He even heard Moses, Elijah and Enoch preach about things. The insights I guess were incredible."

"How thrilling," Whitney said.

"Yeah, and the music! Cliff said the music was unlike anything you've ever heard. He even saw cherubim and seraphim singing before God. Amazing creatures! I haven't seen one of those yet, but Cliff said when I do, my eyes will pop out. I guess they're different than Gamliel, here."

Gamliel laughed.

"You've got to meet Cliff, Whitney," Bob continued. "You only knew him before he got saved. He's a great guy. We went through some harrowing experiences together back in the war. I'm glad I can't remember it much. It's all a little hazy...like it never happened."

Whitney laughed.

"What?" Bob asked. He looked perplexed at Gamliel. "What's so funny?"

"Well, the poor woman has barely gotten a word in," Gamliel replied. "You've been doing all the talking."

"Ha, you're right! I guess I have. I'm just excited to see you after all this time, Whitney. So...what's it like being in the Bride of Christ?"

"Glorious" she replied. "Simply glorious."

"Boy, it must be. Why just the other day after I visited my parents, I got to talking with Abraham, and you know what he told me about the Bride? Well, he said..."

Gamliel rolled his eyes and smiled at Whitney. He knew when Bob got excited about something, he'd be in for some great entertainment.

CHAPTER 117

Throughout the Millennium the resurrected bodies of the saints were slender and vigorous.

They never tired and never got sick.

They needed no food, but could eat if they wanted. They never grew thirsty, but could drink of the sweet waters of the river of life flowing down from the mountain of God.

In addition to the immortal qualities of their bodies, their mental capacities were equally pleasurable. The infinite joy of learning was constant. New truths about God and his creation were inexhaustible, especially the insights they learned of the multiple and diverse attributes of God's divine nature.

With the active life of the kingdom, the timeless bliss of the Millennium sped rapidly to a close.

As written in the Book of the Revelation, the saints of God reigned with Christ during this time for a *thousand* years.

Satan stirred anxiously in the cavity of the Abyss.

His thousand years were up.

The iron fetter fell off his neck and the gate opened to the Abyss.

Loosed from his prison, Satan rallied his principalities and demons to join him at the surface of the earth to do what they did best, *deceive*.

A step ahead of his release, billions of ungodly souls resurrected out of the sea and the land. These were *Gog* and *Magog*. Men and women, both great and small, who once roamed the earth as murderers, liars, fornicators, sorcerers, witches, thieves and adulterers.

Satan quickly went to work on their minds and convinced their bitter souls to rally behind him against the saints of God. For Satan, recruiting the resurrected nations of the deceived was a simple task.

"Evacuate! Evacuate! Retreat to the City of God!" The angelic messengers flew from tribe to tribe, region to region, and city to city warning God's people of the approaching army.

After a thousand years of peace, the message seemed foreign to the redeemed; yet the city fathers, in every region of the continent, told them this day would come.

Prior to the release of Satan and the resurrection of the ungodly, every saint had been transported to the camp surrounding the Great City. Their numbers covered the sides of the long sloping mountain down to the base where it touched the plains. From there the saints watched the horizon with keen interest, awaiting the arrival of the invading hordes of the ungodly.

Gog and Magog came to life on the coastline and throughout the continent. They were as innumerable as the sands of the seashore.

They began their trek across the breadth of the earth, gathering the others as they came, trampling through fields and houses, through cities and towns, relentless in their determination to quench their thirst for revenge.

Finally they arrived en masse, as Satan halted his army at the foot of the mountain of God.

He surveyed the slopes covered with saints. The odds certainly appeared to be in his favor. They looked like defenseless sheep in contrast to the size of his resurrected army with the princes of darkness and demonic hordes in the air.

In smug arrogance, Satan unfurled his great wings to lead the charge. But before he could give the order, the sound of a roaring furnace bellowed overhead.

As he glanced up at the sky, his princes and demons scattered for cover from the descending wall of fire.

"Noooo!" Satan screamed in spasmodic terror. He scrambled to hide like the rest, managing to escape the fire. But something more terrifying approached him. Jesus came riding on his majestic white horse, once again in full gallop, snatching up Satan like a mop. Michael's angels followed close behind to round up his princes and demons who surrendered without a fight.

To the lake of fire the King of kings rode, lifting Satan high above his head. He hurled him into the liquid fire below where Aster and Drakon still bobbed and thrashed in eternal torment.

Michael came, too, with his warriors and tossed their quarry into the lake with Satan.

They shouted triumphantly before Jesus, their mighty

warrior and King. For today they'd seen the last of the enemies of Christ.

CHAPTER 118

Bob watched the whole thing from the mountain.

He had a bird's-eye view of the vast expanse of the plains and the ungodly mass of invaders surrounding their camp.

He was awed by the deluge of fire as it circled the base of the mountain between the saints and Satan's army. Not a hair on his head was singed, nor could he feel any heat from the flames.

He could see the silhouettes of his enemies through the wall of fire screaming for deliverance from the blazing inferno. Many ran into the river to extinguish the flames, but the fire seemed immune to the water.

Finally it ended and the wall of fire lifted like a veil, exposing an endless vista of charred bodies. Bob looked at the smoke-filled air and devastation with sadness. It grimly reminded him of the scene he escaped a millennium ago.

He watched the souls of the ungodly hover above their bodies until something phenomenal happened. In the blink of an eye, the earth and sky disappeared.

Immediately Bob and all the saints were swept into a tunnel of light, back to that place in the fourth dimension called *the third heaven*.

Thrones were set in place.

The Ancient of Days took his seat on a great white throne. His clothes were a brilliant white and the hair of his head gleamed like fine white wool. The throne itself was ablaze with a river of liquid fire flowing out from it into a burning lake of sulfur below.

To the right of the Father sat Jesus, the Son of God, and to his right stood the masses of redeemed saints.

Before them the court was seated and the books were opened, and another book was opened called the *Book of Life*.

The saints and the angelic host were observers at this celestial court, while the cowardly, the vile, the murderer, the unbelieving, the sexually immoral, the liar, the idolater, and those who practiced magic arts—everyone whose name was not written in the Book of Life—stood before the great white throne awaiting their trial.

One by one they stepped forward to hear the remotest details of their lives being read to the Ancient of Days. Every wicked thought, every blasphemous word, every wicked deed in the dark or in the light; all of it was brought to the attention of the court.

There was no excuse, no place to run, no lawyer to defend and no way to deny the naked recorded truth.

Nothing was hidden in this court.

The most embarrassing and disheartening of all their sins, however, was the repeated occasions of ridicule, blasphemy and blatant rejection toward those who had tried to reach them with the gospel of Christ.

Every account of their rejection of truth would serve as tormenting memories of the opportunities they had to avoid eternal separation from God.

At the close of the record of each person's deeds, another book was opened with the question asked, "Is his name written in the Book of Life?"

"No, Lord! His name is not found."

"Then throw him into the lake of fire!"

At this, many cried out in an effort to defend themselves, saying, "Lord...Lord...didn't I prophesy in your name? Didn't I drive out demons and perform many miracles in your name?"

But Jesus could only reply, "I don't know you. Go from me, you evildoer!"

In this fashion the court proceeded, unconscious of time in a timeless dimension. Untiring and meticulous in sorting through every account of every individual.

Beneath the throne, in the lake of fire, the screams of the tortured damned grew louder and louder as soul upon soul was added to their number. Like Aster and Drakon, the new bodies they received were bodies that would never die. Bodies that would feel the excruciating pain of worms and fire consuming their flesh, perpetually shedding like snake skins, only to renew again and be eaten and burned once more.

Their tongues, eternally swollen, would never be quenched by water.

Their eyes, continuing to see, would forever gaze on the hopeless surroundings of human agony.

Their noses, continuing to smell, would forever be tortured by the odor of burning flesh and the rotten-egg smell of the gases of burning sulfur.

Their ears, continuing to hear, would never drown out the vexatious sounds of piercing screams and agony.

This is the price they paid for rejecting the love of God.

This is the price they paid, for the temporal pleasures of sin.

This is the price they *preferred*, in their former life, over the price of the blood of Jesus.

This is the debt they owed, when the Cross would have canceled it out upon their acceptance of Jesus Christ as their Savior and Lord.

CHAPTER 119

It was all brand new. Everything!

A new earth. A new universe. God replaced it all!

Bob stared in awe at the beautiful new planet speeding toward him. It was considerably larger than the former earth, with significant similarities, like the vegetation. But then, not everything was the same. For example, he immediately noticed it had no ocean, though there was an abundance of lakes in various sizes.

Bob descended rapidly, along with the heavenly host of angels and saints, into the atmosphere of this luminous new planet.

Every saint and angel was there from the millennial kingdom, touching down like feathers onto the surface of this huge mountain—a mountain broader and taller than any mountain from the former earth.

It rose with a gradual sloping base that covered four thousand miles in diameter. On top, a vast plateau, perfectly square, spread fifteen hundred miles across.

Gamliel told him this.

After the myriad of saints and angels arrived, Bob glanced up at another breathtaking sight.

The Holy City, a new Jerusalem, slowly descended out of heaven, flashing and glowing like a crystal clear stone of jasper. It set down on top of the mountain covering the entire plateau. It was made of pure, transparent gold, like glass filled with the radiant glory of God.

Then *a voice* from the throne in the city cried out,

"Now God's home is with men and women, and he will live with them. They will be his people, and he—living among them—will be their God. He will wipe every tear from their eyes—for in this place they will never see death, never know sorrow, never hear crying, and never feel pain. That is all in the past, for the order of all things old, is gone."

Then God said from his throne,

"Look! I have made everything new!"

With Gamliel at his side, Bob followed the procession of saints up the gradual slope into the City. He was ecstatic.

"Would you look at the size of this place!" he said to Gamliel. "How big do you think it is?"

"Precisely fifteen hundred miles high and fifteen hundred miles across. The walls are two hundred and sixteen feet thick."

Bob stared at his celestial friend. "Now how did you know that? We just got here."

Gamliel chuckled. "The Bible. It's there in the Scriptures."

"Oh, you're really funny today."

"So, do you want to hear the rest?" Gamliel asked.

Bob smiled and folded his arms. "Sure. Go ahead."

"Very well."

Gamliel loved to impress the saints with facts about the works of God. He was always prepared to answer their questions. "The wall," Gamliel said, "is made of jasper and built on twelve layers of stones. These stones are ornamented with precious gems and engraved with the names of the twelve apostles. The first stone layer of the foundation is made of jasper, the second is sapphire, then chalcedony, emerald, sardonyx, sardus, chrysolite, beryl, topaz, chrysoprase, jacinth, and the twelfth layer is made of amethyst."

"Wow, you're good," Bob said teasing him.

"Thank you. The gates themselves, twelve in all, are pearl, engraved with the names of the twelve tribes of Israel. Three of the gates are positioned on each side of the four-square city, facing north, south, east and west."

Bob's attention became diverted by the beautiful warrior-like angels he saw at the gate. Gamliel told him there was a guardian assigned to every gate.

"When do they shut those huge doors?" Bob asked.

"Never. They'll always remain open to the nations and rulers, so they can come at any time to worship God and perform their holy service."

Bob and Gamliel moved through the gate into the city where the light appeared brighter than the noonday sun. All the light on the new earth came from God's glory, just as it had in the Millennium.

Inside the city walls, the expanse was so high Bob couldn't see where it ended.

Before them the main street was wide and made of pure transparent gold that looked like glass.

"Look at that," Gamliel said, pointing to a crystal-clear river of water. "That's the water of Life."

The river cut through the middle of the main street where the *tree of life* touched both sides of its banks. "That tree," Gamliel said, "will bear twelve crops of fruit every month."

"Can you eat from it?"

"Of course."

"And where's the temple we had in the Millennium?" Bob asked.

Gamliel smiled. "There isn't one. The Lord God Almighty and the Lamb are the temple."

Bob stared at the streets of gold. "You know what, friend? I thought I'd seen the best of the best that day I died...when you took me to heaven. Then, God out did that by giving me an immortal body and renovating the earth into a glorious paradise. So, I thought *that* was the best of the best, and even better than heaven. Now, God's outdone himself again. Bigger, better and more beautiful. Now how much better can it get than this?"

Gamliel laughed. "Our God will never stop surprising us with *better*. That's always been my experience from covenant to covenant, age to age, and creation to creation. I've never seen him return to the former way he did things. It's always on to something better. He likes creating better. That's the way he is. That's how he does it. He'll dazzle us through all eternity with his amazing love and power."

Gamliel's description of the attributes of God got him so wound up he decided to shout, *Glory to God!* and even danced a few steps. Bob and those nearby couldn't help but join in, dancing and singing praises to God.

When they finished rejoicing, they continued their stroll through the city and stopped to browse the glorious new sights.

Suddenly, two pairs of hands grabbed Bob from behind.

"Hey, brother!" a couple of familiar voices said in unison.

Bob turned around. "Cliff! Martha! Where've you guys been?"

"Sightseeing, like you," Martha said exuberantly. "Isn't it all glorious!"

"Yeah," Malloy said. "We haven't stopped praising God since we've been here. We can't get over this place."

"It is amazing," Bob replied. "God is here showering us with blessing, revealing more of his splendor—"

"Yeah, and it's a good thing the Lord gave us these bodies at the resurrection," Martha replied, "or I couldn't handle all the excitement and energy I live with. I would have burned out long ago in my former body."

Gamliel listened curiously to the conversation, unable to relate to their human experiences. Yet he loved to listen to them. Their expressive gratitude was always contagious to his own emotions. Every time they rejoiced about God, he had to jump, too.

Now they had a whole new world of adventures before them. A whole new Earth and universe to explore, even for Gamliel. He had never experienced a brand new cosmos like this.

CHAPTER 120

As Bob talked to Martha and Cliff, the crowds began to stir. A procession of the Son of God approached them down the golden street of the city.

"He's coming, Jesus is coming!" came the whispers spreading from group to group through the multitudes of saints.

The threesome and Gamliel turned toward the crowd as it parted to make way for the King.

Whenever Jesus came by during the Millennium, Bob always felt a radiant love flow out of him to the people. On many occasions he got to experience the joy of talking with Jesus, himself, and drinking from the rich, deep fountain of wisdom that flowed from his lips.

As the Lord passed by, Bob noticed twenty-four men walking beside him. Half of them were the twelve apostles who served the church when Bob became a Christian. Nathan Kelly was among them.

The other twelve were the apostles of the Lamb from the first days of Christ's ministry on Earth. Bob once had the privilege of talking to Peter and John and the other disciples back in the Millennium.

Immediately following them, another multitude of saints walked close behind. Among them were the 144,000 men who ruled with Christ over the nations. They were easy to distinguish by their unique splendor and the iron scepters they carried. They followed the Lamb wherever he went. The others among them were members of the Bride of Christ who lived and ruled with Jesus in the new Jerusalem.

"Look!" Bob said to Martha and Cliff, "There's Jack and Rhonda, Shayne and Laura, and Whitney. If it hadn't been for their persistence to help me, I wouldn't be here."

Cliff and Martha agreed.

As the procession of the Bride passed by, Jack Mitchell waved at them.

Bob waved back, thanking God in his heart for sending that man to rescue him from the fire.

Suddenly, a throng of hands lighted on Bob's shoulders. He turned to discover a number of people crowding around him. Some of the faces he recognized, others he knew by his spirit, but had never seen before.

One by one, they stepped up to shake his hand.

"Hi, Bob, I'm Tony. You prayed with my brother to receive Christ and he led me to Jesus the next day. Thanks for getting my brother saved. If it wasn't for you, he and I wouldn't be here."

"Hi, Bob, I'm Sally. You gave me your testimony and left me a tract. You couldn't stay long, but after you left I read the booklet. I prayed the prayer in the tract and Jesus saved me. The next day I died in a tremor after the great earthquake. If it wasn't for you talking to me, I wouldn't be here. Thank you, Bob."

"Hi Bob, I'm Dan. You prayed with me to receive Christ after you dug me out of the rubble from the earthquake. You had just prayed for salvation yourself and told me about it. I was scared and needed some answers, quick. You shared your experience and then asked me to pray with you. Thanks for telling me about Jesus, Bob. I wouldn't be here if it wasn't for you."

"Hi Bob, I'm Stephanie…"

The line seemed endless as saint after saint came up to Bob, thanking him for snatching them out of the fires of hell and eternal damnation. This had happened to him a number of times back in the Millennium, but he didn't realize there were so many others that his life had touched.

Only moments ago, Bob wondered how God could make things any *better* than this. But, true to God's nature, this was another one of those better experiences.

———

Gamliel stood beside Bob, listening to each account of those saved directly or indirectly by Bob's brief Christian walk on the first earth. Though it was difficult for him to perceive the depth of emotional gratitude coming from these humans, Gamliel knew he would have eternity to learn from them.

Like all angels, he longed to know everything he could about the *mystery* of the ages—when Jesus came to earth, died and rose again—so that the world, through Christ, might be saved.

THE BEGINNING

The Spirit and the Bride invite you to come! And let those who accept—invite others to come!
Whoever is thirsty, you are welcome to come. And whoever wants to may take the gift—the water of life—freely (Revelation 22:17).

Any correspondence to the author may be sent to:

JZ Publications, Inc.
P.O. Box 816
Fairburn, GA 30213-0816

To order this novel in any quantity you may call
our 24-hour on-duty operators at:

1-800-917-2665

THE AUTHOR

Jay Zinn was born in Dayton, Ohio on January 24, 1951, and grew up in the small farm community of New Carlisle, Ohio. He attended the Dayton Art Institute as a teenager, and after graduating from High School, attended the Central Academy of Commercial Arts in Cincinnati. He later joined the Air Force and worked in hospital administration. In the military he was influenced by the Jesus Movement and became a Christian, January 9, 1972.

After he was saved, Jay's desire for a career in art was still in his plans, but a call of God to preach came to him in the summer of '73. He went on to study for this calling and became an ordained Pastor in 1975. He pioneered his first church at the age of 24 and pastored in that church for seven years. After a total of 16 years of "actively" pastoring two churches—plus three years organizing and teaching a part-time Bible School in Oregon—Jay is now an itinerant speaker, teacher, author, and published artist.

The Unveiling evolved out of twenty-three years of Jay's study on end-times. He teaches end-time seminars and has taught extensively in the books of Daniel and Revelation.

He holds a Bachelors degree in Biblical Studies, a Masters degree in Theology, and a Doctorate of Ministry from Logos Graduate Schools in Jacksonville, Florida. He is currently working on his second doctorate from Logos—a Ph.D. in Theology.

His bride, Roseann, has been a loving companion and co-laborer in the pastoral ministry since 1974. They have two adult children, Angie and Aaron, and a beautiful grand-daughter, Michaela.

Revelation Chart

To maximize your "Revelation" experience in this book, follow and read the scripture references below as the events unfold in *The Unveiling*.

7 Seals

1. White Horse (Spirit of Revival - Jesus the Conqueror - through the Gospel) - Rev. 6:2
2. Red Horse (Spirit of War - worldwide) - Rev. 6:3-4
3. Black Horse (Spirit of Famine - worldwide) - Rev. 6:5-6
4. Pale Horse (Spirit of Death - 1/4th of the earth through 4 destructive agents: sword, famine, plague, & wild beasts) - Rev. 6:7-8
5. Martyrdom (5th seal - 5 = # of suffering) - Rev. 6:9-11
6. Celestial Signs (Sun- black, Moon- blood red, Stars fall [meteor shower?], great earthquake) - Rev. 6:12-17
  • Stagnation/no wind or fresh air (four winds held back from blowing) - Rev. 7:1
  • Sealing of the 144,000 - Rev. 7:2-8 • Martyrs coming out of great tribulation (from harvest ingathering) - Rev. 7:9-17
7. Silence in Heaven (Wedding of the Bride/opening of God's judgments on earth) - Rev. 8:1-5

7 Trumpets

1. Hail, fire, mingled with blood upon the earth (1/3 of trees and vegetation burned up) - Rev. 8:7
2. Great burning mountain cast into the sea (1/3 of sea - turns into blood, creatures die, ships destroyed) - Rev. 8:8-9
3. Great burning star -Wormwood (1/3 of rivers/springs turn bitter - many die from drinking it) - Rev. 8:10-11
4. Sun, Moon, Stars smitten (1/3 of day & night [8 hrs.] complete darkness) - Rev. 8:12
  • Announcement of 3 woes - eagle [angelic] warning in conjunction with last 3 trumpets - Rev. 8:13
5. Falling Star/Locusts (fallen apostle [Antichrist] given key-demons loose 5 months) - Rev. 9:1-12 (The 1st woe) - Rev. 9:12
6. 4 angels loosed from Euphrates/200 million demon army (slays 1/3 of man) - Rev. 9:13-21 (The 2nd woe) - Rev. 9:12; 11:14
  • Parenthetical Events: prelude to the 7th trumpet beginning to sound in: Rev. 10:1-11
7. Finished Mystery (Rev 12:1-16) - 7th Trumpet begins to sound - Rev. 10:7
  • This begins the last three-and-a-half years of Daniel's 70th week prophecy (includes everything in chapters 11 - 20).
  • The church is measured/outer court Christians given to ungodly gentile nations to trample under - Rev. 11:1-2
  • Two Witnesses [Moses & Elijah] bring judgments to the earth/spark Jewish revival/comfort to martyrs - 11:3-13
  • Satan is cast out of heaven (The 3rd woe) - Rev. 12:7-12
  • Bride gives birth to the manchild /Manchild caught up to God's throne (see Rev. 14:1-5) - Rev. 12:1-5
  • Satan goes after the Bride who is taken out into the desert - Rev. 12:6, 14-17
  • Antichrist receives fatal wound and rises to full reign/makes war on the saints/overcomes them - Rev. 13:1-9
  • False Prophet (makes image /initiates worship of Antichrist / initiates 666 - mark of the beast) - Rev. 13:11-18
  • Rev. 14 - 144,000 redeemed male virgins/follows the Lamb in heaven/2 Harvests/Winepress of wrath
  • Rev. 15 - Seven angels with seven bowls (vials).

7 Bowls (vials)

1. Poured on the earth - painful, malignant sores, ulcers, boils break out on the recipients of 666 - Rev. 16:2
2. Poured on the sea - turns to blood and destroys all ocean life - Rev. 16:3
3. Poured on the rivers/springs - turns to blood for bloodthirsty people - Rev. 16:4-7
4. Poured on the sun - intense heat scorches men - Rev. 16:8-9
5. Poured on the throne of the Beast (Jerusalem headquarters in Palestine - cloak of darkness) - Rev. 16:10-11
  • Two witnesses-Moses & Elijah-are slain in the streets of Jerusalem
6. Poured on Euphrates River - dried up/3 demons/gathers kings for battle of Armageddon - Rev. 16:12-15
7. Poured on the air - Rev. 16:16-21 (thunders, lightning, earthquake/flattens mountains-isles/hailstones).
  • Rev. 17 - Shows us "Mystery/Babylon the Great/Mother of Harlots/Abomination of the earth"
    (Harlot Church reigns during three-and-a-half years supporting the Antichrist & killing the saints)
  • Rev. 18 - Harlot Church is judged by God who turns Antichrist and 10 kings on her/Harlot destroyed
  • Rev. 19 - 2nd Coming of Christ./Battle of Armageddon
  • Rev. 20 - Satan bound 1000 years/Godly resurrect/Christ reigns 1000 yrs./Great White Throne
    (ungodly-other dead [vs. 5]- resurrects at the end of the 1000 years/they are Gog & Magog)
  • Rev. 21-22 - New Heavens/New Earth/New Jerusalem